W9-BQS-595

"A strong, true voice.... McNamer writes poetically, with restraint and insight, and in doing so, elevates this novel above the ordinary."
—*Los Angeles Times*

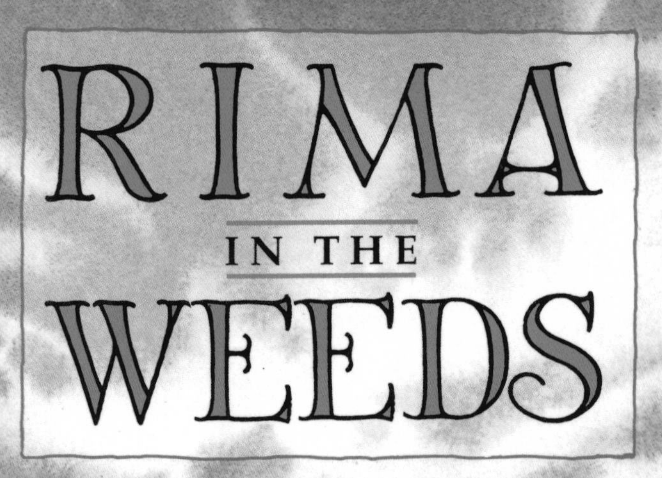


A Novel

DEIRDRE McNAMER

## Critical Acclaim for *Rima in the Weeds*

"A thoroughly engaging book....Those moments that transform you forever are rendered in this first novel with aching clarity." —*New York Newsday*

"An intense and beautiful first novel....Even for an East Coast urbanite reader, Deirdre McNamer makes Madrid feel like home...the town lies somewhere between Lake Wobegon and Twin Peaks." —*Washington Times*

"McNamer captures the citizens of Madrid with a quick, sure hand....Margaret is a purely wonderful character."
—*Chicago Tribune*

"The spirit of the northwestern plains is in her people....A beautifully moving tale about abandonment and healing, the conquest of fear and the resurrection of hope."
—*San Francisco Chronicle*

"Wonderfully observant....A resonant, beautifully written chronicle of small-town life and dreams."
—*Orlando Sentinel*

"An amazingly realistic, ultimately haunting book...vibrant and genuine...readable and thoroughly satisfying."
—*Milwaukee Journal*

"Margaret's longing to understand the mysteries of Madrid is reminiscent of that felt by the young women in another small town: Winesburg, Ohio....McNamer has a firm grip on her little Western town and...fashions an intricate web of the lives in Madrid." —*New York Times Book Review*

"Richly layered....A chilling and powerful window into adolescent sensibility." —*Seattle Weekly*

"McNamer has made a fine beginning as a novelist....She sees...the inner spirals of loneliness and despair which often spin fastest in women who are on the economic margins, not exactly bereft of purpose, but often left to invent one for their lives." —*Los Angeles Times*

"A captivating story....Finishing *Rima* means hoping McNamer already has a good start on her next novel."
—*Denver Post*

"Written with an aching wisdom, this first novel slowly and methodically lays open one woman's fear and loneliness and then documents her refusal to give in."
—*Booklist*

"McNamer captures in beautiful prose the harsh realities of Montana life." —*Library Journal*

# RIMA IN THE WEEDS

a novel

*Deirdre McNamer*

HarperPerennial
*A Division of* HarperCollins*Publishers*

A hardcover edition of this book was published in 1991 by HarperCollins Publishers.



First HarperPerennial edition published 1992.

*Designed by Cassandra J. Pappas*

---

The Library of Congress has catalogued the hardcover edition as follows:

McNamer, Deirdre.
Rima in the weeds / Deirdre McNamer.—1st ed.
p. cm.
ISBN 0-06-016523-5 (cloth)
I. Title.
PS3563.C38838R5 1991
813'.54—dc20 90-39207

---

ISBN 0-06-092262-1 (pbk.)
92 93 94 95 96 MV/HC 10 9 8 7 6 5 4 3 2 1

*For*
*Bryan Di Salvatore*
*and for*
*Burke Patrick McNamer*
*(1952–1985)*

# *Prologue*

## October 22, 1962

The Hi-Line Investors Corp.—Skeet Englestad, Johnny Medvic, Ken Peterman, Doc Hansen, Earl Vane, and Dick Reitenbush—huddled over coffee, the day of the big blockade, to decide, finally and forever, what to call their new steak house.

The chin-to-chin showdown with Castro had them all stirred up, and they spoke with the hushed urgency of generals. Their first choice of a name, the one they'd been running with, wasn't going to work. The Tiki Room? Suddenly it was safe and ordinary, like something named by wives. And this was no ordinary bar and restaurant. This was part of the overall ability of the United States of America to call a bluff.

Here's why. This particular supper club would be a rendezvous point for the boys who manned and serviced the Minutemen—150 nuclear missiles the Air Force was burying, right this moment, beneath twenty thousand square miles of Montana prairie. It would be an officers' club, in a sense. Part of this country's military capability. You could look at it that way. And now, with the Cuba deal, you had an actual military operation under way—those missiles were Kennedy's ace in the hole—and there was just no way, given the situation, that Tiki Room seemed right.

The Hi-Line Investors were three wheat farmers, a chiropractor, a banker, and the city clerk and recorder. They all lived in Madrid, a town of two thousand, give or take, on the Montana Hi-Line, the sparsely settled rail corridor across the plains, near Canada. What they had in common, besides the fact that they'd all grown up in Madrid, was the war: the Second World War. Everyone except Earl Vane had done a stint, stateside or overseas, and they remembered it as the most alert, the most achingly clear-cut time of their lives. To them, these new missiles were an extension into the future of that old exhilarating preparedness. A reminder of danger and a fast heart. The Minutemen. The prairie became a cover for hair-trigger weaponry. It buzzed. It joined the larger world.

Sure it was a gamble, this restaurant. Especially since it was five and a half miles south of town, out on the prairie where the missiles were. But what wasn't a gamble that was worth a damn in the first place? And it was chancy, sure, to stage the grand opening in the winter. But you needed time to get the kinks out before the spring and summer rush.

Right now, the name was the thing.

A military term seemed the way to go. Right for the times, and right as a hats-off type of thing to these missile people. The Firing Range? You'd have your double meaning there, with this suggestion of a kitchen range and steaks and such.

The Rocket?

You want to show these boys from the base that you appreciate their business, that five thousand missile workers is a goddam shot in the arm for your local economies. That a few naysayers don't represent the sentiments of any particular community at large. They will say these things, a few of our local people, about being a target for the Russians, and why should the Madrid area be a target for the Russians. Why are people in this area more expendable than people in someplace like Seattle, Washington? is the kind of thing they will say and write in letters and so forth. They will say they don't want to be a light bulb on some Russian general's map.

But you've always got these people, the naysayers. A decent person is proud to be a target if it's in the service of his country. You can be an ordinary area with a population of two people per square mile that no one knows about, especially since the oil fell off, or you can step out there and be counted. Where would we be if no one had volunteered for the war? Where would we be, for that matter, if no one took a chance on a new business? Where would we be if no one was willing to stand up to Khrushchev and put themselves on the political map?

The Target?

There's the matter of a name with some spunk. But there's also the consideration of your outdoor sign to go with the name. You want something simple and big, without expensive lettering. Something that makes you say the name to yourself, right off. Something that people don't have to sit around and figure out.

From an investment standpoint, there won't be beaucoup bucks for the decor. There will be a serviceable building that has a California-type atmosphere inside. An officers'-club-type atmosphere, with some booths and some candles in glass bowls. For a nice mood. But the line has to be held on expenditures, because these guys will be here for, what, a year more, the construction people, and then you'll just have the people who are in charge of the missiles, the ones who sit down there in those little rooms beneath the grass and the crops. And your maintenance people. And hopefully, by then, a stable local clientele. But it's a gamble, you bet. The point being, keep the up-front expenses down.

A military type of name. Something with some pizazz, some pride to it. Something that lends itself to an officers'-club type of idea. Then a sign, to go with it, that you're going to notice. A sign that doesn't cost an arm and a leg to light up after dark.

# Chapter 1

March, that year, was full of wind that rolled across the world with a sound as clean and lonely as rushing water. It rocked the stripped cottonwoods, hurried clouds across the sky, sprayed gravel against bare legs. You walked into it with a forward tilt.

Margaret Greenfield lay in bed, listening. At night, the wind was an ocean that whooshed forward, ebbed for the span of a train whistle or a dog's bark, whooshed again. She let it wash over her, safe on shore in a way that did not, then, feel temporary.

She lay beneath her warm blankets and the wind died a little. And then it sounded as if it were ruffling a huge sheet. This made her think of her mother's wedding veil. Margaret's parents, Roy and MaryEllen, had gotten married eleven years earlier, in the windy spring of 1951, a year to the day before Margaret was born. As soon as MaryEllen stepped out of the church, a gust blew the veil straight off her head. One black-and-white snapshot in the album shows her standing on the church steps, laughing, her shiny dress blown tightly around her hips, her pretty hand grabbing for the veil. Another shows the veil alone against the branch-crossed sky, a square of gauzy white, solitary and willful. And then more pictures: the veil wrapped around a bare branch; two men in suits climbing a single ladder, cigarettes clenched in their teeth. And another, the last, of the two men again. One is hatless and grinning; the other has a shadow over his face. They are on the ground, the veil stretched triumphantly between them. By then, MaryEllen has disappeared from the pictures. She has gone off to be a wife.

Margaret didn't know why a certain kind of wind at night made her think of the veil in the air. It was just one of those cases where two things stuck together. Whenever she smelled a Big Hunk candy bar, for instance, she thought of the movie *Cat People.* She must have eaten a Big Hunk when she saw it at the Rialto. But she had eaten them at other movies too. Who knows why they were linked to a specific one? A single nougaty whiff, and she could see every scene. She could see Irena, the beautiful, shy woman with a panther inside her that took over when she was made jealous or passionate. It was an old, simmering curse. When the panther sprang to life, Irena couldn't help what she did. She couldn't remain human if she tried.

To raise money that spring, Margaret's catechism class sold plastic cylinders with a figure of the Virgin Mary inside. They were beige and looked, on the outside, like foot-long rockets. A seam ran from base to tip, and it parted like cathedral doors to reveal the praying woman inside. They cost two dollars apiece. Anyone who sold three of them got to name an African pagan baby who would be baptized by missionaries when the money was sent in. Margaret sold six and named her babies Audrey and Gidget.

Trudging on Saturday mornings from door to door, selling the Virgin rockets, Margaret gathered evidence of something she already felt in her bones—that Madrid, where she lived, was not just a gappy little town on the northern Montana plains. Far from it! It was a place of layers and mysteries, of hidden rooms and muffled dramas.

Selling the rockets, she saw, through a slat in a venetian blind, an old man in red boxer shorts vacuuming a carpet. She heard Mr. Badenoch, the meek grade school principal, singing in a heartbreaking voice from beneath a car in his garage, and she watched a three-legged dog with a bow on its collar hop through a tunnel in some bushes.

She was invited into a living room where everything was covered in plastic—the lamps, the couch, even an arrangement of plastic flowers. A woman in a pink apron sat her on the crackling couch. The wind moaned beneath the eaves as the woman poked through a change purse for money. A young man in an old man's bathrobe and slippers padded through an adjoining room carrying binoculars.

She saw an immense salmon-colored Cadillac waiting for her to cross an intersection and remembered suddenly that she had seen it in a dream with palm trees and warm sand that trickled through her fingers, a dream so happy she woke laughing.

But this was the most mysterious of all: One morning she knocked lightly on the door of a yellow ranch-style house on Skyline Boulevard, her rockets in a shoe box under her arm, and heard a woman's distant cry. "So who *are* you, anyway?" she heard. "Who *are* you?" It seemed to come from behind several doors, from behind thick castle walls. It seemed to be shouting at a deaf person, a crowd, the entire town. "I have no idea," it wailed, "who you could possibly be."

On the day of the airplane ride, the second Saturday in April, Margaret woke to silence. No wind, none at all. Not even the usual breeze. This put a flutter of apprehension beneath her rib cage. If there was no wind, not even a breath of it, what would lift the small plane off the ground? What would boost it into the sky? She climbed out of bed carefully and tried to feel nonchalant. She phoned her best friend, Rita Kay, who had arranged the plane ride—the first for both of them—and asked whether she had any worries about the strangely silent skies. Rita Kay hooted at her.

"It doesn't take wind," she said. "It takes air. And there's always air. At least there was the last time I checked." This was a new expression of Rita Kay's: "the last time I checked." She had borrowed it from her older brother, Eugene, a small teenager who had already wrecked two cars, and she said it in a blithe, proprietary way that wounded Margaret a little.

It was a glittering, suspended morning. Sun shot off the small patches of ice left from the last cold snap of the season. The silent air made the sparrows too loud. Rita Kay's father fiddled with the radio dial as he drove them to the airport, skimming the tops of voices and music the way the plane would soon skim above the solid, comforting earth.

The rides were part of a fund-raising effort to repave the airport runway. Rita Kay had seen the ad in the paper and pestered her parents, and Margaret's, until they said yes. Now she bounced triumphantly on the seat, picking slivers of pink polish off her tiny fingernails.

Margaret pressed her nose against the cold window and devoured scraped-looking stubble fields with her eyes, noticing for the first time how anchored and substantial they looked.

The airplane was intensely red and white and black, and it was parked just outside the doors of the metal hangar at the Darrell Johnson Memorial Airport. Bob Ronechek, the pilot, squatted beside it in a large plaid overcoat, examining one of the wheels. A large sign on the hangar wall said WEEKEND RIDES. $10 FOR 20 MINUTES YOU'LL NEVER FORGET.

Rita Kay's dad pointed at the sign. "Aren't you getting a little carried away, Bob?" he said. Bob laughed and shrugged his big plaid shoulders.

The minute he slammed the doors shut, Margaret knew she was trapped in a horrible mistake. It was the sound of the doors, light and plastic. Incredibly light. She was sealed inside a toy, and a man she didn't even know was going to aim it straight into the sky.

I should jump out now, she thought. It will be embarrassing, but I'll be alive. The only doors, though, were in the front, and Margaret had been placed in the back. Rita Kay sat in the co-pilot's seat next to Bob and craned her neck out the window. She turned and grinned at Margaret. Bob pushed a button that made the plane roar and shake. He placed headphones over his ears and muttered into a microphone. He checked the seat belts. Too late. Margaret shut her eyes and consulted her vision of heaven.

For as long as she could remember, everyone up there had been peering over a bank of snowy clouds, monitoring the world with gentle smiles. The old God was flanked by his immediate family and friends, who watched with him: Mary, a pretty blue oval; Jesus, thin and pale-eyed, resting his young man's beard on the old man's shoulder; the Holy Ghost, wings stretched like a quivering silver canopy over their heads. And then all the rest, fanning out to the edges of the sky, tall to short, babies on the end, saints and martyrs and grandparents and orphans, robed and peaceful, looking down with encouraging eyes at her, Margaret, and the rest of the heavily turning blue world.

She knew the vision was too pretty and simple, like a Christmas card—that the details were probably more obscure and elaborate—but the feel of it remained. They were a big surprise party that would welcome her with quiet cheers when she died, providing she had not somehow pitched herself into a canyon of soul-killing sin. That's why it wasn't so bad to die young. You had less time to mess things up. When they wanted you, you should be happy to go.

"Not yet," she hissed at them angrily, surprising herself. Bob put a second pair of earphones on Rita Kay, who squealed with pleasure. The little plane began to move slowly toward the runway, rocking a little from side to side. Margaret stared at the floor. She imagined rows of powerful, hurt eyes. Then she gathered herself and spoke again. "I do *not* want to be with you. Stop looking at me." Bob glanced over his shoulder and lifted one earphone away from his head. "You want something?" he shouted. She shook her head. No, she mouthed. Nothing.

Bob slowed the plane, turned it a quarter turn, stopped it. He turned a handle on the ceiling, then pushed a lever, and the motor roared more alive. The sound grew, a terrible winding up until it screamed like a monster mosquito. The little capsule felt as if it would explode. One more notch and the seams would burst, spitting them all onto the concrete.

At the last moment, he pulled the lever in again, and the sound trailed away. They crawled to the runway. He checked their seat belts again and did a jaunty thumbs-up. He pushed the lever, and the engine started to climb, but this time they were moving with it. Faster, faster. The ground blurred. Everything blurred. And then, just as it seemed they would never make it, that they would go roaring into a fence or a field and explode in flames, the earth dropped away from them like a stone, releasing them to the liquid sky. Small tears seeped from the corners of Margaret's clenched eyes.

The little plane circled and climbed. Then Bob lowered the nose so that it felt horizontal and announced above the roar that they were circling back over Madrid. Margaret opened her eyes and looked down, expecting an intricate little city, somehow made roofless by the plane's spying height. Finally, she could peak down pathways, into shaded corners, over hedges, through doorways. It would take hours to see everything down there on earth. Her home.

But Madrid lay on the immense animal back of the earth like the pieces of a miniature board game or a smashed raft. It was thin and gappy and had a dull, cardboard look to it. Nothing stood out except the oil tanks and the Lutheran church steeple and the Saddle Club arena. The rest was just shadowless little boxes and the gray lines of streets. If a town could be bald, Madrid was that. Bald and terrifyingly small.

"How 'bout that, girls?" Bob yelled above the roar of the engine.

Rita Kay had her nose and hands pressed to the window. Her yellow fluff of hair looked electric. "I see my house!" she screamed. "I see Debbie!" Debbie was her elderly Persian cat.

"You can't see Debbie," Margaret said in a low voice. "You can't see anything." She felt sheer, bone-hollow disappointment. There was nothing wonderful about Madrid. The whole place looked flimsy and temporary.

"What?" Rita Kay shouted, snatching her eyes away from the window for a second to look at Margaret. Margaret shrugged dismissively. She tried to feign eagerness by looking out her own window. Beyond the town were great stretches of buff-colored grass and striped wheat fields, dark fallow soil alternating with pale stubble, reaching in shallow waves to the skyline. A couple of cars inched like bugs along Highway 2, and some freight cars sat by a gleaming clump of miniature grain silos.

Her vision reached so far that the horizons curved downward. And there was nothing sheltering on that earth except the row of mountains on the far western edge of everything. Madrid was lost at sea, Margaret thought, and didn't even know it.

The ground rose up to them. The little wheels bumped it hard, jumped a little, bumped again. Then they slowed and the engine died, and they were parked in front of the hangar. Done.

"Can I steer next time?" Rita Kay said coyly to Bob. Her cheeks were bright pink.

"Why not?" He turned in his seat. "How did you like the ride?" he said to Margaret. "You look a little green around the gills."

"Fine," she said, looking out the window.

He let them out, and Rita Kay ran to her father, a short, smiley man who sat in the car, listening to the radio. She began to chatter. Margaret fixed a mild smile on her face and waited to get home. Up there in the plane, during the span of a few terrible minutes, she had felt everything change. She had pushed herself away from heaven, from those faces who wanted her to come to them and be happy forever. And she had seen the bareness of earth, how it really was when you got a good look. Where did she belong now? Where did she want to be?

Riding her bike, a few weeks later, Margaret passed the Thorpes' large grassy yard. The sun had shone hard for several days, and then there had been an afternoon of rain. The Thorpes' lawn was dotted with mushrooms. Margaret slowed her bike and got off. She turned and wheeled it slowly past the grass again, studying it.

Some mushrooms were poison; some weren't. She thought she knew, from science, what the most poison ones looked like. But there was one kind that mimicked a safe mushroom, and it could grow anywhere. She stood over three mushrooms growing near the sidewalk and examined them. They looked safe. They also looked like the ones that looked safe but weren't.

Then Margaret did something so strange she felt she was doing it in her sleep. She glanced around, saw no one, knelt quickly to the sidewalk, and put her nose to the tip of one of the mushrooms. She sniffed its dried-leaf scent. Then she very deliberately ran her tongue over its velvety surface. And she very deliberately took a delicate bite from its edge. And swallowed it.

She stood up slowly. Slowly, she climbed back on her bike and began to pedal toward home. She held herself very straight, imagining the moonlike particle, tooth-marked, entering her stomach. Was she the same as before? Or was she on the edge of death? She tried to feel her body from the inside, tap it for clues. But her racing heart drowned out everything else. It could go either way. She might live to be a grandmother. She might collapse before she had traveled three more blocks.

Never had she ridden her bike like this. Her fingers fit perfectly in the grooves of the plastic grips. Her leg muscles stretched and tightened in a perfect, gliding rhythm. Her own stiff wind blew her bangs straight up. A small dog darted to the edge of the sidewalk and veered back, but Margaret had already swerved and straightened. Her reflexes were faster than the speed of thought. She pumped faster, eyes as wide as she could make them, fear zinging joyfully up her backbone.

The mushroom dissolved in her stomach and she felt it seep into her bloodstream just as she skidded, fishtailing, into the long driveway. She threw her bike down and ran into the open garage to stand behind the tall box the new refrigerator had come in. She stood, hidden, until her heart quieted. She gave the mushroom time to do its work. Nothing happened. She was alive.

Inside the house, her mother handed her a peanut-butter-and-jelly sandwich, and Margaret burst into tears.

Through the long summer, she felt the slow growth of this runaway force inside her. She craved danger and fled from it. She cried, sometimes, for no reason. And her legs ached at night. She didn't know what it was. She saw Rita Kay almost every day, but Rita Kay wasn't interested, the way she used to be, in make-believe scenarios that went on for days. She didn't want to play jungle girl, or career girl, or movie-star divorcée, which she pronounced div-or-cee-ay because it was French. She wanted to ride bikes or swim. She wanted to talk about boys.

Margaret found an old pile of *Time* magazines in the basement and leafed through them at night in her bedroom. She always read the Medicine section first.

She read about an aircraft mechanic in California who could stop his heart for seconds at a time, whenever he wanted to. His fear was that he might not be able to start it again, but so far he always had. "Although yogis have claimed to be able to control the heart," *Time* said, "there are no well-documented cases in medical literature of an individual stopping his heart at will. What enables Mechanic Swenson to turn the trick is still a mystery."

She read about a family dinner at Orville Fjeldt's farm near Idaho Falls. Grandma Fjeldt served some beets that a neighbor had brought over. She thought the beets weren't sour enough, and she said so, out loud. Something was wrong, but she couldn't put her finger on what it was. As it turned out, the beets were too sweet because they contained a deadly toxin.

"Last week, because of the beets, Orville Fjeldt was dead," the article said. "So were his brother Kenneth Fjeldt (after lingering more than a week in an iron lung) and daughter Ramona, 15." A photo of Kenneth Fjeldt in an iron lung accompanied the story. The caption said, "Grandma wanted more vinegar."

The new fifth-grade teacher, Miss Schmidt, walked into class on the highest spike heels Margaret had ever seen. She had pale skin and red hair and didn't smile. She was very young, and from Massachusetts.

Miss Schmidt began each day calmly, severely. But inevitably something happened that made her excited or angry, that caused her cheeks to flush wildly. Sometimes it was a stumbling answer or a thrown spit-wad. Other times, she would stare out the window at the playground, and the town, and the prairie beyond and get angry about nothing at all.

"Do you know how this town got its name?" she demanded one day. "This town got its name because a big fat railroad official picked it off the globe." She was shouting a little. The class kept silent, watching her. "Like this."

She walked briskly to the corner of the room, her spiked heels clicking, grabbed the big globe from its shelf, and placed it on her desk so they could all see clearly. Her face was blazing and sickly.

"Like this," she snapped, and she put the back of one hand dramatically over an eye. With the other, she spun the globe. She waited a second or two, then let her finger pounce. Bending over the frozen globe, she peered at her finger. "Aha!" she said, her voice deep now, like a fat man's. "Glasgow! Let's name this railroad stop Glasgow!" Susie Appelt tittered, because she used to live down the road in Glasgow. Their teacher was spinning the globe again, jabbing. "Aha! Well, we've got a bunch of little towns near this finger. Where's the closest big town? Yes! Here we are. Le Havre. How about if we just call the next one Havre? Is that all right?" Margaret and everyone else nodded carefully. The wind made the windows shudder and clanged the cable on the flagpole outside.

Then, without even spinning the globe, Miss Schmidt dove with her index finger straight down to Spain. "Madrid!" she cried. "There's a good name! There's a dandy!" She fixed her pale eyes on the children. "Is Madrid a good name for this little outpost on the prairie? This little fort?"

"Yes," said Julie Jackson softly. Two boys giggled.

Miss Schmidt ignored them. She stared out the window again. No one moved. "Is anything wrong with Madrid?" she whispered, turning back to them. Then her eyes filled horribly with tears and she ran out of the room.

The next day, severe and contained, she told them the Russians had missiles in Cuba that were pointed right at the United States, ready to go. President Kennedy had told Khrushchev to get them out of our backyard or else. Not only were the missiles pointed at the United States, but most of them were probably pointed at Montana, at Madrid, because of the big missile system that Malmstrom Air Force Base was installing beneath the Montana rangeland and wheat fields at this very moment. Margaret felt her blood pick up.

She went home for lunch and found her mother grim-faced, listening to the radio. Margaret wondered aloud if Madrid was a target for all those Cuban missiles that were ready to blast off. Her mother looked at her, and her eyes filled with tears. "Oh, honey," she said, and hugged Margaret tight. "Say a little prayer. This will turn out all right." Then her face, which was round and sweet and comforting, got braver looking. She tilted her chin up a little. "Eat your cheese dream," she said. "Don't worry." Cheese dreams were grilled cheese sandwiches made out of French toast, with syrup poured over the top. They were Margaret's favorite meal, and she knew she was eating them, right then, because of what was happening in Cuba.

She wasn't worried, though. She was thrilled. She said a little prayer, but she didn't really mean it. All day, she heard the excitement in her own voice. She thought she could hear the faint underground buzz of Madrid's own missiles, ready too.

She liked the idea of the missiles and all those wires connecting them, even though Susie Appelt's horse had fallen into one of the ditches they had dug for the cables and still favored a hind foot. The missiles made the ground you walked on seem important.

But then she walked into her house after school and smelled baking cookies and furniture polish, and she remembered an incinerated bird she had seen inside the shell of Rev. Olson's burned-down house, and she was washed with remorse and fear. Not yet, she thought.

Remembering, vaguely, a saint's story, she pocketed a small bottle of her favorite cologne, Intimate, and peddled her bike to the large garden behind the hospital. There, she poured the whole bottle over the feet of the statue of the Virgin Mary. And she prayed, earnestly this time, that everyone would calm down.

The garden was empty. The last frail, wine-colored leaves clung to the bushes. She watched the cologne drizzle across the stony toes of the Virgin and plunk into the dirt below. And as the earth soaked up the liquid, she closed her eyes. She seemed, then, to be standing not on the broad firm ground but on a very high rail just wide enough for her feet. If she tipped off one side, she would land in a pile of straw. If she tipped off the other, the straw would be knives. She was up there alone, the wind in her ears. Her mother didn't see the danger. Rita Kay didn't. No one did.

She stood for a long time like that. A squirrel chucked. The bushes whispered. She felt herself begin to lean. She put her arms out for balance. Then she felt herself falling and her eyes jumped open, catching her just in time.

# Chapter 2

Dorrie Vane climbed the iced-up steps to the Empire Builder, on a day so cold it burned, and turned sideways to maneuver her bulky load through the narrow door: Sam in one arm, his huge diaper bag and the green plaid suitcase in the other, the bulging purse provisionally wedged between elbow and ribs. Her face was frozen. Sweat trickled down her sides beneath layers of prickly wool.

Both were red-eyed. They'd spent that last night in Dorrie's echoing apartment on the old iron bed, the only piece of furniture she hadn't been able to sell. Sam had wakened often, as if startled, then cried himself back to sleep. Dorrie had listened to the heavy Chicago wind pound against the windows, watched it skitter pieces of two years across the front of her mind—a chalkboard covered with the lineage of the House of Tudor, a tinsel-covered jade plant on the sill of her cubbyhole in the alumni office, light glinting off a saxophone, warm water running down her legs, the dark hair on Rader's wrists. Memory was no different from dreaming. It survived in non sequiturs and shards, all the accents on the offbeats.

By the time the train began to click out of Union Station, her damp skin had chilled. Frigid air seeped through invisible cracks around the frosted window, and she knew she wouldn't be warm again, not from the inside out, for the next twenty-five hours. That's what she would remember about leaving—how she looked out at colorless warehouses and a tangled expanse of shiny tracks, sniffed the downy hair on her baby's head, and felt her skin turn cold.

The man across the aisle was young and wore an Army uniform. He handed her his *Sun-Times* with the random eagerness some people have when they're starting trips. She took it and gave him a small, keep-away smile.

Dean Rusk was about to announce the resumption of underground nuclear testing in Nevada. A "left-hook blizzard" in Minnesota had stranded a family in their car, freezing the grandmother to death. An international team said all missiles would soon be out of Cuba. Joan Baez had played for a crowd of ten thousand. None of it interested her much. She read the thick newspaper only to prolong the feeling of being a Chicagoan, even as the train pulled her back home, a child in a red wagon.

Sam finally slept. The soldier got up, announcing that he was going to find a sandwich, maybe a beer. He asked Dorrie if he could get her anything and threw a practiced grin at her. He was very good-looking when he did that—rakish, great teeth, confident of a response. Dorrie shook her head and looked very slightly past him until his face tightened, and then he was gone.

She tried to nap, riding the gently rocking train, feeling the poison move in as it always seemed to when she let herself drift. It began as a small liquid ache in her lower throat, then grew and spread—into her arms, her stomach, her womb, her legs. Sometimes it made her whole body pucker and contract.

At St. Paul, she decided to call. The soldier came back and stretched his legs into the aisle. He avoided her eyes. His shoes were the shiniest she had ever seen. She stepped over them carefully, Sam in her arms.

What did she want to say? She didn't know, even as she dialed. Yes, she did. She wanted to say, very clearly, Why don't you remember anything the way I remember it? How can you leave me out here in the cold, making me pound at you like a crazy person? She wanted to expel the venom that made her knees rubbery and tightened her voice to a squeak. The phone rang distantly, and she thought of a disk of skin-colored rubber, a beam of light lasering through a pinprick hole in its edge. She thought of a baby the size of a chess piece, sliding down that light beam, laughing.

Sam had started to whimper as soon as they stepped into the sour booth. He got louder as Dorrie dialed, louder still as she listened. She tried to jiggle him quiet with her free arm. By the time there was an answer, he had reached a despairing wail. "Hello? Hello?" came a high, lithe voice. "Who is it?"

Dorrie stayed silent. She heard the woman listen, heard her put her hand over the mouthpiece and murmur something over her shoulder. To *him*. She heard a stereo playing Brubeck. "Is this a joke?" the woman asked, too cheerfully. For an answer, Dorrie put her baby close to the mouthpiece and let him howl at his father until the line went dead.

The train crossed all of Minnesota and North Dakota in the dark. The countryside had simultaneously emptied and grown dim until it finally became indistinguishable from the night sky—vast blackness pricked here and there with a light, the train clicking blindly into its center.

A pretty white-haired woman in the next seat forward snored softly. Her husband sat in a small pool of light, flicking the pages of a paperback. Dorrie nursed Sam and murmured to him, calmer since the call. That's it, she thought. That's the last of it. Please, let's sleep now.

But her baby whimpered and twisted. She examined his pink, old man's face and wondered again what he was. Sometimes he seemed to be a hidden part of her that had somehow wandered to the surface, where it clung, wanting back in. Other times, he felt like a simple mistake, a sack of groceries that someone had inexplicably shoved into her arms as she waited in a theater line. But then there would be a wave of pure love, and he would become, for a few minutes, all that could ever matter. That was rare, though. Her guilty secret.

She wrapped another blanket around him and took him away from the other passengers to the dome car, a clear, elevated bubble where she could see the hard stars and the glow of the engine when it curved in the distance. A boy and girl sat in the dim forward reaches of the empty seats, their wheat-colored midwestern hair bobbing gently. They opened cans of something and murmured in low voices. Then, at some point, they stopped talking and sank, rustling, into the tall seats. She heard a small moan.

Dorrie had meant to think on the train about what she would do when she got to Madrid. How long it would take to finish her Incompletes. How it would seem without Rosemary, her mother, who was apparently gone for more than a few weeks this time. Where she would look for a job. How she would convince Earl, her father, that she and Sam needed their own place to live. But where would that be? Where did an adult woman without a husband live in Madrid? When she envisioned the town, she couldn't see anything but families in boxy family houses.

She had meant to think about all these things on the train, to map out a plan for the next phase of her life, write it down in a small leather book she had bought for that purpose. But she was too tired to care. She spread the blanket over Sam and herself, listened without curiosity to the hard breathing of the teenagers, and finally slept.

By Williston, the wide sky had turned to pewter with peach-colored streaks. High piles of dirty snow flanked the tracks. A brakeman walked past the car slapping huge mittened hands together, his breath a cloud before his mouth.

Dorrie and Sam descended the narrow stairway to the coach car. It looked like a small battlefield of slain dolls. A fat farmer couple had thrown an orange afghan across themselves and slept furiously, heads thrown back, mouths open. Two small girls lay side by side across a pair of narrow seats. An old man with woolly blue socks hunched, contorted, against the icy window.

The soldier's legs were stretched into the aisle again, shoeless now. He snored quietly, open-mouthed, his smooth, stubby-fingered child's hands folded on his chest. Dorrie stepped over him, into her own seat, and changed Sam's diapers while footsteps crunched back and forth outside the windows.

The Williston passengers filed on, and Dorrie knew, when she saw them, that she was back West. There is a kind of weathered innocence in the faces of rural westerners, she remembered. They look simultaneously young and old. The young ones have beat-up surfaces and the old ones retain something untouched, something in their expressions that makes you feel obligated to protect them. It's a look that can make you angry at them. They don't have the closed, self-sufficient look that people have in Chicago, say, the look Dorrie had wanted badly for herself.

Maybe it wasn't even their faces so much. Maybe it was the way they moved—as if they could take up as much room as they wanted. Slow, gawky, curious. Bumping against people in crowds because they haven't developed voices in their heads that tell them to keep moving at all costs.

One of the new passengers was a young woman holding the hand of a small sleepy-faced boy. Her pink curlers were battened down with a yellow chiffon scarf. She had a little girl's mouth and an eruption of acne on her chin. The two of them wore jeans and cowboy boots. The boy wore a quilted parka, his mother a heavy leather-and-wool letterman's jacket.

She stowed all their belongings under the seat except a square pink makeup case, which she balanced on her lap and sprang open. *Mustangs* was lettered across her back. She shrugged out of the coat, removed her scarf, and began to yank out the pink picks that held her curlers. The boy stood in the aisle and watched her, sucking his finger.

She brushed her hair, back-combed it violently, and aimed a foot-long can of hair spray at it. Eyes squeezed shut, she released the pungent mist, waking the old couple behind her. They batted their hands in the air, flailing dreamily, then sank again into unconsciousness.

The girl got up and walked hand in hand with her child toward the tiny water closet in the rear of the car. Dorrie watched her, admiring the long legs in faded blue jeans, the slim squared shoulders, the hand-tooled belt with a large silver buckle. Not those things, individually, so much as the overall effect. The way she moved so strongly and capably, as if she knew where she was. She would be the one who vaccinates the calves at branding time, Dorrie thought. The one who rides a horse and throws bales and cooks and plays with her little boy and makes love to her young, sunburned husband—then wakes up the next morning, ready to do it all again.

The cowgirl and her little boy came back up the aisle, teetering from side to side, as the train gathered speed. The stop had stirred everyone up and they were blinking and fidgeting around and peering out at the bright prairie. The sun was just over the horizon and had caught the frost in the air so that it shimmered, lighting up the waking faces.

She stopped at Dorrie's seat.

"How old is he?" she said in a flat, uncurious voice.

"Three months. Thirteen weeks."

They both watched Sam for a moment, and he did a strange thing just then. He opened his eyes wide, fixed them on the ceiling, and closed them again.

Dorrie and the cowgirl looked at each other and made mother faces, as if to say, That's the kind of thing they'll do from time to time. You just never know.

"J.B. and I," the girl said, nodding at her sleepy-faced toddler, "are going to Spokane. To the hospital in Spokane, which I've never been to. I've been to the downtown part, but not the hospital."

J.B. handed her the blue rat-tailed comb he had in his hand, and she ran it absentmindedly through his hair, bracing herself against a seat for balance.

"My husband J.B., the first J.B., has them cutting on his knee. He's got this piece of bone running around in his knee, and they're going to cut it out." She made a small swordlike motion with her comb in the air.

"I could feel it with my fingers—the bone that was

running around. Here it was." She touched the comb handle to the side of her knee. "Then, maybe a day later, *there* it was." She moved the comb to the other side of her knee and looked up so Dorrie could register surprise.

"He went out to Spokane to visit his brother, and the whole thing flat gave out on him. So now he has to get that bone cut clear out. And J.B. Junior and I are going out there to hold his hand and see the Ice Capades."

J.B. yawned widely. "It's like a circus on ice," he said in a small voice.

"Hey, J.B.," the girl said briskly, as if she were greeting an adult on the street. She shepherded him to their seats and took the inside one. J.B. began to tug his snow boots off. The girl didn't help him, though it took a long time. When he had finally yanked one of the boots off, he sighed dramatically and told her he was hungry.

"We're gonna eat as soon as you get yourself together, J.B.," she said. "And don't talk like that. I can't hear you when you whine."

"Then how come you answered me," he said, his cleverness beginning to wake him up.

"Don't get smart, J.B.," the girl said kindly. She rustled around in a paper sack, and J.B. started munching a sandwich.

Dorrie decided, at that moment, that she would become like this cowgirl. That's all she wanted. To be brisk and innocent and capable, to be allied in some straightforward, affectionate way with her child. She was sick to death of herself and the way she kept fingering her wounds, as if that would tell her how they had happened. Now she just wanted to go along and keep her eyes open and do her part. She told herself those things, as the train ate up the miles. She used those words.

A few miles east of Havre, just past noon, the train pulled into a siding to wait for a late train from the west. Some of the passengers rustled around in their sack lunches; others headed for the dining car. When Sam had a crying fit because he'd had to be still for so long, the soldier across the aisle got up noisily, hissed through his teeth, and left the car. He had turned sullen and disheveled.

Usually, Dorrie would have hated to stop like that, just a few hours from home. It would have felt like getting stalled in traffic. But she wanted a pause, a deep breath, before she faced whatever waited for her. To the north, white flatness, then a line of rust-colored willows along the Milk River, then more white and Canada. To the south, the Bear Paws. They were surprising mountains, three rounded peaks rearing out of the plains like that, gleaming in the noon sun. They weren't far from the spot where Chief Joseph and his winter-frozen Nez Percé finally surrendered to the hounding cavalry—within sight, almost, of Canada and safety.

During one of her episodes, Rosemary had checked out everything the Madrid library had on Chief Joseph, and read it all, and made a pile of notes. Maybe she still liked him. Maybe she thought about Joseph's near escape when they picked her up along the railroad tracks and took her in the state pickup back to the hospital at Warm Springs. You wouldn't know, one way or another, from Earl's letters. *Your mother,* he wrote once, *does not tell me what she is thinking. She does not seem unhappy or happy, so I can't answer your question about that. But of course there are these episodes, these upswings, which as you know cause her to roam away, if she can, and put herself in danger.* They wanted to keep her longer, this time, to monitor various combinations of the drugs and the electroshock. She wouldn't be at home when Dorrie arrived.

Her father's brief letters over the past couple of years had been distracted, intense, elliptical. A cold snap had caused the marquee on the Rialto Theater to *shatter on its own, just like that, out of the blue.* A wheat crop had *exceeded all expectations, despite the grasshopper situation, which I'm sure you can appreciate.* Malmstrom Air Force Base was installing a huge new missile system, underground, and some of the silos were near Madrid. *Each missile has the firepower of twenty Hiroshimas,* Earl wrote. *And you or I will have a difficult time even telling they are there.* He and some other Madrid businessmen had opened a steak house, *We've named it the Bull's Eye,* south of town.

He usually ended each note with a brief update on the Communist-orchestrated encroachment of the federal government. *Now it's fluoridation, for our own good,* he wrote, double underlining. *We must be ever vigilant. We must be on our guard.*

The last few times Dorrie had seen Rosemary, she had seemed distant, pleasant, careful. Rosemary and Earl spoke functionally or not at all. She and Dorrie talked about small things, when they talked. She didn't answer letters, not even when the baby was born.

When Dorrie told Earl about her pregnancy, his letters stopped for a while, like a long, drawn breath. Then they had a terse exchange about her plans, and he sent her five hundred dollars. When she told him the baby had been born on October 22, he wished her good health and briefly summarized the Cuban missile crisis. When she told him she was out of a job, out of money, out of her scholarship, and was coming home, he sent her a pamphlet about provocateurs in the Department of Health, Education, and Welfare who pretended to be concerned about tooth decay and children's health but were really just conditioning the public to be malleable. On the pamphlet, he had written her arrival date—25 January 1963—and this message: *January 25 is confirmed. I will be at the station. Your mother remains at Warm Springs.* No signature.

* * *

Sam slept deeply on the seat beside Dorrie. The sun flashed, blazing, off a metal barn roof in the distance. The sky was an enamel blue, bisected by the white stream of a fighter jet—a trainer from Malmstrom—that seemed to climb straight up. A thin layer of snow covered the ground, but the wind had swept much of it away so that the underlayers showed through—the buff-colored grazing range, the alternating dark and light of the strip-farmed wheat land. Dorrie had almost forgotten about all this muscularity and sweep: how it had made her feel, sometimes, a peculiar combination of puniness and possibility. How that had seemed, in better times, a thin kind of faith.

Suddenly expansive, she turned to the boy in the Army uniform. "Where are you going?" she asked him. He had seemed to grow younger and more upset with every mile of the trip. Now he was eating some Cheetos, crunching loudly, looking out the window. He seemed not to hear her so she repeated the question.

"Me?" he said loudly. And he automatically tried his come-on smile, then remembered he didn't want to use it. He made his face neutral. "Fort Lewis, out on the coast," he said shortly. "Been home on leave."

"Will you stay there?" Sam was awake now, and he, too, peered at the soldier curiously. Rather, he watched the boy's face, moving his eyes when the boy moved or gestured. Tracking him.

"Not if I can help it. One of my two best friends from high school ended up in Germany. The other one went to a special school, and he's an adviser at Cam Ranh Bay right now. That's in South Vietnam."

He watched Sam, who had extended his right arm stiffly so he could watch his own tiny fingers clench and unclench.

"How come he does that?"

Dorrie told him she had no idea. He put on his

soldier hat then, and retied his shoes, and they didn't talk again.

A bank of clouds moved in from the west. They met the slanting sun, and the world thickened and dimmed. The wind had come up, too. Dorrie saw a man in an overcoat hunched against it outside a grain elevator. Tumbleweeds shuddered between the strands of barbed-wire fences. A small herd of horses turned their backs to it, and their manes and tails rode the air. Powdery snow moved across the ground like smoke.

In a meandering, singsong voice, the cowgirl's son was naming things he saw, pointing at them with a toy pistol. His mother napped. "There's a corral," he crooned. "Horse. Another horse. Another horse. Stubble field. Mmmmmm. Nothing. More nothing. Boxcar on the other track. Two boxcars. There's a road. There's a fence around a missile. *Pow!* There's a teeter-totter oil well. There's nothing. . . ."

The train slowed and passed a crossing for a county road. A red pickup truck waited there, its exhaust billowing into the frigid air, and Dorrie caught a glimpse of two people in the cab—a hatless man with thick mittens and a small girl wearing a woolly red scarf.

"There's a pickup. *Pow!*"

Dorrie piled all her luggage on one seat and went back to the dome car with Sam. "There's a baby," the young boy chanted softly.

Madrid was scattered low in the gray winter light, a spare jumble of buildings. Behind the town, far to the west, the small cutouts of the Rockies lined up iron-colored across the horizon. The river cut through the prairie on Madrid's near edge. Beyond it she saw the white square of the drive-in theater and the spire of the Lutheran church, the two black oil tanks to the north, the small stockyards and rodeo arena to the south.

The train whistle wailed. They would arrive at 4:10—on time. Snow began to spit from the sky, and she was grateful that her father would be there to meet her and take her in the old Oldsmobile to a warm house with carpets and sheets. She wouldn't think now about how it would be between her and Earl, or what a stir Sam would create.

The train started across the Madrid trestle, the clicks and rumblings brittle and airy now because there was no ground beneath them. Dorrie closed her eyes and felt the train slow down. Then the ground came up beneath it again, and she was home.

Earl wasn't at the station. Dorrie waited inside for ten minutes, feeling something close to hatred, then called the bank. They said he was at a meeting, so she gathered up Sam and the diaper bag and her oversized suitcase to walk the seven blocks home.

They walked straight into the wind—past the implement dealership, the Stockman's, the secondhand store—to Main. Sam was shocked into silence by the cold. When Dorrie breathed through her nose, the air sealed her nostrils together. At the intersection of Main and Central, she slid on a patch of ice and dropped the suitcase to catch her balance. Sam began to cry, and a voice called to Dorrie, by name, from a red pickup.

It was the pickup she'd seen at the intersection east of town, and the man with the big mittens on the wheel was Roy Greenfield, the young doctor who had married the high school home economics teacher, who had given Dorrie her pre-college physical.

He tossed the luggage into the bed of the truck, and Dorrie and her baby got into the front with the little girl. He introduced her as his daughter, Margaret, and said she was almost eleven now. The heater fan was on high, the radio played "Johnny Angel," and Margaret sucked solemnly on a Big Hunk. She had a shy, pinched-looking face. Tan-colored braids draped down her shoulders from beneath her woolly red scarf.

"Welcome home," Greenfield said jauntily. "Both of you."

Dorrie didn't know what he'd heard about her or Sam, or about why she was back. But she knew he wasn't going to ask questions. That was Madrid decorum. You didn't have to account for anything that happened a good distance away. Which didn't mean people couldn't speculate behind your back. They would. They already were.

Greenfield, though, had a sort of reserve that made her think he wouldn't do much of the talking. He was a good-looking man—short, wiry, with large dark eyes and a smile that twisted a little and made him look alive and sarcastic. He wore a big sheepskin coat, dirty jeans, and cowboy boots. And he smelled like a horse. A good smell. In the doctor's office, he'd smelled like rubbing alcohol, standing down there between her legs in his white doctor's coat.

Margaret stole long, obvious glances at Dorrie from beneath her straight, grave eyebrows. Dorrie felt young, flat, shaky. She tried to smile and couldn't. They turned up Skyline Boulevard, Dorrie's street, and Margaret blurted out that she'd like to hold the baby.

Dorrie handed him over, expecting Sam to protest, but he rode serenely in the girl's arms until they pulled into the empty driveway. Greenfield took the bags to the front step, then got back into the truck. He and Margaret and Sam calmly watched Dorrie from behind the semicircles on the freezing windshield while she got the key from beneath the ceramic flowerpot, where it had always been.

# Chapter 3

Margaret had known at the crack of dawn that something important was going to happen. From the minute she woke, that January day, she felt the faint prickle on the back of her neck that told her something was coming. But she couldn't get a reading about whether it would be a good thing or a bad thing. She could only stay alert and hope for the best. "Jesus, Mary, Joseph, make it be something good," she whispered, tracing a cross on her cold bedroom floor with a bare foot.

This was the way she had gradually decided to deal with God and the saints, in the nine months since the bleak and terrifying airplane ride. She wouldn't give them any reason to think she was ready to die and be with them, because they might take her up on it. But she would shoot up small prayers on a regular basis—ejaculations is what they were called—to indicate her basic good intentions, her frequent need for help. She often accompanied an ejaculation with a small gesture—a bowed head, a cross made with her foot—to give it punch.

She noticed the prickle again and thought, It could be anything. Nothing would surprise her anymore, not since she had found out that people who barely existed, one moment, could become the secret center of your life, the next. Just like that. Overnight. You could have a dream, just a dream, and you could wake up sick and ecstatic with love. No one had mentioned any of this.

She'd had the dream two months earlier, on November twenty-fourth. The day before it happened, she put on a sweater and her big head scarf with the horse picture on it and started down the frozen alleyways toward Rita Kay's house, four blocks from her own. It was Thanksgiving vacation, and she had the feeling Rita Kay might be organizing something—Kick the Can or Run Sheep Run.

At the far end of the first alley, she saw a boy and girl, high school age, leaning together against a sagging wooden garage. The girl had her back to the garage and the boy faced her. He was taller than she was and wore no coat, just a T-shirt and jeans. His arms were muscled like a grown man's and they were propped against the garage wall, the girl between them. They smiled at each other in a glittering, challenging sort of way.

Margaret thought this looked interesting. She walked a little farther, then stopped. They didn't notice her, so she slipped behind two tall garbage cans, crouched, and watched.

She thought the girl looked almost exactly like Audrey Hepburn in *Green Mansions*. She had the same delicate, big-eyed face but a thinner, tougher mouth. She wore ordinary teenager clothes—jeans and loafers—but she had, on top of them, the most beautiful fringed leather jacket Margaret had ever seen. It was the color of butter and had very long, very thin fringes—rows of them across the front, along the bottom, and flowing beneath the sleeves like a shawl.

Margaret crouched lower. She could almost make out what they were saying, but not quite. The girl tilted her head back and shook her bangs out of her eyes. She laughed. The boy leaned in closer.

Then they both stopped laughing. The girl raised her hands and put them on the boy's bare arms. The wind skittered down the alley and blew the leather fringes of her coat straight up, suspending them for a second or two. Then the fringes dropped and the boy put his hands behind her neck and kissed her for a long time, leaning into her.

Margaret watched them. First, she felt as though she had stumbled upon a piece of entertainment, an odd skit, and regretted that Rita Kay was not there to see it too. But then another feeling took over. Her eyelids drooped, and she felt a delicious languor as she focused on the softly swaying fringes.

It was the same hypnotic feeling she sometimes got when she watched someone do something complicated with great care—like the time Mrs. Flickinger in the first grade had shown her how to fold paper and cut it to make a snowflake. Mrs. Flickinger had long fingers and was very quiet and graceful. Margaret remembered watching her hands as she folded a sheet of white paper this way, then that, and how she had cut very slowly into the paper, making small diamonds, half-moons, commas. She had felt an intense dreaminess come over her as she watched, something that was not a tired feeling at all but made her want to watch what she was watching, forever.

When the teenagers left, she stayed behind the garbage cans for a while and thought about fringed jackets. It seemed to her that she had never noticed fringed jackets before, and now they seemed like the best kind of coat a person could have. She wanted one badly. Rita Kay had a red plastic coat with plastic fringes on it, but that was nothing close. Margaret wanted a soft leather one like the girl's in the alley. The fringes would have to be very long, like hers, the longest fringes you could get. That way, they would be slightly startling. They would wave under your sleeves like water. They would float on the wind.

That night, she dreamed that she and a crowd of neighborhood kids were playing Hearts and Go to the Dump in a large pink living room. Then everyone except Margaret and Woody Blankenship put their cards down and left the room.

Woody, in real life, was two years older than Margaret and lived on a corner across from the high school. He was lanky and freckled and had a silver front tooth. In real life, Margaret had never thought much about him. He was just one of the loud, vaguely irritating older boys who screeched around on their bicycles and sometimes hit a baseball through someone's window when they played in the vacant lot across the street from Margaret's house. Some of them had started to carry black combs in their shirt pockets and ask girls out on dates.

In the dream, after everyone else left, Margaret and Woody Blankenship turned into dancing partners. But it wasn't normal dancing. Margaret stood still, facing Woody; then she sprang into the air, right to the ceiling, in a businesslike manner. She jumped high and then he did too, arms folded away from his body like the cossack in the school's filmstrip about the Russians before they were Reds. They bounded upward together, faces close, and landed lightly on their toes.

Then they were at the top of a hill, a long and grassy one, wrestling in a comradely way, like boys. They threw each other efficiently to the ground and rolled slowly down the long hill, arms around each other. At the bottom, they stopped. Woody was quietly stretched along her body, breathing lightly in her ear. His freckled fingers circled her wrist. They looked at each other, that was all. Woody's mouth was open slightly, and light winked off the tip of his silver tooth.

When Margaret woke, she felt as though something very fragile had been tucked inside her rib cage so that she had to breathe carefully. Something like the hollow, painted egg a neighbor's mother from Czechoslovakia had given them last Easter. Before Rita Kay accidentally crunched it, the egg swirled with glossy stained-glass colors. And it was so light, when you held it, that it felt as though it weren't there.

She lay in bed and stared at the floating bars of sunlight on the ceiling. She reviewed the dream over and over, taking it in little sips to make it last. Her vision about the night things that went on between men and women was fuzzy and involved some kind of friendly but dignified agricultural procedure in which seeds got planted for babies. This was something else altogether. How could she have regarded Woody Blankenship so casually, so blindly, all this time? These *years.* How had she lived just a few blocks from him and failed to realize what a wonderful coincidence that was? She was almost afraid to move. Afraid that the dream, disturbed, might fly away and leave her with ashes on her tongue.

But it didn't. She began, that day, to imagine herself through Woody Blankenship's eyes. She peered into the mirror at her solemn face, her dark eyes, the khaki-colored braids hanging over her shoulders. She smiled at the image, and the smile was for him. She took stairs two at a time, and ran down them the same way, and imagined Woody's frank approval of her strong legs, of her enthusiasm and skill. She didn't feel as if she were being conceited. She felt as if she had been led into a brighter light so that she and the Woody in her dream could see each other clearly for the first time.

She began to walk past Woody's house several times a day, not too fast, not too slow. It, too, had changed forever. Before the dream, it had been a small gray house with a couple of scrawny bushes in the front yard. Now it was the place that held Woody.

Once, walking past his house in a light snowfall, she saw some T-shirts hanging, frozen, on the line in the backyard: Woody's T-shirts. The rigid, Woody-sized shapes put a lump in her throat, and she walked faster. Just then, the aluminum door flew open and Woody and two friends came sprinting out, puffing warm clouds of air. Margaret's face froze and she fixed it straight ahead, willing her pulpy legs to move faster, pretending she was walking too fast to notice him or stop, because if she did—if she looked at him and talked to him—her secret love might spill right out of her eyes and he would see it and be taken aback.

Margaret hoarded her thoughts about Woody. She measured each day by the evidence it produced of him: a glimpse of Woody in person, or of one of his friends, or even of his dog, an arthritic Labrador named Penny.

Sometimes she lay awake at night murmuring ejaculations. Sacred Heart of Jesus, have mercy on us. Mary, Queen of Heaven, pray for us. She shot the words heavenward against the possibility of loss.

By Christmas, she felt she had been thinking about Woody Blankenship forever. She was skittish and too thin. Her parents gave her long, inquiring looks, which she avoided.

She couldn't stop thinking about him, and she didn't want to stop thinking about him—her mind without Woody would feel bereft. But she couldn't help remembering, sometimes, her earlier life when she wasn't odd, or uneasy, or in love with anyone. She thought about the summer before last, say, the one when she was barely nine, and she was washed with nostalgia. How blithe she had been! How easy it had been to lose herself for hours at a time.

She remembered that summer as a buzzing, dreamy one, especially during the long afternoons. Flies droned against screen doors. Sprinklers swished quietly. Mrs. Richie, the only adult in town who rode a bicycle, pedaled slowly in the heat, her knees scissoring up and down, stately and ridiculous.

There had been a lot of cotton in the air, that summer. The cottonwood trees, scattered here and there in Madrid, had cottony pods that burst open all at once, sending silky tufts of the stuff through the air like slow-motion snow. When she thought about that summer, she sometimes saw herself as a smiling figure in a snow-filled paperweight.

She and Rita Kay had spent hours, that summer, in the weeds behind the Assembly of God church, playing Rima the jungle girl. The weeds were pale green and shoulder high. They had grown up where Rev. Olson's house had burned down, and no one had bothered to cut them. They offered shelter and shadows and a beautiful rippling light. If you crouched down, no one could see you from the sidewalk. You had your own green world.

The two of them had seen *Green Mansions* at the Rialto the day school got out. Rima the jungle girl had black hair, long and silky. She ran gracefully through dense foliage and shafts of sunlight, ministering to injured animals who became tame in her presence. At times, she would hear in the distance the faint, plaintive cry of the jungle explorer who loved her and wanted her for his wife: "Reeeee-maaa. Reeeeeee-maaa." But she didn't answer because she had to be free.

Rita Kay had to be coaxed into playing Green Mansions. Usually, she wanted to play something more real, like Teenager, so they could put on the lipstick she had stolen from her mother's makeup drawer. But Margaret insisted, and she patiently coaxed Rita Kay in her lines. They had to pretend they were identical jungle-girl twins. Margaret named herself Rima and Rita Kay named herself Wanda.

They talked to each other in a brief and formal manner, as wild girls would, who were not used to human talk.

Margaret might say in a solemn Rima voice, "Perhaps, if we do not run into too many snakes, we shall gather melons for a salad." Or she would turn to Rita Kay and say, with quiet fervor, "Wanda. Where on earth could this young monkey's mother be?" Margaret liked to say "Where on earth" then. She still did. Her own mother always said "Where on earth," and Margaret liked its scope. "Where on earth are your socks?" Margaret's mother might say. And Margaret would think of a small pair of white anklets draped on the Eiffel Tower in Paris, France, or hanging from a crooked branch, halfway down the Grand Canyon.

Two huge things happened the day school started after the Christmas break. Miss Schmidt was gone. No more red hair, clicking spike heels, teary temper. She had gone back to Massachusetts to rest. The new teacher, Mrs. Cole, looked like a wrinkled brown berry and had taught in Madrid, on and off, since she was a girl.

At recess that first day, Margaret and Rita Kay and some other girls stood in a shivering circle and watched some boys play basketball. Woody was one of the boys. Margaret examined him without seeming to, careful that no one noticed. She hadn't even told Rita Kay about him because Rita Kay would somehow give the secret away, though she would try not to.

Woody moved faster than any of the others. He leaped, he dribbled the ball, he grinned and shouted and flashed his silver tooth. And then, just before the bell, he got the ball again and dribbled it, fast and low, right over to the clump of girls. He stopped, grinned, and held it two-handed, ready to pass. "Catch," he said, and threw it right at Margaret.

She caught it, shocked. Then the bell rang, and as it did, something came over her, and she began to bounce it slowly toward the basket. She heard Rita Kay giggle. She felt Woody's eyes searing her back. She lobbed the ball at the netless hoop. It hit the rim, rolled slowly around it once, twice, and fell in.

Woody made a piercing whistle with his fingers and retrieved the ball. He smiled at her, right at her face, seeing her. And then he grabbed her hand and hoisted it aloft like a referee at a prizefight, and then he was gone.

Margaret kept the hand on her cheek all afternoon. It was her left hand, so she could seem to be leaning on it while she wrote with the other. Once or twice she put the hand over her mouth and quietly kissed it.

She and Rita Kay went to the Saturday matinee to see *The Man with the X-Ray Eyes*. By then, Margaret had been in love with Woody for seven weeks, and she had been thinking about the basketball incident for thirteen days. It made her so hopeful, she woke each morning with her heart racing.

Margaret scanned the crowded theater excitedly because she had a feeling Woody would be there. Small dramas were in progress: a boy with a burr haircut standing up to throw a spit-wad at three huddled girls, the manager's stolid figure heading grimly toward the spit-wad thrower, the smell of popcorn and the distant blipping sound of it, the intimate light, the deep red velvet curtains, the squeaking seats—all of it seemed to Margaret furtive and alive in a way she hadn't noticed before.

*Divorce* showed first because the manager liked to show old movies before the new ones. Kay Francis was a career girl who came home to her small town and fell in love with a married man. She stole him away from his wife. She couldn't help herself. She had to follow her heart.

Between movies, Margaret saw a head turn and Woody's profile, way down in front. "There's Woody Blankenship, clear down in front," she whispered to Rita Kay.

"So what?" said Rita Kay. "Why are you whispering?"

"Well, I just noticed him down there," Margaret said lamely. "He's right at the screen. How can he see from so close?" She laughed gratuitously and happily.

"Look!" said Rita Kay, sitting up straighter. "He's on a date!"

She pointed at the head next to Woody's, a blond head. Woody was tugging gently at the hair on that head, a very long braid that was trapped between the girl and the seat. The girl leaned forward and Woody lifted the braid and dropped it free behind the chair back. It was the longest braid in town, several feet long, and Margaret knew who its owner was: Christie Murphy.

Christie Murphy whispered something in Woody's ear, then hit him playfully on the arm. Rita Kay chattered, and Margaret realized that she was chattering something back, but her brain and face felt as if they'd been put in a freezer. She wanted to weep. Instead, she opened her eyes wide and fixed them on the yellow braid, studying it, until the lights dimmed, the curtains hummed up, the manager yelled at everyone to be quiet, and the movie began.

Ray Milland was a scientist who developed a formula that made him able to see through the surface of things. At first, it was an exciting scientific discovery, and funny at parties because he could see women without their clothes. But then it turned horrible because he couldn't go back to normal and his whole life was wrecked by something he thought was going to be wonderful. In the end, he screamed and screamed because he wanted to stop seeing and couldn't.

When the lights went up, Margaret peered at Christie Murphy. She watched her stand up and move to the aisle. Then she mentally subtracted Christie's hair, the dramatic wheat-colored rope, and she knew—she saw—that the hair was crucial to Woody's interest. Christie Murphy was ordinary without the hair. She was powerless. But that long swatch of silk, fastened a foot from the bottom so that a brush of tail remained, the heft of it swinging like an arm, that was Rapunzel. That was something a boy would want to climb.

Margaret grieved. She plotted. She measured her hair, which was at least a foot shorter than Christie's. She made bargains with God and the saints. She began to speak in code to them. She tacked "God help us" after some of her sentences, trying to sound offhand like her mother did when she said it. But each time she spoke the words she accompanied them with a vehement wish that Woody would toss away Christie Murphy like she was a pair of tattered sneakers. She had cramps in her heart.

On the day she woke up knowing something big was going to happen, a Friday, she felt her parents scrutinizing her closer than ever. This is what happened when you were an only child. They always examined you. You always had to deflect them.

"What's wrong with you?" her dad asked at lunch. "Why so mopey?"

"I think I have trench mouth," she said, grabbing the first thing that came to mind.

"Trench mouth."

"The Anderson twins have it, and we aren't supposed to drink out of the drinking fountain." She felt herself flailing a little. "But I forgot and did it. And I think I got it, God help us." She shot the anti-Christie prayer fiercely heavenward.

They gave her their long looks, and she pretended to read the back of the milk carton. Her father got a flashlight out of his doctor bag. He tipped her head back, pulled her jaw open, and looked around. Nothing, he said. Maybe a touch of tonsillitis. He felt her forehead. Then he slapped her lightly on the cheek.

"I'll knock off a little early this afternoon. Why don't you come with me, after school, to take some feed and salt to the horses?" he said.

"I also have a pain here." She pointed to her sternum. The pain was real. It felt like tuberculosis, which *Time* said was cropping up again in the West.

"Eat your sandwich," her father said. "Baloney cures everything but a broken heart."

She munched silently, trying to swallow past the large lump that had grown in her throat. If he only knew. God help us, if he only knew. With that, Margaret was so overcome by the accumulated strain of Woody, and the poignancy of her distance from her blind, childlike parents, that she ran weeping from the table.

In a few minutes her father knocked on her bedroom door and entered with her heavy winter jacket in his hand. She put it on, let her mother tie a big woolen scarf around her head, and shuffled, drained, back to school. Whatever the day held, it was probably bad.

* * *

After school, they drove a mile east of town on Highway 2, then crossed the railroad tracks, heading south on the county road. Nothing bad or good had happened yet. The sky was low and gray and looked as if it would soon begin to spit snow. Margaret shut her eyes and pretended she was Kay Francis, beautiful and strong enough to steal a man from an undeserving wife. Yes, it was wrong. But it was love, and she was an outlaw who must follow her heart before she repented later and saved her soul.

Margaret's father always whistled in the car, and he was whistling now, softly, through his teeth. "K-K-K-Katy, beautiful Katy, you're the only g-g-g-girl that I adore. . . ." Margaret used to laugh when he sang the words, and she knew he was whistling so she would remember and cheer up. But that was years ago, when she was seven or eight. She managed a wan smile and felt as though she were petting a big, earnest dog.

The road moved slowly up and down, across wide undulations of mostly empty land—stubble fields, pasture, all of it bordered with barbed wire and covered with a thin layer of snow. They passed the Bull's Eye steak house, then went three more miles and turned left. A mile farther and they were at McCoys', where they pastured the horses. Margaret's father opened the gate, hunching against the stiff wind, and nodded at her to drive the pickup through. She scooted far forward on the seat and drove through the gate. He shut the gate and got into the passenger side. Margaret drove them past the rickety wooden ranch house, past the tall yard light and a pile of irrigation pipe and a car without tires, through another barbed-wire gate, which lay open.

Margaret aimed the pickup across the bony pasture, and they bumped along toward a small coulee in the distance where the horses liked to gather out of the wind. She drove intently, competently. Her father sometimes helped her with the big stick shift, but she was otherwise on her own. There was something absorbing and calming about driving, always. When she drove, she felt lighter. She felt expansive and generous and at home in the world.

She craned her head over the steering wheel to scan the prairie with real interest, looking for the horses. "Where on earth are they?" she asked.

She shut Woody Blankenship and Christie Murphy inside a big box with a ventilated lid. They scratched and yipped, but they were out of sight for the time being.

The three horses, two mares and a colt, were lined up nose to tail at the foot of the coulee. Margaret and her father walked up to them with oats and a block of salt, and the big animals surrounded them, puffing sweet horse breath on their faces, shifting their weight from foot to foot, nickering softly, nudging Margaret's scarf, shielding her with their big auburn bodies from the cold.

Her father threaded a rope through the colt's halter and led him around so he'd get used to the feeling. He talked to him calmly and picked up one foot to check an old wire cut. Then he turned the colt loose, and it raced around the larger horses in exuberant little crowhops. The colt belonged to Margaret. She had named him Mister Red because of his coppery coat and the white sock markings, about as long as men's socks, on his front feet. Then she found out from her teacher that Mister Red was *Señor Rojo* in Spanish. So she called him that, changing the last part to Ro-*ja* because it sounded better.

Margaret touched the velvet noses of the two mares and peered into their dark eyes. She put her cheek against the warm neck of the old one, Midge, and left it there for a few moments, smelling the horse's gentle grassy breath.

The skittish mare, Pokey, short for Pocahontas, was

her father's roping horse. Pokey whirled suddenly and aimed a petulant kick at Midge, who flattened her ears and kicked back. Margaret jumped out of their way and watched the three horses trot away into the wind, their manes blown high like flags. Pokey kicked at Señor Roja and missed.

Margaret loved her colt, even though he was only a year old and she couldn't ride him until he was grown. She loved him simply because he was going to become a tall, powerful horse. He would be beautiful. It was in his blood. She also loved him because he wasn't a coward. She watched him run in close to Pokey, then veer off joyfully when she flattened her ears and snapped at his air space.

"Run, Señor Roja, run!" Margaret yelled. "You're a jealous little witch, Pokey," she called. She changed the word to bitch, under her breath, and said it five or six times.

On the way home, light snow began to fall. Fence posts flew past. Then a teeter-totter oil pump that wasn't moving. They passed the Bull's Eye again. The neon arrow was on, now, and pulsated in the darkening afternoon light.

They passed a missile site, a short distance from the road on a small rise—a circle of high steel fence around four insect heads, black periscope-looking things that peered from the ground at each other.

They stopped at the train crossing for the Empire Builder from the east, and it roared past, trailing the sound of its own shrieking whistle. Margaret leaned into the dashboard and watched the windows as they flew toward Madrid, each holding a stranger's head. Someday she would be one of those heads, gazing calmly upon someone like herself who watched.

They stopped for gas at the edge of town, and

Margaret's father talked forever to someone in the garage about something. Then they drove slowly down Main.

Margaret saw her first. "Who on earth is that?" she said, pointing to a woman in a long pale coat and a strange black hat. She carried a huge suitcase and a bundle that looked like a baby. She was walking almost sideways, trying to protect the bundle from the wind.

Margaret's father looked hard and pulled the pickup over to the curb. "It looks like Dorrie Vane," he said, and reached to roll down the window. It was iced stuck, and he worked at it for a few seconds.

"Who's she?"

"A girl who went to college in Chicago. She's coming home with her baby for a while. Must have been on the train."

"Where's her husband?"

"Her dad says she's divorced."

The window cracked open. He rolled it down, using two hands, and called to Dorrie.

Of course. Margaret almost said the words aloud. Of *course,* this is what the day had been holding—this appearance of a divorcée, out of nowhere. One of the train windows was now empty, and its occupant was here in their midst.

Margaret watched her approach the pickup, and her heart hurried. She was gorgeous. The funny hat was made of felt, with a brim, and it had cloth attached to it that pulled over her ears and tied under her chin. It looked like a bullfighter's hat with a scarf on it. No one in Madrid had a hat like that.

The white coat flared from shoulder to hem, so that it would have stood out if the divorcée had twirled around. She also wore black gloves and black leather boots. It was all perfect. And her face fit the dramatic clothes. She looked like a cross between Audrey Hepburn and Jackie Kennedy and Kay Francis.

Margaret slid over toward her father to make room for Dorrie and the baby. They climbed in with a rush of frigid air.

Here we are, Margaret thought as they drove slowly through town and the adults talked. Two heart-sick loners in the same pickup in the same town. What had brought the divorcée home? What was her former husband like? What tragedy had made her face so pale beneath the wide black hat? Where was her hair? How long was it?

Margaret examined the baby, who was staring back at her. She needed some way to show the divorcée that she was her ally in Madrid. She tried to do it by brain waves, looking at Dorrie's face and sending her the message, *I, too, have an ache in my heart. You have a friend in me.* But Dorrie only glanced at her and smiled tiredly and looked back at the street with a strange, half-awake look on her face.

Margaret leaned against Dorrie's arm just a little. Then she tried brain waves again. Then she had a rush of courage and asked if she could hold the baby. She took him as if she held babies all the time, sending a message to him not to cry. He didn't.

With the baby in her arms like a shield, Margaret deliberately thought about Woody. He seemed farther away, though she knew he would come back. She wondered what it would be like to talk to him, whether you could see his silver tooth very much when he talked. And when she thought about that, the tooth, she felt a nauseating wave of love and despair. She held the baby tighter and wished that she were the one who was held. She tried not to think about Woody's hand on Christie's braid. About the pure, blind luck of having the longest yellow hair in Madrid.

# Chapter 4

Earl Vane had a particular sound during the winter. He left his black overshoes unfastened, and the buckles jangled like horse tack when he walked. He also limped, so one footfall was very slightly louder than the other. Holly Hopper, the town librarian, heard him coming before she saw him; heard the door slam and the faint clinks of his buckles coming toward her quiet stacks of books.

Today she was all alone. Even Elmer Davidson, who usually napped and read the newspapers until closing time, was gone. Someone had taken him to the VA hospital in Spokane for gallbladder surgery. Not that he would have been much help.

She didn't look up until the jingles stopped and she'd had time to arrange her face in an expression that she hoped was crisp. The radiators ticked. She smiled carefully.

"Hello, Holly." His face was ruddy from the cold. His thinning hair lay in strips across the bald part of his hatless head. He was smiling. That was the funny thing. If you didn't know what he was there for, you'd think he had such an open, well-meaning face. Boyish, even.

He had a magazine in his hands, and he began to flick through it like a depot clerk through a timetable, deliberately licking his forefinger with each turn of the page.

"I'd like to show you something, Holly. I know we've talked about this before, and you don't see it quite my way." His voice could take on a crackly Jimmy Stewart twang sometimes. "But I'd just like you to read this when you have some time. If you would."

This was the way it always started. He'd act hang-dog, hoping she'd just roll over and let him disrupt her whole system of doing things. He leaned over the desk, inclining his head toward the magazine in a kindly way, sliding it toward her as though she'd asked to see it.

"This one." His finger pointed to a headline that said McNamara and Associates.

"This is going on right under our noses, Holly." He began to read aloud: " 'Defense Secretary Robert McNamara has ties to three organizations which are known to have Communist membership, and yet our President, for reasons of his own, chooses to ignore this fact. Are some oversights deliberate? You be the judge.' "

He looked up, pained. "This is the kind of news the liberal press is muzzling. It needs to be made available to the people in this country. The people of Madrid." He swept his eyes quickly around the little library. "And they aren't going to get it if you hide it from them, Holly."

"I'm not hiding anything. Anyone in this town can come into this library and check out *American Opinion*.

Anytime." She felt her voice rising. "It's right there on the shelf with the other magazines. Right there in its normal place. No one's hiding anything."

"Well, I guess what I'm saying, and I know you've indicated you don't agree with me on this"—he drew his eyebrows together—"I guess what I'm saying is, this kind of news needs to be out there where people are going to notice it right off. It's too important. You've got all these other magazines—your *Harper's* and *Atlantic* and whatnot—and they're just dupes, you know. They're part of the overall blueprint, well meaning or not, which I don't think they are. But that's neither here nor there."

He fumbled in the pocket of his big wool overcoat and took out a small banner bordered with American flags. *American Opinion* was stenciled on it in large block letters.

"What I'm suggesting is this, Holly. You keep *American Opinion* on the magazine shelf where it always is, but tape this above it. So people will know. So they won't have to hunt. I think that's a pretty good compromise, don't you?"

She looked at him then, not answering, trying silently to convey her weariness and irritation. They'd been through all this before, and what was the point? Every other time, she had smiled and been conciliatory and evasive, because this was her first real job and she didn't want a businessman, a friend of several board members, on her bad side. She hadn't changed the magazine display, though.

This time, she had the very distinct sixth sense that he was just going through the motions before he took the matter to the library board. But she'd had a bad week. Her boyfriend Randy had told her she was one of his best buddies, quote unquote. That, plus feeling weak all the time from her diet. So she just didn't care about Earl and his magazine. She really didn't. In fact, she silently dared him to go to the board.

He probably wouldn't even have the guts to tell them he wanted her fired because she wouldn't redo her whole magazine arrangement to make a special spot for his Bircher rag. No, he would just absently stroke the flag pin on his lapel; he would just look sorrowful and say he was concerned, as a taxpayer and businessman, about the youth and inexperience of Madrid's librarian. Something like that.

He smiled at her again, and she saw how haggard he was. Something white clung to the corners of his mouth: milk of magnesia? Who knew? As Randy would say, it wasn't a pretty sight.

It was amazing how Earl Vane had aged in less than three years. How his bad hip had tilted his walk farther and farther to the side. Holly still remembered the first time she saw him, at the Trail's End parade in 1960, her first summer in town. She remembered how much younger and nicer he had looked, and she could hardly believe it now, the way a whole different person could lurk beneath the surface.

The Trail's End parade that year was the largest ever; that's what everyone told her. Fifty-four different floats, and horseback riders, and so on. She could still remember the exact figure because so many people repeated it to her. They thought she'd be impressed because she was from Williston, North Dakota, which was almost a city, really, so she'd be expected to know a big parade when she saw one.

Trail's End Days got its name from the fact that Madrid, once a trading post on a lightly traveled route to Canada, had been the last fort where alcohol was available in abundance. Every post north of Madrid—then called Fort Jamison—was drier. So it wasn't really the end of the trail, but it could easily have seemed that way.

Holly had tried to act impressed with the celebration because she was new to town, but it was really just the usual kind of thing: horseback riders dressed as cowboys or Indians, pioneers trudging along on foot, the Shriners driving midget cars, a Future Farmers of America float made out of chicken wire and paper napkins.

The second to the last person in the parade, that year, was a very small man she later knew as Gabriel. He was from Puerto Rico. No one knew why he had come so far north all alone. He was the only person in town who ever spoke a foreign language, not counting the Hutterites, who came to town on Saturdays—identical in their printed scarves and long dresses, their hats and black jackets—to buy supplies and candy.

During most of the year, Gabriel hired out as a gardener and odd-job man—he did the library lawn—and he wore clean khaki work clothes and spoke softly in broken English. But at Trail's End Days he looked like one of those Japanese paper flowers that bursts open in water. Brilliant clumps of crepe paper covered his straw cowboy hat. Streamers of paper flowed from the hat and from his serape. His shoes were white bucks, and they had paper flowers on them too. He walked slowly, his narrow brown face tipped upward in a kind of trance, shaking his streamered tambourine, crooning softly to himself in Spanish.

At that 1960 parade, Gabriel was followed by a woman who looked, to Holly, a little bit like Jackie Kennedy. This woman was older, with a wide streak of gray in her dark hair, but she had a similar classy, size-six look. She wore a matching rose-colored skirt and sweater, high heels, and a single brilliant yellow rubber glove, which she moved in a slow crescent through the air like a prom queen. She also passed out pamphlets with that yellow hand. She gave Holly one. It said something about weeds, about killing the weeds in Madrid.

Holly remembered staring at the woman and giggling nervously, like those around her. You wanted some kind of clue to the joke—a placard, a bunny tail, flippers on her feet—something to signal her role as a clown so you were free to laugh. But it wasn't there. Gabriel crooned softly, oblivious. The woman waved again, serene and robotic, and took off her shoes so she could carry them.

That's when Holly saw Earl Vane for the first time. He ran out on the street and grabbed the elegant, stocking-footed woman by the elbow. Then he walked a few steps with her, as if to get her used to the feel of him beside her, and steered her onto the sidewalk, through the line of curious spectators.

Holly never forgot his face. It was so vigorous and panicked. She thought of it each time he came in now, just a few years later, an old man with white in the corners of his mouth.

"*La Boca*," Earl said jauntily, pointing to a photo of Eleanor Roosevelt. Holly scanned the column: "Communist sympathizer . . . political prostitute who pretended to altruism . . . liver-lip mouth. . . ."

"Eleanor Roosevelt died a few months ago," she pointed out to Earl.

"Right," he said.

Was she, Holly, the only one who knew Earl was a lunatic in a business suit? Couldn't anyone else see it? Couldn't his business partners at the Bull's Eye, the new supper club, see it in his shaky smile, his speeches and flags?

Holly and Randy went to the Bull's Eye sometimes on Saturday nights. Randy taught American Government and shop at the high school. He didn't know much about books; it was a complementary relationship that way. He was the one who knew all about sports, and who everyone was, and what was going on in Madrid for fun.

The Bull's Eye was five and a half miles out of town, out in the middle of nowhere. It didn't look like much from the outside, just a Quonset-like building, windowless, with a very large orange neon arrow on the top. But the inside had a California theme of some type—a couple of big fake palms, glittery ceilings, drinks with names like Skip and Go Naked. Some of the guys from the base were usually there. They came from all over the country and had the accents to prove it, so the place seemed kind of lively and Williston-like. And the steaks were good.

Right before Christmas, Randy took Holly out to the Bull's Eye when the Missilaires band was playing. That was the night she got her first real insight into Earl Vane.

She and Randy drove around and drank a six-pack before dinner, so she was pretty looped when they got there. She didn't drink much, normally. But she knew she was getting serious about Randy, and she didn't know how she should express that. With him, she could never seem to say what was on her mind because he always made everything into a joke. So she drank three beers so she could make her own jokes.

The Bull's Eye had a photograph on one wall of a missile being fired. And it just struck Holly as funny, the way smoke or steam made a big ball on each side of the rocket. She started laughing, she couldn't help it, and asked Randy if that photo reminded him of anything. He looked at it, not seeing anything at first, then told her she had a dirty mind and he liked that in a girl.

That was the time she saw Earl Vane sitting alone in the bar, drinking coffee. She caught a glimpse of him through the beaded curtain that separated the dining room from the bar, and he looked lonely, through the beads. She thought of the way she had seen him, a couple of times, sitting at his desk at the bank discussing a loan or something with a customer. How he had looked, then, like a perfectly reasonable, slightly tired guy. She decided maybe it was time to talk things out a little. He had already been into the library twice to give his commie speech to her, and they seemed to be at a stalemate. Maybe, in a bar setting, she could get him to lighten up about it and stop bothering her.

She told Randy she'd get them a couple more drinks and headed into the bar. She'd been drinking Metrecal for two weeks and knew she looked pretty good. She saw one of the missile guys, Steve McClintock, standing at the bar. He sometimes took out Kay Bean, the typing teacher. He was good-looking in a Dick Van Dyke kind of way, and a really honest, heads-up guy, too. You could tell.

She gave Steve a big smile, ordered the drinks, then turned to Earl and said, "Hi, Earl," chancing the first-name familiarity because she was a little high. He looked up and she recognized that, for a moment, he had no idea who she was. And it wasn't because of the Metrecal. Then his face clicked on and he said hello, very coldly. Then he left his seat and walked right out the door. Well, okay, kiddo, she thought. I tried.

Now, when he came into the library, she saw that it was all an act: the smile, the soft twangy voice, everything. It was all show. He had his agenda and he was ready to roll right over her, whatever it took. For weeks now, he had made her worry about her job. He had made her tired. He had made her pick fights with Randy. Earl Vane had a way of turning everything sour. She tried to picture him as a little boy, as a young man in love—anything eager and happy and exhilarated—but the picture wouldn't come.

She pointedly closed the *American Opinion* and handed it to him. He shrugged and sauntered stiffly over to the magazine shelf—*clink, clink*—and heaved a large sigh. He unbuttoned his topcoat and thumbed through the *Ladies' Home Journal*. The *American Opinion* banner dangled out of his coat pocket. Here came the speech.

"It's sad," he said loudly. "We can't see beyond the ends of our noses. We shrug. We let it pass. We listen to the lambs cry peace and don't recognize the wolves beneath. The wolves at our door, the wolves who want to rip apart the very fabric of American life!"

He flicked through the glossy pages and shook his head softly. "It's really pathetic," he said. "We believe anything they tell us—de Gaulle, Nasser, Nehru—the crypto boys. Members of the international Communist conspiracy. Definitely. *But*"—and he jabbed his finger vaguely—"they were directed, early in their careers, to go underground"—he pointed at the linoleum library floor—"and emerge—as Republicans, Democrats, Monarchists, Social Democrats, or Socialists. Their task? To further the consolidation of the conspiracy's power over their respective countries, as well as furthering the conspiracy's world strategy."

He whirled to face Holly, eyebrows lifted. "It's sad as hell," he shouted. "Most people have no idea who they're dealing with. What's beneath the smiling faces on those jokers. Certainly you don't, Holly Hopper. And you know what? I feel sorry for you."

She felt a blast of cold air and three little kids ran in, stomping their snow boots on the floor. She heard the train whistle too, the 4:10 Empire Builder. The wind had picked up and was blowing a curtain of snow across the windows. Earl looked out the window at the sound of the whistle, as if it reminded him of something but he couldn't remember what. Holly watched his face and let her fury heat up a few notches.

The kids ran back to the far stacks. Holly walked over to Earl. She looked at him as hard as she could.

"Don't you dare feel sorry for me, Earl Vane," she said. Her voice was very low. "I know exactly what I'm dealing with." She wished Randy could hear her too.

Earl's face clicked off.

"You steal magazines, Mr. Vane," she whispered. "I've seen you." She jabbed her finger into the arm of his coat. "You're a common thief," she hissed. "You take magazines you don't agree with. I've seen you." She sensed her own momentum. "I don't want you back here. I don't care who your friends are. I don't care if you own the Bull's Eye. Don't come back. Until you get me fired, this is my library. And I want you out. Now. Do you understand?"

A little girl with curly red hair ran up to her and asked where the Nancy Drews were.

"You're a sick young lady," Earl said, his head craned upward and to the side, as if he were having trouble swallowing.

"You wouldn't have it any other way," Holly answered, turning away from him to shepherd the little girl back to the other children.

She listened to his boots leave. She felt queasy and triumphant. For once, she'd said what she'd wanted to. She'd called it exactly as she saw it.

# Chapter 5

Dorrie walked through all the rooms of the house with Sam in her arms, and he was quiet, examining everything too. He had the look he sometimes got, of an avid old man alert to random disaster. The rooms were smaller and mustier than she remembered. Drawn flowered curtains; the large brass ashtray, tall as a telephone stand; glass coffee table. All the same. On the table, the china figurine of a Victorian lady with parasol, head tilted coquettishly. Rugs of ashy rose. Walls of pale green. The large blue couch. And those details a solitary man will lay on the surface of a woman's house: dish towels spread to dry on the counter, a stack of newspapers in the corner, unopened cans of food on the kitchen table.

Her parents' bedroom had changed. One of the beds was now covered with tall stacks of magazines, books, newspaper clippings. The other was unmade, its covers stretched over a trunk at the end of the bed so the sheets could air. It was a habit Earl had borrowed from his own dour parents, leaving a bed stretched and open and ghostly—dispelling its vapors, sanitizing the contents until someone climbed into it again.

Her basement bedroom, a dim room paneled in knotty pine, had summer clothes in the closet and smelled like mothballs. It was cold. She turned on the baseboard heater, changed Sam, and put him stomach down on the bed, surrounded by pillows and her old stuffed animals. He whimpered quickly, then slept.

Upstairs, she opened the living room curtains, though it was getting dark now and the wind blew sandy-sounding snow against the picture window. She searched for a drink but found only a very old bottle of vermouth. It was far back in a cabinet next to an unopened pack of her mother's Winstons. Dorrie didn't smoke, but she lit one of the cigarettes and set it in an ashtray where she could smell it. Then she made herself a cup of tea, sat at the kitchen table, and waited. She heard a dog bark somewhere, the wind, the distant rumble of the furnace. That was all. She always forgot how deadly quiet Madrid was.

The teapot had just boiled again when she heard the click of the front door, the faint jingle of Earl's overshoes, his puffing breath. He stood in the door of the kitchen, one hand on the frame. "There's my girl," he said stiffly, pulling the old greeting out of some time when Dorrie was very young. It sounded rehearsed.

"Hi, Dad." He had lost weight. His face was drawn. He had something white in the corners of his mouth, and it gave him a helpless, seedy look. She waited, brittle, for his apology.

"I got hung up. I'm sorry I didn't meet the train."

"It was a long, cold walk," she lied.

"I had a very important meeting."

There was an awkward silence. He looked around for the baby. She made herself another cup of tea. He retrieved some milk of magnesia out of his overcoat and took a gulp. Sam cried faintly from beneath the house, and they both jumped.

An hour later, the three of them sat in the dining room of the Bull's Eye. Dorrie ate a steak. Earl ate something on a skewer. They were both exhausted and careful. The waitress, a very pale, hard-eyed woman with a name-plate that said GLORIA, seemed to sense this and tended to them briskly.

"He was living with another woman," Dorrie finally said, pushing her platter away. "He was a bar musician." A big man with bowlegs was dropping coins into the jukebox at the far end of the dining room. They listened to the faint *ping* of quarters.

"This is a disappointment, Dorrie," Earl said stoically.

"I would say so. Yes."

Sam, lying in a bundle on the seat of the booth, whimpered and twisted impatiently. Dorrie braced him with her hand.

"What are your plans?"

"My plans are to forget him."

"I mean your plan of action, Dorrie."

She felt tears at the corners of her eyes and a pure, powerful anger. She closed her eyes so it would pass or weaken, but it didn't.

"Action? Well, my *action* so far has been two days on the train. Then my *action* was to lurch home in a blizzard with a freezing baby and a huge suitcase. That's about all the action I've got in me at the moment, Earl." It was the first time she had called him by his first name, and the cruelty of it shocked both of them. She handed him the squirming baby and walked quickly to the bathroom.

Gloria the waitress stood at the mirror, applying mascara. Her mouth was unconsciously pursed, and her stance emphasized the sleek curve of her hip beneath its sheen of black rayon.

She yelped. "Christ! I just poked a huge glob of eye gunk straight into my eye." She whirled and poked her face close to Dorrie's. Her gaze was aimed frantically at the ceiling, and her thickly coated lashes blinked rapidly.

"Can you see a contact lens? My vision is all fogged over in that eye. Jesus H. Christ. It probably slid up over my eyeball. It's probably on its way to my brain." She blinked hard and pulled her eyelid up, her eye inches from Dorrie's.

"Look at the floor," Dorrie said.

When Gloria did that, Dorrie could see the edge of a very blue contact lens.

"Put your finger right on it," Gloria said, pulling her eyelid farther back.

"On your *eye*?"

"Uh huh." Her breath smelled like cinnamon and cigarettes.

Dorrie very slowly touched the tip of her finger to the edge of the lens.

"It's okay," Gloria said. "I touch my own eye all the time, putting these things in. Go easy, though! Now move the contact very slowly toward the main part of my eye." Dorrie did what she was told, amazed at this stranger's trust.

"Okay . . . okay . . . there!"

Gloria blinked a few times, hard, and flashed Dorrie a big smile. Her sharp features softened, and Dorrie could see that she was much younger than she looked. The mascara wand was still in her hand and she held it, forgotten for a moment, like a conductor's baton.

"Gotta run. Thanks." She gave herself a severe once-over in the mirror, poked one side of her blue-black bouffant hairdo up a little higher, took a hungry drag of a cigarette propped on the counter, threw it in the sink, and was gone.

"I could work here," Dorrie said to her father, surveying the murky red dining room, the sparkling ceiling, the plastic palm trees in the corners. "I could find an apartment and work here, nights. I'd be with him most of the day. I'd find someone to babysit him in the evenings."

Earl had a pen in his hand and doodled on his paper napkin, the lines deep in his forehead. He was left-handed. Light winked off his wedding ring. Sam monitored the tiny flashes from his perch on Dorrie's lap.

"The house is probably big enough for us all," Earl said dubiously.

"You could get me on here. You're one of the bosses, right? I'm sure they could use another waitress most nights." The dining room had nine other customers, at the moment. "This is a week night. It's snowing."

"Don Bledsoe has some apartments above the drugstore. I don't know if he takes babies."

"We couldn't live with you, Dad. I mean, we could. But it would be hard for all of us. Because of Sam. Because he sometimes doesn't sleep much. You would have no peace. And Mom. When she comes home." Her voice trailed off. He rustled busily in his pocket.

"You're an adult. I think we can safely say that." He corrected himself. "You have the responsibilities of an adult."

He wrote a check for the dinner bill. He wrote a second one, for a thousand dollars, to Dorrie. She took it, thanked him without looking at him, and they stood up to go.

Sam breathed gently. Dorrie lay awake in her knotty-pine room in the basement, thinking about the face of the waitress, Gloria. The white face. The lacquered blue-black hair. The bright aqua eyes, raccooned in black. She was like one of those geisha dolls people keep in glass boxes. She thought about Gloria's husky voice, something about that voice. And then she remembered, in a rush, the way a diver pops up through the water's surface, that Gloria had once been a bouncy-haired girl named Ticker.

Ticker was a senior at Madrid High when Dorrie was a freshman. Ticker wore braces, then, and had a full, rosy face and longish brown hair. She ran with a group of kids who were rumored to call themselves, privately, the Swamp Cats. They were fast. They were greasers. Their families didn't have much money. But Ticker went out her entire senior year with Murray Medvic, a guard on the basketball team, blond and angular, the son of the biggest wheat farmer in the county. So it didn't all hold together. Murray wasn't the Swamp Cat type.

Dorrie remembered the way Ticker and Murray lounged by the lockers, hazy-eyed and cocky. She leaned against the wall, a finger curved through Murray's belt loop. He faced her, hand propped on the wall, snapping his gum.

Ticker's mother, Bernice, a large, fierce-eyed woman, was the morning waitress at the Homestead for years. Ticker's younger brother was Buddy, Buddy Beauchamp, the one in Dorrie's class. The one who died. Yes.

Buddy had sandy hair and pale blue eyes, but he

must have been part Blackfeet because he was buried fifty miles away on the reservation on a very cold day in November.

The Beauchamps—there were three kids but no dad—lived in a tarpaper-covered basement out by Wickman's Oilfield Supply, one of a half dozen houses in town that never got much above the ground. Someone said the house didn't have an indoor bathroom. Living in town, and they still had to use an outhouse. They had to run outside in the bone-clattering winter to use an outhouse.

The older Beauchamp boy was deaf and never went to school, and they sent him away somewhere when he was sixteen.

When Bernice left for work every day, she put two loaves of white bread on the counter, and Gloria and Buddy and the deaf one, before he went away, ate margarine and sugar sandwiches after school. Dorrie's friend Sandra Shepherd knew the details from her older sisters. Dorrie thought about Gloria's sugar-white face and knew she was remembering right.

A few other older kids came back, when she tried to remember them. Kenny Harte, winning basket at the tournament, girlfriend named Peggy, father killed in a tractor accident. Linda Fritz, sat on the boys' laps on the choir bus, Mormon, Pep Club president. Valerie Leno, moved to Madrid from Arkansas, mother taught piano, sister a cheerleader who got pregnant.

The Swamp Cats. They drank beer in cars parked out by the highway department's gravel pits or, on summer nights, in Old Maid's Coulee, where they could sink beneath the surface of the prairie, away from the sheriff or his deputy. The girl Swamp Cats were also called Swamp Kittens. All the Swamp Cats gave themselves nicknames: Ticker. V-8. Deano. Cinder. Their initiation ritual was to run across the railroad trestle on the east edge of town. It was an iron trestle with no rail—a hundred feet high and more than a hundred yards long—that connected the cutbanks on either side of Wolf River. The river itself was narrow and shallow. If you fell, if a train came, you were finished. That was the ritual, to run across naked, at night, from the Madrid side to the prairie side. That was the story.

Buddy Beauchamp had lifeless hair and a chubby stomach that pushed against his shirt buttons, making them gap. His face was pinched and old, and he wore eyeglasses that were too small for his face. His chin jutted out. He looked at once pugnacious, fragile, and puffy.

He had a terrible temper. Once, he started pounding on another boy at recess and his face darkened to an unnatural rose color and he screamed like a cornered animal. Another time he threw his glasses to the ground, and they broke, and he stomped them into little mounds of glass.

He had a crush on Jon Duke, the center on the high school basketball team. He pasted a newspaper photo of Jon in his notebook and wouldn't take it out, even when the others saw it and pointed and snickered behind their hands.

Buddy mocked fervor by his extension of it to such lengths. Teachers and others saw it as their duty to defuse him. But when Mr. Richards, the principal, took Buddy to the little storeroom at the end of the hall and smacked him hard with a ruler, Buddy didn't turn silent and refuse to cry, like some of the boys did. He wailed as if the world held absolutely nothing for him, and the sound seemed to fill the whole school and float out over the town.

His outbursts marked him and made the other kids stay away. He embarrassed them. He was unseemly and transparent. He wore his futile, off-key passions on the outside where they could be seen and punished.

Dorrie and Buddy were both part of a group that left in four station wagons, one Saturday morning in the dead of winter, to go to a grade school basketball game fifty-five miles west of Madrid at Eagle School on the reservation. The principal at Eagle was the cousin of the coach at Madrid, and he had set up an elaborate playing schedule with eleven different teams from as far as a hundred miles away.

The coach had made Buddy the manager of the grade school team to give him something normal to do. Dorrie and five other eighth-grade girls were the cheerleaders.

They drove through a ground blizzard, the low sideways wind wrapping the car in gauzy layers of snow. For a while, it was so bad that the kids on the passenger sides had to open the doors a little and call out when the car drifted too close to the edge of the road. Sometimes the wind died for a moment, revealing a sky above that was a hard, calm blue.

The school gym was an abandoned cafeteria room with a wood stove, the room's only heat, fixed to the middle of the playing floor. Half a dozen spectators sat on benches with their parkas on, rubbing their hands together against the seeping subzero cold. The stove hissed and crackled.

A whistle blew and the boys broke their huddles to sprint onto the floor. They moved stiffly, frantically, from the cold, and smacked their hands together to warm them. Because of the stove, the game was played near the edges of the floor. When the boys dribbled backward or sideways, they shot their eyes over their shoulders to fix the position of the stove, which seemed to glow.

The cheerleaders had put together outfits of tan

pleated skirts and shapeless royal-blue sweaters ordered from Sears. They had also ordered large C's, for Coyotes, and sewn them on the fronts of the sweaters. The letters were so large they pulled down the sweater necklines to reveal the girls' bony collarbones.

"Chickalacka, chickalacka, chow chow chow!" the cheerleaders yelled into the chilly, hollow-sounding room. Their only fans were the four parents who had driven the station wagons and eight-year-old Debbie Westermark, Kiki Westermark's little sister, who had an excessively deep voice, deeper than any boy's. "Chow, chow, chow," she barked, a beat behind, in her croupy voice. A couple of adults on the Eagle side of the room laughed.

"Boomalacka, boomalacka, bow wow wow!"

"Wow, wow," barked Debbie.

"Chickalacka, boomalacka, who are *we*? The Madrid, Montana, Coyotes, yessirr-*ee*!" And they threw their pompons high into the air, caught them, and tried to finish up with splits, although Renee Howard was the only one who could get all the way to the floor.

Only Buddy looked absolutely at ease. Everyone else was yelling, or huddled against the cold, or bounding with strained expressions on their faces across the floor, their legs goose-pimpled. But Buddy paced back and forth along the sidelines, absolutely happy, wearing a nappy gray sweater that was too small and showed part of his stomach. Whenever a boy was taken out of the game and sat puffing on the bench, Buddy rushed over with towels and water and a sweatshirt to fling over his shoulders. He ministered to his charges as crisply and tenderly as a young nurse.

Off-court, in the harder world of school and playground, Buddy began to brag. One of the things he started to say was that he personally knew three Swamp Cats: his older sister, Gloria, whose friends called her Ticker;

his seventeen-year-old neighbor, Roger; and Roger's friend, who was also named Roger. He started insisting on this knowledge, on the playground at recess, walking home after school. He would say that he personally knew those three Swamp Cats, and then the other kids would hoot at him and jeer, and Buddy would get red-faced and eventually begin screaming and kicking. But he kept bringing it up.

Swamp Cats set fires, he said. They stubbed their cigarettes out on the faces of unsuspecting children who camped in backyards during the heat of the summer. More than a few Swamp Kittens got pregnant and had to go away to have babies. His own sister, Gloria, was a Swamp Kitten. She was, yes she was.

Swamp Cats and Swamp Kittens were normal people during the day, he said. It was only at night that their Swamp Cat side came out. The rest of the time, they were like anyone else. They were your cousin, your babysitter, your sister, your brother.

Bernice told the coroner she shook Buddy's foot shortly before 6:30 A.M., then went to work. The foot was hanging over the edge of the top bunk where Buddy slept. She shook his foot and then she drove to the Homestead Cafe in her drafty old Rambler, which she had some trouble starting that morning. She let herself in the kitchen door on the alley, got the creams and syrups ready, called in Elmer Davidson's order, then sat at the counter and smoked a cigarette and glanced at the paper, waiting for the breakfast flurry.

This is what Dorrie thought about, lying in her bed in the basement. That Bernice had flicked through the paper, drunk a cup of coffee, fixed a smile on her big capable face, and started taking orders—while her son lay dead at home. She had proceeded in absolute ignorance toward impalement. Dorrie thought of a story she once heard about two college kids in a boat on rough river water. The one in the prow turned around to find his buddy vanished. "I had been laughing and yelling all by myself and didn't even know it," he told the reporter. "Try to think about that."

How long had she been ignorant with Rader? How long had he been gone before she knew it? She curled up against the rush of poison. She tried to exhale it.

Sam breathed gently next to Dorrie in her white teenager's bed. She touched his warm little head and pulled the covers higher over him. She listened to Earl creak the floorboards of his bedroom upstairs. Her casement window, when she got up to push it open an inch, groaned with the cold.

# Chapter 6

Rosemary Vane was once a handsome, sometimes beautiful, woman. She was tall, fine-boned, slim, with glossy dark hair. A single white streak had mysteriously appeared when she was just nineteen, and it swept back dramatically across the crown of her head. Her eyes were her most expressive feature—gray and wide-set under full, winglike brows. She had delicate, apologetic shoulders, long fingers, beautiful white feet.

Until the fall of 1957, Dorrie's sophomore year in high school, Rosemary was a careful person. Their house was waxed, polished, ordered. The toilet water was deodorized and blue. The Kleenex box had a crocheted cover. Ironed sheets and folded towels were stacked neatly in scented cupboards. Recipes were filed in a flowered metal box. Flower magnets held grocery lists to the refrigerator door. She did certain housework on certain days and never varied the schedule: laundry Tuesday, ironing Wednesday, shopping Thursday when the grocery sales were on, floor-waxing Friday, and so on.

She had a placid, flat temperament, and her exchanges with Earl and Dorrie were parceled and functional. How had their days been? Was it time to winterize the car? Who won the basketball game?

Dorrie seemed to remember a time when her mother had been imaginative and animated, had told her stories, had laughed. But that had been years and years earlier, if it had been at all. She wasn't sure. She also knew something had *happened* to Rosemary before she was married, but she didn't know any details and was too afraid to ask.

Rosemary had a hysterectomy when Dorrie was eight, and after that she took a nap every afternoon. Earl treated her as though she were very slightly crippled. If she missed a nap, he reminded her to go to bed early. They slept in separate beds in the same room.

When she woke from a nap, Rosemary had a cup of coffee and leafed through her *McCall's* or *Good Housekeeping* before she started to make dinner. She clipped things and filed them in a drawer with labeled folders. "Canning: Do's and Don't's." That was one Dorrie remembered, because Rosemary never canned anything, either before or after she saw the article. "How to Pack A Suitcase for a Man." That was another. She sipped her coffee, and scissored it out, and slipped it into a folder labeled TRAVEL.

Rosemary drove a hundred miles to Great Falls on a Friday in late September of 1957, and she bought a red woolen coat. It was a clear hunter's red, calf length, with a stand-up collar. A beautiful coat. And it was enormously expensive. Dorrie saw the price tag. It cost as much as a large piece of furniture.

During the next week, Rosemary charged a number of other things at stores in Madrid: a kitchen table and chairs, carpet for the bathroom, new curtains, twelve T-bone steaks, a large radio, and a black off-the-shoulder sweater. Earl protested each purchase more vehemently and made her take the radio back, because they already had three. "What's *wrong* with you?" he burst out, pointing at it as if it might explode. She shrugged excitedly.

Dorrie was so deeply shocked by all this—her frugal, orderly, calm parent on a spree—that she pretended she didn't notice. She tried to spend more time at her best friend Sandra's house, where it was very noisy and cheerful.

Rosemary began to wear the red coat around the house, draped over her shoulders. She looked frightening and beautiful. One night she served dinner by candlelight, her white shoulders and long neck naked above the black sweater. "There!" she said, her arms spread as if to embrace them both, her voice exuberant. "Isn't this nice for a change? Isn't this better?" Earl watched her warily. He said nothing about the sweater or the candles. He asked if she'd had her nap. Later, he mentioned something to Dorrie about this *thing,* this strange animation, happening before, long ago, before Dorrie was born. He said it was dangerous. He made a phone call to Rosemary's brother in St. Paul. He dug his thumbs exhaustedly into the corners of his eyes.

For the first week and more, Dorrie was aghast at this new version of her mother, embarrassed for her. She wanted her to return to the person she fully recognized. But as she sat at the candlelit table with her parents, she watched her mother's face and realized that *this* person, *this* Rosemary, might be the real one. Perhaps she had been waiting, radiant and alive, all these years. And now that she was out, was here, wasn't she the one who should stay?

"This *is* better," Dorrie announced, looking straight at Earl. He shook his head sorrowfully and bent over his food.

For the next few weeks, Rosemary was springy, happy, bursting with energy. She seemed, for the first time Dorrie could remember, to be truly interested—even fascinated—by her own daughter. She looked at Dorrie kindly, directly in the eyes. She asked her about her life, how she *felt* about school and her few friends. She praised her, told her she was lovely and unique, and anyone who didn't see that was a fool. A fool.

This was at a time in Dorrie's life when she felt almost monstrous. She was taller than most of the girls in her class and slumped to mitigate both her height and the breasts that seemed to expand heedlessly, day by day. Sometimes she framed her face with her hands, pursed out her lips, and widened her eyes. And when she did that, she told herself she would look like a fashion model, with the right makeup. Nobody else ever said that, though, and she knew she was, to the world, tall and quiet, sarcastic if you knew her, big-breasted, slumped.

Rosemary gently pushed back Dorrie's shoulders. "You're gorgeous," she said. "You really are. You'll see that I'm right." And Dorrie adored her for it, though it was a stranger speaking.

With each day, Rosemary got more flamboyant and careless. She ignored her old routine. Dust started to accumulate. Dishes piled up until Earl and Dorrie started to do them. "Come on!" she'd say when Dorrie walked into the disheveled kitchen after school. "Let's go for a drive!" And they'd get into the car and drive out of town fast, to the airport, maybe, or just along county roads. Rosemary squinted at the road and asked Dorrie strange questions. "What do you think about Sputnik, zooming around up there, peering down?" she asked. "Do you think we are turning into our own guardian angels?" Another time she looked sideways, gently, at Dorrie. "Sometimes," she said, "I feel that I am you."

Those kinds of remarks carried small danger flags with them, but Dorrie closed her eyes. She made a long interior leap, choosing this new version of her mother over Earl's nervous gloom. And the weather—the last gorgeous, metallic days of autumn—seemed to support her choice. Gusts of wind blew the last gold leaves out of the scattered trees in veils. The Rockies had new, snowy tops and gleamed in the far distance. In the mornings, hard frost covered windshields and sidewalks. The sun came up and made the ice crystals brilliant.

There came a day, though, when it all turned into something else. Dorrie came home from school to find her mother yelling on the phone. "What do you mean by that, Ruth?" she screamed. Ruth Allen was a neighbor. "What do you mean by that, I said. Say what you mean. You never say what you mean. You never have." She held the phone in the air for a minute, then slammed it down and stalked out of the room without a glance at Dorrie. There was the sound of running bathwater, and the click of the bathroom door lock, and she stayed there for two hours. At dinner, she wanted Dorrie and Earl to recite anything—a poem, a speech, a part of a speech—that they knew by memory. Neither of them could remember anything.

She decided to paint an intricate border of fleur-de-lis around the ceiling of Dorrie's bedroom, which is why Dorrie moved downstairs to the basement room and then stayed there because it felt removed and comprehensible. The project was chaotic and fumy, and Rosemary abandoned it in disgust when the stylized flowers wouldn't turn out right. She painted over the flowers.

She bought a second television set and installed it in that room.

And then the footsteps began. Dorrie woke one night to hear squeaking footsteps directly overhead. They moved across the floor in the direction of the kitchen. Then she heard running water and the faint slam of one cupboard door, then another, which surprised her because any late-night walking around by her parents should have been brief—to the bathroom and back, to the kitchen for a glass of water. But these footsteps kept moving. Back and forth across the living room, which was directly above Dorrie's room, down the hall to the bathroom, back to the living room, into the kitchen, over in the direction of Dorrie's old bedroom, then into that room, which was now a den.

They paused there, and Dorrie heard the hum of a test pattern from the television. Then silence. Then the footsteps again. They were light and even, which meant they were Rosemary's. Earl's were slower, weightier, and his bad hip gave them a slight lurch.

Dorrie lay bolt awake, straining to hear something more that might explain those steady, quiet steps. But they were as tense and aimless as a cat's in a cage. And while she listened, she realized that she had been expecting them. All these weeks, she had been expecting them.

Night after night, they continued, and a heaviness settled in Dorrie's stomach that made it difficult for her to talk much, to eat, to respond to her mother anymore. With each notch that Rosemary speeded up, day and night, Dorrie seemed to slow and flatten. She had the sense, sometimes, that a fuel transfer was taking place, and she was the one who would end up empty.

One day, after school, Dorrie went into the high school gym alone to look under the bleachers for her lost rabbit-furred gloves. She couldn't remember sleeping at all the night before, because of the pacing, and she felt teary and light-headed. As she searched under the bleacher seats, stooped, she heard slow footsteps. She peered through the slats and saw Buddy Beauchamp walking across the gym floor. His footsteps echoed, and he moved up on his toes to make them more quiet. She watched.

On the other side of the gym, there was a life-sized cardboard cutout of Jon Duke, made by Reinhart's Photo Studio when he set the school's point-scoring record for a single season. It was black-and-white and showed him grinning, his arms folded confidently across his basketball uniform.

Buddy walked up to the cardboard Jon Duke and looked at it. Then he slowly put his arms around the cardboard and rested his face against Jon Duke's chest. He stayed like that for a long time.

Dorrie breathed shallowly. Before these long weeks with Rosemary, she would have been shocked. Now she just wished him away. Away. And eventually he did leave, the sounds of his shoes echoing a little in the huge room.

Three days later, Buddy died. At home, in an iron-framed bunk bed. His sister Gloria had spent the night at a girlfriend's. His mother Bernice had left the house without knowing. The coroner said it was a rapid, acute pulmonary condition. Dorrie saw Buddy in the gym on Monday. On Friday, he was lying in a suit on puffy white satin at Cavanaugh's Funeral Home, his stubby fingers folded over his chest. They had smoothed some kind of oil on his nappy hair, but it still wouldn't lie flat. He wore his glasses, and his small mouth was imperfectly rouged, like an old lady's. Dorrie and Sandra and some other classmates went to visit him and left in absolute silence.

"Your father is a hero, you know," Rosemary whispered to her one morning at breakfast, after Earl had gone to work. "He threw himself in the path of a car and saved the life of a neighbor child. Years and years ago. He threw his body on the little boy's, and they rolled to the curb." She made an end-over-end motion with her long fingers. The red coat was draped over one thin shoulder. "That's how he hurt his hip. The bone was broken in three places. He walked with canes when I met him."

"I thought it was arthritis." Dorrie felt as if they were arguing over the plot of a movie they'd both seen several times.

"You *thought* it was arthritis, because your father just let you think that. And of course it *is* arthritis, but it's a heroic form of it. It has a known cause." She pushed her hair back impatiently. There were dark circles under her eyes. "He is a very, very modest man," she said bitterly.

The next day, Rosemary plucked out half of her thick winged eyebrows. The day after that, she plucked out all the rest and replaced them with arched pencil lines. She looked perpetually amazed.

Earl, who usually ate lunch at the Homestead with bank people, began to come home at noon to check on Rosemary. He brought hamburgers from the A&W and they threw their greasy wrappers in a sack, which Earl took outside to the garbage on his way back to work. He tried to take Rosemary to Roy Greenfield, their doctor, but she refused to go. Dorrie heard arguments from their room at night. Crying. More walking. And one night, a slammed door, and the car engine starting, then their voices in the garage, and the engine turning off. She couldn't sleep, waiting for what would happen next. Would the car start up again? Would it leave? She couldn't remember the last time she had really slept. Teachers asked if she was sick.

One night, Dorrie heard the footsteps again, back

and forth, back and forth. Then they stopped and began to come down the basement stairs, fast. Her blood began to pound in her temples. She imagined her mother in the dark with those eyebrows, or perhaps, if she'd washed the pencil off, with no eyebrows at all.

"What do you want?" Dorrie shrieked, just as the footsteps got to her closed bedroom door. She heard fast breathing on the other side of the door. She flicked on the bedside lamp and jumped onto the cold floor to face the door. "What do you want?" she screamed again. She heard Earl's heavy footsteps over her head.

"I'd like some company, Dorrie," came her mother's low, rapid voice from behind the door. "I have a number of things to talk to you about. I've been thinking. We have talking to do." She was panting.

Dorrie flung open the door and grabbed her mother's arm and yanked. "Come in," she yelled, her voice trembling. "Come in and talk and talk and talk." She gave the arm another yank. Rosemary lurched toward her, then tipped suddenly to the side, and fell, with a sharp cry, onto the floor. They heard the bone crack.

Rosemary couldn't stop walking. She walked out of the hospital that night and they found her a half mile out of town in her hospital gown and slippers, scuffling through the season's first powdery layer of snow. They gave her drugs and kept her in the hospital. But she couldn't stop. She got outside again, in the middle of the afternoon, and fell on a patch of black ice, badly bruising her hip and the elbow of the arm that wasn't broken. They took her more than two hundred miles away to Warm Springs, the state hospital, where she got electroshock treatments.

And when they brought her home she was the first Rosemary, the original Rosemary, again. Paler, with brownish circles under her eyes, but basically what she had been before "this lengthy episode," as Earl called it. She was quiet and contained and took naps again. The only real evidence that something had happened, besides some gaps in her recent memory, was the cast on her forearm.

Dorrie couldn't bear to look at the cast. When she did, she felt monstrous. It was a discovery: her own fear, taken far enough, made her lethal.

The cast was the only obvious token of that long autumn. They all behaved as though it didn't exist. And one day Earl drove Rosemary to Dr. Greenfield's office, and when she came home, it too was gone.

Two and half years later the walking started again, that soft, relentless creaking overhead. By then, the three of them—Dorrie, Earl, and Rosemary herself—had encased themselves in separate lives. Dorrie studied in her room in the basement. She got good grades and began to think about good colleges. She carhopped at the A&W in the summers. She turned down a couple of dates, and then no one asked anymore. She kept the same two girlfriends—Sandra Shepherd, a red-haired girl with white eyelashes who worshiped Fabian and felt tormented by her large, loud family, and Rhonda Lynch, quiet and studious, who was semiengaged to a Mormon missionary who was away for two years in Japan.

Dorrie kept Sandra and Rhonda away from her house and her mother, though Rosemary, most of the time, was as polite and distant as a servant.

Earl went to the Elks Club more often and joined a couple of Elks committees. He went to some meetings of the John Birch Society with Skeet Englestad, a fellow Elk. Then he subscribed to *American Opinion*, the Birch magazine. He became a member of the Society, then head of the local branch. He worked late or had meetings four or five nights a week.

Rosemary took longer naps. She joined a book club, then quit it because they were reading *'Twixt Twelve and Twenty* by Pat Boone. She got very few phone calls. Dorrie suspected Rosemary had done something at the book club, made some kind of odd remark to someone. Because, although she looked and dressed and moved like the old Rosemary, there was, since the hospitals, something odd and antagonistic on the edges of her. She read and smoked late at night in the den, and sometimes you could hear her laugh to herself, and it was a harsh, knowing laugh. Sometimes she slept in the den, wrapped in an old blanket. She went through her files one day and dumped all her magazine clippings in the fireplace and burned them. When things wore out—light bulbs, the shower curtain, the ironing board cover—Earl replaced them.

The summer after Dorrie graduated from high school, there came a day when Rosemary's voice climbed a half pitch and then another; and she began to move faster and confide in them, her voice higher and faster; and she stopped taking naps, and stopped doing the dishes, and she arranged the clothes she wore in new ways—she tied a long scarf around her waist, she fastened her hair with a rhinestone clip she'd found in the Safeway parking lot. She smiled and was busy and she bought something new every day, small things, paid for with the grocery money, because, after the last time, Earl had revoked her charging privileges all over town.

Earl and Dorrie watched her, trying to cool her down with their eyes. They spoke to each other in edgy, conspiratorial tones, like scouts in enemy territory.

Then came the night-walking. And the circles under her eyes, and the desperate vivacity. She poured over the weekly newspaper as if it were in code. She saw that the county commissioners had held a meeting to discuss weed control along the county roads, and she shouted excitedly about the weeds they'd missed right under their very noses, right in town, in every single vacant lot, behind the Assembly of God church, along the railroad tracks, on more than a few lawns.

"They're taking over!" she said, snapping a fingernail against the newspaper. "You don't even know they're growing, and all of a sudden there's nothing else!" One afternoon she went to the commissioners' meeting, hoping they'd discuss weeds. Earl showed up to complain about some problems with the magazine section at the library, and he saw her sitting there, ready to speak. He turned white, grabbed her by the elbow, and took her home.

Earl had begun to make the meals, and he mashed the powerful tranquilizers with a spoon and put them in Rosemary's food. After a few days, she knew what was going on and threw a plateful of stew across the dining room just as the paper boy showed up at the door to collect. She sent the boy away with no money and whirled to face Earl. "How would *you* feel if I pressed a pillow over your face and watched you kick?"

A small cat had begun to come to the back door in the evenings, seeking food. Sometimes Madeleine, their old terrier, ran the little cat off, but most of the time she let it sit there, as if to see how long it would silently beg. The little cat looked as if it had recently belonged to someone.

Rosemary hated the cat, although it didn't yowl or whine. It just appeared silently and crouched on the step. It was August, now, and hot. The kitchen fan clattered. The cat, through the screen door, looked like a small tan sphinx. Rosemary tried to run it off with a broom, but it always came back. Sometimes it walked daintily up to the screen, braced its front paws on the door, and stretched. Just that.

"Don't give it anything," Rosemary said urgently to Dorrie. "It will never leave."

"It's never leaving anyway," Dorrie answered in the flat, lofty voice she had adopted.

"It could, though," Rosemary said unsteadily. "We shouldn't give it a reason to stay."

Three days later, Rosemary walked downtown and marched in the Trail's End parade. She had stayed up all night, doing something in the den. Dorrie and Earl walked to the parade together, thinking she was finally asleep behind the closed door.

She was at the very end of the parade, all dressed up, marching, smiling. She wore a yellow rubber glove on one hand, and used the tip of one rubber finger to peel off each pamphlet before handing it to someone on the sidelines. Between pamphlets she waved. The pamphlets were hand-lettered. They said: KILL THE WEEDS BEFORE THEY KILL MADRID.

When Rosemary climbed slowly into the Oldsmobile so Earl could drive her to Warm Springs, she wore her long red coat, though the day was already hot. By now, it had become a broad joke, a costume.

Dorrie, who had been packing for college, watched them leave. She watched her mother's beautiful hair, with its single streak like a tendril of smoke. She watched her lean against the dashboard, holding it with both hands, while Earl slowly rotated his torso and backed the big blue car into the street.

# Chapter 7

The girls on her dormitory floor had the skittishness of small-town girls in the city. A number of them had grown up on farms or in towns as small as Madrid, and the leap to the University of Chicago made them so dizzy they were almost hysterical.

Dorrie's roommate, a solemn blonde from a town of seven hundred in Indiana, quit school the third week and went home to marry her boyfriend. The next roommate carried a little book with her everywhere, which listed calorie counts of every food. She passed it around at meals in the huge clanging dining room, so everyone could tally everything.

Dorrie didn't know exactly what she had expected when she left Madrid, except that she had seen, in her mind, gleaming tracks that headed due east across the plains to burrow their way, eventually, into a green and windless place, an oval of spreading trees around a fort-like building with something Latin and pure-hearted over the portal. *Lux et Veritas.* The vision had a vivid schematic look to it, like a drawing in a children's primer. You wanted to jump inside it.

She felt disappointed at college, and old. She realized that she had felt old for a long time. It was just that she noticed it more now, living under the same roof as others her age. She spent long hours in the library, trying to read herself into the Renaissance or Jane Austen's parlor—anyplace that took her a long way away. But eventually she always had to go back to the dorm. And there they were, in their cluttered cells, with their curlers, notebooks, cigarettes, damp nylons, photos of boyfriends and movie stars, stuffed animals, fashion magazines, radios, weekly newspapers from home. Every night, they rinsed out their girdles and bras and nylons, and put curlers in their hair, and rubbed cream into their faces. Each morning, they unwound the curlers and combed and dressed and stood before the full-length mirror in the bathroom, one by one, a hand on a wool-skirted hip, a finger blotting a lip, an anxious glance over a shoulder at a hem, a little shriek at something someone said, slammed doors, off to class.

The roommate with the calorie book cried, sometimes, in her sleep.

They stood there, Saturday and Sunday mornings, brushing teeth, poking meditatively at a blemish, talking about a party the night before, their young skin pale under the harsh fluorescent lights. And there might be one of them, a little apart, down by the end of the row of sinks—GiGi Gordon, say, or Helen Key—who had deep circles under her eyes and a contained, older look to her, though she was just a freshman too. And you knew she had done it, made love, the night before, with—who knew?—because GiGi slept around, and no one knew much at all about Helen.

They had stepped—a GiGi, a Helen—outside the communal virginity of the fourth floor of the girls' dorm. They did not share information about where they had gone, what they had done before they slipped back, just before curfew. They had simply stepped away from the pack, and the others were giddy and censorious. Some saw them as versions of compulsive gamblers or kleptomaniacs—people with embarrassing compulsions that put them at great risk. Look at the possibilities: the wrong husband, a shoddy reputation, a home for unwed mothers, quacks with dirty knives. Everyone knew a forced-marriage story, a back-alley story. Who'd risk it?

Dorrie, though, felt a secret envy sometimes. She wondered what it would be like to slip something forbidden, maybe costly—a diamond, a silver necklace—into your pocket and just walk off like you owned it.

What a slut! they said about a Gigi or a Helen, as they milled around in their slips under the cold lights.

Rosemary, at Christmas, reminded Dorrie of someone who had stepped in for the drunken star—tentative and unrehearsed, but pointedly calm.

None of them mentioned the Trail's End parade or the hospital. Not a word. It was another Rosemary who had marched in a parade wearing a dazzling smile and a rubber glove, who had paced and wept and stayed up all night penning warnings about weeds. That particular Rosemary was gone, but they knew she was lingering in the wings, ready to run out under the stage lights if she thought she had been given a cue. So there were no cues, nothing that acknowledged her past behavior or the curtained presence of her other.

The Rosemary in attendance was subdued and cooperative. Although her movements seemed to occur without her full participation, she cooked meals and cleaned the house, and even found a tree she liked at the Christmas-tree lot near the Texaco station and brought it home so Earl could spray flocking all over it. When it was all white, they strung blue lights on it and hung on its branches metallic balls that were the same pale blue as the sofa. They turned on KMON radio to hear the carols. "Perfect," Rosemary said when Earl plugged the lights in.

From time to time, she seemed to blink herself more fully into the room, and then she would ask Dorrie a question about college, her classes, what Chicago was like. But the electroshock had wiped out some of her recent memory, so she sometimes found herself at a loss. She didn't remember that Dorrie lived in a dormitory, for instance. She forgot who John Kennedy had run against for President, though she knew he was about to be sworn in.

And Dorrie wasn't much help. She had tried, that first time, to ally herself with the talkative, confiding, charming, ultimately rampant version of her mother. And it hadn't worked. It had become grotesque. She had broken her own mother's arm. Since then, she had developed a habit of silence around both her parents, and come to feel their mere presence as an interrogation. Their effect, if not their aim, was to crack her heart, to bring her to her knees. And so she withheld herself, to stay strong. She muttered stripped, rude answers to her mother's labored questions, unable to help herself.

That Christmas, Earl bought Rosemary a camera with a self-timer, so you could set it on a tripod and scurry around front, and it would take your picture on its own. On Christmas morning, Rosemary fixed French toast, and they went to the Methodist service, though Earl wanted to change churches because he'd discovered that the new minister, a twenty-six-year-old from Boston, had socialist connections. The day was very cold and clear and silent, and they walked the four blocks to the church over snow that squeaked like Styrofoam. The church was on a rise, and when they got there they could see the edge of town and the snow-blazing prairie stretching for miles. They squinted into the reflected sun. Their breath puffed white. Earl limped heavily up the steps.

Rosemary wore her red coat, but it looked different now, because Earl had bought her a large fur collar to attach to it. It draped over her shoulders like a shawl, and was the skin of a long, thin, pointy-headed animal that looked like Dorrie's idea of a lynx, though neither Earl nor Rosemary could say, for sure, what it was. The pelt circled Rosemary's sloped red shoulders, the eyes open and beady, the teeth biting the feet.

After church, they sat on the couch so Earl could try the new camera. It was a quiet house. It always had been, until Rosemary's episodes. But now, as the shutter buzzed its ten seconds, and they sat together stiffly, the three of them, Dorrie thought she had never heard such silence. And when she saw the photo, a week later, it was so brutal she tucked it in a pocket, then ripped it up and threw it away.

It was overexposed. Their faces were dead white, and the flash had given Dorrie and Earl red lights for eyes. They sat on either side of Rosemary like Martian guards. The family. All three of them had their hands folded identically in their laps. Rosemary stared slightly off to the side, her lovely strong face dominated by her dark, deep-set eyes. The flash had missed them. They weren't red. They were alive and eloquent. What am I doing in this place? they said. How did I get here?

Helen Key sat just ahead of Dorrie in microbiology class during winter quarter, and one day she turned around and asked to borrow some notes.

Helen had somehow managed to move out of the

dorm—freshman girls generally weren't allowed to—and they studied for the midterm together at her apartment, three plant-filled rooms on the third floor of a pre–World War I building near the campus. They studied at a table lit by an old brass lamp with a rose-colored shade. They drank coffee, and Helen played Louis Armstrong, turned low, on the record player, and once, turning up the volume to hear his grand and demented voice, they listened to Dylan Thomas reading his own poems, and Helen kept her eyes closed the whole time.

Helen was from Two Forks, a tiny town in southwestern Illinois, and she said its name with mock terror, pulling up the neck of her big turtleneck sweater so that her dark eyes peaked over the top.

Microbiology was Dorrie's last class on Mondays, Wednesdays, and Fridays, and Helen began to invite her over for dinner afterward, a time or two a week. Helen's lover, a bearded graduate student named Ben, stayed at the apartment a couple of nights a week, so he was often there at dinner too. Dorrie liked him. He looked like the philosophy major he was—solemn, inquisitive, old-eyed—but he also had a clear, young laugh that burst out of him at odd times and made everyone else in the room laugh too.

He and Helen were serious students, both of them. They read the Russians, the Freudians, the Marxists. They had long, arcane discussions, curled up stocking-footed on the couch. I love the boy madly, Helen said dryly in his presence. And it was clear to Dorrie that she did.

Ben was a rhythm-and-blues fan. Sometimes he played a drumbeat on the edge of the table with his index fingers, listening to something he liked inside his head. He had recently discovered a three-man band in town—they played at a bar called Pinocchio's—and he brought the piano player to Helen's for dinner, one Monday in February. He had run into him at a record store.

His name was Bill Rader, but no one used his first name. He was lanky and low-voiced and wore a tweed driving cap. That's all Dorrie noticed at first, as she stirred the spaghetti sauce on Helen's tiny gas stove. They came in, Ben and Rader, bringing with them a cloud of dampness. It was raining hard, and the wind had come up and was scraping a black branch against the kitchen window. The spaghetti sauce burbled and puffed.

Helen covered the card table with an old bedspread and lit a big candle in a wine jug. They drank wine and ate spaghetti in the dim, flickering room with the storm beating on the walls. Helen told a story in her secretive, sly voice, and Ben's laugh soared high, and they all laughed with him. Rader sat at Dorrie's right, and their knees accidentally touched under the small table, and then it happened again at the end of the meal, and his leg didn't move away for a long time, and hers didn't either.

He didn't talk much. He smelled warm and clean-sweated, with something pungent and male on the edges. His damp wool cap hung on the corner of his chairback. His hand rested on the table, pale and long-fingered. She imagined it moving rapidly over a keyboard. His face was narrow, almost gaunt, and his eyes were crinkled at the corners.

After dinner they drank inky coffee and more wine, and at some point she and Rader made some kind of friendly bet and shook hands elaborately. Strong hands, he said appreciatively. Pretty woman, strong hands. Almost to himself. And then somehow, their hands still clasped, they had their elbows on the table and they were doing an exaggerated arm wrestle, Helen and Ben cheering them on, which ended when Rader, with a dramatic howl, let Dorrie slam the back of his hand onto the table.

Got you, she pronounced, her face flushed with wine and what was going on between them. Got me, he said gently, leaning back in his chair to look at her, their hands still clasped.

A week later, Helen asked Dorrie to move in with her. She needed help with the rent and also wanted company. Ben was leaving soon for Oxford, where he had a fellowship. Ben told Dorrie about a part-time job as a secretary in the alumni office, which she applied for and got.

So, suddenly, life was different. She was leaving the dorm. Helen had forged a voucher that said they were cousins and their parents gave them permission to live together off-campus, for financial reasons. Dorrie had a job that would give her some money of her own. She had a roommate who wore black tights, black clothes, who was studious and elfin and dignified. She had the feel of that tense handclasp, which she called up again and again for the fluttering pang it always gave her. This feels right, she said, carrying a box of clothes up the crumbling front steps of the apartment building.

She sent word to Earl and Rosemary that it would be difficult for her to come home at spring break, because of the job. Summer was doubtful too. She hoped all was well.

At dinner one night, Ben mentioned that he'd run into another guy in Rader's band. "Rader," Ben reminded Helen, pointing to the spot at the card table where Rader had sat. "Did he seem married to you?"

A week before Ben left, he and Helen and Dorrie went to Pinocchio's to hear Rader's band. The bar was dim and seedy, with wooden floors and a bandstand so dark she could see only his hat, bent over the keyboard behind the long piano. It was a Wednesday night, and the crowd was scattered and relaxed. The band sounded subdued, dilatory, plaintive. Helen waved to Rader, but he didn't see them.

They ordered drinks. Ben and Helen huddled together, heads almost touching, mournful and revved up. How can you leave me, Helen said tenderly, just when I'm getting to know how weird you really are? Her hand rested on his thigh. How can you go off to launch a brilliant career, leaving me here to be the breadwinner?

One of Helen's uncles from Two Forks owned a bar and restaurant in the Loop, and he'd offered Helen a hostess job. She was going to join Ben in England when the academic pressure lifted a little, maybe by Christmas. That's going to be *months,* she moaned. Every day will be a little death, he promised her.

Dorrie leaned back against the vinyl seat and peered through the dark. She could see very little, really, except a bar of light here, a glow there, a struck match showing the flicker of a face. It was like driving in the dark in the country. The evidence—what you *saw,* actually—was nothing. A shape, a line of stripes, a light from a distant window, the conelike bars from your headlights, illuminating the barest shard of the world. Anything at all could jump out and run you off the road. The darkness beyond your headlights could be a cliff, for all the evidence there was to the contrary.

Rader suddenly hunched over the piano and ripped into a long solo rag that made people lift their heads sharply, then rock them and murmur, Yes! His hands flew, he jumped, he tipped his face back and closed his eyes and nodded his head, pounding out the beat with a hard left hand. And when he was done, people whistled through their teeth and slammed their hands on the tables. Dorrie drank her beer fast and tried to listen to Helen and Ben.

At a break, Rader walked through the tables toward the bar at the back. He bent over one of them and kissed a woman with blond hair. Dorrie's face flushed. Ben called out.

Rader's face was even thinner than Dorrie remembered it. He sat next to her again and asked her how she was, shaking her hand, tilting his head in mock gentility. She did the same, and saw him register the soft parry with appreciation. He hardly glanced at Ben and Helen, who started their own quiet conversation again.

It was as if she and Rader already had a history, Dorrie thought; something had already happened between them. "I've missed you," he said, smiling crookedly at the sound of the words. Helen threw Dorrie a sharp, curious glance.

"You sound good," Dorrie said. They took long sips of their beers. She pulled a sweater around her shoulders, and he reached behind her neck to pull her long braid gently over her collar. Someone on the stage called to him, and he got up. "Come back sometime," he said. "I mean it."

Ben left. In early June, when Chicago was brisk and watery, Helen flew to Japan for an abortion. Dorrie rode with her on the bus to the airport and watched her walk into the huge plane, a small straight figure in black. Though she talked as if she was familiar with everywhere interesting in the world, Helen had, in fact, never been much of anyplace except Two Forks and Chicago. Once, an aunt took her to Los Angeles. But she had never been on an airplane. Not once. Not until the day she walked onto the big jet and flew to a clinic in Tokyo. Four hours after it was done, they put her on another plane, groggy and bent with cramps, and she flew round the clock once, and then she was home.

She went to Tokyo, she told Dorrie, because she knew of a girl from Two Forks who had gotten an abortion in Chicago, three years earlier, in a room behind a homeopathic medicine store. She had gone back to a motel room and bled to death. Helen had heard there were other, safer places now, but she wasn't willing to take a chance. Her doctor told her about Tokyo: told her how to do it, where to go. Her uncle paid and said he didn't ever want to hear about it again.

The uncle had been a tail gunner during the war. He was the only other person in the family who had ever been to Japan.

Helen never told Ben about Japan, and Dorrie never asked why or brought it up at all. But she felt grieved by the whole experience, in some odd, personal way. It had the feel of a disaster—as if Helen, in ending the pregnancy, had wiped out all memory of herself and Ben, the way electrodes on Rosemary's head had erased everything that seemed to make her briefly happy.

Helen took Dorrie to her doctor, and they were both fitted for diaphragms. Life goes on, Helen said. He wouldn't have to be a husband, Dorrie thought, as she put hers in her drawer.

She used it the first time with a law student she had dated half a dozen times, a handsome, serious guy who wanted to be a foreign diplomat. He talked well. He was bright. And one night Dorrie invited him to dinner, and when he asked if he could stay, she said yes.

He told her afterward that she shouldn't have let herself be used that way. And he apologized for himself, too.

They retreated from each other so quickly and completely that they were genuinely shocked when they happened, every couple of months, to run into each other on campus. Dorrie thought his reaction seemed wildly out of proportion to the event itself, which was, for her, disappointing.

Helen started work at her uncle's restaurant. She slept late, and when she got up she was sallow and snappish. She put on weight and bought a small television set for the apartment, which she watched before she went to work. She mentioned once that she'd heard Ben had gotten accepted in the Ph.D. program at Berkeley. She had stopped writing to him after Japan, and when he called once, she had said something to him that made him never call again. When she told Dorrie about the Ph.D. program, she said, "Ben, oh, Ben," and shook her head like a bitter parent.

Then, as suddenly and shockingly as she had gone to Japan, Helen told Dorrie she was getting married. In three days, at the courthouse. He was the manager of the restaurant. Dorrie had met him once. His name was Harold. He was heavy-lidded and fortyish and overly polite. He had a teenage son who helped move Helen's things out of the apartment.

The day she left, one of those September days that feels like high summer but has a slanted, burnished light to it, she and Dorrie sat at the sunlit card table and drank coffee. Helen sighed deeply and looked around her. Dorrie had put a couple of new prints on the wall and installed a bright blue writing table, but it was otherwise the same place she'd moved into just six months earlier. And Helen? Helen, in that bright September light, looked pale and stubborn and tired. She wore bright clothes: a white blouse, a pink cotton skirt, sandals. She looked like somebody from Two Forks, Illinois. They hugged, when she left, but avoided eyes. "It's all yours," Helen called over her shoulder as she left. "Don't lose touch."

That night, Dorrie went to Pinocchio's alone.

# Chapter 8

"Let's go wild," Rita Kay said in a bored voice as they scuffed down the sidewalk after school, kicking small rocks ahead of them.

"How?" said Margaret.

"Do you have money?"

They rifled through their pockets and came up with the money they'd saved by eating candy bars instead of the cafeteria hot lunch.

"I've got my barf-lunch money," Margaret said helpfully.

"Fine," said Rita Kay, pulling a folded dollar bill from her shoe. "So do I." They pivoted quickly and began a slow trot in the opposite direction, toward Main.

It was a damp February day, warm enough for sweaters. A chinook, a long, warm wind from the west, had come to town the day before and raised the temperature almost forty degrees. The brittle, dry-ice world had turned cheerful and soggy. Snowmelt gushed into the drainpipes. Dirty slush flew onto the sides of cars. Everyone peeled off heavy winter coats and gloves and aimed their goose-bumped skin at the sun. It was a rehearsal, a promise that summer existed, even if it wouldn't actually arrive for another four months.

At Bledsoe's Drug, Margaret and Rita Kay slid into a booth and ordered marshmallow Cokes. Margaret loved booths. They were like train cars in the movies, where you got your own little room to sit in, away from everybody else. She liked the feeling that she was still short enough that the top of her head didn't reach the top of the booth—although that was clearly temporary. She was growing so fast she could feel her bones inch along her bedsheets at night. They ached a little when they did it. And then she'd get up in the morning, hold her arms and legs out before her—and, yes, they had grown. Not enough that other people would notice right away, but enough that she did, whose bones they were. It was awful. She'd read an article in *Time* about a new operation that could make you shorter. What they did was cut a chunk out of your leg bones and let them heal back together. It was for people who didn't want to be so tall: women, especially, who didn't want to be taller than their boyfriends, or who couldn't get boyfriends in the first place, because they were so tall. She thought about the operation at night, or in the morning before anybody else was awake, and felt her bones stretch, notch by creaking notch.

She had the sick knowledge, sometimes, that she was a toned-down version of the farm boy with the bad gland. His name was Jay-Jay, and he was a patient of Margaret's father. He was just eleven, and he went to a country school, so she hadn't actually seen him for herself. But she heard her father talking on the phone with

Jay-Jay's mother, Mrs. Tweet. He told her the boy had a gland that was not working right, and that was the explanation for his "rampant growth." Margaret remembered that hard, wild word: rampant. She saw a monster boy with his head among the lower branches of a tree. There was talk of gland surgery to slow him down.

"How big is he now?" Margaret asked loudly, when her father got off the phone.

"How big is who?"

"That boy with the bad gland."

Her father looked at her curiously, then knitted his eyebrows in irritation. "You're awfully curious about someone else's medical problems," he said.

"How *big?*" She could hear the whining insistence in her voice.

"He's six-foot-one," her father said. "And growing." He smiled reassuringly at her.

"Sounds like me!" Margaret said, trying to sound sprightly, stretching out a thin arm to show how short her sleeve was.

"Hmmmm," he said. "You'll have to go some to catch Jay-Jay Tweet."

She scrunched down lower in the booth and jammed her straw into the gooey marshmallow, which lay like a piece of shiny plastic on the surface of her Coke. Coke gushed out, spilled over the side of the metal fountain cup, and fanned lazily across the table. Drops of it plunked onto the floor. They both put their noses close to the table and watched its course. When it began to tap-tap onto the floor, they looked at each other with identical moron eyes. They made identical elaborate moron shrugs. This made them explode in a fit of giggles. When they tried to hold them back, the giggles burst out of them like farts, turning the laughs to small shrieks. They clamped their hands over their mouths as the black-aproned waitress strode over to them.

She was an older woman, far older than their mothers, with a strong, droopy face and steely hair. Sparkly eyeglasses hung from her neck on a chain. She plodded over to their table, a large rag in her hand.

"Having some trouble with those Cokes?" she said in a gravelly, unreadable voice.

They muttered and stared at the table. Rita Kay kicked Margaret lightly, so she'd have to look up. And when she did, Margaret burst into giggles again. She closed her eyes tight and tried to stop, afraid that the waitress was going to yell at her, maybe even kick them out. But she couldn't stop. She couldn't. She felt the most horrible, delicious combination of pressures, and the inevitability that the giggles were going to win. Her face grew hot. There was nothing she could do. Her giggles turned to a full laugh. And she laughed and laughed. She laughed, head against the vinyl back of the booth, until tears ran down her face. She felt ecstatic and outrageous, aware that the waitress and Rita Kay were watching her curiously while she laughed all alone.

When she opened her eyes, the waitress was wiping up the Coke, shaking her head. Rita Kay was staring at the ceiling, a sly, dreamy smile on her face. The waitress walked away, shaking her head some more, and came back with a fresh drink.

"Here," she said gruffly. "Try again." She walked off slowly, shaking her head.

"Here!" Rita Kay hissed, staring cross-eyed at the new Coke with its fresh new layer of marshmallow. "Try again!" But the moment was over. Margaret just smiled now. The wild giggles were gone. She langorously drew her straw over the surface of the marshmallow, then licked it off. She was happy, for the moment. She was sitting in a tall plastic booth on a springlike day with her best friend Rita Kay. The waitress wasn't going to kick them out. It was blue-skied and sunny outside and smelled like mud and clean sheets. She was in Bledsoe's Drug, and she had recently learned that the divorcée, Dorrie the divorcée, lived right upstairs in an apartment. Maybe she was up there now, elegantly sipping her own marshmallow Coke.

She ran over in her mind, again, the afternoon they'd given Dorrie and her baby a ride to the yellow house on Skyline Boulevard—the same house, the very same one, where she had heard the strange cry when she was selling the Mary rockets almost a year ago. "So who *are* you?" That eerie woman's voice. And Dorrie had walked right through the door, straight into the mystery.

Margaret sat for a moment, perfectly still, her straw resting on the marshmallow layer, and had a peculiar thought. She thought: I will never, ever, be doing this exact thing again. I could come here again and have a Coke. Rita Kay could be with me. We could get the giggles and spill the Coke. But *something* would be different. It would be a different time of day. A different day. A different season. Her own mood would be different. The waitress's mood would be different. Never, ever, ever, ever. The words repeated themselves over and over, for the next few seconds, as she sat very still, her eyes and ears wide open. She felt the way a dog will look when it has its head cocked to one side, its body frozen, its ears pointed straight ahead. She felt that small, heart-catching lurch an elevator gives when it is starting up.

They paid for their Cokes and ambled over to the toy and accessory section of the store. There they found a small bin of plastic baby rattles that were shaped like huge diamond engagement rings. When you shook the rattles, they made a hissing, sandy sound, and the gold dust swirled slowly through the clear diamond part like something half asleep. The rattles were rings for giants. They fit over the girls' wrists like bracelets.

"These are so *coooool,*" Rita Kay exclaimed in the exasperated teenager's voice she had been affecting lately. "I mean, they don't look like rattles when you have them on your wrist." She looked sharply at Margaret. "*Do* they?"

"Nope." And she twisted her wrist this way and that to make the gold dust move.

A man stood by the shelf of stuffed animals, watching them. It was Elmer Davidson, the bum, sort of, who was always reading in the library and murmuring strange things to himself.

"These are *so cool,*" Rita Kay repeated, groaning with exaggerated pleasure. She looked boldly at Elmer.

He had an old suit on, and a shiny tie with a picture of a leaping fish on it. His face was ashen and whiskered, his eyes mild and watery. His shoes were bedroom slippers.

"Are you going to buy those big ol' rings?" he asked in a high, cracking voice.

Rita Kay stretched her arm up high and let the big rattle slip down her arm. She scrutinized it, as if she were trying to make up her mind.

Margaret looked up at the colorless old face. She could hear his wheezy breath. "No," she said, slipping the rattle off her arm to put it back in the bin.

"We don't have any money," Rita Kay announced, staring hard at Margaret because this happened to be a lie. They had enough for one of the bracelets, at least. Elaborately, regretfully, she removed hers and put it back in the bin next to Margaret's, casting a sideways glance at Elmer.

He was digging deep into a front pocket of his baggy pants, his face furrowed with concentration. He brought up some bills, a ten and a twenty—crisp, surprising bills that he turned over a few times in his hands as if trying to remember what they were for.

He placed the ten on the counter, then shoved the twenty back inside his pocket, very slowly. And then he called to the clerk in his crackling voice.

He put the change in his pocket, wrapping the silver in a dirty bandanna. Then he handed the rattles to Margaret and Rita Kay, his ropy old hands trembling slightly.

"Here, little ladies," he said. "Now you're engaged. You're engaged to Elmer R. Davidson. Elmer R. Davidson, Junior!" With that, his voice cracked precipitously and he doubled over in a fit of phlegmy coughing. When he raised his head, tears streamed down his cheeks.

"Thanks!" Rita Kay chirped over her shoulder as she walked quickly toward the door.

"Thanks," Margaret mumbled, glancing at his face.

He smiled bitterly. "O tiger's heart," he muttered, "wrapped in a woman's hide."

Outside, they broke into a full run, squealing. They ran across the intersection against a red light, just ahead of a slow-moving Air Force jeep, and speeded toward home, braceleted arms held high, the big rings bobbing and flickering over their heads.

Rita Kay wanted Margaret to stay overnight at her house, but Margaret's mother balked. She fed them Sloppy Joes for dinner, then told Margaret she should call it a day.

Part of Margaret wanted to do just that. She wanted Rita Kay to go home and leave her to her calm parents, her cool-sheeted bed, the whispering sounds of the big cottonwood outside her bedroom window. She wanted to get her new tennis shoes out of the box and sniff their new smell, alone in her room.

Part of her wanted to feel, again, as though she

were still her parents' child, a feeling that seemed to be seeping away with each new day. She felt she was not only growing too fast, she was out-aging her parents in some strange way. Gaining on them so rapidly that they seemed to be losing years, going backward.

She had taken to calling them by their given names, MaryEllen and Roy. Not aloud, but to herself. And when she said those names, MaryEllen and Roy, she felt an odd pang—as if she were reciting the names of beloved pets. She was not like them, when she said their names in her mind. She was the old one.

MaryEllen had very curly dark hair. She fastened it here and there with bobby pins, but the curls sprang away from her head whenever they had an opportunity, like wayward children, or a part of herself that was trying to get away.

She was a home economics teacher before Margaret was born, and still substituted at the high school sometimes. She had put Roy through medical school, teaching teenage girls to sew their own clothes, and cook nutritious meals, and slide onto car seats like ladies.

Margaret knew MaryEllen had always expected a big family. She was an O'Haire from Butte, and the O'Haires all had big families. But it didn't work out that way because it wasn't meant to be. MaryEllen was very religious, in a quiet way, and she accepted the pains that life handed out—far better than her daughter did. She went to mass at the hospital chapel several mornings a week, and she was sweet-voiced and serene almost all the time.

Sometimes, though, she would develop a faint flush on her face that reached down to her neck. And her hair, when she got the flush, would seem to grow larger and wilder, bounding away from her head so exuberantly that she had to tie a scarf around it. And when she looked like that, MaryEllen was apt to get angry at something or go to her room and cry. Once, on the elevator at a department store in Great Falls, she met a man she had known in Butte, and the flush came onto her face. He rode with them a floor, then got out. On the next floor, their stop, the door took its time opening, and MaryEllen kicked it hard.

Those things didn't happen very often, but when they did, Margaret got nervous. She wanted MaryEllen always to be calm and definite, never to have a shred of doubt.

Rita Kay begged for Margaret's release.

"It's Friday!" she said. "We can sleep in. We're going to have a Kool-Aid stand tomorrow if it's still warm, and we have to get ready." She smiled her cutest wheedling smile. "Pleeease can she stay at my house?"

"You girls spend every waking hour together," MaryEllen countered, as she did the dishes. "Don't you think you need a break?"

"No!" Margaret retorted, her own intentions clarified by her mother's quiet opposition. She had felt, in the span of a few seconds, a bleakness, a quietness, gathering around the edges of the day. It had something to do with the sound of the clinking dishes. She imagined how quiet the house would be if Rita Kay left, how she would be left alone to talk quietly to her parents, then think about things like her growing bones and Woody Blankenship and Christie Murphy's tawny rope of blond hair, swinging from side to side, taunting her.

She had stopped praying about Woody. You couldn't make someone notice you by praying that they would. Not in a world full of unbaptized pagan babies, German shepherds biting Negroes down south, Asian jungles on fire. She read *Time*. She knew what was what. God had much larger things to think about, and He didn't even seem to care that much about those, though MaryEllen said that was jumping to conclusions because suffering is a mystery.

She shoved Woody brusquely to the corner of her mind and giggled randomly. Rita Kay giggled too. They always knew the mood of the other person, always knew what the other person was laughing about, and sometimes knew exactly what the other person was going to say. That's why they were best friends.

Margaret giggled again and shook her rattle, putting it close to her ear to hear it hiss and sigh. Rita Kay had told Margaret's mother they got the rattles from a lady who was giving them away at the drugstore, and Margaret had let the lie stand.

The next morning, Rita Kay's mother left the girls alone in the house with Rita Kay's brother, Eugene, and drove out to a friend's farm for an arts-and-crafts meeting. Eugene was supposed to fix sandwiches for lunch and keep an eye on things. But he drove off on his motorcycle as soon as his mother's car was out of sight, his skinny back as small as a child's.

Rita Kay and Margaret ate some Sugar Pops, then got their Kool-Aid stand ready. The two of them had slept in Rita Kay's bed, and Rita Kay, in her snoring sleep, had shoved Margaret right to the edge of the mattress, where she lay awake most of the night. She felt light-headed with exhaustion.

They set up an old card table and folding chairs on the sidewalk, found a cigar box in the basement for change. They mixed up two big pitchers of Kool-Aid, orange and grape.

"Want to see something?" Rita Kay said.

She crooked her finger and motioned Margaret into her parents' bedroom. She pointed at a big dresser drawer, and Margaret opened it. It was full of underwear. Piles of women's underwear in the most unusual colors—black, red, peach, turquoise. There were tiny straps, wide bands of lace, swaths of silky stuff, piles of it, anything you could imagine.

Margaret couldn't match this drawer with Rita Kay's mother, Marie. It was like a costume drawer. Some things, like the underpants, looked too tiny for a grown woman to wear. Plus, Marie was kind of sporty looking. She would want to wear ordinary underwear, white cotton panties and bras, like MaryEllen did. These looked like gypsy or dancer clothes. Where would she wear them? What would Rita Kay's father, who was so jolly and ordinary, think if Marie put them on?

"Let's put them on," Rita Kay said.

"We can't! They're underwear!" She examined the molded bra cups. "They won't fit!"

"Let's put them on over our clothes. Just to see what they look like."

Margaret ran her fingers over a red, silky slip. She inhaled the faint smell of perfume that the open bureau released. She ran her gaze over everything in the deep drawer, a row of slippery folded things in the front, some puffy things in the back. She tried to remember where they were, so they could put them back right.

Rita Kay thrust her hand into the back and pulled out a large black net thing that looked like a ballerina outfit. The bra part was shaped with foam and came to points. It zipped up the back.

Rita Kay climbed into it, fully clothed, and turned her back so Margaret could zip her. "Pick one!" she urged.

Margaret rustled tentatively in the drawer until she found a black half-slip. She put it on over her jeans. Then

she found a red bed jacket trimmed with wide bands of red lace, and she slipped this over her T-shirt. She examined herself in the full-length mirror on the closet door and decided she looked like a Spanish dancer. She found a lacy white handkerchief, which she draped on her head, fixing it with bobby pins. It still wasn't right. She picked through the things some more and discovered another red slip, this one scratchy and full. She took off her jeans and put the red slip over the black one, then slid it down her thighs until the bottom was around her ankles. Now she had a two-tiered Spanish-dancer skirt, black and red. She fastened the slips together with a safety pin and flounced around the room. Impulsively, she grabbed a bottle of cologne from the bureau and doused herself in a spray of sugary flowers.

Rita Kay, by now, had squirmed out of her T-shirt and wadded it into a ball which she inserted between her own boyish chest and the spongy black corset top to make it stay up. She draped a hot-pink robe over everything, leaving it flapping open, dragging on the floor, and stuck her small, splay-toed feet into feathered black mules. She began to apply a frosted melon-colored lipstick to her little mouth. Debbie, her matted old cat, jumped stiffly from a chair to the bureau and watched.

A screen door slammed. Margaret's heart flopped. She looked wildly around the room for a place to hide. Rita Kay froze, the lipstick poised as if she had been writing in the air. The cat thumped to the floor and slunk under the bed.

Eugene burst into the room. He looked like a very small James Dean, although his hero was a new star named Steve McQueen. He wore a white T-shirt and socks, beltless tight jeans, and shiny black loafers. His face was pale and handsome, but his skin was bad that day. He wore his chocolate-colored hair in a flattop with fenders sweeping back on the sides.

Besides his skin, which had its good and bad phases, Eugene's biggest problem was that he was very short for a sixteen-year-old, and the prospects weren't that good. Rita Kay was the second shortest person in the fifth grade. And their parents were short. Marie wore a size 4½ shoe, which was smaller than Margaret's. To make up for his shortness, Eugene had a large motorcycle and a girlfriend named Wendy to ride around on the back of it.

"I knew you two would do something if I left you alone!" he shouted in his cracking voice. He always moved quickly, and he shouted a lot. "Look at you. You are in one deep pile of shit, Rita Kay." He looked the girls up and down. "Where did you get that junk?"

Rita Kay pointed at their mother's drawer with a little smirk. A quick look passed over Eugene's face, a peculiar combination of surprise and eagerness and disgust. And then it was gone, and so was he.

"Fine!" he called over his shoulder. "Don't come crying to me!" They watched him grab a couple of beers from the refrigerator.

"Beer! I saw!" Rita Kay shouted.

"You keep your little trap clapped, Rita Kay," he yelled again, without turning around. The door slammed. His cycle growled to life and roared away with a screech of rubber.

Their close call threw Margaret and Rita Kay into uncontrollable giggles and snorts. "Keep your trap clapped, Rita Kay," Rita Kay mimicked in a tortured falsetto.

Margaret snatched the lipstick from Rita Kay and applied it thickly to her pursed lips. Then she grabbed the perfume and sprayed it at Rita Kay, chasing her into the kitchen. On the slippery vinyl, Margaret slid wildly on her stocking feet, then tripped on the edge of the red lace slip, plunging forward with a little shriek. She heard a long rip and the clunk of the perfume bottle.

"It didn't break!" Rita Kay yelped. "Thank God, thank God, thank God!" She clasped her hands to her foam breasts.

She ran the perfume back to the bedroom while Margaret examined the torn slip, deciding finally just to shift the damaged part around to the back where she couldn't see it.

They each grabbed a pitcher of Kool-Aid and traipsed outside to the cardboard table. Margaret drew a sign—$.15 CENTS—on a piece of paper. Rita Kay ran for Scotch tape, pink robe flapping, and they were in business.

"Sugar in the mornin', sugar in the evenin', sugar at supper *time*. Be my little sug-*ar* and love me all the time." Margaret belted the song at the top of her lungs as she filled a row of paper cups with orange Kool-Aid. The sleeves of her bed jacket flapped softly. Outlaw energy surged through her.

"Honey in the mornin', honey in the evenin', honey at supper *time*," Rita Kay chimed in. "Be my little hon-*ey* and love me all the time." Then they both shouted, "*Put* your arms a-*round* me and swear by the stars a-*buv*, you'll be mine for-*ev*-er, in a heav-un of *luv!*"

A car drove by slowly, its tires crackling on the wet street. A woman stopped and her two small children ran out, coins in their fingers. Customers! Rita Kay raised her robed arms wide, so that the black corset beneath was in full view. The mother stared, then called sharply to her kids. Rita Kay handed them two cups of Kool-Aid and they dashed back to the car, spilling most of it.

"Sugar in the mornin', sugar in the evenin', sugar at supper *time*. Uh-*be* my little sug-*ar* and uh-*luv* me all the time." Their twangy voices followed the retreating car.

And then it was quiet. So quiet. The street was empty. Old Mrs. Thorpe, across the street, carried a sprinkler with infinite care to a corner of her large square of grass and bent painfully to place it on a balding patch, ignoring them. Then she walked slowly, slowly, back along the hose to the faucet and turned it on, creating a little crystalline umbrella over the weather-damaged spot. She was senile and didn't know or care that it was all going to freeze up again in a couple of days.

A door slammed somewhere down the street. A car backfired several blocks away. But everything else—the square pastel houses, the sparrows, even the cottony clouds inching across the sky—seemed to doze.

Margaret and Rita Kay sat shivering on their folding chairs, swathed in pink and black and red nylon, in feathers and lace, reeking of Chanel No. 5.

They heard faint drumbeats, tiny little drumbeats, blocks away, moving closer. They stood up. Now they could hear the screech and groan of brass and wind, awkward and earnest. It had to be the high school band, practicing for the basketball tournament—outside, in February! It drew closer until suddenly, in a frontal blast, it was around the far corner of the block, coming down the street toward the Kool-Aid stand.

The band moved very slowly. Players and instruments seemed stiff and rusty from the cold winter. The huge tuba caught the sun and blasted it back. *Wooonk.* You could hear it, a mournful foghorn beneath the lurching harmonies of the others.

A long sea-green car inched along the street behind the band, caught behind its big wave until the next intersection.

"It's Aunt Candy!" Rita Kay hissed at Margaret. "She's going to tell!" She moaned dramatically, and they both looked down at their outfits, seeing themselves through Candy's eyes. Deep shit! They could hear Eugene's cracking voice, triumphant.

The band stopped inexplicably and marched in place for a minute, then snailed forward again, the sea-green car following it like a dream boat.

"Sugar in the mornin', sugar in the evenin', sugar at supper time!" Margaret shouted it out as loudly as she could. The band had drawn even and was drowning her out. A flute player pointed at them with her flute and laughed. Several others stopped playing and laughed, too.

It wasn't enough. Rita Kay might be trapped, but *she* wasn't. Ecstatically, she climbed up on the folding chair, hitched the black and red slips up a little, cupped her hands around her mouth, and tried again.

"Be my little sugar and love me all the time!" Deep breath. "*Put* yer arms a-*round* me, swear to the stars a-*buv,* you'll be mine for-*ev*-er in a hea-vun of luv!" She closed her eyes and threw back her head. She belted her song, pretending she was a McGuire sister without a microphone, her own voice part of the band, with its big, rhythmic, supporting presence. When she opened her eyes, Candy stood in front of her, livid, gripping Rita Kay by an ear and a silken sleeve.

Candy hauled Rita Kay toward the house and snapped her fingers at Margaret to follow. Margaret slunk behind them, into the house, into the bedroom, where Candy took one look at the open underwear drawer and drew her lips tighter.

"You are in deep, deep trouble, Rita Kay Cotten," she announced, peering curiously at the drawer as if she, too, was surprised. Everyone was surprised at the drawer.

Rita Kay's face had lost its impishness and grown sullen. She snapped her gum loudly and casually picked up the Chanel No. 5 atomizer.

"Drop that!" Candy snapped with a cowboy snarl. Rita Kay placed it slowly, very slowly, back on the bureau.

"Take those things off! Now!"

They disrobed, Margaret struggling briefly with the safety pin on her slips, keeping her back away from Candy so the rip wouldn't show. She slid the slips down and folded them quickly, avoiding Candy's scorching gaze.

"I am disappointed in you girls. Ex-treme-ly disappointed," Candy said sadly. "Get that hankie off your head, Margaret."

It was difficult to feel intimidated by Candy because she was so short, almost as short as Margaret. Margaret went into her habitual slump, so Candy wouldn't feel threatened. Besides being short, Candy had reddish hair, which was fixed perfectly because she was a hairdresser. She had a cute sprinkling of freckles across her nose and a little chipmunk voice, which she seemed to know about, because she was now making it very deep.

"Where's Eugene?" she boomed. Rita Kay shrugged loyally.

Candy jabbed her finger. "You," she said to Rita Kay. "To the bathroom. Wash that junk off your face."

"You," to Margaret. "Home."

Rita Kay ambled off down the hall to the bathroom, head bent, defeated. This was temporary. She would be on the phone to Margaret within the hour. Margaret made her own face remorseful and shuffled out the door toward home. She walked very slowly. The day was growing heavy and cold. The clouds were clumping together and turning leaden at the edges. She felt sleepy.

Her moment with the band, standing high on the folding chair, her borrowed lingerie wafting around her, seemed long past, the moment of a different person. She wondered if that's what it was like to get drunk. Those cartoons of people with lampshades on their heads. Maybe getting drunk was that same feeling of happiness and abandon. And maybe, when it was over, it felt like it had happened years ago, or to someone else.

* * *

A very large, very black baby buggy was parked near the front steps. Margaret looked inside—it was empty—and went into the house. She could hear MaryEllen talking to someone, a woman, in the kitchen. She joined them with a rush of pleasure and self-consciousness.

It was the divorcée and her baby, sitting at the kitchen table as if they belonged there. How long had she been there? What had gone on while she was at Rita Kay's? How did the divorcée suddenly come to be sitting in Margaret's own kitchen?

"What happened to *you?*" MaryEllen asked. "You look peculiar, honey."

Margaret put her hand to her head and realized that she hadn't brushed her hair that morning. One braid was partially unraveled and hung in lank strands. Her shirt was buttoned crookedly. And her mouth—she remembered it with a small shock—was plastered with Tahiti lipstick. She ran the back of her hand over her lips.

She shrugged, at a loss.

"This is Dorrie Vane," MaryEllen said in her teacher's voice. "And this is her son, Samuel. I saw them out walking and invited them in to sample my coffee cake."

"I know who she is." Margaret heard how blunt she sounded, and tried to soften it with a smile, hoping all the lipstick had wiped onto her hand. "We picked them up in a blizzard." She spoke shyly to her mother, fixing her eyes on the baby. "When they came on the train."

"Ah." MaryEllen poured Dorrie more coffee. Dorrie smiled at them both. She hadn't said a word yet, and she didn't have to. She was so beautiful and interesting, just sitting there. Margaret made a mental note to remember everything about her: the long dark hair pulled back from her face with a tortoise-shell headband. Her large, wise eyes. The man's simple white shirt, worn tails out over black capris.

Compared to MaryEllen in her pink-checked blouse and skirt, Dorrie looked simplified, even mannish. She held Sam on her knee in a formal, arm's-length way, as if she trusted that he knew how to behave.

"Dorrie and I thought you might want a little job," MaryEllen said. "We thought you might want to take Sam for a walk on afternoons when the weather is decent. In the baby buggy."

Margaret didn't know what to say. She felt that all her nerve endings were extending from her skin, groping the air. This was news! This was a development! She would have a business relationship with the divorcée. She would go to her apartment, three, maybe four days a week, and actually talk to her. She had known it in her bones, this tie between herself and Dorrie. Known it the minute she saw her walking down the snowy street in her beautiful white coat and bullfighter's hat. She hadn't known how it would show itself, but she hadn't worried. She had simply bided her time. Waited. And now this.

"Okay," she muttered.

"I'll pay you handsomely," Dorrie said, in a low, movie-star voice.

"That's okay," Margaret said, shrugging to show her lack of commercial interest.

Sam faced Margaret and cooed.

"He likes me, I think," she said gruffly.

Everyone smiled.

The next morning, Rita Kay called to say she was grounded for two weeks. She couldn't go out of the house, except in her own yard or with her parents. She also had to give up weeks of allowance money to pay for the rip in the red slip, even though it was Margaret's fault.

Her voice was pale and tiny over the phone, but Margaret knew it was an act. It was her martyr voice that she used when she knew her parents were listening. Margaret felt distant from the whole episode and eager to offer her own news.

"That divorcée above Bledsoe's, you know? The one with the baby?" A tiny grunt from Rita Kay. "Well, I'm going to be her babysitter. I'm going to take her baby on walks." She couldn't conceal the triumph in her voice.

"Why?"

Margaret was stung. "Because she asked me to. In person. She came over to my house and asked me to do it."

There was a pause.

"I didn't tell my mom that you sprayed her perfume all over me and the house." Another pause, and then the imprisoned voice again. "Or that you dropped it on the floor and almost broke it."

"Good!" Margaret said heartily. She wanted out of this conversation so she could think about going to the divorcée's to pick up the baby. "See ya later alligator, understand rubberband?" Their automatic sign-off.

" 'Bye," Rita Kay said.

Sam was asleep almost immediately. Margaret wheeled the big buggy slowly across Main. She walked past her own house, past Rita Kay's house, over toward the Rotary Park. The temperature had dropped again, after the chinook, and the sidewalk was patchy with ice. She hummed a vague little tune, keeping time with the faint screech of the wheels and the little clicks they made on the cracks.

At each curb, she carefully lowered the front wheels, lifted the back ones, lowered them onto the street. Sam slept under his piles of blankets.

She sat on a bench at the park, next to a scrawny lilac bush, rocking the buggy with her foot like she'd seen it done in a movie. She stretched her legs out. They had grown again.

It was a spare park, a full block in size, with no trees yet. Across the way, she could see some boys on bikes, riding in circles inside the empty concrete wading pool. She squinted. One of them was Bobby Hefty, the little brother of one of Eugene's friends. The other, in a bright purple jacket, had his back to her. As he came around the circle, she jumped. It was Woody Blankenship. She slid a few inches on the bench, so that she was slumped behind the buggy but could still see.

Beyond the wading pool, three girls leaned on their own bikes and watched the boys. Margaret squinted again. She couldn't see as well as she used to. But if she made a fist, leaving a tiny peephole to look through, the image sometimes sharpened. She did that.

One of the girls was Bobby Hefty's sister, Laurie. One, an older girl she didn't know. The third was Rita Kay.

Margaret's first instinct was to call out to her, to run over and join them. To congratulate her on getting out of the house. But she held back, because small questions were rising like minnows to the surface of her mind. Why hadn't Rita Kay called her? Why was she with these other girls? There was something closed about them, something secret and revved up, that signaled new alliances. They had drawn their pastel-colored bikes together and stood in a huddle, breaking every now and then to shout some kind of retort or encouragement—Margaret couldn't tell which—to the boys who were zooming around the concrete circle.

It gave her a peculiar feeling. It was like remembering her song with the band. This Rita Kay at the Rotary Park seemed like another person from the one she knew. She slumped down a little farther behind the baby buggy and stared over the top of the handle. Rita Kay was very animated. She waved her hands in the air as she talked, one foot pointed out in that high-school-girl way she liked to stand. Light winked from her big plastic bracelet. Her high-pitched voice carried through the air to Margaret—the tone, not the words.

Woody Blankenship wheeled his bike over to the clump of girls. And Margaret saw Rita Kay reach out and touch her finger to his shirt. What was she doing? Pointing to something he spilled? Plucking a bug off that purple jacket? Whatever it was, they all laughed, Woody too. So casual! So easy! And then Woody leaned over and whispered something in Rita Kay's ear. Margaret opened her eyes very wide, and her heart crumpled. She stared longer. Then she put her forehead onto the baby buggy handle and watched her hot tears plop, one by one, onto the dead brown grass.

Margaret and the divorcée silently agreed to ignore each other's red-rimmed eyes. Dorrie transported the sleeping baby to his crib and rustled in her purse for a dollar.

"Would you like a cup of bouillon?" she asked Margaret, putting a light hand on her shoulder. Margaret didn't know what bouillon was, but she nodded.

She imagined the searing pain that must have produced Dorrie's tears. Perhaps she had received a telegram from Chicago, with word that Sam's father had died. She didn't believe that Dorrie was divorced because she wanted to be. She thought it was probably something more like Romeo and Juliet: powerful families who had almost physically ripped them apart, the lovers' eyes holding each other's to the last. Maybe he had died of grief.

"Did Sam behave?"

"Uh huh. He was fine. He slept the whole time."

"Did you have any problems?" She searched Margaret's face.

"No."

Dorrie left it at that, and Margaret was grateful. Grateful, too, that Dorrie had scaled her own grief to peer down sympathetically on a stranger's sorrow.

"Your apartment is nice," she offered, looking around at the spare room with its yellowish walls and frayed dusty-rose carpet. Chairs had been placed on either side of the window that overlooked Main. They were the only furniture in the room except for a desk that was littered with papers and baby toys. It was an artist's attic, a nun's spare quarters.

"Sit down," Dorrie said, adjusting the venetian blind so that the westerly leaning sun didn't blast into the room.

Then they just sat there for a few minutes, silent. Margaret felt they were both resting. She closed her gritty, exhausted eyes for a few seconds. She could hear Don Bledsoe scraping ice from the sidewalk below, and it sounded like a noise from another season. Sometimes, for no reason at all, during the snowy winter, she would remember the lovely, jetting sound of lawn sprinklers. Or on the hottest summer day, she might think of the soft scrape of a snow shovel. It was like that.

# Chapter 9

Madrid had no buildings taller than two stories, unless you counted the grain elevators and the church steeples, and their upper reaches naturally held grain or bells, not people. Most of the second stories along Main Street were supply rooms for the businesses below, or the offices of a half dozen dentists and lawyers. One two-story building on the edge of town, a narrow, wooden structure that needed paint, had a veterinary office on the ground floor and the VFW club on the top. You reached the bar, the Top O' the Vets, by climbing a flight of outside stairs. Once or twice a year, someone crashed through the rail, but no one ever seemed to get seriously hurt.

The Mitchell Apartments, eight of them along a dim hall above Bledsoe's Drug, were the only places above ground level where people actually made their homes. There were other rentals in town—in the basements of houses, in a pink semicircle of cottages called The Capri, in the trailer courts—but they were all down where the activity was going on. Dorrie would look out her Main Street window in the Mitchell, peer down on the head of a shopper, the roof of a car, and she would feel, sometimes, as if she inhabited a catwalk or a roost, a narrow space wedged between the real Madrid and the sky.

It had been different in Chicago. There, an apartment, even one that was five or ten or twenty floors up, was horizontal with thousands of others, reaching across the city. There was company up there.

The kinds of people who lived at the Mitchell seemed to push the place farther from the life of the town, too. Opal Stenurud, the retired bartender, with her flaring violet lips and quivering Pekinese. Mr. Lovejoy, the stiff-legged old piano teacher who came to town on the bus from Great Falls and stayed three days a week. Dorrie passed him in the hall sometimes as he set out with stricken dignity, on foot, to his students' houses. He had one blue eye and one brown one. Elmer Davidson, the old drunk who spouted nonsense and Shakespeare. "Sweep on, you fat and greasy citizens!" he liked to yell from his window after a long night.

The Mitchell smelled of overcooked vegetables, harsh floor cleaner, old cigarette smoke. As soon as she came up the stairs with Sam, that first day, Dorrie got hit with that smell and remembered, in detail, a day when she was six years old. A babysitter had taken her to these same apartments. To visit some friends, the babysitter said. And there, in one of the apartments—which one?—were five or six unzipped sleeping bags spread on the bare floor, with high-school-age kids beneath them. Boys and girls together, bare arms above the canvas covers. The boy who answered the door had jockey shorts on and a beer in his hand. The blinds were down, and the room was cool and shadowy. Everyone but the boy with the beer seemed to be sleeping. This happened in the morning. The sun had been up for hours.

The babysitter had made her promise to say nothing about this "secret meeting" to her parents. If Dorrie did, she said, the police would come to her door and ask her, Dorrie, what *she* had been doing there. In seventh or eighth grade, she finally mentioned it to Sandra Shepherd. "That was an orgy," Sandra said patiently. "Swamp Cats."

The more she thought about it, the more she was sure her apartment was the one she had visited so many years before. She wondered about those mysterious, dozing kids. Who were they? How had they slept on, oblivious, right above the sunlit business of Madrid? Who had given them the room? Where did their parents think they were? How could they hide in a town so small?

She felt, sometimes, as removed and dreaming as they had been and tried to dispel the feeling with small plans, little schedules she wrote down.

The days were for Sam, with some time to work on her correspondence courses when he napped. Dinner with Earl on Tuesday, the night she was off work. Her evening waitress job at the Bull's Eye, Wednesday through Monday. Gloria was the main waitress and worked from four to midnight. Dorrie helped from six on. She bought an old Dodge with $499 of the money Earl gave her, and drove it back and forth to work, eleven miles round trip. It wouldn't start on cold days until the midafternoon sun had warmed it.

In the evenings, Sam stayed with Mrs. Berridge, an old woman who took in ironing and a few children. Margaret, Roy Greenfield's daughter, had agreed to come by after school, on days when the sun was shining and there wasn't much snow on the ground, to take Sam for a short walk in the big baby buggy that had once been Dorrie's own.

It should have worked. It seemed a system, something with purpose. But Sam was colicky and restless. He woke two or three times a night with a thin little wail, and she had to rock him back to sleep, walking the floor. He had trouble sleeping during the day, too. She had stopped nursing him, because of her job, and cow's milk didn't agree with him. She took him to Greenfield and they worked out a new formula using soy. He told her she should get a good physical too; her color wasn't good. But she knew the problem wasn't her. It was Sam. He continued to wake during the night, and she had to quiet him quickly because someone down the hall had already complained to the manager.

He was up for good by eight or nine, and Dorrie had had four, maybe five, sketchy hours of sleep. Her face in the mirror looked drawn and pale, with blueish circles under her eyes. Sometimes, after she'd had her morning coffee, which she made strong, seeing the whole day ahead, her hands trembled and she felt a surge of panic. She knew it was brought on by the caffeine, but the feeling itself, the fluttering panic, seemed an appropriate response to her situation. The caffeine simply uncovered what was already there.

Sometimes, when Sam woke up, he was dewy and alert, and if he didn't have a bad stomach or a cold, he would stay that way for an hour or two. He reminded her then of a little starfish, tentacles reaching for information. He moved his fingers as if they were underwater, like the Balinese dancers she saw once in Chicago, twisting them slowly to entice something from the larger world. He smiled at her, a crooked little jack-o'-lantern grin, his gauzy blond wisps of hair pushed straight up by the static electricity in his blanket. And then the knot in her stomach would loosen, though it never went entirely away, and she would insist to him, "I love you, Sam. I love you so much. You know that, don't you?" and she would think, I will make this work out; I will make us some kind of life; I will get back on my feet and then we will leave.

An hour later, he would be screaming, his little face contorted and purple. And she'd put him down for a nap and he couldn't sleep. Wouldn't sleep. That's how she often thought of it—that he was deliberately pushing her to the limits of what she could take. She chanted to him sometimes as she tried to fix a blanket over his chubby, flailing legs, her hands shaking. Go to sleep, she singsonged, go to sleep. Her voice quavered. Sometimes he would finally drift off, and she would sit down to her desk to thumb through a text the correspondence division had sent her—she hadn't actually signed up for anything yet—and he would wake and cry, and she'd throw her pencil across the room, and a few times she screamed too. She yelled at him once so loudly that his face went blank with shock before it gathered itself to cry. She grabbed him up to rock him and apologize then, her own hot tears streaming down her face. This is misery, she murmured. I'm only twenty-one. She thought of the girls in the freshman dorm. She thought of the Madrid girls who had married and stayed in town, in houses.

She saw no one she recognized in this baby, except sometimes at night, when he was sleeping. Then he had something stripped and exhausted and old about him that reminded her of Earl. And there was, sometimes, something in his stylized hand movements that was Rosemary. But nothing of Rader. Nothing of herself. Not that she could see.

She developed a way of being in the apartment that seemed one long, silent incantation to Sam to stay silent. If I walk very slowly and deliberately across the room, she told herself, he will sense my purpose, my deliberation, and he will stop crying. Her stomach contracted and she could not eat sometimes, so she made cups of broth from bouillon cubes, making it a small ritual. A cube, half a cup of water at a boil, the dissolving, a careful stir of the spoon, then the rest of the boiling water. If she changed the process by a hair, she felt he would start screaming. She cried herself. She tried to remember the last time she had had a good, long night's sleep. Strange, violent scenarios ran through her mind. Rader in a car crash. Herself in a car crash and Rader hearing about it, remorseful too late. The lady down the hall, the one who had complained to the manager, getting hauled off to the hospital with some indefinite and lengthy illness.

Margaret showed up more and more often, as the winter began to trickle away. She seemed to be growing at an exhausting pace. Her spindly arms hung out of her sweater sleeves. Her shoes were long and narrow and a little run over at the heels. She had begun to wear her straight tan hair in one long braid, the way Dorrie did, and the slicked-back style made her straight eyebrows more fierce. Some days it looked as though she'd tried unsuccessfully to make the braid herself. It was bent and wispy, or falling apart. She was always bending over to pull up the knee socks that slipped down her stick legs.

Margaret seemed to occupy no middle ground. She was either miles away or so close, so focused, that she made you uneasy. Her moods also changed quickly. "You're growing like a weed," Dorrie said once, as she let a smiling Margaret into the apartment, and was surprised by the fearful, hurt look the girl fixed on her. She could be touchy that way.

Margaret seemed able to calm Sam when Dorrie

couldn't, so she was grateful to hear the after-school knock on her door, even on days when the weather was clearly too cold or windy to take him out. Margaret would arrive, her head covered with a big scarf, and Dorrie would invite her in to warm up, knowing she would stay until Dorrie left for work.

They would have a cup of tea, or of bouillon, and Margaret would fix her rapt gaze on Dorrie's face. And then they would talk, about ordinary things, mostly: school, the different groupings in school, what fifth grade had been like when Dorrie was in it.

Sam watched Margaret. If he cried, she looked straight at him as if he'd asked a question. Sometimes he just kept wailing, but sometimes he stopped and gazed back at her, his face pink and wet-eyed. And then Margaret would say something calm and explanatory. "He feels lonely," she said once. And another time: "He doesn't know why he's crying. He just does it." And once, when he stopped crying, then started again and wouldn't stop, Margaret raised her voice above his and said, "I think he dreamed that he didn't feel like crying. Then he woke up all the way and realized it was just a dream." She shrugged when she said that, and turned to squint out the window at the sign on the Homestead Cafe across the street. She put a hand over one eye, then moved it to the other. It was a dim, sleet-filled late-afternoon. "I can see the big letters," she announced. "But I can barely see the little ones underneath. Soup, Burgers, Steaks? They're blurry on the edges. I think I'm slowly losing my vision. I have to go find out." She shrugged again.

"Maybe you just need to wear glasses," Dorrie said.

"Maybe," Margaret said bleakly.

# Chapter 10

Gloria came to work fifteen minutes late and walked in wearing very large sunglasses and no makeup. She announced to Pete, the busboy, that she had a hangover and felt like the Skipper's Special, which was a Bull's Eye joke. She waved at Sully, the bartender, visible through the beaded curtain on the barroom door, and scurried into the bathroom.

Inside, she lit a cigarette and extracted her beauty aids from her oversized purse. First, she removed the net scarf she had tied loosely over her sculpted beehive and surveyed her bare face to check out its status. It was a satisfactory face, unlined, pale. Her mouth was thin, a little crooked. Her eyes were large and wide-set, her best feature. She had a sprinkling of freckles across the nose. Good teeth, since the braces, which took her four years to pay for. Circles under the eyes today. Blemish on the chin. She decided she looked like a tired fourteen-year-old.

She smeared moisturizer over her face and neck in upward sweeps. Then she applied a layer of pale matte base makeup over every inch of skin, even her eyelids and lips. She liked this part. She had neutralized everything, created a clean slate. No freckles, no nothing, no identifiable age. Just a pale mask with very blue eyes peering out.

Lip gloss and a pale pink frosted lipstick, the color of her long fingernails. Cotton Candy, it was called. Cover-up under the eyes, on the blemish. And then the eyes themselves, the major part.

She traced a thick line of liquid eyeliner along her upper eyelashes and the outer half of her lower lashes, curving the corners up a little for an exotic effect. Perfect. She smudged gray eyeshadow across her lids and extended it outward, catlike. She applied one coat of mascara, blinked slowly to make it dry, applied another coat.

She dusted light powder all over her face. Brushed it off with a Kleenex, applied another coat of Cotton Candy on her lips. She gave her hair a final spray and reshaped the spit curls, which were still damp from her shower.

She examined herself again, this time backing away from the mirror to see more. She was tall and broad-shouldered with curvy hips and smallish breasts which she helped out with a conical padded bra. Her black rayon waitress uniform fit snugly. Just right, actually.

Briskly, she replaced her makeup items in her purse, took two more aspirin, squirted the backs of her knees with Emeraude cologne, and stepped into the red, cavelike dining room, ready to go.

Dorrie dropped Sam off at Mrs. Berridge's, weaving through a forest of starched, freshly ironed shirts to deposit him in a playpen. Both she and Sam had colds and were red-nosed and exhausted. He had been irritable and unhappy all day. Nothing she did seemed to comfort him. When she left, she had absolutely nothing to say to him or to Mrs. Berridge, a very large, white-haired woman in a voluminous housedress and men's oxford shoes. Mrs. Berridge was not a jolly woman. She never smiled. But she charged very little, and she handled Sam with no-nonsense ease. He often calmed down when Dorrie handed him over to the huge grim woman, which wounded her.

It was a raw day in early March. Ice lay in small black patches along the edges of the streets. Dorrie drove past the schoolground, hearing the *clang-clang* of the flag-less line on the tall pole. One child spun by himself on a merry-go-round. Another weaved a bike between the monkey bars and the swings. It was past five, and the rest of the playground was empty. The Dodge ran with a little hiccup in the motor. She revved it up at an intersection, listened with a flicker of unease, gunned it, listened again.

Outside town, the countryside was scoured. Nothing green. The barest patches of old snow. Chalky alkali patches visible here and there. Thin cows along a barbed-wire fence. She kept the heater on high and leaned the car into the smacking wind. Her eyes were swollen from her head cold. Her throat felt burned.

The Bull's Eye was out there by itself. You came over a rise, and it was on the right side, a windowless prefab building and a gravel parking lot. The roof was peaked, with a large target fixed to the town side, the one most of the oncoming diners would see. Sunk in the center of the target's bull's-eye was a pulsating neon arrow the length of a man. At night, the light from it made the cars in the dark lot pulse orange, orange, orange.

Dorrie pulled eagerly into the lot. She liked the place. It was always a relief. It was a world without Sam, a world where she knew everything she was supposed to do, where other people's expectations were modest and concrete. She knew many of the customers by name or by sight—someone she'd known from high school, someone's parents, a former teacher, a store clerk—and she smiled at them but made herself too brisk and busy to talk much. The work itself—the movement, the ordering of priorities in her head, the reminders to herself to check a table, reassure them, get the right dinners to the right people—left her no room to think about anything else. She waited tables as though she'd been born for it.

After her shift, she usually had a drink with Gloria. It was a suspended, comforting hour. Gloria had the ability to make almost any subject harmless and matter-of-fact.

She told Dorrie, with elaborate shrugs, about her mother, Bernice: how she had simply left town one day, what a wild drifter she was.

"You were in my brother Buddy's class," Gloria said. "I don't remember you, but that would be right." Dorrie nodded.

"Bernice left a year after Buddy died," Gloria said. No one knew exactly where to find her, though she showed up every now and then, usually with some scumbag.

She told Dorrie about her grandmother up on the reservation, Rosie Two Guns, her favorite person of all time. Rosie was half Norwegian and half Irish, an orphan who had come to Montana with some homesteading cousins from Iowa. She married Ignatius Two Guns in 1900, when she was sixteen years old, and they lived together for fifty-one years before he died. Rosie dressed and talked and acted like any other of the old Blackfeet women, except she had very light blue eyes in her leathery old face. The other women called her Wolf Eyes. Big Jokers, she called them back.

Rosie and Ignatius had five children, four of their own and one adopted white child, Bernice, who was the only one who went bad. Rabbit was on his way toward trouble, but he got killed on an icy highway before he ever got there.

Bernice ran off with an oilfield worker from Cut Bank when she was seventeen, and she had Robert, the deaf one, and Gloria and Buddy before the marriage blew up somewhere down in Oklahoma.

Old Rosie wrote off Bernice when she quit her job at the Homestead Cafe and took off for God-knows-where. She said she couldn't claim anyone who had stopped trying. Gloria puffed out a fast stream of smoke as she told the story, and said she could only agree.

Dorrie told Gloria about having a baby in a large city hospital, alone except for her former roommate, Helen, who brought some flowers when it was all over. How her mother, Rosemary, had never even written to her about the baby but had let Earl speak for both of them; how that had seemed, at the time, a deliberate retaliation for the years Dorrie had kept to herself.

She told Gloria how her water had broken while she stood in line at a huge grocery store; how it streamed down her legs as she abandoned her shopping cart and ran, blimplike, for a cab to the hospital. She had never told anyone that. They laughed at the picture of it.

Dorrie didn't tell Gloria about Rader, because she knew the mention of his name, just that, would release such a flood of hatred and loss that she would be unable to continue talking. Gloria never asked. They didn't mention Buddy again, either.

* * *

Dorrie hung up her coat, surveyed the dining room, and took a long breath. Though business had been slacking off recently, this was the weekend of the Class B basketball tournament, and the place was full. The red vinyl booths along the far wall, and the tables too, had candles that flickered in round glass globes, half of them red, half of them orange, like small campfires scattered in the darkness.

The restaurant had opened in early December for the holidays, but there had been some embarrassing kinks right off the bat, according to Gloria. The cook didn't show up one night and no one knew where to find him, so they had to turn everyone away. All the lights went out in a blizzard, and no one could find the fuse box.

Irwin was hired in January to manage the place. He was from California, where he had supposedly run an officers' club at Vandenberg Air Force Base. He had insisted, right off, on a large neon sign to replace the small light-bulb one that the Hi-Line Investors had rigged up on the painted target. It was one of what he called "the extras that make a difference." He was also concerned with something he called "the presentation." Because a fair number of customers were involved with the missiles, he gave military titles to the steaks, which were what most people ordered. This was a presentation thing. The General was a fourteen-ounce T-bone, the Major was a ten-ounce sirloin, the Amelia Earhart was the ladies' six-ounce filet mignon, and the Skipper's Special was frozen shrimp and some other kind of fish from old-looking packages, deep fried and served with tartar sauce. The steaks came to the tables with plastic rockets stuck in them: blue for rare, red for medium, yellow for well done.

Irwin liked the curtain of clear plastic beads, hanging in strands, between the dining room and the bar beyond. He liked it, he said, because it "enhanced the mystique." Anyone in the bar was revealed to the diners from behind a glittery little curtain, and vice versa.

Irwin was slope-shouldered and thin and wore a huge class ring and lots of Jade East aftershave. His patent leather shoes had cracked in the cold and snow, but he still wore them. He had thinning combed-back hair above a small, tense face.

"I'm not sure what mystique is," Gloria liked to drawl, "but I do know Irwin could use some."

Intimacy, mystique, Irwin kept saying. This place needs mystique. It is a haven. The customers are royalty. And he made Pete the busboy walk around slowly among the diners, carrying a gigantic pepper grinder in his arms like a baby or a scepter. This was another touch that Irwin had picked up in California: a stylized grinding or two on the salad or the baked potato. It made a difference.

At closing, Dorrie walked on aching feet from table to table, blowing out the candles. The dining room smelled, now, like smoke and old salad dressing.

Pete had the vacuum cleaner going in the foyer by the front door. It was the mournful, practical sound of childhood Saturday mornings: the great dispeller of daydreams. The show was over, the motions of attention and service and camaraderie. Now the place was empty and a vacuum was going and Sully had just flicked on a panel of lights along one edge of the sparkly ceiling so Pete wouldn't miss the soda crackers on the orange and black rug, the cigarette ashes on the booths. All the signs of disruption were evident now. All the little messes.

Her sore throat had gotten worse as the evening went on. One side of it felt as if someone had scraped it, over and over, with a small knife. Gloria, too, seemed to be getting something. Her face was flushed, even through her makeup, and a little swollen. She kept putting a hand to her cheek, as if to cool it.

It had been a bad night. A kid Dorrie knew from high school had come in with his fiancée, who looked about sixteen, and his mother, who was in a wheelchair. Dorrie couldn't remember their names, and they knew it. The mother asked her about "poor Rosemary" and peered up at her when Dorrie murmured something vague. Dorrie brought the woman the wrong dinner and had to take it back.

She took a steak sandwich to a customer at the bar, a missile guy, and accidentally tipped all the french fries onto the floor. She bent to pick them up, apologizing, and he told her to forget it. He had a nice smile. Said he knew the cook had another batch of fries in there with his name on them. His name was Steve McClintock. He made a point of telling her that.

Another customer, old Doc Bennett, found a very small Band-Aid deep-fried into the crumbs on his Skipper's Special and made a loud fuss, marching back to the kitchen, where the cook tried to reassure him that the Band-Aid in question was only for a hangnail, nothing worse. "I don't care if the damn thing was on a *freckle,*" Bennett shouted so that anyone in the building could hear. "I don't want it glommed onto my prawns!"

Now all the customers were gone except Curt Wilcox. Dorrie noticed him at the bar, through the shiny curtain strands.

Wilcox closed down the Bull's Eye one or two nights a week. Tonight, he had been very drunk when he came in. Dorrie could tell, even without talking to him. She knew from his overefficient movements, from the way he pulled out a barstool and lit a cigarette. He had sent a firm directive to his soaked brain—no sloppiness—and it showed up like a badge, giving him away.

Wilcox, Major Wilcox, was some sort of commanding officer for the Minuteman missile squadron that fanned out for hundreds of miles from the Bull's Eye. He was in his forties, crew-cut, with a thin mouth, gravelly skin, and surprising soft eyes. He always came in alone. Sometimes he chatted lazily with Sully. More often, he sipped bourbon steadily, with no evident haste, and smoked. When he left, his eyes sagged and he moved as if the floor were mined.

His manner with Gloria and Dorrie was highly polite. He had the suggestion of a southern accent and a habit of saying, "Yes, ma'am," in a way that made Dorrie vaguely uneasy because it was so exaggeratedly deferential. It had an embroidered, antagonistic sound.

Tonight, though, Wilcox was different. He was louder when he talked to Sully. He fidgeted. And, now, with the evening over and the vacuum cleaner going, he swung around on his stool and watched Dorrie through the flimsy, wavery curtain. She saw him in the corner of her eye. She leaned over a candle and blew it out. He stood and rested an elbow carefully on the bar.

"Hey, sweetheart," he called out. She looked up, then moved to another table.

Wilcox walked slowly through the beaded curtain, a cigarette dangling limply between his fingers. His smile didn't move. He stopped very near her and cocked his head in a bleary imitation of a flirt. "Hey, sweetheart," he said jauntily. "Don't you know how to blow out a candle?"

Dorrie felt a moment of confusion, an automatic attitude of helpfulness, as if he had said, "Where do I pay my bill?"

Then the poison on his face registered and she felt weariness on her shoulders like a pair of metal hands. "I can handle it," she said coldly. "Don't worry about it."

She walked to the glowing candle at the next table and blew it out quickly. Wilcox followed her.

"You're fun to watch," he said. "I could watch you forever. But you've got a *big* problem." She moved on.

"Don't you even know how to blow out a *candle?*" he called. Then he looked around the room as if he were waiting for someone who had promised to show up hours earlier. His face took on a random, wits-end fury. "Fuck!" he said, striding over to her. He threw up his hands, gesturing his helplessness to an invisible, sympathetic audience.

"There is a right way to blow out a candle and a wrong way to blow out a candle," he said, dropping his voice, explaining to a child. He grabbed Dorrie's elbow and steered her to the next table, where the last candle wavered. As she began to pull out of his grip, he grabbed the back of her neck, very quickly for someone so drunk, and shoved her head down to the candle. His hand felt huge. "Blow," he said through shut teeth.

Dorrie wrenched her head sideways until her mouth found the inside of his forearm. She bit as hard as she could, feeling her teeth break skin. He shrieked and threw her off. She staggered backward across the floor, then stopped and spit saliva and blood on the rug. She felt her own blood rush away from her head as if a plug had been pulled. For a moment or two, runaway rage took her vision away. She steadied herself against a table and took a napkin from it to wipe her mouth.

"You're crazy, you bitch," he whispered, swaying slightly, staring at the beads of blood on his arm.

Sully had a hand on Wilcox's shoulder. "Hey, sir," he said loudly, as if he spoke to a large rebellious crowd. "Let's call it a night."

He led him by the elbow to the bar, where he wetted a cocktail napkin and gave it to him for the wound. "Put some antiseptic on that when you get to the base," he said.

Wilcox struggled into his jacket, and Sully let him out the back door. It slammed with a tinny sound.

Dorrie sank into one of the booths. Sully and Gloria stood beside her. "Jesus." Gloria looked at her with a mixture of admiration and something close to embarrassment. "That happened fast. You okay?"

Dorrie nodded. She felt that if she spoke, she would throw up.

"She's fine," Gloria said briskly to Sully. "Get us a couple of vodka-Sevens, will you, sweetie?"

She sat down with Dorrie, lit a cigarette, and puffed the smoke out in big circles.

"Judi Westermark came in here at Christmas with some Indian from India that she met at college," she said. "That would have been a month or so before you got here, I think." She thought, and confirmed the timing with a nod of her head.

"Well, Judi brings that guy in here and I thought old Curt was going to have a cow. He kept looking over at that guy—he was real dark, the guy, with those humongous brown eyes—and then Curt said something about diaper heads. Real loud. Judi and the guy were in the dining room and I don't think they heard him. But I was getting some drinks and I did. So I went to the kitchen and I came back and handed him a paper bag."

Dorrie listened. She saw Wilcox's face again, and felt her mouth twitch involuntarily.

"Uh hum. I handed him this old paper bag and said, "Here, *major*. You're hyperventilating. Breathe in this for a while.' "

She opened her eyes wide, innocently, as she must have with Wilcox, then signaled to Sully for another round. He gave them doubles.

"I'm going to get a gun," Dorrie said.

Gloria bit one of her cuticles, then lit a new cigarette and took a long drink. "For here?"

"Whatever."

"That doesn't make sense, Dorrie," Gloria said reasonably. "I mean, it makes sense to *have* one, I'm not saying that. I've got a twenty-two pistol in my car that Sully sold me after I hit that dog. That dog I hit right after we opened? You weren't here. You wouldn't know. I hit a dog that ran out on the road, three, four miles from town, and I didn't have anything to kill it with. It was awful. I had to leave it and call the sheriff's office when I got home. So I have a pistol now." She shrugged. "But. And this is what I'm saying. There's no point in having one here, in the restaurant. What are you gonna do? Shoot everyone who gets drunk? Good luck." She smiled amiably and picked something out of the corner of her black-rimmed eye.

"I feel like hell," Dorrie said.

"You sound like hell. Your throat. You sound like the wrath of God."

They sipped their drinks silently. Sully clinked the glasses a little as he dried them. He whistled "Lady of Spain" and made soft castanet sounds with his fingers on the bar.

"Does my face look funny?" Gloria asked, feeling it with her fingertips.

Dorrie examined the kind geisha face. "It's pinkish," she said. "You look feverish."

"Oh, God," Gloria said, disgusted. "Ace and I spent some time under this old sunlamp I got secondhand in Great Falls. The kind that shine on your whole body? Today. This afternoon." Ace Booker was Gloria's latest boyfriend, a missile worker who manned one of the underground launch control centers. "I made some weird rum drinks with pineapple juice, and I guess we were pretending we were in the Bahamas or something. We sort of fell asleep under that stupid sunlamp. I hate to think what my skin looks like under my makeup. Christ. At least we wore goggles." She probed her face again with her fingertips.

Dorrie started to cry.

"It's okay. Cry." Gloria leaned her head back and sighed sympathetically.

"I broke my mother's arm once," Dorrie said. "She was being strange, and I yanked her and she fell and it just . . . snapped."

Gloria looked at her carefully. "Things happen," she said slowly. She stirred her drink. "Hmmm. Dorrie Vane, one-woman crime wave." She wrote the headline in the air with her finger. "Here. Have an extra that makes a difference," she said, handing Dorrie a rocket swizzle stick. Then she took their glasses back to the bar. Dorrie heard her yelp.

"Jesus H. Christ! My face!" Gloria scooted behind the bar and stepped past Sully, hands on his waist, to peer at her face in the mirror.

"I can't believe it," she wailed. Dorrie got up to see.

In the bright mirror, the white marks of the goggles were pushing through Gloria's makeup like small x-rays. She looked as if she contained a different, very serious person inside her painted face. Sully laughed quietly.

"Poor Ace." Gloria laughed. "Right now, he's

down in the launch control center looking like this." She clicked her long fingernail on the mirror. "Sitting down there, sixty feet under the ground, with little white glasses on his red face." She turned to Dorrie. "Did you know they each wear a little key around their neck? I kid you not. Like a car key. They sit there and watch the lights and whatever. Is something wrong with the missile? Are the Reds coming? Whatever they need to know.

Then, at the moment of truth, they both insert their little keys in the locks. *Click, click.* And they turn them at the same time to set off the missiles. One can't do it without the other. *Click, click.* If *one* went crazy, nothing would happen. But if they *both* lost it at the same time, *pow!*" She followed the long arc of an imaginary missile with her raccoon eyes.

"I asked Mr. Ace Hot-pants what he thought about down there. Not the Russians, I bet. I asked him that, and he gave me this look that took my clothes right off; I kid you not."

She drew a long, comical face. Dorrie's tears started again.

"You're a mess," Gloria said gently. "I guess I would be, too, if I had to bite Curt Wilcox after a busy shift." She put her arm lightly on Dorrie's and led her to their coats, waving over her shoulder at Sully. "Maybe you *will* have to shoot him," she said brightly.

Dorrie tiptoed past Mrs. Berridge, who was tilted back on her lounge chair, swollen ankles high. She tiptoed out again with Sam, waving to the old woman, who always woke for a moment. Sam was sound asleep, his breath thick with his head cold.

At the apartment, she started to put him in his crib, then placed him gently in her own small bed. The windows rattled with the wind. She was chilly and her throat felt scalded. She couldn't swallow without new tears. She felt puckered with fury. Eventually, though, the waking day began to fade. Eventually, her muscles smoothed and she made her way into sleep, her body in a long curve around Sam's, adrift in his sweet baby smell.

# Chapter 11

And he said, Stand over there, by the window, so I can watch you. I love to watch you. The small flame by the bed flicked shadows across the ceiling and walls as she very slowly opened six small buttons, waiting a long beat between each. And then the insect rasp of a zipper, and then a hook, and the clothes lay around her ankles, lit by the night window like the ghosts of clothes. She stepped out of them and turned very slowly, away from him. His soft breathing, and hers, filled the room. She stretched her arms up, holding the window frame, then tipped her head back as his breath drew close.

She ran six blocks to say good night again, in the rain, naked under a long wool coat.

She's just a friend, he said. Then he said it again.

*   *   *

She began to feel, during the daylight hours, as though she had a role in an instructional film. How to ride a bus. How to type in an office. How to take notes with a hundred other students in a lecture hall. How to chatter. None of it was real. It wasn't bad, it just wasn't real. The real part was the click of his key in her apartment door, sometime after midnight. He turned one lock; she released the dead bolt. *Click, click.* Symmetry. The door opened. Sometimes she moved so fast, when she heard his footsteps, that they turned the locks at the same time.

She saw him once in full daylight, near the campus, outside a record store. She was in a slow-moving bus. He glanced at it but didn't see her. It was a cold, blustery day and he stood hunched, hands in pockets, talking to another man, bouncing a little in place. A woman walked by and he stopped talking to follow her with his eyes. His jacket looked too thin; the sleeves were too short. His cap was pulled low over his eyes. He looked aimless and seedy and vaguely criminal. That isn't him, she thought. That's a stand-in.

I know you, he would say afterward. I know every square inch of you. Yes, she said. I missed you so much, before I knew you. I ached for you.

He lived with a woman named Anna. It was complicated. They were friends but basically lived their own lives. She was at a hard place in her life. If he left, she would have no place else to go. He felt sorry for her. But there was nothing between them. Not like this. Nothing to compare. How could she even ask?

They were both edgy. They had a brandy. He took off his jeans and walked around in his undershorts, fanning himself with her Japanese fan, which made them laugh because it was snowing outside.

Anna had given him a scare, he said. They had begun, sometimes, to say her name with neutralizing casualness, as if she were an old pet or a favorite aunt. Anna had told him she was pregnant. But it was a false alarm. He threw his head back and exhaled loudly.

At that moment, Dorrie knew he was leaving her.

She listened carefully. She smiled. She got up and touched his hair. He ran his hand down her hip.

In the bathroom, she smeared spermicide on the diaphragm, folded the slippery circle of latex. Her quivering fingers slid off the edges, and it flew across the room to land on the bath rug. She picked it up, plucked the lint off the jelly-smeared rim, then gave up and washed it and started over. Smearing, folding, crouching, relaxing. Again, it shot out of her fingers.

She washed it again, her eyes brimming, and looked closer. She held it up to the light. There was a pinprick hole near the rim. She stared at it. The bedsprings squeaked. She folded it again and it slid quickly into her body, as if it knew, finally, where to go.

# Chapter 12

Margaret had just gotten her first pair of eyeglasses, perfect cat-eyes, and she was amazed at how much she could see. She lay in the scrub grass beneath a stand of cottonwoods, took them off, and watched the branches turn gauzy and familiar. Then she put the glasses back on, bracing a little for the barrage of detail. Thousands of leaves leaped out, trembling and hard-edged. The narrow river, a few yards away, turned crunchy-looking again. Bird sounds attached themselves to small shapes on high branches.

She didn't know when her vision had started to go seriously bad. It had been so gradual, this nearsightedness, that she hadn't noticed it for a while. At first, it seemed only that a luxurious vagueness had come into her life. Then it had begun to make her uneasy. But this sudden return of all the details was more than she really wanted. It was unnerving. It gave her the same feeling she got when someone explained how something scientific works—osmosis, say, or photosynthesis. The explanations crowded out her imagination and made her feel bleak with information.

The day after she got the glasses, she saw Woody Blankenship leaning against the wall of Bledsoe's Drug with his hands in his jeans pockets, looking as if he were waiting for someone. She was walking along the sidewalk and couldn't avoid him. She said hi, he said hi. She speeded up and walked right in front of him and on down the sidewalk, head tilted back to make her hair look longer.

As she walked on, she felt a strange twinge of loss. It had been too easy. Maybe it was the glasses. She had felt almost nonchalant when she saw him standing there, so sharp and clear. He seemed to wipe out the fuzzier Woody, the one in her dream, the one who stretched along her body and breathed in her ear.

Near the riverbank, upstream, MaryEllen and her best friend, Julia, and Julia's brother from Philadelphia were spreading a picnic blanket and setting up a few lawn chairs on its edge. Julia's children, a two-year-old and a four-year-old, were home with a babysitter because they were in the last phase of chicken pox.

The tailgate of the station wagon was covered with thermoses and Tupperware containers and fried chicken. With her glasses on, Margaret divined almost every detail of the lunch. Squinting, she saw the pattern on the Dixie cups.

Julia wore loose slacks and a billowing blouse the color of cotton candy. She transferred food from the tailgate to the picnic blanket with oiled, backward-leaning movements. Her baby was due in two weeks, and Margaret was grateful for the possibility of crisis that Julia brought with her. She had a feeling the baby would be born here at the Rising Wolf rodeo, an hour's drive from any town. It wasn't impossible.

She imagined all the chaos and urgency if the baby came. She would have to help. They wouldn't be able to ignore her, because she already knew about babies from her job wheeling Sam around town. Now that summer was here, she sometimes wheeled him to the swimming pool and parked the buggy near the wire fence so they could watch the swimmers. Rita Kay was always there with her new friends, blue-lipped from the unheated water, racing down the concrete walk to dive again from the medium board. Margaret still couldn't dive. Wheeling Sam was a small relief from having to think so often about trying.

As she approached the adults, Margaret scrutinized herself briefly in the car window. She noticed very little except the new glasses. It was as if a hidden, sober part of her was emerging. The fully adult Margaret. The Margaret who would be able to explain osmosis, who would be tall and explicit and solemn.

She took her chicken and potato salad and sat down on the grass next to her mother. MaryEllen ran a hand through Margaret's long, buff-colored hair, so different from her own, which looked, at the moment, like the pelt of a small animal, short and alive. Margaret's was like a different species of hair, more languid and distant.

MaryEllen and Julia and Julia's brother, whose name was Aden, sat in the sun, munching, talking lazily. Aden looked a little like Robert Kennedy. He was explaining himself to MaryEllen, who listened, head cocked to the side, as she cracked a hard-boiled egg.

"I'm thinking about the Peace Corps," he was saying. "That's one possibility."

In the near distance, beyond several rows of cars whose roofs glared in the sun, Margaret could see the small split-rail arena where the rodeo would soon start. A buoyant announcer tested the tinny sound system. "Test, two, three, four. . . . Can you hear me over there, Bob? Raise your hat if you can. . . . Test, two, three, four." Some of the contestants galloped their horses around the arena, warming them up, kicking up little twisters of dust.

Margaret's father, Roy, and Julia's husband, Red, were riding around in the arena. Roy was entered in the calf-roping and team-tying. Red was entered in the team-tying and bulldogging.

"Or the Forest Service," Aden said, looking appreciatively toward the mountains. "No one told me you people had this at your back door."

Margaret wished Dorrie and Sam were here, so she would have something to do, someone interesting to talk to. She had thought about bringing Midge, her old mare, to ride around on so she'd seem like part of things. But she didn't actually like to ride Midge that much. She liked the way horses looked and acted, more than she liked to ride them. Maybe it would be different when Señor Roja was trained. For now, she just liked to look at him and imagine what it was like to be so fast and brave.

Between MaryEllen and Aden sat Julia, a big-bellied queen, her square face flushed. Margaret wondered why Aden looked so relaxed when he was so out of place. She felt embarrassed for him: for his slacks and white sport shirt; for his canvas shoes that weren't even sneakers, much less boots; for the fact that he was probably the only man around who wasn't at the arena. His forearms were covered with black hair, a soft layer that reached down to the tops of his hands. That was strange, too, though it might be ordinary in Philadelphia.

He stretched his long legs and let them rest a few inches from MaryEllen's neatly crossed ankles. MaryEllen told them a little about the history of the place where they sat, how it had been a Blackfeet summer camp a century earlier. "And you can see why," she said, making a wide circle with her hand.

It was, indeed, a gentle spot, with its small, clear river, the tall trees on either side of the water, the little breeze that skittered through, lifting a corner of the blanket, rustling the summer-dried leaves, then stopping so the leaves could bake drier. Margaret munched potato chips. No one seemed to need to speak.

At that moment, Roy and Red—pink-cheeked, dusty, excited—clattered up on their tall sorrel horses. The rodeo would begin in a few minutes, so they didn't even get down to eat. MaryEllen handed up sandwiches and beer. The men ate rapidly. Their horses, Pokey and Boone, stepped softly in place, as if they too were anxious to be off.

"How're you feelin', sport?" Red said to Julia between munches.

"Fine," she said softly, rubbing her hand over her big belly. She was a tall, big-boned woman with an ordinary face that changed entirely when she smiled because her smile was so wide and white-toothed.

Red spit on the ground. He was large and freckled, with eyes like a nice dog's, earnest and thoughtless. You looked at him and thought of something that crashed through bushes and underbrush, something that thought about one thing at a time. He liked to tease Margaret—called her stringbean and, now, four-eyes. She liked him because he was loud and real and made the world seem like something anybody could handle.

Roy was quieter and smaller. He had a smart face that looked a little tense under his broad cowboy hat.

Sometimes he looked as if he wore a costume when he came to rodeos because, most of the time, he wore his doctor's clothes—slacks, starched white shirt. Margaret could tell that he wanted something Red had. Rudeness, maybe. Because Red was very rude. He drank too much and stayed away from home. Once, Julia had come over to their house, red-eyed, late at night. She and MaryEllen sat in the kitchen and talked in low, sad voices about something Red had done when he went to the livestock auction and stayed four days. Margaret had listened to them through the grate in her bedroom floor.

Pokey nickered softly. Julia kept her hand on her belly and closed her eyes. Aden lit a cigarette and leaned forward, toward her, his hairy hands clasped.

"What does it feel like when the baby turns inside you?" he asked his sister. Everyone looked at him. Margaret blushed.

"When the baby does what?" Red asked loudly, looking around for clarification.

"Turns," Julia said. "In the womb."

Red rolled his eyes, swallowed the last of his beer, and lobbed the empty can at a paper sack, making the shot. "Let's go, Roy. Girl talk." But Roy was watching MaryEllen, who studied Aden in a completely unguarded and curious way, as if someone had just told her something amazing she never expected to hear. Her face was flushed. Margaret took off her glasses and cleaned them rigorously with her shirttail. She didn't like this moment.

"When the baby turns?" Julia smiled her lit-up smile. She cocked her head to the side and thought for a minute.

"It feels like falling in love," she said. No one responded.

"You know. Like the inside of you is doing an underwater somersault." She laughed ruefully at her inability to explain herself. But Margaret understood her, because of the Woody dream. And so did Aden, she thought, because he smiled in a satisfied way. MaryEllen still looked curious, as if the question hadn't been answered. She smiled at Julia, willing and uncomprehending. Julia shrugged again.

Red turned his horse briskly and trotted off to the arena. MaryEllen stood and handed Roy a candy bar for quick fuel later on. "Gotta go," he said unnecessarily. And she patted Pokey's nose, and he was off.

Margaret followed the men on foot, heading for the crackling loudspeaker. "Merlin Chatham is our first roper," it quavered. "Buddy Connell on deck and Joe Whiteman in the hole." It was an island of tinny sound amid the calm swish of the river, the hot breeze through the trees, and the faint, sharp sound of children playing among the parked pickups on the far side of the arena. Margaret crawled up on the splintery fence near the busiest end of the arena where the chutes were and the pen that held the bucking horses. It was very hot now, and the heat wavered up from the pickup hoods and the tin roof of the little hot-dog stand.

In Madrid, the mountains were small, two-dimensional points that marched along the western horizon. But here, at the Rising Wolf rodeo, they were near and gray. They had a hunched, big-shouldered look, like thunderclouds or buffaloes.

Margaret watched her father and Red team-tie a big steer. They raced behind the animal on their tall horses, Red reaching forward to rope the neck, Roy scooping his lariat across the ground to snag two feet. They stretched the steer out flat, and all the men and animals panted while horns honked and the people in the bleachers clapped.

She watched the barrel racers with their straight, pretty backs, their brilliant blouses and short whips. She watched a huge steer come charging out of the chute, horns wide and aloft, and Red galloping his horse behind it, then alongside. Then he was hanging off the side of his horse, then leaping through the air, grabbing the horns, planting his heels in the ground, twisting, twisting the massive leather neck until the animal thudded dustily to the ground.

Margaret sat on the fence and watched. It all repeated itself. The first go-round. The second go-round. Horses dashed out of chutes, calves speeded down the arena, men circled their long lariats in the air and leaped onto horned steers, dust devils skittered across the dirt, car horns honked.

As the afternoon wore on, a sense of distraction and driftiness entered the crowd. Kids with Popsicle mustaches and small cowboy boots ran around in packs, darting between parked cars. A baby wailed. The arena filled with short, intense engagements, but the overall feel of it was timeless, full of the smell of river trees and dust and the dry whir of grasshoppers.

Young bucking horses with names like Thunderbolt, Staircase, So Long, and War Paint milled around a holding pen. Then one of them, a splashy pinto, did something very strange, even for a raw young bucking horse. He reared up and raked his hooves against the old rail fence, drumming it with his hooves, trying to make it break.

This spooked the other horses. They began to run around the narrow enclosure, whinnying. The rearing horse pawed at the rails.

Red appeared. He had a stiff leather strap in his hand. He climbed up on the fence, leaned over, and hit the rearing horse, hard, on top of the head. *Crack!* Margaret could hear it plainly. At the same time, her father rode up to the fence on his horse. "Where is your mother?" he said quietly.

"At the car."

"She's missing everything."

Margaret ran back to the car. Aden had a Kool-Aid pitcher in his hand and was pouring the Kool-Aid into three Dixie cups. They were all laughing softly.

Margaret interrupted loudly, rudely.

"The rodeo's half over, Mom." Her voice was accusatory and shrill, even to her. "When are you coming over?"

MaryEllen looked sleepy. She gave Margaret a gentle, satisfied smile. "Coming, sweetheart," she said. Her hair had become a mass of wild ringlets. There was a challenging lilt in her voice, and Margaret knew it wasn't meant for her.

Her mother turned back to Aden. "And what makes you think that I would think something like that? What gave you that idea?" Her face was alive and unruly, like her hair.

Margaret tugged at her hand like a very young child and pulled backward as hard as she could. She knew she was acting like a brat, but she didn't care. She felt trapped and hysterical, like the bucking horse Red had smacked on the head.

She pulled backward, trying to raise her smiling mother to her feet. Then her sweaty hand slipped out of MaryEllen's, and she crashed into the side of the station wagon. Her glasses flew off and landed in the potato salad. And when she saw them there—sunk into the lumpy mess—she burst into tears.

Aden scooped them out of the salad and cleaned them off with his handkerchief. But Margaret didn't put them back on.

"Come on!" she screamed at her mother, her voice shaking.

"Margaret," her mother said sharply. "Stop it. Calm down." Margaret walked off toward the trees and sobbed, but she felt as though she had gotten through the worst part. She had managed to wake her mother up, so that she was talking again in an ordinary, familiar tone of voice. She didn't mind that it had taken some screaming and tears. It had to be done.

She put on her glasses, which smelled faintly of mayonnaise. Then she and her mother walked together toward the arena.

"That Aden guy has hair on his hands like a monkey," Margaret offered. "And he's a wimp."

"No, he's not," MaryEllen said briskly. "You're wrong." And they found places to sit on the rickety bleachers.

Roy sat with two other cowboys on the fence rail, across the arena. He waved widely at them, and Margaret felt another burst of anger at her mother. This was where MaryEllen belonged. She should have been at the bleachers long ago. MaryEllen waved back serenely. Everything seemed to be fine. And then it occurred to Margaret that she was the one on the outside. That, although she was the person who was keeping everything smooth, they were oblivious to her efforts.

A few clouds had bunched together directly above the arena and were taking on a blue-gray tinge, but most of the sky was still a clear hot blue. The announcer's voice wavered onto the air. He kept up a jovial stream of patter than sounded intimate, like a card player in the next room.

"Tough luck for that cowboy," the tinny voice said when a bronc rider landed hard on his face.

"Hey, Lorraine!" This was too loud, and the loudspeaker screeched. "You sure you clocked that cowboy right?"

"Hey, Rosco," he called down to the clown, who was twirling dizzily beneath the announcer's platform. "Keep your shirt on."

He never stopped. It was as if he couldn't bear to leave the airwaves empty. He had to keep talking, up there on his frail little perch, had to keep hearing his ordinary voice come back at him from somewhere else, enlarged.

Red was holding court at the far end of the arena near the chutes. He stood at the center of a half circle of cowboys. They all spit a lot in the dirt. A few had cans of beer. They stood with their feet apart on their high-heeled boots. They took furtive-looking drags on their cigarettes and threw them curtly away. They wore Levi's, and brightly colored shirts, and leather hand-tooled belts with enormous buckles that flashed in the sun.

A small dog, a border collie, ran between the men, ducked under the holding pen, and nipped a bucking horse on the heels. Red picked up a rock and lobbed it at the ragged dog, which yipped away, tail between its legs. But it came back a few minutes later, as if it had no memory. And this time it darted straight into the pen and stirred up the horses so that they ran in circles.

When the dog ran out of the pen, Red lunged at it and gave it a kick, a kick so hard that the dog flew into the air and landed, rolling, in the dust. Then Red picked up a stick and lobbed it at the animal, which ran yelping out of the arena. He returned to the group of men, popped open a beer, tossed his head back, and roared with laughter at something someone said.

Margaret kept her eye on Red, keeping track of him. She felt in her bones that he had started something rolling. She looked at her mother to see if she saw the danger, but MaryEllen was folding a bandanna, tying it around her wild curls, putting on sunglasses to watch the rodeo. The timekeeper, the lanky woman the announcer called Lorraine, leaned over the rail on the announcer's perch to say something to a man on the ground, and Margaret felt another small flutter of dread, as if it were she who was high above the ground.

MaryEllen's head was tilted back, receiving the sun. Then the clouds covered the sun for a minute and her mother's face went into shadow.

"I feel kind of sick," Margaret announced. "I don't feel right."

"You didn't get enough sleep last night," MaryEllen said, putting a hand on Margaret's knee and waving with the other at Aden, who was mounting the bleachers. He had pushed his shirt sleeves farther up his arms. There was a sheen of sweat on his face. His teeth, when he grinned at them, were as white as Julia's.

He stood in front of them, blocking the view. "Julia is taking a nap," he said. "I thought I better see what this is all about." He sat down next to MaryEllen and looked out on the men and horses.

"It's almost over," Margaret said sullenly.

The three of them watched together. Roy rode past—he was one of men who helped riders off their bucking horses—and looked sharply over his shoulder at them.

Something was going on in the chutes. Margaret saw a wild-eyed horse's head above the wooden gate. It was the pinto again, the one who had tried to break the fence. Then the head disappeared and there was shouting, and the rider leaped for the side of the chute as the horse crashed to the ground and flailed its hooves against the narrow enclosure. Red leaned down from the side of the chute and pulled the horse upright. The white-faced rider eased back down on the animal, and the gate flew open and they were out.

The pinto ran out fast, then stopped, put its head down, and kicked its hind feet almost straight up. The rider, leaning far back, stayed on. Margaret was silently cheering the horse. He reminded her of what Señor Roja would do if someone cinched leather around his flanks and raked him with spurs.

"Here's a tough customer," came the echoing voice from the announcer's box. "This critter tried to crash out of the holding pen earlier this afternoon. Whoa! Look at that!"

The horse had stopped and stood stock-still. It didn't move. The rider raked it with his spurs. Nothing happened. Then Margaret saw her father climb down from his horse, pick up a rock, and lob it at the horse's feet, as if he were skipping a stone across water as hard as he could.

"Don't! Stop it!" Margaret's voice was piercing. It seemed to follow the horse, which had broken into a straight gallop and was running around the arena crazily, like a fly in a bottle.

It ran toward the fence and reared high. The rider fell over backward and lay for a few moments in the dirt before picking himself up to run. The horse continued to attack the fence. Its hooves crashed through the brittle rails, and then the rest of its body followed, sinking heavily into the broken wood. The big animal rolled forward and sideways, and when it came up again a large stick protruded from its neck.

The horse staggered across the arena as if drunk. It stopped and stood in place, head almost to the ground, the stick like a buried sword.

MaryEllen tried to cover Margaret's eyes. "God help us," she moaned. Aden stared.

A clump of men ran out and stared at the horse. Then one of them trotted back to the chute area and came back with a gun. They all stood for a moment, looking at the wound and at the blood that now flowed from the ears and nose. Then the man with the gun, a fat man in a pink shirt, stepped back, raised the pistol, and shot the horse once in the head.

Margaret wailed.

MaryEllen took her arm firmly and steered her down the bleachers and away from the arena. Margaret turned once to see her father and Red bent over the dead young horse, putting ropes on him to pull him away.

They drove home in the rain. Through Heart Butte, past the abandoned boarding school, across the Two Medicine River, on home. Margaret rolled down her window to smell dust being tamped down by moisture, that particular smell that is more like dust than dust. Her parents were silent.

A week later, a baby boy was born to Red and Julia. A week after that, they all gathered at the church: Red, Julia, and the baby, their other two children; Margaret and her parents; Aden.

Aden was going back to Philadelphia that afternoon. He wore the suit he would travel in, and his hair was slicked down in a way that made him look very young. His clothes fit badly.

Julia handed the baby to Aden while they waited for Father Malone to get ready. The baby whimpered a little, and Aden jiggled him back and forth, awkwardly. He looked uncomfortable. Father Malone thumbed through his black book and checked the water level in a small crystal pitcher at his side.

MaryEllen and Roy stood close together. Ever since the Rising Wolf rodeo, they had been different with each other. Margaret had noticed something new in the way they said goodbye in the morning: a longer touch of MaryEllen's fingers on Roy's fresh-shaved cheek, a softer sound in their voices. Roy looked like a doctor today in his gray suit and white shirt. He held his arm lightly around MaryEllen's waist, and she leaned into it a little. She wore a crisp linen dress and a straw hat.

Julia looked tired and a little puffy. The four-year-old and the two-year-old, Mitzi and Jake, rustled and poked each other. Red looked restless too. His face was sunburned and the balding parts of his head, usually covered with a hat, were white. His corduroy sport coat was too small to button. His cowboy boots were dirty and unpolished.

Aden jiggled the baby tentatively, and it began to cry. Red reached for the baby, and it cried louder. Red's big freckled fingers splayed across the gauzy blanket.

Margaret knew she needed to speak. "Why don't you let the mom hold him," she said to Red, trying to sound cute and whimsical. It was the wrong thing to say. Everyone looked at her. But Red did pass the baby to Julia.

The prayers began. Margaret closed her eyes for a few seconds, opened them. Then the baby's fuzzy head was tipped back over something that looked like a giant birdbath, and Father Malone called him in Latin from limbo into the world.

# Chapter 13

A half hour before the eclipse of the sun, Dorrie ran into Marie Cotten at the Inland Market. Marie, who had to be in her mid-thirties, still looked like a high school cheerleader. Ten pounds heavier, perhaps; more fixed, more permanent looking. But still short, lithe, and ripe in an adolescent sort of way.

She and a schoolgirl version of herself stood at the checkout counter. They both wore turquoise canvas flats, white capris, and pink sleeveless blouses. Marie's hair was a filmy bouffant; the girl's was pulled into a fluffy yellow ponytail. Marie shook some Sen-Sens into her hand and they both picked at them daintily, nibbling one tiny soapy square at a time.

"Dorrie Vane," Marie drawled, making her large eyes wider. Dorrie brought her grocery cart to a halt and smiled. Marie was the oldest Shepherd girl—seven or eight years older than her sister Candy, thirteen years older than Dorrie's old friend Sandra.

When Dorrie and Sandra were still in junior high, they had found a packet of damply worded love notes from Larry Cotten to Marie, in an old box in the attic, and the discovery obsessed them for months. The notes had been written years earlier, when Marie and Larry were in high school, and they were much more interesting than Marie and Larry in the flesh. Marie became, through the notes, revolting and wonderful. And her power held, these years later.

"This is—"

"Rita Kay," Marie said, pleased. "Getting big. Too big for her britches."

Dorrie remembered actual phrases from the love notes: explicit, agonized.

"The sun's gonna disappear by one-fifty-seven P.M.," Rita Kay announced. She held a large cardboard box with a hole cut out of one side. "This is my Sun-scope. I'll see it in here." She gestured with her eyes. "It will be a little tiny eclipse, about the size of a dime. It will shine through this little pinhole above the head hole." She showed Dorrie the smaller hole. "I'll be watching the sun turn dark." She paused. "Inside here."

Dorrie politely examined the box. This, then, was the Rita Kay that Margaret referred to so elliptically and bitterly.

"We're having a Hawaiian luau this evening!" Marie said in her commanding, popular-girl voice. "Why don't you come? Bring your dad if you want. He could use a little fun. Larry ran into a couple of missile guys at the Bull's Eye last night, and he invited them too." She winked conspiratorially. "Fresh blood!"

* * *

Dorrie put her groceries away and felt the day turn heavy and quiet. The Bull's Eye was closed two days for something Irwin called inventory, though she didn't know what they would tally. She was free to go to the luau, and it seemed, suddenly, like a good idea. She checked her watch, pulled the curtains open, and peered up at the sun.

When she was a child, she now remembered, the sky had turned a gray and salmon color and all the noise had bled away from the afternoon, like this. She had stood on the street curb, surveying the nauseous sky, and a golf ball of ice had landed at her feet, bounced once, and rolled to a stop. It was a pure surprise.

She ran into the house with it and showed it to Rosemary, who didn't believe it had appeared from above. "You froze that in the freezer," she said. Two or three minutes later, they were both on their stomachs under the dining room table listening to the huge hailstones crack into the roof. It was like being inside a wooden box that giants were pelting with boulders. One stone shot horizontally through the living room window like a bullet fired from the street.

When it was over, two big windows lay in shards on the rug, and Rosemary was laughing. "We're under siege!" she shouted, picking her way gleefully through the glass. Dorrie had never heard her so excited.

Sparse traffic moved along Main: a bright yellow truck from Weaver's Furniture, loaded with three plastic-covered couches; a teenager on a motorcycle; a dark blue Air Force jeep. The light turned and the vehicles stopped and waited, the motorcycle puny between the other two.

And then, as Dorrie watched, it was as if a large cloud moved in front of the sun. She stood at the window and kept her eyes aimed down at the street. Several people came out of stores onto the sidewalk, holding their cardboard viewers. They stuck their heads inside the boxes and turned their backs obediently to the sun. Daylight disappeared then, rapidly. It was as if a bulb had blown out in a movie projector, darkening the film to twilight, or a record had slowed from 45 to 16 rpm, turning the sound thick, muddy, dark. Main Street turned to early night.

She knew that if she looked at the sun, it would be a dark disk, framed by something lighter. She remembered the term suddenly: penumbra. The less dark region. Helen had named a smoky gray cat Penumbra. "It means 'almost shade,' " she had said, reading the big dictionary. "And after 'almost' it says, 'See *passion*.' " She had looked up, at that, and made her eyes big with surprise.

The streetlights flickered on in the darkness, then flickered off as the darkness began to leave. It was over. The day was growing bright again. Cars zoomed down Main. Clerks shouted joyfully across the street to each other.

Earl didn't want to go to the party. He had research to do. Dorrie didn't ask what kind. She knew. She also knew that the strange afternoon might have set him on edge. He would be reminded, again, of the enemy's acid-eyed intents.

He didn't want to go to a Hawaiian party, no. But he paused after he said that, and he made a startling offer.

"Why don't you drop Sam off, and I'll watch him while you go to the party," he said. They were drinking coffee in the kitchen. "We could wait until he turned in for the night, and then you could go."

"He's at Mrs. Berridge's," Dorrie said. "I dropped him off while I did errands. I could just leave him there."

"Whatever you think." His voice had retreated.

"Mrs. Berridge says he's been waking up about eleven every night. I could leave him with you and come back before then."

"Well, maybe it's not such a good idea. Let's forget it. Some other time, maybe."

She knew he had dismissed her. She thought of him, as he would be later in the evening, bent over his magazines, writing in the margins, in a house that made no sound.

"Dad." She paused, wondering what she was about to say. "Dad. This last year. Mom's problems this last year. What were her complaints? What bothered her the most? Was it me? Was she worried about the baby? Did she think I'd slid off the edge of the earth or something? Or was it something big, like the color of the kitchen being tragically wrong?" She heard her own flailing anger.

"It wasn't you," Earl said, rubbing a hand over the strands on his crown. "It wasn't you at all." He let that float in the air for a few moments.

"It was me," he said. "She's been claiming, when she gets like this, that she doesn't know me. Doesn't have any idea who I am. After twenty-four years of marriage, she doesn't know me. She keeps screaming it at me. 'Who are you?' Over and over. A real shriek. 'I'm your husband, Earl Vane,' I'll tell her. 'That doesn't tell me anything,' she'll say. 'That doesn't tell me a damn thing.' And then she starts in again. Loud enough for the neighbors to hear. She was quite abusive this last time, but then again she wasn't in her right mind, so you can't take that at face value."

He paused again, for three long beats. Four.

"It wasn't you at all," he said quietly.

* * *

The pistol was in a holster on a shelf in the basement storage room, next to a baseball cap and a wicker fishing creel. They were like a museum display, Dorrie thought. The artifacts of an earlier era, another person.

In the far past, she and Earl had gone target shooting. He smiled during that time in his life. He put soda pop cans on fence tops and showed her how to shoot them off. That's my girl, he said when she did. He wore the baseball cap.

The pistol was unloaded, but that didn't matter. She put it in the bottom of her big purse. Its weight felt innocent. It felt like remembered protection.

Dorrie walked through the wicker trellis into Larry and Marie's backyard. The sounds of "Lovely Hula Girl" drifted out of the record player. "Lovely Hula Girl, I'm in a whirl, crazy over you. . . ."

Don Bledsoe, the drugstore owner, was swaying his hips back and forth, carving a woman's shape in the air with his pudgy hands. Card tables had been set up, a dozen of them, covered with identical flowered tablecloths. Each had a centerpiece of an orange glass globe over a candle, ringed with paper flowers.

The yard itself was spare, as most of the yards in Madrid were. After the first greening of June, most people just let the grass turn brown, watering only the spots that threatened to burn up entirely. By August, when the river was very low, there was usually a ban on watering much at all. The flowers turned dry and rustled in the breeze. The grass crackled underfoot.

Marie had planted a short border of geraniums along one wall of the peach-colored house. They were crisp and faded. Among the stalks were small ceramic statues of a mother rabbit and three babies.

For this party, she had gone all out. There were the tables. There were three tiki torches. There were streamers stretched from the clothesline to the gutter of the roof, with paper lanterns hanging from them. They batted back and forth in a stiff little breeze. Ukelele music wafted among the lanterns and the lights and the voices, among the men in jeans and flowered Hawaiian shirts and the women who had wrapped a few yards of flowered material around their bodies, leaving their pretty shoulders bare. It was a chilly evening for July, and they were beginning to put sweaters on. Some had real flowers bobby-pinned behind their ears.

Bledsoe spotted Dorrie and ceremoniously placed a paper lei around her neck. "Where's your outfit?" he bellowed.

"Quit!" said Marie, giving him a playful punch in the arm. She wore a sarong of brilliant red flowers on a white background. "How is she supposed to have an outfit when I only informed her of this little gathering this afternoon?" She adjusted Bledsoe's lei. "Didn't even know she was back," she lied easily.

"Nice party," Dorrie said, drawing her cardigan closer around her shoulders as two large drops of rain hit her on the head.

"Stop!" Marie scolded, shaking her finger smartly at the streaky sky. The drops stopped.

"Gee, I wish Sandra could be here to see you, hon," Marie said as her eyes roamed to a smoking barbecue. Beyond the smoke stood three men, tall, young, and clipped. "But they're in the middle of harvest down south, and she won't get back to town until Christmas, I'm guessing. Little sister Sandra and the orangutans." The week after high school graduation, Sandra Shepherd had married one of the Miller boys, and they farmed an uncle's place in Oklahoma. She sent Dorrie Christmas cards each year with a new photo of the family. It was up to three kids.

"Rita Kay," Marie called. "Get a Mai Tai for Dorrie. Quick like a rabbit!" She clapped her hands. "I want you to meet those good-looking guys," she said to Dorrie in a stage whisper.

Lieutenants Steve McClintock, Fred Schermer, and Jay Gunn introduced themselves formally when Marie led Dorrie to them, nodding gravely as they did so, speaking in soft southern and midwestern accents. Jay's had a distinct Appalachian twang on top. They wore pressed slacks and muted sports shirts and looked—in that flickering, florid gathering—tall and straight and sober, even with the paper leis around their necks. They were stationed at Malmstrom. They worked with the missiles. Jay called her ma'am.

Dorrie reminded Steve that she had spilled his french fries in the Bull's Eye bar on a particularly bad night. He remembered and grinned. "I heard it turned into a worse one," he said. "Wilcox," he said to Fred and Jay, reminding them. They all shook their heads. Of course, everyone would know, one way or the other.

Uneasy, she asked them where they were from, how they liked Montana, what their jobs were. Jay was a maintenance worker on the missiles. "I'm the handyman," he said cheerfully. "Don't want one of those babies to short out!"

Steve and Fred worked in launch control centers. They sat sixty feet under the ground in a reinforced concrete bunker, with a partner, for twenty-four hours at a time. Steve's partner in the LCC was Ace Booker, Gloria's sometime boyfriend.

"Did you grow up here? Are you a Madridian, would you call it?" Jay asked.

"Yes," she said. "This is home." They all took sips of their drinks at the same time.

"What do you do down there?" Dorrie asked. The question had a surprising, insinuating tone, and she felt her face redden.

Steve and Fred looked at each other and shrugged elaborately. They looked very healthy and confident. Like the boy on the train, when he first got on.

"What do you *think* they do down there?" Jay twanged. "They defend the land of the free."

"And the home of the brave," Steve sang.

Margaret walked through the trellis with her parents. She said hi shyly to Dorrie and waved stiffly to Rita Kay, who was over by the barbecue.

"Rita Kay's mom is giving me and her five dollars to be servants for two hours," she told Dorrie. "She doesn't know we're not friends anymore. My parents made me do it." Roy and MaryEllen ignored the pointed remark and waved at friends.

Rita Kay and another girl were peering at the barbecue, their heads inside the billows of smoke. Bledsoe and two other men peered too. Marie fluttered behind them, touching them lightly on their backs, their shoulders. One, then the other. Her husband, Larry, was over by the lilac bush, adjusting the flower behind Kathy Bledsoe's ear.

"Where's your Hawaiian outfit, Margaret?" Dorrie said, touching her own lei.

"I had one, but I took it off. It was stupid. I had to wear a sweater with it because it's so cold, so then it looked stupider, so I changed back into my jeans." She was having a bad day. She looked miserable and distant as she set her chin and walked into the crowd.

A few minutes later, she was back.

She waved a thin arm toward a cluster of men in brilliant flowered shirts, their faces lit by the glow of the paper lanterns.

"Those men over there are talking about Communists. That's all they're doing is drinking these Mai Tais and talking about Communists. They think the Communists are going to put poison in the water and tell everyone it will make them have good teeth."

"They're scared," Dorrie said. She saw Earl's veiny hands, scribbling, scribbling. His hunched, tired-looking shoulders. The silent house.

"They don't look scared," Margaret said, surveying them. Bledsoe, who was weaving slightly, said something and they all laughed. An older man shook his head ruefully. Another took a long drag on a cigarette. Their faces glowed. "Do you think any of those guys can predict the future?" Margaret asked.

"No. They think they can. But they can't."

"I think I can predict the future."

Dorrie looked at her closely. "You? Why?"

Rita Kay called to Margaret from within the barbecue cloud. She hoisted a flaming skewer over her head. Margaret waved impatiently.

"Why, Margaret?"

"Because you know that rodeo I went to a couple of weeks ago? Well, a horse got shot. I didn't tell you that part. And I knew it was going to happen. I had this feeling it was going to happen. And then it did."

"You knew a horse was going to get shot."

"Well, I didn't know it was going to get shot. But I knew *something* bad was going to happen. Ask my mom." She gestured vaguely across the yard where Roy and MaryEllen talked to a very large silver-haired woman who sat in a lawn chair. "I told her, but she didn't believe me. I told her way before it happened." She pushed her glasses up her nose. "And then the horse went bananas. And they shot it."

Margaret stopped talking and gazed out over the party. She began to hum a thin little tune. Dorrie waited.

"And now I'm scared that if I think about anything scary—like poison in the water, or the missiles going off, or something—that I'll make it come true. So I just try not to." She glanced quickly at Dorrie, her face pinched.

Dorrie knew she was being asked a question.

"Bad things happen," she began slowly. "And sometimes we fear that they'll happen before they happen. But that doesn't mean we *make* them happen."

"Whenever I think I'm going to do a belly flop off the diving board, I do one," Margaret countered bleakly. "Almost every single time. I know it's going to happen before it happens."

"That's different. That's because you're scared. You imagine something, and it makes you so scared your body doesn't work right. And then the very thing happens that you're scared of." She didn't know what to say next. "It's important not to be scared," she said lamely.

"Well, how do you *stop?*"

Dorrie didn't answer. Across the yard, Rita Kay was signaling imperiously in their direction, but Margaret ignored her.

"I'll have to think about that one," Dorrie said. *How do you stop?* She made her voice lighter. "Meanwhile, you're not going to turn the water poison or make the missiles go off. Believe me. Okay?" She smiled at Margaret, knowing she owed her more. "I'll think about it, and we'll talk about it when you come over to the apartment, okay?"

Margaret started across the yard.

"We'll talk about it, Margaret," Dorrie called.

Margaret turned. "What about if you're scared of

Communists?" she shouted in a high, angry voice. "Isn't that just like being scared of a belly flop, so you make it happen?"

Heads turned and everyone fell silent for a moment. Ukelele music gurgled from the record player. Someone giggled nervously; then one of the men made a comment that Dorrie couldn't hear, and several people laughed, and the party noises came back.

Marie put on a new record and glared at Margaret. She looked tired and chilly. "Larry!" she snapped. He was whispering something to Kathy Bledsoe. Marie stood back and pointed dramatically at the barbecue with a long red fingernail. "The shish kebabs!"

Dorrie watched Margaret walk, slightly pigeon-toed, through the crowd of flowered bodies. Her lank hair hung down her back, a tortoiseshell barrette clinging to a few strands at the crown. She looked gawky and plain, a missionary among the hopped-up Hawaiians.

Margaret looked around uncertainly, then walked slowly toward Rita Kay and the other girl, who were jostling around next to the barbecue, paper leis swinging. They had spatulas in their hands and were pretending to sword fight. They ignored Margaret, who parked herself next to them in an odd, mournful slouch, her eyes fixed meditatively on the shish kebabs.

That morning, walking to the Inland Market, Dorrie had seen a homely young man in a business suit, alone at a wooden table outside the Tastee Freez, hunched eagerly over an ice-cream sundae. He looked so young and combed and motherless—so vulnerable—that she had to turn away. What had he done all day? Sold encyclopedias? Vacuum cleaners? Delivered pamphlets for the Jehovah's Witnesses? He had made her so sad she couldn't look at him.

Someone bumped into Margaret from behind—Dorrie saw her body lurch—but Margaret only glanced mildly over her shoulder, then turned her eyes back to the smoking grill.

Dorrie took a gulp of her Mai Tai. Her throat ached as it always did when a day was beginning to feel intolerable. She was furious, suddenly, at Margaret. Why did she have to deal with a moony, overwrought little girl on top of everything else? She looked up. Margaret hadn't moved. Stand up straight! she wanted to snap at her. At least until you really have something to worry about. Wait until you really see what's going on. *Then* you'll have something to slump about. Her own voice in her head sounded shrewish, small, self-dramatizing.

She closed her eyes for a minute, breathed in somebody's powdery sweet perfume and a whiff of smoke that had threaded its way across the yard, and gave in to her own thin rant. Where am I? she thought. How did I get here? How long was I a kid like Margaret, living ignorantly in a yellow house that's only four—no, five—blocks from this spot?

She thought of the prairie, stretched like an open hand, Madrid a freckle on its tawny surface. Where did I go before I landed back on this little dot? Where is Margaret going? How is she going to survive, if she lets her fears run away with her like this?

How could I have been a child who didn't even suspect that my family was rupturing, bleeding internally, or that, when I left town, I was attached to a long, long rope that was going to yank me back, hard, when I'd made a big enough mess on my own? How could I be standing on this spot, an adult, with my fatherless baby sleeping down the street in a stranger's house, with a leg-aching job at a prefab building with a flashing arrow on its roof; in a windy little know-nothing town where the sun blinks out in the middle of the day, and a bunch of adults pretend they're Hawaiians in a scrawny little backyard rimmed with tiki torches; with a father, at home, who slowly rubs Ben-Gay into his searing hip joint while he flips through magazines for evidence of systematic deceit, endemic deceit, deceit that creeps silently into a wife, a government, changing them from the inside out?

How had it come to this? The slumping Margaret was Dorrie herself. She stared at the girl and hated her. She listened to herself and wanted to be able to laugh, but she couldn't. Heartbreak was real. Fear couldn't be wished away. It had killing power. It was flattening her too. Weighing her down, sometimes, to the point where she could hardly lift her eyelids. She thought of the cowgirl on the train. Didn't she have hardness and disappointment and cause for self-doubt in her life? Didn't Gloria, for that matter? Sugar sandwiches, a tarpaper roof, dumped by Murray Medvic when his rich-farmer parents decided she brought him down? Gloria, who talked about going to business school, talked as if her time in this town was limited, a stopover, when everyone knew—everyone—that if anybody ever grew old alone in Madrid, it was going to be Gloria Beauchamp, her geisha-girl face gradually freezing solid. Didn't Gloria have her own little string of tragedies? And wasn't she able, like the young mother on the train, to muster up some kind of useful spunk?

They could; she couldn't. It was as simple as that. She was losing ground.

While all eyes were focused on Don Bledsoe doing a purple-faced hula, she ducked quietly through the rickety trellis into the darkened driveway. Steve McClintock stood alone at the end of it, the back of his pale shirt glowing faintly in the dark. He turned, zipping up his pants, and threw up his arms in mock embarrassment, catching a finger in his paper lei so that it broke. Paper petals floated to the concrete.

"Even Hawaiians have to pee," she said.

"Where are you headed?" His voice was stiff and jaunty.

"Home."

"Where's home?" Alcohol had added a layer of volume and joviality to his voice. He walked toward her, broad-shouldered, steady, mindlessly at attention. He wore his civilian clothes like a costume.

She waved vaguely toward the north, which caused them both to look briefly at the sky. The wind still blew, but the clouds were gone and the sky was blasted lightly with stars. Why couldn't he be someone else? she thought. Someone besides this strong-jawed, crew-cut Boy Scout who sits out there, under the bunchgrass, in a buried concrete room watching a panel of lights. Or whatever it was they did.

"I'll walk you," he said, offering his elbow in a courtly drunken gesture.

She started to say no, to think of an excuse. Then she thought about Margaret's mournful, defeated face, and she took the arm. She fought her own retreat. He felt solid and warm.

They walked through the quiet streets. Steve whistled almost imperceptibly between his teeth. She smelled his cloying aftershave. She stretched her stride to match his. Neither had much to say.

"Where are we going? To your house?"

"No," Dorrie said. "To my babysitter's." She felt him register the information.

"You have a kid."

"A baby. He's nine months old." She paused. "And, no, I'm not married. Not now." She let the implication of a marriage and divorce stand. It was easier that way, with this person.

"He's wonderful," she added, surprised at herself. "The baby. He's the center of my life. He's what makes the most sense to me." Steve made a small vague noise of agreement.

Mrs. Berridge sat in her plastic recliner, her swollen ankles aimed at the blue light of the TV. She called them in, when they knocked, but didn't say anything after that. Mrs. Berridge had circulatory problems and never talked much at the end of the day.

Sam was asleep in a crib next to his stroller. Dorrie tucked him into the stroller, and she and Steve walked back into the night, the stroller squeaking faintly. Sam craned his head briefly, whimpered, then slept.

We look like a little family, Dorrie thought. Out for our midnight stroll. Dad works in a concrete room, sixty feet under the dirt, his fingers on buttons that could bring on the last big eclipse. Mom mostly wrecks things. And when she's not wrecking things, she works at a restaurant called the Bull's Eye, where she feeds huge steaks to people like Dad. Baby sleeps. When he isn't crying, Baby sleeps.

She laughed shortly and felt her eyes sting. She was so tired she could barely walk. She felt a little dizzy. Steve glanced at her but didn't break his pace. He started whistling through his teeth again.

At the door, she gave him directions back to the party. He looked at her solemnly, as if he planned to kiss her, then extended his hand. She shook it stiffly, her other hand on the stroller. And then he walked away, tall, broad-shouldered, clean-lined, definite. And she watched him. His heels made a clicking sound. He walked into the lavender darkness, looking like the only human on earth.

*　　*　　*

Upstairs, she undressed Sam, put a new diaper on him, and wrapped him in his gauzy summer blankets. The cool breeze crackled the metal blinds.

She pulled the blinds all the way up and sat at the window, holding Sam. A car screeched farther down Main, out of her line of sight. A car door slammed and some kids shouted. Then it was quiet again. A police car glided through the intersection.

The phone rang and she answered it. There was shallow breathing on the other end, but no voice. She said hello again, then realized, with a shock of adrenaline, that the caller wanted it this way: wanted the breathing silence and a scared woman's voice. She slammed the phone down.

Still holding Sam, she went into the tiny kitchen and ran herself a glass of water. She drew the empty pistol from the bottom of her purse. Sam stretched and shuddered in his sleep.

She turned off the kitchen light and the living room light and sat back down in her chair at the window, Sam on her lap, the gun in her hand, which hung loosely at her side. She swung it a little, testing its weight.

# Chapter 14

Steve McClintock left the launch control center, the big door thunking behind him, and took the silent elevator to the surface. He was off work for four days and not due at the base until the next day.

It was a dusky summer evening that smelled like wheat. Ace, his LCC partner, stood next to the jeep, changing rapidly into jeans and a madras shirt. The seven o'clock sun slanted across the prairie, and cloud shadows moved across the grass like ghostly rafts.

Steve stretched and arched until his back cracked audibly, then reached for his off-duty clothes behind the jeep seat. He changed, combed his hair in the rear-view mirror, and they were off to the Bull's Eye, a few miles down a road that began as gravel, turned into pavement for a mysterious mile or so, then became gravel again.

Coming out of the ground—going topside, as they put it—was like landing a plane. Up there above the clouds, all you saw were your instruments and the featureless atmosphere. Descending, you received the detailed world. The same thing happened, in reverse, coming out of the LCC. You left a cockpit room of instruments and a co-pilot and nothing much else to look at and emerged into shifting light and smells: wind, people, random sound.

But, more and more, topside, Steve felt the flimsiness of what was above. Sometimes he felt as if he had climbed to the top floor of a skyscraper where cleverly painted cardboard sets had been arranged to look like a country scene. You could move around freely—along wheat fields, down deserted country roads, even into Madrid or back to the base—but you knew the city, the engine, was beneath you: all the pods, beehives, circuitry.

They drove straight into the sinking sun. Ace had his mirror sunglasses on and his arm outside the window, his hand flattened like a wing, riding the air. He clenched a cigarette in his teeth. Ace was bright, but he was a slob. Too much hair oil, too-eager eyes, a slyness, a calculated circumspection around the brass: the look of a cop with a juvenile record.

And Ace was his, Steve's, superior. He would be the one who got the call, verified the code, decided this was it. He would insert his key into the firing mechanism and nod at Steve to do the same. He would request the second confirming order. *Tock, tock,* the hands of the clock, and then—yes. Now. They would look at each other, Ace would nod, and they would turn the keys to the right a quarter turn. And then the missiles, high as five-story buildings, would roar out of the farmland, level out gently, and race fifteen thousand miles an hour to Russia with their cargo of incinerating light.

Steve reached into the toolbox behind the seat, took out a bottle, and put it between them. This was a special occasion, Ace's twenty-seventh birthday. They sped along, windows down, taking pulls from it.

Gravel crackling, pinging against the floor of the jeep. The piercing gurgle of a meadowlark. That flowery, cereal smell of the wheat. They were both in good moods. Ace let out a long libidinous howl. Steve took his cue and speeded up.

The front door to the Bull's Eye was propped open to let in some air. The restaurant was supposed to have air-conditioning, but it hadn't been installed. Gloria had told Ace it wasn't coming at all, because it cost too much. This was supposed to be the summer business peak, but something was going wrong at the Bull's Eye, customer-wise. Nobody seemed to know exactly what the problem was. Irwin was gone a lot.

The place did look deserted. A typical Friday night like this should have had wall-to-wall cars in the lot by seven-thirty. There were four. "Terrific!" Ace protested, slamming the jeep door. They walked around the side and through the bar door.

Sully had a big fan going, the kind that moved back and forth. He sat at one end of the bar, reading a *Playboy*, the hair on his forehead lifting straight up each time the fan's path reached it. Dorrie and Gloria sat at the bar in their waitress uniforms, fanning themselves with menus.

The only customers, visible through the beaded divider curtain, were Holly Hopper, the librarian, and her boyfriend, Randy something, from the high school. They were hunched toward each other and seemed to be arguing. Every now and then, Holly turned sideways in her chair and stared at the ceiling, looking for help.

Ace and Gloria went into a big exaggerated clinch, and Gloria kissed Ace loudly on the neck. *Mmmm-wah!* she pronounced. Dorrie smiled and said hi to both of them in that quiet voice Steve liked. She had circles under her eyes, and her skin was very pale. He tried to imagine her biting Curt Wilcox and couldn't imagine the version he'd gotten from Ace. Wilcox could be a jerk, probably had been. Something had happened. But he couldn't see Dorrie drawing blood.

"Beers for the birthday boy," Steve announced. And Sully set them all up, even though Gloria and Dorrie weren't supposed to drink during their shift. It was hotter than hell. No one knew where Irwin was.

Holly and her boyfriend came into the bar to pay, and Holly made a point of saying hi to Steve. She always did, though he couldn't remember ever being introduced to her. Someone had mentioned her name, so he called her by it, though he didn't know anything about her except that she was the librarian. She would like to know him better, he could tell, boyfriend or not. But she wasn't his type. Too stocky and sisterly and blunt. Too something.

A group of six came in the dining room door, then an older couple right behind. Gloria and Dorrie moved through the beaded door out to the dining room, their nylons and uniforms making some kind of female swishing sound.

It was true, he thought, as he watched them. There were basically two kinds of women in the world, besides the Hollys. Gloria was one kind; Dorrie was the other. Gloria was cheerful and artificial, up front, sexy in a blatant, matter-of-fact kind of way. Steve had known lots of women like her. They were easy, in every sense of the word.

Dorrie was more reserved and mysterious, the kind of woman you could think about and want. That walk home from the Hawaiian party had been strange. He'd been a little drunk, but he knew something quiet and promising had taken place. She didn't talk much. Seemed kind of sad, which he usually found attractive, if the woman was also pretty. Which Dorrie was, in an irregular kind of way: slim and full at the same time; very pale; even features and wide-set eyes; glossy dark hair, hanging down her back in a thick braid that was severe and old-fashioned beside Gloria's gauzy, hair-sprayed helmet.

She had a quality of suffering about her, and some surprises too: the incident with Wilcox, whatever had actually happened; her baby, and the quiet way she lifted him into the stroller.

He didn't like talkative, flamboyant women like Gloria. He didn't mind having them around, but he didn't like to have much to do with them intimately. They were too *present*. He liked women like Dorrie, who encouraged protection and kept you reaching for something.

Gloria was very quick and efficient. She got her customers set up, took their orders, and scurried back to the bar, where she kept an eye on both customers and kitchen through the beaded door. One of them had to stay out in the dining room, just to make it look like someone cared, so Dorrie did that. She moved wearily, adjusting napkins and salt shakers and other things that didn't need to be adjusted. Steve watched her without seeming to.

"Let's go," Ace urged. "This place is a goddam tomb. Let's go into town. Maybe we'll come back later."

"What's in town?" Gloria asked, flirting.

"Humans," Ace said shortly. He was on his fourth beer and was adding shots. His knee jiggled, a nervous tic. Gloria grabbed the bar cloth and elaborately rubbed at a small spot on the front of her uniform.

She asked Steve for a cigarette. He gave her one and tried to light it, but the fan passed by just then and blew out the flame. She looked up and smiled her slyest smile. "Try again," she said, she cupping his hand with both of hers until the cigarette caught. Ace played imaginary bongo drums on the bar.

Steve always felt a faint blend of antagonism and nostalgia when he sat down at the Bull's Eye because Sully, the bartender, looked almost exactly like Thomas Kinlan, the rector who had thrown him out of St. Dennis Seminary. The same tufted, graying, eagle eyebrows. The same ruddy cast to his narrow face. The same pale, scoured eyes. And something beyond the physical, too. What was it? A lethal playfulness. Something whimsical and terrifyingly solitary.

Sully was apt to burst into a few bars of song while he dourly wiped the big gray cloth across the top of the bar. Kinlan had a similar somber flippancy, little bursts of mania that did very little to mitigate the steeliness and seemed like an insider's joke. Steve never understood it; he was a literal kind of person by choice. It seemed self-indulgent and a waste of time to function any other way.

Steve joined the seminary because he wanted to be a soldier. He had been prepared to deny himself, to try to create a just and clear-cut world, to suffer and hone himself. He had been prepared to give up women. Women were not on a level with soldiers. Soldiers, strong ones, didn't need them.

Freddy Murphy, also from Des Moines, a pudgy high school acquaintance, had entered the seminary at the same time Steve did. He brought a stupid, soft, scared look with him that just got worse as time went on. Steve hated it. After a while, he hated Freddy, though he tried not to. Freddy in his cassock, getting fatter every day. Freddy confiding his doubts, his fears—did he have a vocation? could he sustain this choice?—to Steve. He was soft, emotional. He had no place there. He was not a soldier for Christ. He was the weak link who brought everyone down. Steve was ashamed that they were from the same town. Freddy would never survive.

Steve sat by himself in the dining room one day, reading. Freddy plopped himself down next to him, his needy fat face eagerly searching Steve's. "I'm feeling all these doubts, Steve," Freddy said.

Steve felt his face harden. He looked up coldly and gave it to him straight, as a favor. "Then get out, Freddy. Go home. Do us all a favor."

Freddy's face flushed a shade deeper. He looked at Steve with his big deer eyes. And then, horrifyingly, he began to weep. "I'll never fit in there, either." He sobbed quietly. "You of all people should know that. We're alike in that way."

That's when Steve jumped up, ran around the table, grabbed Freddy by his cassock, and punched his face as hard as he could. He felt the cartilage bend and crack. Freddy fell to the ground, pulling Steve with him, and they rolled around on the wooden floor of the dining room in their long black skirts. Freddy kicked; he grabbed at Steve's eyes. Steve hit him again, this time in the ribs. "You stupid cripple," he murmured as he did it. And then arms were pulling him off, and that was pretty much it.

He could have stayed if he'd offered an explanation and apologized. But he wouldn't. That would have been moral capitulation.

Kinlan fixed those blasted eyes on him from across the big desk and stated the terms. Steve stared back and shook his head. And he felt himself move, at that moment, into a lonelier sphere but a truer one. He had done the right thing in the wrong company. It was time to leave.

After that, he had gotten on the bus and just traveled around the country, getting himself mentally prepared for whatever came next. He carried weights in his duffel bag, stayed in cheap motels, and worked out every morning. He was in training, he was hair-trigger ready. He just didn't know for what.

On that trip, at the Amarillo bus station, he saw the most beautiful woman he'd ever seen. She was just nineteen or twenty, with huge eyes and a soft full mouth and long auburn hair. She held the hand of a toddler and smiled sadly at Steve as she climbed the bus steps. Two days later, he joined the Air Force, and a year after that he got the highest score in his class on the test for potential missileers, the people manning the Minutemen.

Eight-thirty, almost nine, and the Bull's Eye dining room was empty again, except for the Hanricks, who lived on a big prosperous farm a few miles away. They had come for their usual Friday night dinner, the Skipper's Special, which Irwin now wanted everyone to call the Skipper's Choice, because Special sounded bargain basement. The Hanricks always dressed up, always looked ruddy and scrubbed. Their farm was impressive. A big windbreak all the way around. A half dozen grain silos inside the enclosure. The peak of an ample white and red house. And then the fields, geometric and strafed, stretching out from that lush, padded, orderly compound for miles. An English country garden on the moon.

One of the missile sites was about a mile from the Hanricks' house. At the Bull's Eye bar one night, Fred Hanrick was having a quick blast with the boys when he called down the bar to Steve.

"What are they doing to that thing out there?" Hanrick yelled cheerfully.

"What thing is that?"

"That thing they hauled out on that big truck. Looks like they're replacing whatever was in the ground. Big secret! You could see that outfit comin' from ten miles away—your truck, your little tank deals, your helicopter overhead."

"I really couldn't say anything about that."

Hanrick hooted and slapped his hand on the bar. He turned to the guy next to him. "Damnedest thing you ever saw. I'm lookin' out past my hay pasture. See this truck, this friggin' *convoy*. Look out a few minutes later, and they've got the damn missile tipped up on its end. Looked like the Washington Monument out there in my alfalfa!"

"I'm outa here," Ace announced. "I don't have to be twenty-seven years old, sittin' in some piss-ant little prefab out in the middle of fuckin' nowhere." He was so drunk his words slurred.

"Fine with me," Gloria said brightly. "We're going to close early. But it's still fine with me." Ace was pacing back and forth in front of the jukebox.

Dorrie had come back to the bar after the Hanricks left, and she sat down wordlessly next to Steve.

"I'm going to town. Hell, there's nothing there. Maybe I'll go all the way to Great Falls," Ace said to Steve. "I'll take the jeep. You can come along, partner, or one of these lovely ladies can give you a ride to the trailer. I'll go someplace and have a birthday party, and maybe I'll drop myself off at beautiful Miss Gloria's when I'm done." He snapped his fingers, head bent, hearing invisible dance music.

On nights they didn't have to be at the LCC or the base, Ace and Steve sometimes stayed at a trailer in a small court a mile from the Bull's Eye. They chipped in with another guy for the rent.

"I'm thinking really seriously about business school," Gloria said airily to Dorrie, as if she were continuing a conversation.

"Now?" Ace demanded. "You're going to business school this fuckin' minute?"

Steve wished he were at the trailer, alone, cleaning his rifles, watching TV, killing a six-pack.

That was the next project on his list of summer projects—clean and oil the rifles he kept at the trailer. He thought about the good feeling he'd have when that was checked off his list and his rifles were all gleaming and in good order. He had three of them, all bona fide antiques that he had got at various gun shows around the country. They were beautifully made. One of his other projects was to make a new case for them, the kind with a glass front.

He wished he were at the trailer, or even down in the LCC. He liked the clarity of that underground room. The absolute systemization. The sense of clear cause and effect. It was beige and hard and readable. And it was a room of hidden power.

The politicians ran around on the surface, making statements, holding their meetings, eyeing the red phone from time to time. Khrushchev, the fat fool, banged his shoe on his desk at the UN. We will bury you! Well, surprise, sucker. We're already buried. We are this country's ace in the hole. And we can come screaming up from the grave at any time. You make one real bad false step. You try another Cuba. And we rain your death down on you from above.

A tumbleweed trips one of the sensors, and a light goes on, and security's roaring down the road to check it out. That's how ready.

Below ground, the game was vigilance, survival, discipline, a crucial functioning of lethal systems. It was undeluded men willing to do the dirty work for everyone else. Topside, all the stakes were relatively trivial. Topside, it was mostly little games. With women, with guys like Ace, nights like tonight. The kind of aimless search for entertainment that was no small task in someplace like Madrid, Montana. None of it was to be taken seriously. You got laid. You drank some. And you could do all that, guilt-free, if you had a larger mission. That's what growing up seemed to be. Finding that larger mission.

Sully had put his *Playboy* away and was breaking rolls of change into the cash register. "Zing! went the strings of my heart," he sang softly, as he rapped the rolls on the edge of the drawer.

"Maybe we should just close the place up and have our own party on Ace's corpse!" Gloria suggested. Ace had passed out on the bar, his head deep in his folded arms, snoring like a child.

They heard the screech of tires. The door flew open and three teenagers burst in.

"Hey! Keep the noise down in here!" one of them said, looking around at the empty bar. He was small and looked like James Dean with acne. He swaggered up to the bar. "We need two six-packs of Bud," he said, slapping the money down, his eyes off behind the bar somewhere.

Sully gave him the look. "For your dad, out in the car?"

The kid blushed and rustled briskly in his pocket. He extracted a wallet and flipped it open to a driver's license that said his name was Eugene Cotten and he was born in 1940.

"Save it," Sully said, bored.

"He looks young because he's had an easy life!" a tall kid with a yellow baseball cap piped up. "He's a midget who's had a very very easy life."

"Fuck you, Wilson," the kid said, whirling around.

Ace raised his head very slowly from the bar, turned it carefully, and squinted at the newcomers.

He turned it very slowly back to Sully.

"I need two six-packs of Bud, Sully," he said.

"No, you don't."

"Yes I do. They're for me. I'm taking them to the trailer, this very minute, to have for breakfast. I mean it. It's my birthday and I want two sixers for my birthday hangover breakfast." He fumbled in his pocket and laid the money on the bar. The kids watched.

"Take him home," Dorrie murmured to Steve. Gloria sat on a barstool, filing her nails, humming loudly.

The kid with the baseball cap squinted at the license in Eugene's open wallet. He put a hand on Eugene's small shoulder. "It's his birthday today," he announced. "He's *not* twenty-two. He's twenty-*three!*"

# Chapter 15

Gabriel, the handyman, got out of bed at five o'clock, when the sun was just a rose-colored streak across the dark. He dressed in his everyday work clothes and sat on his sagging front steps to drink three cups of inky coffee, humming to himself between sips. He hummed a Spanish song about a woman who is like a rose.

As he hummed and sipped, the sky flushed a deep pink, then became silvery gray with peach-colored streaks, and then the sun glided up onto the prairie like the eye of God. Nothing else moved except the throats of the sparrows, who called back and forth to each other from the tall branches of two cottonwoods down the street. Once, during a silence, Gabriel heard the more distant sound of a meadowlark—two piercing notes, followed by a gurgling figure-eight—and the sound was so extravagant and embroidered, so unlike the blunt American sparrows, that tears of homesickness glazed his eyes.

He finished his coffee, rinsed the cup, then slowly began to arrange his parade clothes. He spread his suit on the bed, the shabby suit he had worn when he left Puerto Rico in the rain in 1943. On it, he pinned looping garlands of vivid crepe paper, shoulder to ankle, the loops smaller as they descended. He took his old cowboy hat and his white buck shoes from the shelf. On them, he pinned bushy crepe-paper flowers, which he had learned to make from directions on the paper package.

When it was done, when the suit and hat and shoes and serape were brilliantly crusted with red, green, and orange paper, he arranged the rustling garments on himself and waited for parade time.

Gabriel, who was fifty-two years old, could count on his hands and feet the number of times he had been with a woman in the twenty years since he arrived in Madrid. He had kept to himself, trying to disappear into the blank American inland, trying to forget the trouble back home, then the betraying cousins in the heartbreakingly misnamed city of angels, the numb bus ride to this place with only its name and its remoteness to recommend it.

After he began to believe that no one was coming for him, he started his own circumscribed celebratory tradition. All year, he was a teetotaler. He was neat, orderly, simple. He kept to himself. But in August, at Trail's End Days, he dressed up in a costume he thought he remembered from a long-ago parade in a town that smelled of the ocean, cooking oil, and his mother. He dressed up with care, and he marched in the Trail's End parade. And then he got drunk on rum. For the past six years, he had topped off this solitary adventure with a visit to La Reina Perrilla.

La Reina Perrilla was his name for Opal Stenurud, who lived above Bledsoe's Drug with two Pekinese, which looked like women's wigs that had sprouted tiny feet and snouts. Opal had red hair, rhinestone eyeglasses, and vermilion lipstick that she applied in two high points over her upper lip. She was quite old; Gabriel didn't know how old, but he suspected she was old enough to be his mother. She had been the bartender at the Plains Lounge for a number of decades. Now she drank there on Friday nights, and for three days straight during Trail's End Days, and no one saw her anywhere else except at the grocery store or Bledsoe's, her dogs hoisted under her arms or racing ahead of her on rhinestone leashes, their tiny claws clicking furiously.

After their first Trail's End night, Gabriel and Opal didn't even try sex. But they had somehow managed to forge a gentle understanding which carried them back to Opal's apartment, one night during every Trail's End Days, to drink and carouse until morning. Opal liked to put on a voluminous lime-green peignoir and her matching mules, then dance around the room, her dogs in her arms, while Gabriel sang and clapped. Sometimes she hung a large rose-colored scarf over the lamp, for atmosphere, and sprinkled it with her Evening in Paris perfume. She drank Black Velvet and Coke.

Gabriel drank his rum slowly, straight from the bottle, and it worked on him like an infusion of the Holy Spirit, releasing his tongue in profuse and magical ways. He sang songs he didn't know he remembered: nonsense songs he knew when he was five and six years old, lewd teenage ditties, solemn hymns to the Virgin. He described every detail of rooms he hadn't seen since he was young, while tears trickled down his leathery cheeks and over his smiling mouth. He referred darkly, elliptically, to his banishment and the reasons for it, and he muttered, in Spanish, that fate was a cruel mistress and sorrow was a bottomless well. La Reina danced slowly, and drank her Black Velvet and Coke, or sat on the arm of Gabriel's chair and stroked his coarse gray hair while her dogs—Prince and Princess—daintily chewed the cuffs of his pants.

Toward dawn, they stretched out on the ruffled bedspread, Prince and Princess draped across their ankles, and Gabriel raised Opal's liver-spotted hand to his lips and gave the palm of it a fumy kiss. And then they slept open-mouthed for a few hours, he in his crepe-paper garlands, she in her frothy, lime-colored robe.

After he woke, near noon, Gabriel would delicately negotiate the stairs to the street, wincing with each step, and make his way home, where he had a few cups of coffee and went back to bed.

The next day he appeared in his khaki gardener's clothes, pressed, sober, and quiet. He wheeled his cart, filled with garden implements, down the streets to his yard jobs. When he passed anyone, he nodded deferentially. Now and again, he passed Opal Stenurud on Main Street, as she and her dogs made their brittle way. He nodded. She nodded. And that's how it was for another year.

# Chapter 16

Candy Shepherd Kampen opened the Paris Hair Salon six months after her husband Teebow fell into a mountain of winter wheat at the grain elevator and suffocated, leaving her with a life insurance policy of $30,000 and two kids. Everyone always said how spunky and tough Candy was. They said it even before Teebow suffocated.

Candy was only four feet, nine inches tall—the shortest of the Shepherd girls—but she was perfectly proportioned in a sturdy kind of way. She had a tough little freckled face with a lower jaw that stuck out just a shade too much for prettiness, and her eyes were small and smoky looking. She was very dense and compact, and she moved rapidly, snapping her head this way and that.

In high school, Candy was the head twirler in the band, and at half-times during Friday night football games she did a solo performance with a flaming baton. It was something to see. She wore a sleeveless silver-spangled outfit with a band of red trim around the tiny skirt. Her white boots were also plastered with silver spangles and had fluffy red tassels that leaped around like long tongues as she high-stepped onto the field, her bare arms goose-bumped from the cold, her short dark hair ruffled like a bird's.

"Look at that little gal," big men in thick jackets murmured to each other as she marched smartly onto the center of the turf, her twirling baton a circle of fire around her little hands, her muscled legs pumping forward. The band, sitting in the low wooden bleachers, played with shaky verve, but Candy didn't need them. She was the whole show.

When she reached the center of the field, she braced her legs and tossed that short piece of metal, both ends flaming, high, high into the black air. She watched it come down, end over end, toward her expectant face. One arm was cocked casually on her glittery hip, while the other reached out, at exactly the right moment, and scooped the blazing metal rod out of the air. And kept it twirling. End over end, it never stopped.

The crowd roared. "That little tiny gal," the men murmured. She did it again and again; then one last time, spinning herself around with a flourish before she made the catch and dashed off the field, a last flash of silver, into Teebow's waiting, warmed-up pickup.

Candy had peach-colored hair now, which she wore in a wide bouffant, flipped up at the bottom and anchored with a stretch headband. She worked in an aqua rayon smock and black slacks, standing on a metal box to reach the tops of her customers' heads. She had fine crow's-feet in the corners of her eyes, and her hands were dry and scoured looking, with large bleached patches from the hair chemicals.

On Saturdays, she did three of her regular customers in the morning, then closed around noon. Gloria was her eleven o'clock, the last one. Gloria lived in a small apartment behind the Paris and had known Candy for years, so they usually tried to wind up Candy's work week on a festive note. Sometimes Candy ran across the street to get them cinnamon rolls and Seven-Ups from the HiWay House. Sometimes they spiked the Seven-Up with the vodka hidden at the rear of the comb-and-scissor drawer.

Candy liked to try out new styles on Gloria. Sometimes they spent a half hour or forty-five minutes just leafing through the style magazines while they smoked and sipped. It was peaceful in the Paris when you were the last appointment on a Saturday morning. This was Trail's End weekend, so things were livelier than usual. But the parade was over, and there was the feel of a lull.

Gloria came to her appointment straight from bed. Just threw on some clothes and rushed down the little hall carrying a piece of toast, all her makeup in a big purse. She felt jangly, cranky, and mildly hung over. But the smell of bleach and neutralizer and stripper and hair spray, mingled with the smoke from Candy's cigarette and the faint sugary smell of a cinnamon roll, made her feel better. She entered the shop with mild sleepy blinks and a gravelly greeting to Candy, who just nodded. Candy didn't talk much when she was working. That was part of the peace of it. She'd answer, sometimes ask a question, but she wasn't a person who had to chat.

Gloria flopped into the chair and told Candy she wanted her hair all up and she wanted it to last a week. They both knew she meant an elaborate French roll with layered flat curls at the crown and spit curls on the sides.

"It's so damn hot," Gloria said, waving her fingers like a fan. "I can't stand anything on my neck."

It was, in fact, a scorcher. So dry your teeth felt dusty. And hell on contact lenses. Little pieces of grit under the plastic all the time, like tiny, probing knives. Gloria was constantly popping a contact out, popping it into her mouth to wash it off, popping it back in. Her eyes were always pink-rimmed this time of year. She masked the pink with eyeliner, which made her eyes itch even more. But she refused to wear glasses. She prided herself on the fact that, as soon as she went nearsighted, she went straight to contacts.

Candy was smearing lotion onto her face and arms. The wind had picked up a little and was sending a dust devil across the two-car gravel parking space in front of the Paris. The screen door, with its loose catch, tapped nervously.

Candy peered into the mirror to examine a crack in her lip, and Gloria fanned herself with an old *Life* magazine. Then she slowly leafed through it as Candy began to remove the bobby pins from her tangle of blue-black hair. Gloria could feel her neck muscles relax.

Candy shook out Gloria's hair, gently poked through it with a wide-toothed comb, loosening the ratted layers. Then she brushed it slowly back with long pulling strokes so that Gloria's eyelids were drawn back and her head tingled. She closed her eyes and let herself be pulled. The brush felt like a mother cat's tongue must feel to the kitten. It was just on the edge of hurting.

She opened her eyes and studied a photo of Christine Keeler in *Life*. Christine Keeler, the young, dark-eyed fun-time girl. She sleeps with England's Ministry of War. She sleeps with a Russian spy. Twenty years old. A toppler of governments. Sitting in a white suit in an expensive-looking car, straight-backed and ladylike, except for the skirt hitched above her crossed legs, a cigarette poised between long slim fingers, her hair in a poufy long pageboy, her lips parted breathlessly.

"Maybe I should grow my hair out a few inches," Gloria said, studying the photo. She felt a swift pang of envy. She wanted to be Christine Keeler—savvy, powerful, provocative. A small jeweled knife at the throat of some of the most powerful men in the world. And Christine hadn't even had much of a start. She just knew how to parlay what she had. She had guts. She knew what she wanted. That's finally all it took.

Candy tipped Gloria's head back over the sink, hosed her hair with hot water, squirted on shampoo that smelled like lemon floor wax, and scrubbed expertly and thoroughly with her fingertips, making sure she squished soap through every strand to the end. Gloria closed her eyes. She felt Candy stop for a moment and knew she was bending over to examine Christine Keeler.

"You could never wear your hair like that," Candy said flatly, her fingertips in motion again. "It would be all wrong for you. Some people can get away with that length; some can't."

It was a professional opinion. It was final. Gloria knew any argument would go nowhere. Candy would shrug her shoulders. Think what you want to, the shrug would say.

"I think I could," Gloria insisted. "It's still in good enough shape. My hair." She buried her face in the big towel Candy threw over her head and rubbed her hair vigorously, not wanting to see Candy's contradictory eyes. "I don't think there would be a problem," she murmured from the depths of the towel.

"I know your hair," Candy said. "Believe me."

Back at the chair, Candy stepped up on her box. She combed Gloria's hair out gently and wrapped the strands around metal rollers colored an iridescent rose, like a child's bicycle. Then she tied a big net over the curlers and answered the phone while Gloria moved docilely, out of habit, to the big dryer. She adjusted the temperature herself, sat down, and carefully lowered the big hood over her head.

She could hear Candy's husky little voice through the roar of the hot air. "Terri Marie, you're making me tired," she said. "I know we're out of cereal. You don't have to call me up and *tell* me we're out of cereal. Make some toast! Make DeeCee some toast too! What's he crying about? You gave him a taste . . . of what?" She reached over to flick her cigarette in the shampoo sink.

"Tabasco sauce. That's nice. What do you *mean* you gave him a taste of Tabasco sauce? Terri Marie, put DeeCee on." She took a long sip of her Seven-Up. "Now!" she barked.

"Darrell Cody Kampen, what is going on?" she demanded. "What do you mean, she burned you. Are you kids lighting matches?" Her high-pitched voice was anxious now.

"With the Tabasco sauce. She put a blob of Tabasco in a spoon and told you it tasted good." Candy sounded elaborately bored now. Gloria smiled to herself. Candy's voice was faint, like the animated, distant voices you sometimes hear in the background of a long-distance phone call. The hot air blasted her rollers and made rivulets of sweat trickle down the side of her face. She felt relaxed and purged.

"DeeCee," came Candy's distant, sighing voice, "you've got about one *teaspoonful* of brains. I know your lip hurts. Go wash it off under the sink." She paused, listened. "I *know* there's no cereal. Eat toast!" She slammed the phone down briskly, grabbed a broom, and swept the shop floor vigorously, pushing dust and hair out the front door, where it blew away. Then she sat in the styling chair and leafed through a hairstyle magazine until Gloria pushed back the dryer hood and announced that she was done.

Candy stood on her box and expertly took the rollers out, fingers flying, the rollers dropping into a big plastic pocket on the side of the chair. More brushing. Then, section by section, Candy lifted the hair straight up. She inserted her comb halfway up each strand and pulled straight down to the scalp, her brow furrowed and intent. When she was done, Gloria's hair stood straight out from her head like a cartoon electrocution victim's.

She surveyed herself calmly in the mirror, hair straight out, face pale and unmade-up. Candy shook the huge hair-spray can.

"I'm thinking about moving to Great Falls. Maybe Billings," Gloria announced. Then she buried her face in her hands and Candy shot hair spray at her, standing back from the acrid cloud, slit-eyed.

"You are not. Why would you?"

"Business school." The minute she said it, the plan began to take shape. "I wouldn't mind being a legal secretary or something like that. And I wouldn't mind getting out of this town for a while. The Bull's Eye bores me stiff, and I think it's going down the tubes, if you want the truth." She leafed through *Life* to the Christine Keeler article again, then glanced at the mirror to catch Candy's reaction to Great Falls. Candy's face was carefully impassive.

"I thought you already went to business school somewhere a couple of years ago." Candy had a brush in her hand and was very lightly smoothing the outer reaches of the hair. This was the best part—Candy working out there on the edges of the snarls, delicately smoothing, shaping, spraying a spot here, a spot there, gently inserting the bobby pins, shaping each curl with the comb, lifting any flat spots with the rat tail.

"I did." Gloria felt slow, almost hypnotized. "For three months. In Portland. I couldn't stand it out there; it was like living inside a mossy old toilet tank, a dripping one." She smiled a little, pleased with the comparison. What she thought of, though, was not a contained, claustrophobic, quietly dripping place, though it had been like that sometimes, especially in the early mornings when she couldn't sleep. What she remembered most vividly was not the weather. It was her terrifying loneliness over there near the ocean in that city with the wet gray buildings. In three months, she had not once been called by her first name.

They were not good months to be there, the business school's winter term. If she'd waited, she might have discovered that the sun came out. She might have discovered how to meet people socially. But she couldn't bear to stay. The place was, in her memory, a dark apartment in a brick building on a busy street, where she sat on the iron bed and smoked and copied Gregg shorthand symbols and listened to the steady hiss of water from tires flying past. It was standing with a pack of uncurious strangers at a bus stop in the late-afternoon darkness, feeling the dampness soak through the soles of her cheap shoes. It was, most of all, being in a place full of people who knew absolutely nothing about her private or shared past.

No one had any idea that she had gone out with the basketball star of her high school, that she had been a Swamp Kitten, that the Medvics had tried to buy her off—offered to pay her way to business school, right after high school, if she'd get out of Murray Medvic's life. That she'd torn up the money and mailed it back to them, and Murray had dumped her on his own. Even that would have been preferable—that someone knew her enough to judge her.

She was, in Portland, Miss Beauchamp, who sat with twenty or thirty other girls in damp classrooms in a turquoise-colored two-story building, classrooms with cold wooden floors. Learning to type, to take shorthand, to take dictation.

"I left the day I found a dead mouse inside a sack of sugar," Gloria told Candy. "It was a little sack, but the mouse had crawled right in there and then, I don't know, I guess gorged itself and died." She shuddered elaborately. Candy backed off from her hair, when she did that, then resumed her work.

"That was it," Gloria said. "I just packed my suitcase, left the rent I owed, and took a bus back to Montana. Where I have *never*, by the way, seen a mouse in the sugar. I don't know. I think it was the dampness. Maybe it was looking for anything sandy and dry." She thought of a cartoon she'd seen somewhere of a parched man crawling across the sand toward a bar that said Oasis. "Maybe he was looking for the opposite of an oasis."

"Now you've lost me," Candy said. "Here, let's have something to make us smart." She pulled the vodka from the back of its drawer and tipped it into Gloria's Seven-Up can, then her own.

Candy hummed a little tune. A couple of flies made passes back and forth across the styling chair. The screen door ticked. Somewhere in the distance, a car door slammed and a cracking teenage boy's voice called out faintly, "Up yours, asshole!"

"Nice," Candy said dryly. She stood back and released another cloud of spray. *Hisss . . . hisssss . . . shhhhhhh.* It sounded like power brakes on a bus or truck. It sounded like a deflating balloon. Gloria closed her eyes, fighting off a sudden, almost overwhelming, urge to sleep.

* * *

She had wanted someone, anyone, in Portland to call out her name, even look at her with that condescending boy-she's-gotten-tough look. She had wanted to recognize someone, anyone; to be someplace where she could talk to a stranger for five minutes and discover somebody they knew in common. Or who remembered the '58 basketball tournament. Or that horrible blizzard of '57. Someplace where she could get an old car and drive herself around, go visit her grandma, old Rosie, up in Browning, her only relative who cared about her. She had wanted to wake up to space and wind.

The bus ride home from Portland took twenty-six hours. They stopped in Missoula very early in the morning, in the pitch dark, and all the passengers trooped across the street to a motel coffee shop for breakfast. She changed buses there and dozed fitfully, opening her eyes to see dark pine trees, a curving road, the flash of a river. Then the bus climbed up Rogers Pass and descended carefully into a landscape that was suddenly vast and spare and spread out before her like a giant's tablecloth.

In Portland, there had always been buildings or trees or people in the way. Water in the air. She always wanted a very tall ladder to see over all the obstruction. To look around and see where she was. Back in Montana, on the east side of the Rockies, the sun rose up over the rim of the huge table ahead of them and streaked the sky lavender and peach. Then it was up farther, and it crystallized the atmosphere into sugary light. You could see the road five miles, eight, ten miles ahead. You could tell what was coming. Or look back and watch the trail you'd left. I can *see,* Gloria had thought. Christ, I can finally really see.

At Great Falls, the hard ache in her throat had

begun to dissolve. And when they were past the city limits, pointed toward Madrid, she had finally slept.

"I'll go to Great Falls," she told Candy briskly, realizing that she'd just made what felt like a definite decision. "I'll probably quit the Bull's Eye in a month." She liked the way it sounded. As if she made those kinds of snappy, cut-and-dried decisions often.

"But keep that under your hat, Candy, until I tell Dorrie it's firm. She's been a little weird lately, and I don't want to have someone else spring it on her that she might have to handle things alone at the Bull's Eye for a little while. I mean, business is slow. But she might take it wrong. I'll tell her, okay?"

"It's not like I see Dorrie Vane, to talk to," Candy said as she rewetted one of Gloria's spit curls and taped it to her cheek.

"I know. But still."

"In a month?" She sounded exasperated.

"Or two. Depending how things work out."

Candy gave Gloria a hand mirror so she could examine her hair from behind.

"Like weird how?"

The phone rang, and she stepped down from her box to answer it. Gloria took a tube of frosted lipstick from her purse and began to apply it slowly. She hummed to herself, thinking about people in Great Falls who might know people she knew.

"Paris," Candy singsonged. "No!" she snapped. "Leave her where she is. Just *leave* her there, Terri Marie! *You* don't know what to do! *Pussywillow* knows what to do!" She listened, then made her voice very weary and patient. "She's the mother, Terri Marie. She'll get along fine on her own." She hung up without saying goodbye.

"Christ." For a moment her face looked oddly

flushed, as though she might cry. Then she rolled her eyes and threw her little body into one of the customer waiting chairs, her legs splayed in dramatic exhaustion.

"The cat is having kittens," she said. "In her groady litter box. I tear up piles of rags to make a nice soft bed for her behind the hot water heater, someplace she'll feel comfortable. And she just ignores me, the dope."

She sighed, then walked over to Gloria and touched her helmet of hair meditatively.

"I'm gonna reroll the temples here," she said, pointing to the upswept spots she meant. "They'll go flat on you if I don't."

She wetted the hair again and wrapped it around four rollers, a size smaller than she had used the first time. These were metallic turquoise.

"Weird how? Dorrie Vane. Weird how?"

"Oh, I don't know," Gloria said. "She's kind of pale and shaky. Small things just seem to set her off. She seemed okay when she first came back and started at the restaurant. I mean, considering that she brought back a baby, and had to line up sitters, and deal with all that. Plus having Earl Vane for your father. There's a fun guy." They both rolled their eyes.

"Well, when you think about it, how could she be normal? I mean, you know what I mean," Candy said. "Her mother has just completely flipped out. I mean completely. Virginia Palmtree has a sister-in-law who works at Warm Springs, and Virginia says Rosemary Vane is the biggest entertainment there. She has run away something like three times, naked as a jaybird. And she always heads straight for the railroad tracks."

"To kill herself?"

"No!" Candy hooted. "She just waits until a train comes, and then she runs alongside it, laughing her head off, waving at the engineer. The engineer radios the cops, they call Warm Springs, and one of their little trucks zooms down and picks her up. She acts like she's having the time of her life. Can you believe that? Can you imagine your *mother* doing that?" She shook her head mournfully and took a greedy puff of her cigarette.

Gloria actually *could* imagine her own mother doing something like that, wherever her mother was. The last time Bernice was in town, she had taken off her shirt in a bar on Railroad Street, on a dare. That's what Gloria heard, anyway. She hadn't spoken to her for a few years.

She could imagine Bernice doing something like that, but she couldn't see Dorrie's mother doing it. Because she remembered Rosemary Vane, vaguely, as one of those pretty, polite, well-dressed women who were the wives of all the men in town who had any money. A dentist- or doctor-wife type. Clean, contained, modest. She didn't know what she based this on, exactly, because she couldn't really visualize her. She got her mixed up in her mind with Joy Weaver, whose husband owned the furniture store.

"How does she act?" Candy asked again.

"Most of the time, she's fine," Gloria said, trying to back-pedal. "I mean she's hardly the type to go run around on the prairie naked or anything. But she gets real withdrawn sometimes, or she snaps at you, and sometimes she talks to herself. I've heard her. Like in the bathroom at work. Sometimes she's just in there whispering to herself, fighting with someone in her mind. And one time she slammed the wall with the flat of her hand. So hard that a chunk of plaster dropped off. Things like that." She leaned forward to sip from her Seven-Up can. "And then she bit Curt Wilcox."

"*Bit* him? How bad? Where?"

"Bad enough to draw blood, but not bad enough

to straighten him out. He's a real snake when he's boozing." Gloria hooked two fingers like fangs and jabbed them in Candy's direction, making small snake hisses.

Candy went over to the sink to rinse her hands.

"Dorrie's going out with Steve McClintock," Gloria called over her shoulder. "I think *she* thinks I'm interested in him. Which happens to be very, very wrong." She began to put on the rest of her makeup.

"Listen," Candy said. "Just leave those side rollers in until they dry, and stop by the house, quick, before you go to out tonight, and I'll comb you."

Gloria nodded, blotted her lips, and tied an orange net scarf lightly over her towering hair.

"What am I going to do about my hair in Great Falls?" she said, paying Candy.

"I'll find out who you should go to," Candy said doubtfully, avoiding Gloria's eyes. "You just let me know when you're about to move, okay? I *hope* I can find someone for you."

"Okay." She'd have to have someone for her hair. She couldn't live there if she didn't. That sounded weird, even to herself, but there it was.

When Candy wasn't standing on her box, the top of her head just reached Gloria's chin. She squinted at Gloria's hair one last time, frowned, bent one curl a little tighter, then grabbed the spray and gave her a last once-over.

At the Inland Market, Gloria wheeled her cart up and down the aisles. She tried to picture herself rolling the cart up and down the aisles of some strange store in Great Falls, trying to find what she needed. She shopped languorously. Her hair felt good; the vodka felt good. Getting her hair done relaxed her more than anything else on earth. It always put her in a good mood.

"Earth to Mars, Earth to Mars!"

It was Ray Rondini, the butcher, grinning at her. He'd done it before when she came into the store with rollers in her hair.

"Earth to Mars!" he called, pretending his bloody cleaver was a microphone. Then he made a scratchy static sound and gazed off across the store, rapt. "Do you receive?"

"Go to hell, Ray," Gloria said, smiling.

He made the static sound again. "Does spacewoman wish a purchase?" he said in a robot voice. "Of beef?" giving the robot voice a lewd twist.

Gloria drew herself up dramatically, extended her arms, pointed her two index fingers at Ray, and made a wide-eyed zombie face.

"Spacewoman turns meatman to space dust," she said in her own robot voice. "Spacewoman leaving for new galaxy." Then she turned smartly on her heel and pushed down the aisle, swaying her hips a little, just for him.

# Chapter 17

Margaret was good at clues. She could begin to figure out whole scenarios on the basis of just a few scraps of evidence. Sometimes they were scenarios about the future, sometimes about the past. She thought of the dead young horse at the Rising Wolf rodeo, when the clues, separately, had been so frail and unreadable—a glance, a cloud, a low laugh, a rock—and the way they had suddenly fit together, like pieces of a big arrow. Sometimes it was like that. Other times, the clues were obvious, right from the beginning. But most people missed them.

When Margaret thought about Dorrie's previous life in Chicago, she imagined her as a Rima-like figure, moving gracefully through a jungle of steel and crystal. She imagined penthouses, many of them, with huge windows overlooking a field of twinkling lights: penthouses with grand pianos, and white rugs, and women in slinky dresses sitting on low couches, laughing throatily with men in tuxedos. Dorrie had moved freely, confidently among the buildings and penthouses. You could tell. (Clue: the way she stood at her apartment window in Madrid, arms spread on the ledge, her braid swept dramatically over one shoulder, a dreamy look on her face, as though she surveyed a metropolis of infinite glamour and possibility.)

She had made Chicago her turf, and she didn't care about falling in love. She was not looking. She had some other passion. It was something exotic and academic, like jungle plants or Chinese. (Clues: several of the books on Dorrie's shelf—*The Wild Palms, Murder on the Orient Express.*) But her true love was out there too. He followed her through the tangled jungle of skyscrapers; he glimpsed her through his penthouse window, saw her standing silhouetted at *her* penthouse window, and felt that he could see through to her heart, her waiting heart that didn't know it was waiting, until . . .

One day! As he stood at his penthouse window and she stood at hers, she turned, her sequined dress rippling like water, and there in the air, twenty stories above the tumultuous street below, their eyes locked! They both had x-ray eyes because of their great love. They could see across the canyon between the two buildings, straight into each other.

The man, Margaret thought, looked something like Bobby Kennedy. Actually, he looked more like Woody Blankenship—unruly hair, piercing eyes, Woody's silver pirate tooth. But tall, and with a deep, heartfelt voice, and wearing, most of the time, not scroungy jeans and T-shirts like Woody's, but either a tuxedo or one of those sweaters that makes you look like a poet.

Their eyes locked, and then they were deliriously

in love. They ran down spiral staircases to the sidewalk. Dorrie wore a long glamorous coat or cape over her flashing dress, and it flew out behind her like a wing. And then they embraced on the sidewalk, the man leaning Dorrie against the wall. They kissed and kissed and kissed, Dorrie's cape ruffling around them like petals. What joy! Their hearts clattered. They felt that now they were complete. Now the world was what it was supposed to be. They felt as if they had touched an electric fence that didn't shock them but perked them up instead, made them buzz. Those nagging feelings of unease and gappiness—how well Margaret knew them!—were gone. They had melted like snow in a chinook.

They ran down the street to a church, which happened to have rental bridal gowns in an incense-smelling back room, and one fit Dorrie perfectly, so they were married on the spot. And when they said "I do," Dorrie's Rima-wildness bloomed all over her face, then narrowed and became a light that emanated from her eyes and met that coming from the man's. Their x-ray vision pierced to the core of each other. The man's name was Fitzgerald.

But trouble lurked, like fog rising slowly from the low valleys to the sunlit castle. A damp, evil fog that would stop at nothing until it folded itself around their blazing happiness and snuffed it out. The fog was parents—Fitzgerald's parents.

Fitzgerald, as it turned out, had millionaire blood. And there was a rule in their family that any wives had to have millionaire blood, too. Dorrie was completely wrong for Fitzgerald. He pleaded with his family, but they threatened to cut him off without a dime. "I don't care!" he said, slamming the door of the mansion. "As long as I have Dorrie."

So he and Dorrie moved to a garret in a colorful part of town—Margaret thought for some reason of the hunchback of Notre Dame; that kind of neighborhood, near a huge cathedral—and they were poor but happy, and they had Sam.

When Fitzgerald's cruel parents found out about Sam, they went crazy and threatened to have a hit man kill the whole family. Their craziness had to do with the fact that Sam was their only grandchild and due to inherit some great-grandparents' money. It was in the will, and there was nothing the evil parents could do about it, even though they hated Dorrie and didn't want her to have any of it. Dorrie and Fitzgerald and Sam had to get out of Chicago! But by this time Fitzgerald had tuberculosis and had to go to a secret sanitarium in the country.

He put Dorrie on the train, coughing weakly, and they concocted a story about a divorce. Because if she told people back home she was married, they'd want to know about the father, and would ask questions about where he was, when he was coming, what was the matter. Being divorced was kind of a hands-off thing. A clever way to evade questions.

So Dorrie went home to Madrid, which no one in Chicago had even heard of, and waited for word of her beloved, and wrote him letters every day about her and Sam. As time went on, she also wrote about Margaret. "A wonderful girl is assisting me with our son," she told him in her formal and elegant way. "She has long beige hair, the longest I've seen in town. And she is quiet and very calm and levelheaded. I don't hesitate to entrust her with our son. You would like her, Fitzgerald. She has a sixth sense about our situation, I know that. I don't know what in the world I would do without her."

Those kinds of letters flew from Dorrie's pen. Fitzgerald wrote back. (Clue: a small packet of letters under a paperweight on Dorrie's desk.) But then he got too weak to write anymore (Clue: the little pile of letters never got bigger.) So Dorrie got nothing. But she never stopped doubting for a moment that he was out there, thinking of her. She decided an evil guard at the sanitarium was intercepting Fitzgerald's letters. She had faith in Fitzgerald. Why would she need evidence?

It was up to her to carry on, with Margaret's help, until Fitzgerald was able to send for her. Margaret had heard that phrase—send for her—somewhere and thought it sounded perfect. Meanwhile, Dorrie was prepared to defend herself and her baby from anyone who would try to do them wrong, kidnappers for instance. (The best clue: the small revolver Dorrie kept in a kitchen cupboard! She had seen it, one day, when Dorrie reached for their bouillon cups.)

And then Fitzgerald died. (The red eyes.) And Dorrie was left to carry on alone in the world, trapped in Madrid, trying to decide what to do.

The best thing about Dorrie was her bravery, Margaret decided. It was her most queenly quality. You sensed it in your bones, right away.

Sometimes, though, when people have a particular quality, like bravery, they have a hard time explaining how they got it. Dorrie had a hard time explaining bravery at the luau. But that was normal. Why should it make anybody angry? Good horseback riders. They just do it naturally. They don't sit around explaining to themselves or anyone else how they do it. Number one, they don't want to. And, number two, they aren't able to. Because if they explain it, they are putting it up in their heads where explanations come from, and then it doesn't even work.

Margaret had once tried to tell Rita Kay how she should ride a horse. She told her what Roy had said: Pretend that a stick is running from the crown of your head, through your hip, and out the heel of your boot. A stick that can't bend. And when the horse starts trotting, you tilt everything forward a little, keeping the stick straight, of course, and just start your own rhythm: begin-to-stand up, sit down, begin-to-stand up. Then you won't flop around like a sack of oats.

But it didn't work. Rita Kay had listened very carefully—this was when she and Margaret were still best friends—and then she had trotted off on Midge, Margaret's calm old mare, bouncing so hard that Margaret could see a big gap of air winking, winking, between Rita Kay's seat and the saddle. Rita Kay had tilted backward, too, and her toes, in Margaret's borrowed boots, had slid far forward in the stirrups until they pointed downward. It was all wrong, and when Midge shifted heavily to avoid a badger hole, Rita Kay fell like a stone from her broad red back and lay on the ground, squeaking, her breath knocked out. Margaret thought for a moment about Rita Kay lying on the ground, grabbing for air, and felt a wave of loss and pity.

But the thing is, Margaret knew Rita Kay had probably tried to do what she was told. While Rita Kay sat on the ground, red-faced, grabbing her breath back, Margaret climbed up on Midge and tried to follow her own directions. As soon as they reached her mind, though, everything went stiff and wrong. She began to feel like Rita Kay had looked. She lurched, she bounced.

To get back on track, she had to quit talking to herself and just pick one thing to pay attention to. That's what seemed to work. So she paid attention to the shifting horse weight beneath her, the powerful pumping muscles, and she hummed a little song that matched her own rhythm to the horse's. And then all instructions just slipped away and she was doing it right.

Bravery might be like that, she thought. You can't

explain it to someone else. You just get it by focusing on what you want to do, and when all the little voices pop up on the edges and whisper, "You can't, you can't, you'll wreck yourself!" you just stare down your beautiful nose at them. If you're Dorrie, that's what you do.

Margaret watched the Trail's End parade, ate lunch, and picked up Sam at 1 P.M. sharp. She moved him briskly from Dorrie's arms to the buggy, which Dorrie kept in a little alcove on the ground floor by the door to the street. She tucked him in, patted him on the cheek like Dorrie did. She straightened her posture and patted her hair, which she now wore like Dorrie's, in a single long braid.

She wheeled Sam across Main, under the strands of fluttering plastic flags, the kind you saw at used-car lots, crisscrossed over the street for Trail's End Days. At the intersection, a giant white banner with blue sparkly lettering said WHOOP 'ER UP! It was a hot day, and several shops had their front doors propped open because of the heat and the number of people wandering around town.

Margaret wheeled Sam down the sidewalk, talking to him in his own language, which was that of a tiny Mars man.

She also hummed to him softly, "Sugartime" or the theme from *The Apartment*. When she adjusted him or he cried a little or she had trouble negotiating a curb with the big buggy, she sometimes made her voice like José Jiménez's on that record where they shot him into space. "Don' let them *do* this to me!" she said in a little Mexican Mars voice, and Sam seemed to appreciate that.

She kept an eye out for kidnappers, spies for Fitzgerald's parents, and this made her look closely at everyone she passed. In fact, she paid close attention to everything in town—people, bushes, activities in backyards, car crackling down the streets, faint sounds of celebration—as she wheeled slowly along, the buggy clicking delicately.

Madrid looked busy, with the street decorations and all the people who had started to mill around. You could tell the ones who had come in from the farms and ranches. They all seemed to have damp hair and new jeans, except the Hutterites, who always looked the same.

She thought of the way Madrid had seemed from the air, that spring day more than a year ago: how brown and scrawny, what a cardboard look it had had, and how that had been such a blast of bleakness. But maybe it had been her, not the town. Maybe it had been because she was thinking of the real Madrid in Europe, "a glittering city of millions," according to Miss Schmidt, the teacher who had to go back to Massachusetts. Maybe the real Madrid had blotted out the one she was looking at.

And what was her vision of the real Madrid? Well, it was kind of like Chicago, the same jungle of glass and steel buildings. The same penthouses, too, but with different decorations, Spanish-type decorations, which she couldn't quite picture except to see a clay piñata and all the cocktail-party people hitting at it with sticks.

Everyone there looked more or less like Gabriel, the Puerto Rican gardener, but they had nicer clothes. Throngs of them crowded the sidewalks. The men wore clothes like Zorro's: flat black hats, white shirts, and sometimes capes. The women wore lots of red and black flounces and shoes with heels that clicked when they walked. And there were palm trees, too. Every place without a building or a person held a palm tree. The combination of the buildings and the trees made it impossible to see out the sides of the city, clear to the horizon, like you could where Margaret lived. That was the real Madrid.

And when you were in the real Madrid, how did

you feel? There was a pulse. There was mystery and shadow. There was a sense of many people breathing. But the best thing about it was something that was hard to describe and had to do with old buildings and old trees, shade and age. The real Madrid had a history. It was centuries and centuries old and used to lots of things. Nothing you did there could surprise or shock anyone. Not really.

Maybe she had been holding that image so tightly in her mind that she hadn't been able to see her own Madrid very well. And how could she see much of anything, anyway, from an airplane? Like the earth from a spaceship. It wouldn't look so interesting, just a blue and white thing floating out there. There would be no reason for a spaceperson, scanning that distant blue and white ball, to suspect the existence of something like the real Madrid. Or Margaret's Madrid, for that matter.

Or the men down in those missile silos, in Russia and right outside Madrid. What world did they see? It was probably just a buff-colored map with target marks on it. Or a board full of lights. Because when you were underground like that, you were a long way away, like she had been in the airplane, and it wasn't necessarily true that when you saw something from a distance, you saw it better. You couldn't see the people, for one thing.

It was best to look close. For instance, when you looked at Dorrie's apartment at first, it didn't seem like anything out of the ordinary. But when you looked more closely, there were all those clues. Those letters, that gun.

Two boys galloped their horses down the street past Margaret, clattering, kicking up small stones covered with the summer's latest layer of dust-settling tar. Some teenagers in a red convertible with the top down drove by, the radio blaring. The short one in the back seat was

Eugene. He turned his head briefly, as they zoomed past, but didn't acknowledge her.

She remembered all the odd things she had seen when she was selling the Mary rockets. She remembered the cry from the yellow house on Skyline Boulevard, the woman's cry: "Who *are* you? Who *are* you?" And her own thrill of shock when she and her father had dropped Dorrie and Sam off at that very same house, the day they came home on the train. Someday she would ask Dorrie. Who was that woman? she would say. And what in the world was she yelling at?

She took Sam back to the apartment after an hour, leaving him to Dorrie and her sad, brave smile, and her fierce protection. And then she went swimming because it was very hot.

She might see Rita Kay at the pool, she knew, but Rita Kay didn't matter so much to her anymore. Margaret had other friends. Tammy Olson and Theresa VandeCamp were always at the pool, and she liked to swim with them because they spent a lot of time playing mermaid, with their eyes wide open under the water, and not so much time on the boards.

They were at the pool, as Margaret had suspected. So were Rita Kay and her new friends, shivering, blue-lipped, in line for the medium board.

Margaret stuck her toe in the shower, padded out to the pool, and waved at Tammy and Theresa, bobbing around in one corner of the deep end. At least she thought that was them. She had taken her new glasses off.

Then she had a burst of bravery. She marched straight to the diving-board line. She made her face like she imagined Dorrie's face would be if kidnappers burst through the door and she waited for them with the gun.

But she was terrified, so she kept up a steady stream of chatter with some older girl she didn't even know, as the line moved swiftly forward.

Rita Kay was at the head of the line now. She climbed quickly up the ladder and stood for a moment, confidently pulling her suit over her little bottom. The suit had a tiny skirt on it, and she wore a yellow cap with rubber spikes that made it look like a wig. She was now several inches shorter than Margaret, and her body struck Margaret as much more manageable than her own.

Rita Kay didn't hesitate. She put on her flesh-colored nose plug, ran to the end, and flung herself into the air, arms spread in a perfect swan dive.

Margaret reached the wet metal ladder and climbed it, still talking, softly now. Her teeth chattered like a set of wind-up dentures, and she couldn't silence them. When she reached the turquoise, rough-surfaced board, she stopped. The far end of it quivered slightly. A boy in the line yelled at her to hurry up. She gazed at the far end of the pool, the shallow water, the wire fence, and the silvery parking lot beyond, grateful that her pink striped glasses were tucked away with her clothes and the world had gently blurred. The boy called out again.

She knew in her mind what to do. Run to the end, jump once on the springy board, let it boost her upward, then hurl into the air, fingertips touching, head between arms, and let her head tip the rest of her down into those shocking, watery depths. There was no hanging back. Hanging back spelled disaster, the cruel giant's slap of water.

The boy yelled again, joined by another. Sharp, yippy little yells. Her only choices, now, were to back down the ladder, pushing down the girl who had already started to climb it, or chicken out and jump feet-first, or dive.

What was bravery? It was letting the directions go, putting them over somewhere else, and just paying attention to what was going on. If it turned out bad, it would have anyway. If it turned out good, so much the better. Fear nipped at her all over. She tried to stare down her nose at it.

And then she ran. She felt her bare feet slap the rough wet surface of the board. She paid attention. Don't hesitate! The feet came to the end, skittering, little tiny braking steps, then they were side by side, and then she jumped high, throwing her arms skyward so her body would follow. Her feet hit the board again, *sproooooong,* and then she was high in the air again, a squeak jumping from her throat, a little squeaking moan. This was it.

She launched herself, paying desperate, fast-motion attention to the feel of the air and to her rocket arms, the upper parts plastered to her ears, the fingertips crossed, one hand over the other. Her eyes were clenched shut. She felt her body—it felt, top to toe, like a racing heart—felt it tip earthward. And then the sudden disappearance of the surface roar, and the soundless slow-motion descent, down, down, into the place of no breath.

Her fingertips quickly grazed the bottom of the pool; the flats of her hands skimmed along the bottom. She aimed them upward and realized with a sick shock that she had forgotten to take a big breath before she jumped. Her lungs were burning. Up and up, eyes open, through the endless foaming blue-green water. Her lungs were at their limit! She was going to die. After doing a perfect dive—she knew it was perfect—her lungs would be forced open by this terrific pressure, come unsealed. The sharp chlorine water would pour in, and she would sink like a stone to the bottom. Dead.

She took a tiny sipping breath—how could God do this to her!—and burst through the skin of water, thrashing, coughing. She saw instantly that she could very well die in front of a whole pool of people. An adult figure leaped lightly down from his high chair and picked up a long metal pole. Casually, so casually. Her hands dog-paddled frantically. She coughed—great, racking coughs—and he extended the big pole across the water, slowly, like a big blind handshake.

She grabbed it, and he towed her to the concrete shore. His strong, muscled lifeguard arm reached down and helped her out. "Breathe in a little of the wet stuff?" he asked. A very brown teenage girl in a yellow bikini leaned against his high chair, and they both grinned at Margaret.

She crawled up on the concrete, bent over, and coughed some more. Then, shocked to the core by the previous few seconds, she padded, arms wrapped around herself, toward the locker room.

She had to walk right past Rita Kay and her little clump of girlfriends, who were shivering on a bench, their small brown backs aimed to the sun.

Rita Kay's friends, Laurie and Roberta, giggled a little. But Rita Kay just looked at her curiously, her face like it used to be when they were best friends and had just discovered something interesting together, like the dead, bloated cat they once found in the street and poked at with sticks to hear it sigh.

"When did you learn how to dive?" she asked.

Margaret shrugged triumphantly and kept walking.

For the rest of the day, she repeated the dive in her mind, doing it over and over again, the air leap, the plunge into watery silence, that moment on the border of air and water when she knew in her bones she had been successful. She repeated it over and over, smiling to herself like a cat, until the rescue part—that long humiliating pole snaking over the surface of the water—faded out, and only the dive itself remained.

She went to the Trail's End street dance that night with Roy and MaryEllen. It looked like something she imagined from the real Madrid, a corner of it. Strings of warm orange lights were laced across the blocked-off street. At the Main Street end, a bandstand was draped in crepe paper and lit with more glowing lights. The effect was glamorous and pulsating, even before the band began to play. Adults and teenagers and small kids lined the street, the small warm lights flickering across their sunburned faces. They gripped plastic cups of foaming beer, or a hog dog, or popcorn. It was warm. The sky still held a violet and orange streak at its western edge, but it was after ten now, and the rest was dark, with a speckle of stars.

Margaret slowly munched a hot dog and watched her parents dance to some kind of polka tune. Her mother was flushed and pink, in a crisp white sleeveless dress with a big flaring skirt. Roy was looking like the perfect combination of doctor and cowboy. A white dress shirt, creased jeans, polished boots. The two were exactly the same height. Roy held his arm around MaryEllen's waist protectively, and they kind of hopped from one foot to the other to keep time to the music. It was like they were trying to do a fast waltz, and they weren't very good. Margaret felt mildly embarrassed for their clumsiness, especially in light of her recent, inspired dive. But then Roy turned them so that MaryEllen faced Margaret. She saw, to her surprise and puzzlement, that MaryEllen's eyes were closed blissfully. Her mother lurched gracefully among the milling dancers, transported.

Margaret wanted to dance. She scanned the crowd

for Woody Blankenship. She knew how to dive now. Maybe that meant she had also stepped into Woody Blankenship's personal interior spotlight. It could happen. Maybe he would just come sauntering out of that clot of people on the other side of the street and crook his finger at her, give her a big silver grin, and ask her to dance. When she thought about that, she got a peculiar fluttering feeling between her hipbones.

Now the band slowed down. And they played one of her favorite songs in the world, "Release Me." A sting of tears came of Margaret's eyes. She had to dance to this song. She signaled to her father to come and get her, to take her out on the street so she could dance. She *had* to. It was the cap to this odd, dramatic day. It was meant. If she didn't dance, the day wouldn't end right.

But he ignored her. He and MaryEllen. They were on the far side of the dancing crowd. She could barely see them now. Everybody in the world was dancing. Two little girls twirled past, dancing in a fast little stretched-arm circle.

So Margaret just plunged in. She let her arms hang loosely at her sides and began to twirl slowly. The street was so crowded that no one paid any attention to her. A small boy darted among all the legs, banged into her, veered off. She kept twirling. She remembered the time she had twirled around on the playground, eyes shut, and bumped right into Eddie Leary, whose cancerous eyes had been removed as a baby so that he had only slits. What a scare!

She stopped twirling for a moment and looked around to make sure nothing like that could happen again. Then she thought, Well, if it does, it does. And she began to spin again, with the music. She speeded up, and she closed her eyes so that she saw only the thinnest layer of moving shapes and light. She let her head fall back. Her arms floated at her sides.

She spun and spun. And then she stopped—just like that—and opened her eyes wide. And she looked hard at what she saw, an orbiting galaxy of lights and colors and people. They swirled around her still form, swiftly, as if they never wanted to stop.

# Chapter 18

The Missilaires' singer was frail-looking for an Air Force man. He had a prominent Adam's apple and smooth, womanly wrists that stretched too far out of his jacket sleeves. He darted his head around nervously, then came to a decision and planted his legs apart. The band began. He tipped his face into the mike and launched into "Release Me" in a voice so loud and deep that Dorrie jumped.

She and Steve moved into the street, among the others dancing under the orange zigzagged lights. The night was warm and still, perfect for a street dance, and it smelled like horses and popcorn and beer. The blocked-off street was full of moving people. They bobbed and swayed. Feet scraped the pavement lightly, rhythmically. Some of the older couples, the ones who had been married to each other forty and fifty years, moved stiff-backed, torsos untouching, hands grasped politely like strangers.

Dorrie and Steve tried to dance, but it wasn't working very well. Steve guided them steadily among the other couples, keeping competent, wooden time. She couldn't seem to follow. His steps were too long; that was part of it. Every now and then, she had to take an extra half step, a little jump, to match up again.

His hand was planted on her waist. His leading hand was rigid. She tried to relax, to make her own hand, the one he held, bouncy and flexible. That was the secret to successful following—to make that hand, that arm, entirely malleable, to offer it as an indication of what he could expect the rest of her to do. She closed her eyes to listen to the music, to catch the slow, dipping beat. She relaxed her hand some more, tried to bounce lightly on the balls of her feet. Under the right circumstances, she was a good dancer. She didn't even have to think about it; it was as easy as breathing. She and Rader had sometimes danced for a few minutes, perfectly, to nothing more than their own humming. But nothing seemed to work now. She had the sense that Steve had his eyes fixed on a ghostly demonstration couple somewhere across the crowd, and was trying to match his and Dorrie's movements to theirs. Something about his stiff, tipped-up chin made her feel skipped over.

Gloria waved from across the street. The Bull's Eye had closed for the weekend because of the Trail's End festivities. They were civilians for a few days. Gloria stood on the sidewalk leaning against Ace, back to his chest, his arms pulled around her like a cape. Her towering hair made them almost even in height. She smiled brightly at Dorrie. Ace's sly face peered over her shoulder, scanning the crowd. Dorrie waved back. Gloria waved again, unnecessarily. She had been like that lately—agitated, ingratiating. It wasn't like her. The masked, sardonic Gloria seemed to be developing spiderweb fissures, like an old painting. Something was moving beneath her familiar surface, and it made Dorrie uneasy.

At work, the past few weeks, they had been more careful, more hearty with each other. Dorrie tried to think of what it was, what feeling she had been getting from Gloria—and now she had it. Gloria was scared. Something had happened, or was happening, that made her afraid.

Knowing this, Dorrie didn't feel curious or even particularly concerned. She felt, more than anything else, deserted. She counted on Gloria to defuse trouble, to defang it with distance and humor. Pain and bad luck could be filtered through Gloria, and it came out, sometimes, tolerable. But Gloria had to stay impervious, removed, or it wouldn't work. She couldn't falter.

The skinny singer had reached the last chorus of his song. "Release me . . ."—he took the microphone off its stand and held it close to his mouth, bent his knees deeply, then slowly straightened them, twisting his scrawny body upward as he sang the final plaintive, stairstep phrase—"and . . . let . . . *me* . . . love . . . again," which brought him to an upright position, arms straight and military at his sides, head bowed, dramatically spent.

"Load it on, buddy," Steve murmured.

And then Dorrie heard her mother's voice, over her shoulder, through the crowd, the "episode" voice that was so full of life and excitement, so lilting at the edges. Dor-ee, it called. Closer now.

She whirled around to see a woman coming toward her. A very fat woman in floppy knee-length pants and a large yellow overblouse. The woman opened her mouth, and Rosemary's voice came out again. It was grotesque, like a "What's Wrong with This Picture?" puzzle. The wagon has dog's feet. The nurse has a beak.

But she wasn't saying Dor-ee. She was calling Cor-een, Cor-een, her hand cupping one side of her mouth. She stopped in the middle of the street, looked around, called again, her head tipped back. Cor-een. And a little girl in dirty clothes and a runny nose ran up to her from behind, and poked her lightly on the arm, jumping back as the woman turned in sloppy irritation and cuffed the child lightly on an ear. Dorrie flinched as if she were the one who was hit.

The little girl ran toward the bandstand and disappeared around the corner of it. The band members were taking a break. They sat in their powder-blue jackets on the edge of the makeshift bandstand, heads turning in unison as Corinne flew past. Then they turned back to watch another girl who twirled alone, arms outstretched, in the middle of the street. They watched her with mildly curious smiles, as if she were some kind of antic pet.

It was Margaret. Her head was tilted back, her arms flew out from her sides, her long, straggly braid flew out behind her. Her eyes were closed, and she smiled as if she had finally found the right—the perfect—station on the radio dial. Dorrie looked around for someone who might be dancing with Margaret at a distance, a girlfriend, perhaps, who was egging her on for a joke. Someone else involved in this silent twirling. There was no one. Margaret was all alone.

She twirled faster. Then she stopped cold, arms out like cracked branches, and opened her eyes. Dorrie watched her with embarrassment and envy. She wanted to protect her, to whisk her off the street, away from anyone who might laugh. She also wanted her to keep spinning. Don't stop, Margaret, she said to herself. You don't have to.

Margaret's face burst into a wide smile. Her gaze roamed lazily to the band members, to the empty street, to the people milling around on the sidewalks. It grazed

Dorrie but didn't seem to see her. She walked away, wobbling slightly.

"That's my babysitter," Dorrie said to Steve, pointing at Margaret's back. "She takes care of my son for an hour, every now and then. Wheels him around in the buggy for some fresh air."

"Looks like *she* could use some fresh air."

"She's fine. She's a good kid. Kind of a loner."

They watched her thin back disappear among the people lining the sidewalk.

"Out to lunch, more like." He was trying to make conversation, and his tone was jovial.

"She's fine." Dorrie heard the snapping, cold edge to her voice. "She just doesn't care what people think. She's gotten to a point where she just doesn't care. And—" She stopped abruptly.

"Okay, okay!" Steve made a mock defensive gesture, hands before his face. "She's the perfect babysitter." He shrugged. He looked simple and healthy and handsome.

Dorrie laughed uneasily. "I trust her," she said. Down the street, a small fight exploded between two T-shirted boys. They were teenagers, newly muscled. Their white T-shirts glowed in the dim light, and so did their white socks beneath their short, tight jeans. They fought silently, with drunken intensity, until their friends moved in to pull them apart.

Then the band was playing a fast one, which Dorrie and Steve watched from the sidelines, and then a slow one. Dorrie didn't know what it was. Some kind of old-fashioned–sounding waltz. They moved into the street, placed their hands on each other, and tried again. This time, she didn't worry about following or not following. Maybe it was because the rhythm, this time, was slower, statelier. Maybe it was because neither of them was expecting much, or that they had skirted an argument, and that flicker of antagonism—their first—had allied them in some strange way. Maybe it had something to do with the sight of Margaret, alone and unembarrassed. Whatever it was, their steps matched now. They were easy and light on their feet. And when the song ended, they surprised each other with a quick hug.

They threaded their way through the crowd to the booths beyond the bandstand at the far end of the block, passing the fat woman in the yellow blouse. She was dragging her disheveled child by a wrist. "That woman's voice is exactly like my mother's," Dorrie said. Steve made his face look interested. "Sometimes," Dorrie corrected herself. "Sometimes she sounds like that. My mother. At her best. Or worst. Who knows?" He nodded gravely.

Earl stood by the corn-dog booth, talking to his friend Skeet Englestad. Dorrie noticed that her father was hunched sideways, favoring his arthritic hip. He wore slacks and a white long-sleeved shirt, out of place among the cowboy clothes, the hot-weather sleeveless blouses, the T-shirts.

She introduced Steve to him. Told him Steve was from the base, worked on the missiles, and waited for the look of approval on her father's face. But he seemed distracted. The vertical line between his eyes cut deeper than usual. He shook Steve's hand politely and glanced around the crowd. He had propped himself so that very little weight fell on his right leg.

When his eyes returned, he seemed to wake up a little.

"Can I buy you kids a corn dog?" he said.

"None for me," Steve said.

"I'll have one," Dorrie said. She wasn't hungry at all, but was eager at this moment to make her father feel good, to establish a thread of a connection. She wished she could make his hip stop hurting so his face would relax. That would make things easier. Once—when was it?—he had said it felt like being gnawed on by a small animal, that scrape of bone on bone. He wanted to get a steel one someday.

Earl elbowed his way to the counter of the booth and ordered the corn dog. He handed it to Dorrie.

"Don't you want one?" she asked him.

"Nope. I'm not big on corn dogs."

"Here. Have a bite," she said, offering it to her father. It seemed important that he take it. A gesture. He took a bite, chewed politely.

Then several things happened at once.

Gloria walked up to them with Ace, and Dorrie turned to talk to her. When she glanced back at Earl, he was doubled over, trying to cough. But no air was moving through; that was horribly apparent. His face came up and he looked straight at her, stricken. She knew he was having a heart attack. He had been seized, his heart had. He was dying in front of her eyes.

It was a moment of extreme clarity. Death, the great jack-in-a-box, had pounced up, right in the middle of them. Her father's contorted face. His arms pulled to his chest like a new baby's. His eyes open wider than they had ever been opened. His grabbing breath. A horrible, involuntary stamp of his leg.

She grabbed his arm and whirled toward Steve, who was already yelling at someone to get a doctor, jabbing his finger high in the air. Gloria had her hands up to her face. Ace was striding off fast, yelling for help. Her father's heart was going. At this moment. Dorrie just stood there and gulped him in. His face was turning from red to purple. "I'm sorry," she said imploringly. "I'm so sorry."

At that moment, a short, square-faced young woman came striding through the little clot of people who were gathered in a semicircle around Earl. She looked disgusted. Like a kindergarten teacher in a bad mood, she very rapidly placed everyone back from Earl. Didn't push them; just grasped them firmly and set them back. Then she stood at a right angle to Earl, scrutinized him for one odd moment, swung back her clasped, fisted hands, and hit him very hard in the small of the back.

Dorrie moved forward to stop her, and, as she did, a small gagging sound, then a burst of free coughing, came from Earl. He bent over, hands on knees, eyes squinted shut, and coughed long hoarse coughs. And when he straightened up, he was back among them again. His face was flushing pink. His eyes were strained-looking and wet, but they weren't flared open in panic. He had escaped.

A couple of people murmured their relief and drifted away. Those who had moved toward the corn-dog booth, curious about the commotion, turned away. Someone laughed. A little kid began to cry. "Jeez," Gloria said loudly. She waved at Ace, gave him an all-clear sign.

The woman who had come striding like a small giantess through the paralyzed little crowd was gone. No one had even seen her go. She had left as fast as she'd come.

Earl always drove, even though the house was just seven blocks from Main. Dorrie and Steve walked him to his car. The band had begun again, and there was the feel of a party moving into higher gear. The voices that carried to them from the street were higher-pitched. A bottle crashed somewhere.

Earl walked with a deeper limp than Dorrie had ever noticed before. He seemed beaten.

"Holly Hopper packs quite a punch," Steve said. "The librarian with the fist of steel."

"She's not the librarian anymore," Earl said dully.

"I thought she looked vaguely familiar," Dorrie said, linking her arm through Earl's. "Seems to know what she's doing."

It was the first time she had touched him in a long, long time. He seemed shuffling and brittle now. All his bluster, his furtive excitement, his skewed vehemence, had deserted him. Without it, he was old.

They were a block from the street dance now, in sudden quiet. It was as if they had passed out of a crowded room, and now they could hear their own feet on the sidewalk. The sky, the starry sky, came in closer. They saw Earl to his car, watched him drive off slowly.

*Your father is a hero,* Rosemary had said. She said it had happened in Madrid, before the war, when Earl was just ready to start college in Missoula. He walked with two canes when Rosemary met him at the university. When they were married, he walked with one. He didn't go to the war, needless to say.

The child he saved, Joey Witherspoon, a neighbor, got polio from the swimming pool a year after Earl saved his life. For a number of years, Rosemary said, Joey and Earl had a very similar limp. She seemed to attach importance to this. *They looked matched.* Joey died when he and six other drunk sixteen-year-olds in a '49 Ford flew off Dead Man's Curve after the Class B basketball tournament in 1954. Joey's leg brace caught on the door handle, trapping him inside.

Dorrie knew Earl wouldn't have seen any other choice, when that little boy ran into the street. There was no question. Life, when it really meant something, was not ambiguous. You were presented with clear-cut choices, and you didn't waffle. Earl wouldn't have stood there, helpless, if Dorrie had been choking. Earl would have done something.

They walked toward the Rotary Park instead of back to the dance. They held hands. The park bench was next to a large lilac bush, which still smelled, faintly, like its absent blossoms. A single light, halfway across the park, lit up the wading pool, made it an oval of silver in the dark. They heard the dance band, far away.

"I really thought he was dying," she said. She thought of him gone, of her and Rosemary alone in the house. Or maybe Rosemary wasn't coming back from Warm Springs. Twice, since Dorrie had come home, the hospital had been ready to release her. Twice, she had done something to sabotage herself, to keep herself there.

Maybe, if she did come home, she wouldn't be present, not in any real way. Dorrie's visions of her alternated. Sometimes Rosemary was running wild-faced, naked along the railroad tracks. Sometimes she was hunched deep inside her red coat, pale and quiet, with no eyebrows.

When she thought of her mother as two people, maybe more, she always thought of Rader too, though she tried to banish him. She thought of him handing her three hundred dollars and a phone number. How he had looked, then, like someone she had never met. Maybe she and Sam would end up with no one. No one at all. Ever.

Steve put his arm across the back of the bench. She leaned her head back. They both sighed deeply. "Nice night," he said. She turned her head and they kissed. They stopped and kissed again, shortly, tentatively. A long pause. And then again, for a long time, until they needed to stop and breathe.

* * *

They waited at the door. Finally, Mrs. Berridge opened it, her face groggy. The television glowed blue and gray in the room beyond her.

"What are you knocking for?" she said sharply, her voice rusty. "Just come in and get him like you usually do." She looked Steve up and down.

Dorrie took a deep breath and spoke. "I was wondering if you could keep Sam overnight," she said. There was nothing to explain. No one spoke.

"Did he have any trouble going to sleep?" Dorrie said, to fill the silence. Steve seemed to have moved away, out of the small circle of the porch light.

"Nope."

"Well," Dorrie said. "If you wouldn't mind."

Mrs. Berridge looked enormous in the doorway. She nodded stiffly and closed the door.

From Dorrie's apartment, they could hear doors slamming a block away, faint shouts, tires screeching down Main, the dismantling of the dance. Everything would soon be stone silent.

She found two beers at the back of the refrigerator, and they drank them in the dark, sitting in the two chairs by the window.

They tried to talk. He told her that he was going to an antique-gun show in Great Falls. He told her his job in the LCC was boring, but someone had to do it, and she knew, the way he said it, that he didn't think it was boring at all.

Down the hall, amazingly, she heard a frail old man's voice singing in Spanish. Then Opal Stenurud shouted something that sounded like, "Better and better." Someone clapped.

She told him she was only back in town until she could save some money and go back to school. She didn't plan to be a waitress all her life. No, she said, her ex-husband didn't send any help. Yes, she said, her father helped her financially. But she knew she was basically on her own. She wanted to be. That's what she wanted, really.

As she said it, she felt loneliness swell her throat until it closed, and she couldn't talk anymore. She stood up and took his hand and pulled him gently to his feet. He didn't seem to know quite what he wanted to do. She placed his arms around her neck, and her own around his waist, and rested her forehead on his chest.

He left at first light, his movements rapid and business-like. He refused coffee, combed his hair with short, irritated strokes, buckled his watch with one quick pull, kissed her quickly. His footsteps were light and fast on the stairs.

Dorrie put on her robe and made a cup of bouillon. She felt a little sick. There was Mrs. Berridge to face. There was her own growing guilt about leaving Sam all night. And there was the night itself. She had sealed herself off. He had slept for most of it, snoring softly. She had drifted, coming back to more Spanish, more singing, more muffled laughter. She had thought, Maybe this could get better. We could give it a chance.

# Chapter 19

Chocolate Metrecal was the best flavor because it tasted as if it had more calories than strawberry or vanilla, though the count was exactly the same. Holly Hopper alternated sips of it with her coffee. She always put the Metrecal in a glass to make it seem like real food.

Holly lived in the Thorpes' basement apartment, a dim, pleasant place with knotty pine walls and its own separate entrance. Sometimes she went for days with no evidence of the Thorpes except a thin creak of footsteps, the sound of water through pipes, or a brief murmur of conversation. The conversation sounds were rare. They were old people, in their eighties, and seemed to have run out of words.

Holly's eyes were swollen from crying. She stirred the Metrecal bleakly, the spoon clinking against the sides of the glass, and took another sip. Her left hand, the one with two taped fingers, throbbed with pain. What did it matter if she lost seven and a half more pounds? She was leaving town, fired from her first real job. Slinking back to Williston. Breaking up with Randy, her third boyfriend that counted.

Her roommate, a kindergarten teacher named Evelyn, was singing in the shower. She had just gotten engaged to Rugga Maynard, the wrestling coach. Holly listened to her for a moment, then jumped up from the little table, dumped the rest of her Metrecal down the sink, and made herself four slices of cinnamon toast, which she ate very rapidly. One hundred and seventy times four. Two hundred with the extra butter.

"I hope you're satisfied, Earl Vane, you son of a bitch," she murmured as she rinsed her toast plate off and scoured the sink furiously with Bon Ami. "You greasy two-faced thief. You get me fired. You ruin my life when it's barely started. You make me break my diet." She grabbed the steel wool pad, dumped more scouring powder on a persistent spot, and rubbed furiously with both hands, wishing it were Earl Vane's face.

The shower stopped. Now Evelyn was singing, loudly and off-key. "I'm a little teapot, short and stout. Here is my handle, here is my spout." Holly couldn't stand it. She stomped to her room and slammed the door. Then she flung herself on her bare mattress and stared at her pile of boxes.

Her brother Frankie, a rodeo clown, was in town today for the Trail's End rodeo. He was on his fourth year as a clown, the most unappreciated job in the rodeo. You risked your life constantly, while people laughed. That's what you did, day in, day out. The next stop on Frankie's circuit was near Williston, so he was taking Holly and her boxes back in his pickup. They would leave in the morning, early.

* * *

Earl Vane had stood right up at that meeting and lied. Before he lied, he folded his hands, leaned forward apologetically, and told the board he was concerned, as a citizen and library user, about Holly's performance. Concerned. That was the word he kept using.

Skeet Englestad, the head of the library board, said he had heard that some library users were concerned. And he was concerned about that concern. The librarian's position was a responsible community position involving work with children and so on, and influencing the public and so on, where you didn't want people to have concerns. At least, not concerns in the upsetting sense, as opposed to concerns in the caring-about-something sense.

Then Iver Englestad, Skeet's cousin, also a board member, said he would like someone to summarize the concerns. Were they personal, having to do with Holly in particular, or were they just general concerns about general things involving the library, and Holly happened to be part of all that?

"That's the problem," Earl said regretfully. "Those things are impossible to separate. One affects the other."

Everyone on the board nodded.

"Holly Hopper is the youngest librarian we've ever had," Earl went on. "In my twenty years' association with this fine library, we've never had a librarian so new to the field."

Everyone nodded again. Some of them read a memo that had circulated among them before the meeting. It said she was resigning for personal reasons. It didn't say the personal part was theirs, not hers.

There was a long silence.

Holly, who sat by herself in the front row of the board meeting room, felt oddly detached from the proceedings. This was all after-the-fact.

Gene Pepich, the elderly chemistry teacher at the

high school, stood up suddenly in the audience. He slapped his rolled-up memo nervously against his open palm.

"It seems to me," he began in his quavery voice, "that we have a legitimate difference of opinion here between our librarian—who, I might add, comes equipped with better credentials than any librarian we've ever had before—a simple difference of opinion between that librarian and one of our library users." Skeet rustled impatiently in his seat. Iver reached across the table and smacked a fly with his memo.

"May I respond to that?" Earl asked in his nice-guy Jimmy Stewart voice.

"Shoot," said Skeet.

"I wish it *was* just one user," Earl said. "Then I would say, What's the problem? I would be the first to ask that question. But, you see, it's not just one user. It is hundreds of people in this community who feel they are being denied the facts. They feel that important facts about the state of this country are being buried beneath a glut of silly nonsense"—he pulled a *Hot Rod* magazine from his briefcase and held it high—"and subversive propaganda." He held up a *Look* magazine with a title on the cover that said, "We are Winning the Cold War."

Pepich hadn't sat down. He gripped the back of the chair with his ropy, arthritic hands, and he looked very frail. He spoke up. "Who are these hundreds of people? Why aren't they here?" His voice was so high and unsteady it sounded as if he might cry.

Skeet Englestad swept his hand around the tiny meeting room, past the board members and the nine people in the audience.

"Well, Mr. Pepich, where would we put them?" He chuckled comfortingly. Iver and Vivian Crookshanks, the other board member, chuckled too.

"Let me assure you," Earl said, nodding emphatically. "They're out there." He pointed out the window. And he sat down stiffly, briefcase on his lap.

"May I say something?"

"Of course, Holly," Skeet said warmly.

"Earl Vane steals magazines." She scanned the room, trying to look at each person straight on. There was dead silence now. Her voice seemed to echo in the room. "Those magazines he has in his briefcase. I think if you'll check, you'll see that he took them from the library. They are not checked out to him. I did not loan them to him. He took them."

Silence again. Then a faint shuffling, as people moved in their seats, adjusted themselves. Everyone looked embarrassed for her. Earl's face was flushed and stalwart. He turned his head to her and shook it with elaborate sadness. The board members studied the table in front of them. They pretended to read their memos again.

"That's all I have to say," she said and walked out.

That was the long and short of it.

For a week or so, Holly waited to see whether anyone would protest. Write a letter to the paper. Anything.

Nothing happened. She got two weeks to tie up loose ends, and they replaced her with Marion Cowper, the wife of the Church of God minister, who had a degree in elementary education that she'd never had a chance to use.

So now it was Sunday of Trail's End Days, her last day in town after three years in this place. Randy was taking her out for a hamburger at the A&W tonight. What a farce. He hadn't even addressed the fact they were breaking up. He said he didn't know what he was going to do when she was gone, and he really hoped they wouldn't lose touch. Those were his exact words, and he didn't even look that sad when he said them. It was like hearing someone when you're in the future and they're in the past. Hearing from that perspective how fake they sound, and saying to yourself, "Can't you *hear* that? Can't you hear how he's faking it?" But you still pretend to believe him. She was already in the future. When he said those words, she almost got sick on the spot, she felt so burned. But she also knew that she was going to forget Randy Simpson. He was not the man of her dreams, put it that way. She knew that. Right now, though, it didn't help.

Of course, it had to be Earl Vane whose life she probably saved. Out of two-thousand-some people in town, it had to be Earl. And it had to be her. Right at the dance with all those people milling around and getting in the way. And of course, no one else seemed to know what to do. Stand there with your finger up your nose while a guy is choking on a corn dog. That was about their speed.

There he was, munching on it, standing by the corn-dog stand when the band was taking a break. Then he looked up and saw her, and he couldn't look away fast enough. Then—classic Earl—he pretends he didn't try to duck her, and gives her this big lying smile, and starts to say something. And suddenly he's doubled over coughing, and then his head comes up and he's got this stricken look on his face. Anybody would take one look at that face and know he had the corn dog stuck in his throat.

And anyone with half a brain would have done exactly what she did, which was run around behind him, clasp her hands together in a fist, stand sideways, and smack him on the back.

She hit so hard she heard her fingers crack. She heard Earl give a little whooshing sound, then there was an awful little pause, and then he was coughing like a normal person and the color was rushing into his face.

It was disgusting. Earl Vane. Her sworn enemy. First he basically kicks her out of town. Then he almost croaks on a corn dog and she, Holly, of all people, has to be the only one with any presence of mind. It was disgusting. The whole place was disgusting. That piece of corn dog flying out of his windpipe, that was extremely disgusting. One corn dog with ketchup: 850 calories. A whole day's allotment.

# Chapter 20

Lights on a surface. Runway lights of lights. Rosary strands of lights. Pockets of lights. Single lights. Lights prickling across the edgeless sky and scattered across the earth, the earth lights inverted stars, visible only to the avengers on each side, the men who sit at the big boards and watch.

The earth from the moon would be the ignorant earth. The blue and white one, the one without the hidden lights, so fresh and eager, the continents once locked together like spoons. From the moon, that earth—the great mother—would rise up over the horizon like something so immense and essential it could never end.

The wheat fields he drives through to get to the LCC, and how green and bright-wet they were in June, waving in the spring breeze like a painting, but better.

Everything beneath that quiet beauty is wires. Not

just his part of it, all of it. It is a bad dream. It reminds him of an old movie where a man, a man who looks to be flesh and blood, a *polite* man, collapses, is hit by a taxi, and the ambulance people rip open his shirt to reveal—wires. There were many people who had trusted that man, who thought he was sensitive, kind, even funny. They had trusted and liked something that could be turned on and off like a vacuum cleaner. After that, no one knew whether the man had *really* been sensitive, kind, funny, and so on, or whether they simply needed him to be those things, needed it so badly, for themselves, they had missed the fact of what he really was.

The underpinnings of the big blue earth smell smoky and acidic. The nostrils don't like this smell; it sears them. He is down there among the wires, trying not to breathe too deeply. And then he is in a wire-lined hall, which seems to lead from his LCC to another. He steps into the hall and sees a small dog, a collie just like the one he had as a kid. Skippy, for God's sake. The same half-cocked ears, flopped over at the tips, silky. The same black circle around one eye, a target. The same dog eagerness.

Skippy trots into a far doorway of the echoing, sulfur-smelling hall with its tapping metal pipes, its pings and taps, and the buzz of something through the wires. He stands in the light of the doorway with his head cocked sideways. He's curious.

This is the bad part. Steve calls Skippy in a high, boyish voice. "Here, Skippy. Here, boy." Skippy looks around, blissfully alert, waiting for one more cue.

Steve squats down behind a large diesel-smelling barrel so Skippy can't see him. Now he whispers, "Here, Skippy! Atta boy." Skippy cocks his ears once more, then gives a joyful bark and runs toward his hidden master, and as he runs, as he gets closer and closer, he crosses a thin beam of light razoring across the hall, a thin blue beam of light, and it throws him back, teeth bared, all the hair on his body sticking out, his eyes horrified. He glows for a second or two, and a terrible shriek comes from his mouth. He is shrieking Steve's name! *Steve,* he screams. And it's the sound of pure loathing and the knowledge of betrayal. Then he falls, fried, his mouth open, his teeth black.

That is the kind of dream to wake you shouting.

# Chapter 21

The calls usually came after 3 A.M., and they always came when Dorrie and Sam were alone. This time, she let it ring three times, four, lifting the receiver only when Sam began to whimper. Nothing again. Just his steady breathing. His. She knew it was a man. Every time there was a call, she saw Wilcox, small-eyed and drunk, staring at the scar of her teeth on his arm.

Wilcox still showed up at the Bull's Eye. But after that night he had never again acknowledged her presence on earth. Once, not long after it happened, he had sat in the dining room with two other officers, and she had asked for their orders. Wilcox pretended no one had spoken. Dorrie asked again, and the other two ordered, their embarrassed eyes fixed on the menus. Wilcox stayed deaf, smiling pleasantly at the two men, until Dorrie sent Gloria over.

Her hand on the phone was clammy. He was still there. She waited. Then she spoke into the receiver, her voice low and shaking with fury. "You stupid two-bit drunk. You little tinhorn general. If you ever call me again, I'm going to walk right up to you at the bar and blow your groggy brains all over the wall." She heard a click. "That's a promise," she whispered, hanging up, tears starting down her cheeks.

Sam began to cry. He pulled himself to a standing position in his crib and clung to the bars, sobbing. Dorrie picked him up and walked him around the room, bouncing, crooning to him, wiping her tears on his terry-cloth sleeper. He cried louder. For the past few days, he had been red-eyed and almost inconsolable. A door slammed down the hall, and she waited for the footsteps to her door, putting her hand lightly over Sam's mouth to cut the sound. The footsteps went the other direction, down the stairs to the street. Sam, who had been shocked into silence by her hand, cried again. He didn't just cry; he shrieked.

She wished, suddenly, for Helen—Helen as she was when Dorrie first met her, the Helen of those first dinners in the old apartment building near campus. Helen before she gave up. But the thought of Helen gave her the thought of Rader, and she flew from it, her stomach doing a sick flop.

Jiggling Sam on her hip, she put the teapot on for bouillon. She wished Margaret was at the door. Margaret would make Sam quiet. She would look solemn and avid. She would feel the fear that was in the room, right now, and she would give Dorrie an eager look that said, Yes, it's here, and now what shall we do?

"What are you thinking?" Dorrie crooned to Sam, whose crying had finally dropped to a whimper. "What is making you sad? Did you have a bad dream? Were you afraid someone would hurt you?"

She held him, sipped her bouillon, and watched the dawn sun light up the face of the Homestead Cafe across the street. Miraculously, he fell asleep. She took him to bed with her, and they both slept hard until the phone rang again, just after eight.

She snatched it up, listened for a moment, heard nothing.

"You jerk!" she shouted. "You coward! Hiding behind the phone, too scared to come out. You're scum. I spit on you."

"Dorrie?" It was Earl.

"What's wrong?" Her voice was a little scream.

"What's wrong with *you?* Who did you think I was?" His voice was slow and shocked.

"I've been getting some strange calls."

"Well," he said slowly, "I don't like that."

She closed her eyes. "Oh, I do. I love phone calls that scare the shit out of me."

"No need to be sarcastic, Dorrie. Or to use unbecoming language."

*Unbecoming.*

"I called"—he plunged in fresh—"because I have some information about your mother." He waited. She's dead, Dorrie thought for one wild moment.

"Your mother is coming home. The people at Warm Springs say they have come up with a combination of medications—two new ones, I believe—which seem to keep her focused on reality. They want to monitor her progress for two more weeks. Then we can go down and get her."

"Did you talk to her?"

"Yes," Earl said, and his voice grew warmer. "I

think she might be all right, this time. I think maybe they've got it licked. But I was wondering something."

*Got it licked.*

"I was thinking it would be good to have someone here in the house after she comes home. While I'm at work, and so on. You and the baby could move in for a while, is what I was thinking. Have your old room in the basement, and we'll rig up some space down there for a baby room."

Dorrie made her voice very deliberate and calm. "I come in pretty late at night." No response. "You'd have to get Sam to bed. You and Mom." The word sounded strange.

"Well, now, I think we could work these things out. We could talk about your waitress job. Maybe a better job could be keeping your mother company for a while. I think that would warrant some compensation. I'm not sure the Bull's Eye is the best thing. I'm not even sure the Bull's Eye is going to be able to stay open as much. Some changes are going to have to be made in the Bull's Eye operations, as I'm sure you're aware."

"I'll get back to you, Dad," Dorrie said. "Sam's making a ruckus." Sam stood quietly in his crib, watching her.

The car honked beneath her window around noon. Shave and a haircut, two bits. She peered out and waved at Gloria, who was leaning against the driver's door, smoking. The day was already hot enough to soften the tarred spots on Main. A redheaded boy at the intersection poked a small oval of tar with a stick, then lifted it so he could study the gooey strands.

"Ace couldn't come," Gloria announced as Dorrie struggled into the front seat with Sam in one arm and a large sack of sandwiches, chips, and beer in the other. Gloria wore cat-eye sunglasses and had on cinnamon-colored pantyhose beneath her Bermuda shorts, to make her legs look tan. A small run had started at her left ankle.

"He said he had to work on his pickup," she added skeptically. "Big emergency. It'll break down if he doesn't fix something this minute." She snapped her fingers, tossed her cigarette disgustedly into the street. "So the one day we all have off, probably forever, he's busy."

"I'm exhausted," Dorrie said, ready to tell Gloria about the phone calls.

"You do look like something the cat brought in," Gloria agreed. "Well, I say we dump the kid, pick up Steve, and go dip our toes in the reservoir." She rapidly adjusted the sun visor and lit another cigarette. "Get smashed. Watch the world go by." She jammed the old Rambler into first and took off. The cans and bottles in her big cooler made a clinking sound.

Mrs. Berridge had a television game show turned loud. The audience screamed and clapped ecstatically. Her little house was warm, with the smell of hot starch, and her big loose face was flushed.

She sat Sam on the couch between two piles of clothes and folded her arms.

"We need to have a little talk about this arrangement when you get back," she said. "I don't do overnights, you know. It's been three times. That isn't what I do."

"I'm not leaving him overnight. It's just for the afternoon."

"It's been three times, overnight," Mrs. Berridge repeated stolidly. "This isn't what I do." She had a trace of a Scandanavian accent, and it made her *s*'s sound like small hisses. "I think this arrangement, it is not working."

"I won't leave him overnight anymore," Dorrie said. A wave of panic and guilt made her keep talking. "I apologize. You won't have to keep him all night. That was a mistake. I had some things to work out; to discuss. Some problems. With my friend." She finished lamely. "My friend Steve."

Mrs. Berridge batted the air as if ridding herself of a pest. "We will talk," she said, with a shooing motion. "Go."

Sometimes a day begins so badly that all you can do is pick a point in it and pretend you're starting a new one. Dorrie rubbed a cold Budweiser bottle across her forehead, then popped it open to drink as they headed south of town. Gloria turned on the radio and squinted through her cigarette smoke at the dial, trying to find something that fit the mood they both wanted to have. Bobby Vinton was singing "Roses Are Red." Gloria sang along for a few bars, then found "Telstar" and left it there. They sped along the road, windows down to stir the heat, listening to the space tune—a tune for metal cylinders circling invisibly in the limpid summer sky, peeping.

Gloria stuck her hand out the window and aimed her third finger upward, jauntily. This struck them both as hilarious and they laughed, each burst feeding the other's, until they couldn't laugh anymore. It felt nostalgic. This was the old Gloria.

The day was beautiful when you looked around at it. Speeding up and down the low swells was like flying, swooping. The wheat fields were pale yellow and dense as fur, ready to be cut. The sun drenched everything with light. She saw a woman in a red-checked shirt riding a bicycle down a long rutted driveway to the mailbox at the road, and she looked like the essence of purpose and optimism.

They drove across a dry creek bottom, where a hawk dipped out of the sky and skimmed a stand of full-leaved willows. Four small antelope sprang into the air and bounced past the leaning shell of an old homestead into a coulee beyond. There was so much light that the Rockies, far off across the flat-looking plains, were washed of color and almost invisible.

Dorrie opened her eyes wide so the light would come flowing into them, too, and erase the dark, uneasy places filled with Mrs. Berridge's folded arms, Curt Wilcox's puffy eyes, Earl's ratcheted walk. Tick-tock rooms, the hiss of an iron, the tiny clatter of a beaded curtain, footsteps over your head.

Steve's trailer, the one he sometimes used, was one of eight in a treeless, U-shaped park a mile from the Bull's Eye and four miles from the launch control center. It was blue and white, perched on large wooden blocks. His Air Force pickup was parked outside. A small collie napped in its narrow shadow. Steve stood on the step in a white T-shirt and faded jeans, shielding his eyes.

"There's a couple of beauties," he drawled politely.

"Beauties with beer," Gloria said, pointing to the cooler on the seat.

Gloria swatted Steve on the seat of his jeans with the *Mademoiselle* magazine she'd brought along. Dorrie hugged him quickly, oddly shy in front of Gloria, and he pecked her on the forehead. They had slept together three times, but he remained a stranger to her. In bed, he was silent, strenuous, and quick. She had the sense that she disappeared for those minutes—that she could have been anyone or no one—and that she reappeared when it was over and he had opened his eyes. He ignored, without apology, her tentative attempts to postpone, to linger, to murmur the language of skin and hunger and capitulation. And, to her own surprise, she had quickly stopped trying and had let herself gutter out. Why? She wasn't sure, except that the decision, if it was that, carried with it an odd relief. This was not someone who could unravel her.

Out of bed, he was usually easy and friendly. He seemed smart and competent. He was good-looking, in a tall, clean-sweated, broad-shouldered, Eagle Scout way. This was not a person who would look like a criminal, a fugitive, in the daylight. He was a daylight person. He belonged there.

Four well-polished, old-fashioned rifles rested on a rack above the television set.

"Nice guns," Gloria said, handing him a beer. She took some pale lipstick out of her huge purse and slowly applied it, dreamily pursing her lips as if she were alone. She had changed when they got to Steve's. She had become careful and arch. This was another aspect of her recent twitchiness. She took steps, with men, to make sure they were aware of her. Dorrie had noticed it at the restaurant—Gloria's old automatic flirtations had become conscious ones.

Steve had a large fan propped on the lunch counter, but it didn't seem to be cooling anything off. The trailer was impeccably neat, but it had a close, bloated feel to it, apart from the heat. The orange flower print on the sofa cover was huge. One corner was filled with barbells and a jump rope. The ceiling was so low she could almost touch it. The shag carpet grabbed at her rubber thongs.

She stood by the screen door, sipping her beer, while Steve lifted down one of his rifles to show them, the one he'd discovered a few weeks before at a second-hand store in Great Falls. "Great Falls has tons of good stores," Gloria said eagerly. She seemed very interested in the rifle. She leaned close to him, asked questions.

The beer and lack of sleep were making Dorrie sleepy. She gazed through heavy eyelids at Steve, who was holding the rifle aloft to show Gloria its underside. He looked like the statue of the Revolutionary War soldier, the Minuteman, that she'd seen in a Chicago park the day after she met Rader. A day filled with beautiful lazy snow.

The water of Tiber Reservoir quavered in the heat. Half a dozen straggly trees on the bank, the only ones in sight, cast stringy shadows over an unruly gathering. Small children darted here and there like gophers. A very old lady wearing a straw cowboy hat napped in a lawn chair. A priest in a Roman collar rolled up his sleeves to slice a ham.

Dorrie, Gloria, and Steve decided to drive back to the Bull's Eye intersection and turn south toward some unposted rangeland that Steve knew about. It dipped down to a small creek and a stand of trees, he said. The heat had made them silent. Gloria hummed "Telstar" and clicked her long fingernails against the steering wheel. Steve sat next to her in the front seat because of the leg room. Dorrie sat in the back.

Gloria pulled over to the side of the road abruptly.

"No peeking," she sang softly as she stepped out of the car and pulled her shorts off. She tugged at the cinnamon-colored pantyhose, pulled them off, and tossed them dramatically in the ditch. She wore turquoise underpants.

Slowly, she pulled her shorts back on, easing long, slim, dead-white legs through the holes. She fastened the button and zipped them closed, gazing meditatively across a plowed field.

Dorrie watched her. Steve looked at her too, then turned away to fiddle with the radio. But Dorrie had seen his face. It was eager and a little flushed. It was a look she didn't think he had in him, especially not for Gloria. When he and Dorrie talked about Gloria alone, he referred to her as his pal. He made fun of her in small ways, of her nest of hair, her talonous fingernails, her bumpy relationship with Ace.

Gloria got back into the car. In the sunlight, she looked smaller, softer than she did in her black rayon at the Bull's Eye. You could see how fine-boned she was, how her makeup covered peach-fuzz skin. She looked, in profile, soft and pugnacious like her brother Buddy had. Buddy, who died. She reached over and took Steve's beer from his hand, took a long drink, and gave it back to him. "Ah," she announced. "That's better. Tan legs aren't worth roasting to death."

Steve smiled and shook his head as if he couldn't believe her. He fanned himself sturdily, absentmindedly with the *Mademoiselle*. He'd found a Canadian station, Calgary, coming in clear. Brubeck was playing "Take Five."

Dorrie took a sip of beer and had to gulp hard to make it go down. She felt as if she were watching Gloria and Steve from behind a glass window, as if she were riding in a taxicab, behind a wire-reinforced window, through a very dangerous part of a big city. I'm dead tired, she told herself. It makes me panicky. She saw that Gloria's bare arms were beautiful. She saw that Steve saw this. She tried to focus on their separate smells. Gloria was hair spray and hops and small powdery flowers. Steve was machinery and warm bread and cigarettes. She herself was tanning cream and sweetish underarm sweat.

Steve put an unlit cigarette between his teeth, slouched a little, and rested his head against the back of the seat. Dorrie leaned forward so that her nose lightly touched his head. He jumped, startled, and hit the glove compartment button with his knee. It fell open.

"What have we here?" He drew out a .22-caliber pistol.

"As if you wouldn't know, Mr. Gun Nut," Gloria said, smiling lazily. "That would be a weapon, honey."

"I meant, why is it here? You been fending off attackers?"

"I am a lone woman in a cruel world," she murmured sorrowfully.

He twirled the barrel. "It's loaded."

"Well, it wouldn't do much good if it wasn't. I'm not a very good bluffer."

"I bet you aren't." He put it back in the glove compartment.

"Does anybody want to do a little target shooting?" Dorrie called from the back seat. She wanted the car to stop. She wanted to be out of the back seat, out in the air, with them. She remembered what a good shot she was, those long years ago when she and Earl used to shoot at cans and bottles, somewhere out here in the country. She needed to show this skill to Steve and Gloria.

"Does anybody want to *eat*?" Steve called. "This place with the trees is probably three, four miles."

"Let's stop," Dorrie said. Gloria shrugged amiably. "I don't have any more bullets," she said.

"Six is enough," Dorrie said. "I need to stretch. C'mon. We each get two."

They passed the Bull's Eye and its empty parking lot. The building looked shabby in the sun. Gloria gave it a hard look. "That place is going down the tubes," she said. She sounded, for a moment, as tired as Dorrie felt. Three miles down the road, they turned off on a gravel road, heading east. The road passed a white farmhouse with a yard full of machinery, then went up a long rise and descended. The barbed-wire fence, along it, seemed to stretch forever. Sweat trickled down their foreheads, beaded lightly on their upper lips. Gloria's eye makeup had smudged softly around the rims of her eyes, making them softer, smokier.

There was not a house in sight now. Not a barn or car. Nothing but a line of fence, a line of telephone poles, and beige scrub grass bordering strips of pewter-colored dirt and buttery wheat. Any creek bottoms or trees were sunken, invisible, beneath the wide tan surface. The sun had begun to lean slightly, and the mountains, which had been washed out by the drenching midday light, were now visible. Gloria, Steve, and Dorrie stepped out of the car into the heat and a whirring undertone of grasshoppers.

A young, auburn-colored colt, with a thick coat and two long white socks on his forelegs, stood alone against the fence. He put his head over the wire, watching them.

"Okay, I have a confession." Gloria held the gun in both hands, laughing at it. "I have shot this thing exactly once. When I bought it from Sully, he took me out behind the restaurant and showed me what to do. But I'm not what you might want to call an expert." She giggled and looked to Steve for help.

A grouse flapped up just then behind her, from the barrow pit, and fluttered away, a foot or two off the ground. Gloria whirled around at the noise, tracking the gun past Dorrie and Steve.

"Jesus!" Steve shouted. Gloria whirled back, retracing the gun's path. "Gloria!" Steve and Dorrie shouted at once.

No one said anything for a few moments. A small gust of wind blew a stiff section of Gloria's hair away from the rest. She patted it back into place.

"Okay." Steve was using his quiet instructor's voice now. "That's lesson number one. You don't wave the goddam thing around like that."

"I wasn't expecting a major flapping behind me. Sorry."

He raised his eyebrows. "Lesson number two. Keep the weapon pointed at the ground until you're going to use it. Keep your fingers around the butt, away from the trigger." Gloria giggled. Dorrie saw that Gloria and Steve were both drunk, though she herself felt stone sober. They'd all been drinking beer since Steve's.

Gloria would get giggly, but nothing worse. She could hold it. Dorrie had seen her knock back four or five stiff ones after a busy shift and walk to her car without a misstep, back the old Rambler slowly, roar off to town fast. She'd never had a wreck.

Steve, though, could get angry when he drank—in an encompassing, abstract kind of way. It was surprising. Last week he had waited in the Bull's Eye to take her home after work, and he had drunk more than usual. On the drive to town, he had talked in a low, steady voice about people who "didn't make the grade." He appeared, at first, to be referring to Ace, his partner in the LCC, but others quickly came in: a swim coach in high school, his older sister who was divorcing her husband after fifteen years of marriage, a mechanic who had worked on a car five years earlier. The people piled up, gathered from every part of the country, every era of his life, until it was clear to Dorrie that the people weren't the problem. Not specific people. It was something else. Some tendency he saw in life to set him up, then disappoint him. She was one of the disappointments too. She was just beginning to realize that.

Steve climbed through the fence and put the sack of their empty beer cans near a post. The horse trotted off, then stopped to watch from a distance. Steve walked to his left about thirty yards to another barbed-wire fence that ran at right angles to the one along the road. He put a can on a fence post, then walked back to the car.

"This was your idea," he said to Dorrie. She climbed through the fence, and he handed her the pistol. He returned to the car to lean against the passenger door with Gloria. "Hold it with both hands, sight your target inside the notch, and squeeze the trigger," he called.

"I know what to do," Dorrie retorted. "I've done this hundreds of times before." He looked genuinely surprised. "I couldn't tell you how many times I've done this before."

He shrugged. "Two shots apiece," he said.

Gloria feigned terror, grasping Steve's arm with the tips of her lacquer-nailed fingers.

Dorrie held the pistol in two hands and sighted. She couldn't see the can very well. Sun was flashing off it, and her eyes were beginning to brim with tears. Sweat trickled down the back of her neck. A shiny cylinder in the notch of her gun. A shiny thing to blow away.

She looked up to clear her sight. A white jet stream, a chalk mark across the sky, lengthened silently.

She blinked hard, trying to remember the feel of shooting. Earl had stood behind her, his arms around hers, his hands on her hands. She had stretched out her arms, squinted along the barrel. The can was a glimmering jewel, worth her fiercest concentration. Her father was strong, respectful, interested in her competence and her happiness.

Over her left shoulder, she heard Gloria giggle. Heard Steve say something in a low voice, and Gloria giggle again. She shifted slightly to the left to see past the can's glare. Her teeth were clenched so tight her jaw ached.

"Fire!" Gloria shouted.

The sound cracked the air.

The can flew off the top of the post. Steve and Gloria clapped and whistled in the far distance.

I am alone, Dorrie thought. I am a long long way from them. Alone. She walked slowly to the sack of cans and retrieved another. Steve was lighting Gloria's cigarette. Dorrie ran to place the can on the fence post and returned to her shooting position. She was panting hard. Her throat ached. They would go home after target practice and Rosemary, in those days, would give them a smile and make them dinner. Sometimes someone would even tell a joke. Their home seemed quiet and ordinary. She didn't know then. She had no idea that Rosemary, two, three years later, would be standing outside her bedroom door, whispering, muttering, her eyes wide beneath her absent eyebrows. We must talk, we must talk—

Dorrie cut her off in mid-sentence. The bullet jumped out at it, and the can was gone.

She ran, gasping, to the sack of cans. Her face felt stiff, like a mask. Blood thudded in her ears. She reached for another one.

"You're done," Steve called sharply. He and Gloria still leaned against the car. She looked up from the cans and saw that they saw her tear-streaked face.

"Dorrie," Gloria said, her voice wary. "What's wrong? Are you okay?"

Dorrie raised the gun in both hands and stretched it toward them. They froze. She studied them with an odd sense of leisure. Snow statues. Steve was flushed.

He looked thin-lipped and bulky. Gloria was dead white. Her mouth was slightly open and her hand made an involuntary shooing motion.

"Put your arms around each other," Dorrie ordered. They looked at her, at each other, blank, confused.

"Do it!" she screamed.

They placed their arms around each other woodenly, ineptly, as if they were embracing posts.

"Stay like that," Dorrie said flatly. Gloria's eyes were squeezed closed.

Dorrie put the can on the fence post, walked back, checked Steve and Gloria. They were frozen. Gloria's eyes were still closed.

Buddy had walked up to the cardboard cutout of Jon Duke, the life-sized photo of Jon Duke in his basketball uniform, and stared at it. Buddy's stomach was pudgy, his shirttail hung out. He had a small, terrified smile on his face. He moved closer. He glanced quickly over his shoulder, his thick glasses catching a shard of light and bouncing it back. The smile went away. His face became white and solemn. And he gently put his arms around the midriff of Jon Duke, rested his cheek just above the large M of his basketball suit, and hugged him for a long time, eyes closed.

Dorrie glanced over her shoulder. The colt watched her, then loped in closer, and stopped. It had a sturdy, deep-chested build and moved with head-tossing grace. Dorrie jumped in the horse's direction. "Get!" she screamed. The horse ran for a few steps, then stopped, curious.

She turned and fired at the can. It sat on the post undisturbed.

"Sit there," she screamed at it. "Do what you want! You'll get hit! You think you won't, but you will. You're a fool, a fool. . . ." She ran out of words and her eyes fogged again. "A blind fool." She fired through the blur, and the can flew into the air.

She lowered the gun and turned around. She looked up at the hard sky, bluer now as the sun notched slowly toward the earth. The jet stream now reached into infinity. Steve and Gloria slowly dropped their arms from each other. The colt took a few steps forward.

Dorrie raised the gun. Steve and Gloria reversed their movements to put their arms around each other again, as if their arms were attached to Dorrie's. The horse stopped. The grasshoppers stopped. And the faint breeze, too. The white jet stream stopped. For a beat or two, Dorrie's heart stopped.

And when it started again, everything came roaring out of the underground part of her. She felt something red start at her feet and move up her legs, through her womb and her heart, through the saddest part of her throat to her forehead, where it glowed and screamed like a siren and sent part of itself back down her throat and through her shoulders, down her arms and to her fingers. Her iron mouth opened. There was no going back. All nerves were ready to fire. She cried so piercingly that the world turned to blood.

"I loved you!" she howled. "I loved you. And you *threw me away.*"

And she pivoted, aimed, and shot the colt through the head. It thudded to the ground and lay there, its side shuddering. She walked up to it, her ears ringing, and she fired her last bullet.

It was over. She dropped the gun. Gloria screamed faintly somewhere. Dorrie buried her face in the darkness of her hands. His running footsteps paused, the fence wire squeaked, the footsteps started again, muffled, crunching on the grass. She let herself go limp and he plowed into her, slamming her head and shoulder into the prickly, rock-hard earth.

She surfaced to the sound of her own moans. He lay across her knees, gasping. She tasted dirt, then blood. Then everything began to hurt.

# Chapter 22

Margaret would think later about driving up that long rise with her father, the gravel road lifting so gently you didn't sense it was tipped at all while you were driving along it. If you walked on it, you probably wouldn't even feel yourself going uphill. The only clue was the nearness of the horizon. If that road hadn't been slanted, you'd see for miles. You'd be able to see anything that was coming.

They drove along the road, the day before school started, to go feed the horses. As they drove, she thought of herself—how she had *been*—just a few weeks before, on Trail's End weekend. Diving so cleanly into the swimming pool, walking triumphantly past Rita Kay, dancing in the street. Climbing, finally, into her small bed under the eaves. Sinking into sleep, absolutely happy, with a peculiar added kind of happiness that she got, now and again these days, and which was related to her new knowledge that happiness was a live thing that moved around: moved away, came back, left again. She used to think happiness was like a doorstop she saw once when she was selling the Mary rockets, a doorstop of a little sheltie dog, made out of some kind of heavy plaster or maybe even iron. You just propped it where it belonged, and it stayed there. It was cute, but you couldn't really *like* anything like that, not as a pet. So why did they make it look like a pet, so eager and wide-eyed? Why did they even pretend it was? It was like a pet that would never go away. She used to think that happiness, the best kind, was something as immovable as that dog doorstop. Now she thought it was maybe more like a real dog.

She shook the pan of oats on her lap and sniffed them. She took a couple and picked at them with her teeth, trying to extract the part inside that they made flour from. She took a couple more and popped them unhusked into her mouth. Roy whistled through his teeth. Gravel hissed against the bottom of the car, occasionally topped by the hard ping of a larger rock. They climbed the long rise, and she shifted to the front of the seat, slowly chewing oats, ready to scan the countryside for the horses, once they'd topped the hill. Sometimes they were right by the road. Most of the time they weren't. You had to drive back to McCoy's, through their jumbled farmyard, and out onto the big pasture, looking.

"It's a scorcher," Roy said. "We probably should have waited until the day cooled off a little." He took off his hat, shook sweat off the band, and put it back on.

"Scorcher in the mornin', scorcher in the evenin', scorcher at supper time," Margaret sang loudly, shaking the pan of oats to keep time. "Uh-*be* my little scor-*cher* and love me all the time." She tossed her head around, shook the pan of oats, then caught an oat in her throat and coughed wildly and exaggeratedly to dislodge it. She pretended she was gagging. She wiggled around on the seat. She made cross-eyes at Roy, and he grinned at her, shaking his head. They topped the rise.

When Margaret saw the car at the edge of the road, a quarter mile ahead, she hoped there had been some kind of accident—just a little one with no one hurt—so she and Roy could come to the rescue. Then she saw the people walking around. Then she saw the horse lying on its side.

"What the hell?" Roy muttered, accelerating the pickup.

There were three people standing by the side of the road, and they seemed to be having an argument. One of them ran away from the other two, but the man caught her and pulled her back. The horse didn't move, didn't jump to its feet, didn't kick with his hind legs and run as fast as he could from those dangerous people and their car.

"Run," Margaret whispered fervently, trying to propel the thought to the unstirring horse. "Run!" She buried her face in her hands. "Please, please," she whispered, and looked up. Everything was the same, but closer.

"Stay here," her father said curtly, coming to a stop some distance from the other car. He slammed the door and loped toward the three people, who were huddled together now. A woman and a man held another woman between them. They were having a hard time doing it, and their faces were wild and strained. The horse didn't move. He lay on the other side of the fence, not far from it, his furry red coat glowing dully in the long sunlight.

Margaret got out of the pickup and ran over to the barbed wire. The horse had white socks on his front legs. "Señor Roja!" she screamed, leaning into the barbs. "Señor

Roja! Get up. Now!" Her voice became a shriek. "Move, Señor Roja!" He didn't. Blood had pooled on the ground beside his neck. She saw that now.

Roy yelled something, but Margaret ignored him. She crawled through the fence and ran toward the open-eyed horse, her own screams in her ears. She stood over him. He looked frozen but alert, like a toppled statue of a rearing animal. Upright, his white socks would have been pawing the air.

This had happened before. At the Rising Wolf rodeo, she had stood and screamed; she had seen a young horse shot, its eyes forever open from the blow. And she had known through much of that hot, dreamy day that it was going to happen. Not that a horse would get shot but that something bad would happen. And it did. And now it had happened again. Now it was her own horse. Her brash and glowing horse. Who was supposed to grow up.

She stood over him. For a moment, she had the odd sense that she had shot him herself, and she actually looked down to see if there was anything in her hand. Then she squatted down and touched Señor Roja's slim white foreleg, his trim young hoof and she left her hand there, her eyes closed against the glare.

A woman wailed. It was a long, diminishing cry—like someone dropping off a ledge. The people by the car had moved apart, and Margaret could see the third woman now. Dorrie. Dorrie Vane. Margaret's first, fleeting reaction was utter relief. Dorrie was here; she would know what was happening.

But this Dorrie was someone else. She leaned awkwardly against the side of the car and wept freely, great sobs, her face contorted and horrifying. The other woman and the man held her, one on each arm, as she cried out and struggled weakly. Roy sprinted back to the pickup.

He returned with his doctor bag, and he held a needle up and filled it from a little bottle and gave it to Dorrie in the arm while she just stood there and cried. She had a large scrape on her cheek. Some of her hair had come out of its long braid and hung in strands around her face.

Margaret walked very carefully back to the pickup and got in. She watched them place Dorrie in the car, everyone very businesslike and quick. The man huddled with Roy and talked quickly, then ran around to the driver's side of the car and jumped in, slamming the door. The car turned around and drove off, very fast, toward Madrid. When it passed the pickup, Margaret bent her head and stared at the floor.

She sat very still while her father got into the pickup, silent and grim-faced. She felt him looking long at her. She felt his hand on her head, just resting there. Then he started the pickup, turned it around, and drove slowly down the road. Margaret didn't move.

"I'm going to take you home, honey," he said. "Then I'll come back and get him away from the road." She nodded.

As they drove home, she thought of Roy coming back alone. He would loop his lariat around Señor Roja's back feet. Then he would tie the other end to the pickup and slowly drag the animal's weight over the bumpy scrub grass. They would inch over the earth. After a long time, they would reach a shallow coulee. The other horses, Midge and Pokey, would be there in the scant shade of a willow bush, swatting their tails. Their ears would go forward, absolutely alert. They wouldn't move. They would be too shocked to move.

Then Roy would untie the rope and drive away. And Señor Roja would stay behind, to be picked apart by the crows, dried away by the wind. Frozen and made into chalk bones.

They said Dorrie was crazy. That's what MaryEllen said to Roy, at night in the kitchen. Their voices floated upward through the grate in the bedroom floor, and she heard MaryEllen say it. She imagined Dorrie in a jail, shackled, and it made her glad and empty at the same time.

"What a crazy, what a *senseless* thing to do," came MaryEllen's bereaved voice. "Why would she do something like that? Just flip, like that? It sounds like her poor mother all over again, God help us. I hate to say that, but it does."

MaryEllen was using that expression more and more. She'd say, I hate to say this, and then she'd say it. Even Margaret knew it was a form of polite anger, worming its way out of her sweet-faced, sweet-souled mother. She tried not to think about it.

"I sedated her," Roy said. "They're keeping her a few days in the hospital. Maybe she just needs some rest."

The owl in the tree outside Margaret's window hooted once. Hooted again. Her parents voices fell silent.

"We'll see tomorrow," Roy said. "We'll see how she is, see what the story is here. From what that Steve guy told me, sounds like a possible assault charge. If he and the other gal want to pursue it. He says Dorrie was waving that gun around, pointing it at them, God knows what all."

"It's so *sad*. Was she drunk?"

"Don't think so. Didn't shoot like she was drunk. Hit 'ol Señor Roja right beneath the ear. Christ."

MaryEllen moaned a little. "Poor Margaret," she

said. "How on earth is she going to make a shred of sense out of this?"

Her bedroom was a cave. When she pulled the blind down in the morning, nothing came in except a watery bar of light at the bottom of the window. It moved forward and backward across the hooked rag rug when the breeze pressed against the shade. Margaret stared at it and tried to become hypnotized.

She heard the small, faraway shouts of kids starting back to school. MaryEllen peeked in the door, and she pretended to sleep. Her bedroom was a cave. It had a fern floor. Her bed was made of soft ferns, too, and some jungle animals lay curled at its foot. A small silver monkey. Two lion cubs. A calm, nonpoisonous snake.

She would sleep, and then she would nibble for a while on some jungle fruits. And then she might sleep again. She would stay for a while in her dappled cave, the jungle plants muffling any sounds from the outside, wrapping her in their soft perfume.

Any humans who tried to find her would be out of luck because the cave, from the outside, looked like nothing more than a small slope covered with a bunch of tangled weeds. You had to know exactly where it was. And even then the animals might not let you in.

She could lie on her bed and read magazines, or pull the covers over her head and pretend she was lying in a coffin. People filed past her—Rita Kay, Dorrie, Woody—bent with remorse at the way they'd wounded her.

A note from Dorrie came, and she put it in her Chinese puzzle box until she could figure out what to say back. She had a small, permanent-feeling ache in her sternum. She missed another day of school.

Her parents bought her a present to cheer her up. A jacket with short, blunt fringes—the wrong kind, the ugly kind.

On the third day, she woke to the sound of the phone. She heard MaryEllen's cheery voice talking to Julia, asking about the baby. Asking about some broken ribs that Red had. Outside, the garbage man slammed garbage lids. The wind blew the shade out. More light came in. The shade slapped. *Slap, slap.* The lids clanged. The man swore. MaryEllen hung up the phone and turned on the radio. A jolly voice announced the Swaperoo and Bulletin Board. A fighter jet broke the sound barrier with a sound like clipped thunder. Margaret left her room and went to breakfast.

She had a headache again, and it felt like something more serious than eyestrain or a cold. She emphasized that fact, without actually mentioning the word meningitis, but MaryEllen just told her she better hurry because she would be late for school.

"My arms feel kind of . . . heavy," Margaret said, stretching them out on the table so MaryEllen could see how lifeless they were. Her hand hit the Sugar Pops, then caught the box quickly before it spilled. She flopped her arms to her sides with a sigh to convey that the quick catch had been an extra effort and a fluke. "And my neck, too. Plus my headache."

"What do you mean, heavy? Don't slump, honey."

"Heavy like they're starting to freeze." She looked up at her mother carefully. "Or get paralyzed. It might not be serious, but if it *was* serious, I'd feel like this, before I knew I had it. Had something serious."

She stared glumly at her mother. MaryEllen stood with a cereal box resting in her arms like the roses of a beauty queen. Her unruly hair was tucked under a yellow scarf. She was neat and sweet and clear-eyed—MaryEllen as she should be, in crisp slacks and a checked shirt, slim-ankled, uncurious, serene. She ran her fingers through Margaret's snarled ponytail and told her to be ready for school in ten minutes.

The teacher was Miss Mamie Stenurud, the sister of the red-haired lady with the Pekinese dogs who lived down the hall from Dorrie above the drugstore. She was as gray and sensible-looking as her sister was outlandish. She wore glasses with a chain on them and had a sad, collapsed face, with no chin. She had put a color photo of President Kennedy on the wall, just behind the flag-pole. It was a bad photo, like one from a movie star fan club. His skin looked sick.

Rita Kay and two of her new friends were in the class. Rita Kay wore nylon stockings and had small new breasts. She also had a huge new purse. Margaret saw her take some white lipstick out of the purse and put it on while the other girls watched.

# Chapter 23

Three days after Dorrie shot the horse, Gloria visited her at Madrid Memorial Hospital. It was a streaky-skied evening, warm, still. After that endlessly long day of the solstice in June, the days seemed to shut down in leaps. Now it was early September, and the pale sky was striped with burnt orange by eight o'clock. Gloria drove more carefully than usual, because she was quite drunk. The Rambler had cratered—something with the fuel pump—and she had Candy's old sea-green Pontiac.

Sully had called her that morning to tell her the Bull's Eye was shutting down for a week or so. The owners, he said, wanted to discuss some changes in operations and also whether any changes of a renovation nature needed to be made in the interior space. She asked for a translation. It means they're going broke, he said, but you and I aren't supposed to know that.

She had told him Dorrie was sick with a bad flu, so he asked her to pass on the information. Would she relay it? She would.

There were some reasons Gloria was drunk. She was off work with nothing to do; her job was going down the tubes; Ace was down in the hole, and he didn't give a shit about her anyway. Not really. Also, she was nervous about what she'd find when she visited Dorrie. She was curious, but also angry and panicked in a detached kind of way, the way you feel when you remember a fearful dog that snapped at you. It's not that personal, really; the dog has been conditioned to snap at anyone. But it's still a shock. Whenever she thought about standing out there on the prairie, wrapped around Steve McClintock, expecting to get shot, she felt her bones turn to rubber. She had never, ever, felt more alone in her entire life.

But she didn't hold those moments of pure terror against Dorrie in any permanent kind of way. She had known something was coming, that Dorrie was under a lot of pressure of some kind and was walking some kind of edge. She knew it wasn't personal. And now, drunk, she was very curious. Had Dorrie flipped completely? Shouldn't she know about the Bull's Eye closing for a week, in other words probably forever? Wasn't she, Gloria, one of Dorrie's only friends, maybe her only friend, in town?

The hospital was very small and very quiet. She asked for the room number at the desk, then walked down the linoleum-floored hall to the left wing, passing a bird-faced nurse and no one else. A number of the rooms were empty. Somewhere, an old man argued in a high, panicked voice with someone who didn't respond. The place had the cramped, stale feel of a very clean salesmen's hotel.

Dorrie seemed to be sleeping. She lay stretched out on the thin white bed in the airless room, eyes closed, hands folded on her stomach. The other bed was empty. When Gloria stepped lightly through the door, Dorrie opened her eyes.

"Hi." Her voice was flat and matter-of-fact. It gave Gloria a weird feeling because it reminded her of the way people were with each other after they had sex. The way men usually were with her. All that tumult and abandon, switched off, turned flat, with daylight. Another person, a cold and bored one, stepping in to replace the sex person.

Dorrie sat up on the side of the bed and pushed her hair back impatiently. "They really make you feel wonderful in this place," she said dryly. "They wouldn't even give me a hairbrush. Maybe I'll poke my eyes out with the bristles." She shrugged, gazed for a few seconds at the floor, then looked up briskly.

"I'm sorry about the other day, Gloria," she said. "I didn't mean it personally." She smiled briefly at the sound of the words.

"I didn't take it personally," Gloria said. She was nervous so she got up and walked around the little room, peered down the hall, looked out the window. "Oh, God," she said, heaving a huge sigh. "You're not missing anything, believe me. It's completely dead out there." She flicked her fingers in the direction of the window. "And now Sully tells me the Bull's Eye is closing for the whole week, maybe longer."

Dorrie looked up in mild surprise.

"He told me it's for 'renovations,' " Gloria said, her voice heavy with sarcasm. "The place is going tits up." She paced slowly around the room again, pretending to be curious about the monastic furnishings. A bird cheeped outside the window. Someone started up a lawn mower, not too far away. She felt a great rush of panic come over her. What was she going to do, if the Bull's Eye really was a goner? She would have to make a decision about Great Falls before she felt ready. The panic grew.

"Is that the can?" she asked suddenly, pointing at a door. Dorrie nodded.

Inside, Gloria ran the water, opened her big purse, and took three large gulps of vodka. Then she flushed the toilet, rinsed her mouth, and went back into the room. The alcohol quickly began to blunt the edges of her panic, but it also made her feel stifled in the tight little room. She opened the window.

"What are you going to do, if they close?" she asked Dorrie.

Dorrie shrugged. "Maybe we could be A&W carhops," she said sleepily.

"Right."

Dorrie lay back down on the bed, hands behind her head. Gloria sat down in the plastic visitors' chair but couldn't stay there. She got up again.

"I'm definitely going to go to business school in Great Falls," she said. Dorrie didn't answer; her eyes blinked sleepily. "I've been thinking about this for quite a while, you know. It's time." She moved over to the window, heaved it open more, lit a cigarette, and dangled it outside. When she took a puff, she bent over and twisted her head out the window to reach her hand.

"They'll kick you out," Dorrie said mildly.

"Out of business school?"

"Out of *here.* A drunk and smoking person visiting a hospital patient who's crazy enough to do anything. Nice combination."

"I'm not drunk," Gloria said as crisply as she could manage. "I had a drink or two with my dinner. And who are you to be talking about any certain kind of behavior, anyway? You're the one who tried to shoot me. Threatened to kill me."

Dorrie's face turned pale and set. Gloria stubbed out her cigarette on the ledge of the window and threw it out on the hospital lawn. There was a very long silence.

"When are you going to business school?" Dorrie asked. "That's a good idea. It really is."

"I'm going when I'm ready to go," Gloria said tightly. "I'll keep you up to date on every detail." She snagged her purse from the chair, losing her balance a little as she reached for it. "I just wanted to tell you about work. We're history at the Bull's Eye."

"Fine," Dorrie said, closing her eyes exhaustedly as Gloria left the room.

Gloria drove slowly on the pavement toward the airport, sipping vodka from the coffee cup she kept under the seat. She speeded up and quietly mimicked Dorrie's voice. "Fine," she said. "Fine with *you*. Because your banker dad can just hand you a big banker wad of bills to tide you over. Why should *you* care, you spoiled little bitch?" The sun was almost down now, and she drove straight into it, squinting. She felt terrified. She thought of Portland, her apartment there, and how it might be like that in Great Falls. Alone in an apartment, strangers in the rest of the building. No one at the grocery store who knew her. No one to do her hair. She touched her fingers to her airy bouffant. Telephone poles flew past. She passed two kids loping bareback on their horses. The Melhoffs' place. The Dumontiers'. The Rideouts'. She knew them all. Who lived where. This was hers, this road, these little edge-of-town farms, this wheaty twilight. If she ran off the road here, someone would come running out of one of those houses, and when they found her they'd say, "My God! It's Gloria Beauchamp! Someone get some help quick!" Or, if she wasn't too hurt to move, they might carry her gently into their living room and put her on the couch. And when she came to, they'd call her by name and make her sip something to revive her. They'd cover her with a blanket and stroke her forehead. "Gloria," they'd say. "What in the world happened, honey? On second thought, don't try to talk. You just rest. Everything's going to be all right." That would never happen in Great Falls.

At the airport, she turned around and headed back to town. She drove through the main intersection and kept going, east on the highway, then over the railroad tracks, and south toward the Bull's Eye. The car drifted toward the barrow pit, and she corrected it too sharply, causing the big old thing to fishtail. When it lined out again, she speeded up.

She thought she'd go by Steve's trailer court and see if he was off. If he wasn't at the base or down in the LCC, he might be at the trailer. Maybe he'd have some ideas about what made Dorrie go berserk like that. Actually, that isn't what she thought. What she thought was hazy, but it had something to do with being fellow survivors. They could sit down on the couch, or maybe out on the step, and have a drink or two on this hot, empty, Indian-summer night and just kind of hash it over. Because they both could have gotten shot. They could both be dead right now. That made them have some kind of link.

The old Pontiac roared down the road. She passed an oncoming car, then nothing. The road, the whole countryside for that matter, was hers. She sipped her vodka. Her headlights arrowed into the darkness.

When she reached the trailer court, she dimmed her lights and drove slowly around its single horseshoe. No one was outside, but most had latched only their screen doors, and she could see small portions of the trailers' glowing interiors, the flash of blue television light off the walls. Steve's was dark, and she felt a sharp pang of disappointment. He was at work or on the base. Or maybe he had just gone to bed. It wasn't that late. Maybe he couldn't sleep—who could, after the other day?—and would welcome someone who could talk about the whole thing. In some corner of her mind, she knew the alcohol was thinking for her, but it wasn't so weird or outlandish, this idea of rousing him. She knocked. She called his name softly. Nothing. Just the motor of her running car, too loud. It sounded like a big motorcycle.

She hit the door flat-handed and called a little louder. Nothing. She moved along the side of the trailer to the window which she thought was probably the bedroom. She slapped the wall. "Steve!" she yelled cheerfully. "Goddammit!" Next door, a baby's climbing wail came from a window, and she heard stomping footsteps. The door flew open upon a very pale man in boxer shorts. He looked stunned and furious, like a child whose friends have tied him to a tree and gone off to play.

"What the fuck are you doing?" he cried in a strangled voice. The baby's wail climbed a few more notches. "You goddam stinking-drunk bitch. Get out of here before I call the cops."

"I'm looking for a friend," Gloria said with slow dignity. The man hissed through his teeth and slammed the door. She slowly got into her car and slowly drove back onto the country road. She speeded up then, and kept going south, toward the Bull's Eye. She came over the rise and saw it sitting there, the sign lit, the parking lot empty. When she saw the glimmer of a light cracking through the back door, she almost wept with relief. Sully or someone was there, maybe waiting for a ride.

She pulled into the gravel lot, brakes squeaking a little when she stopped. A big CLOSED sign was on the front door. She walked around back. A CLOSED sign hung there too, but she could hear a radio playing. Sully must be doing something. Checking off supplies, moving equipment out, who knew? Where was his car? That made no sense. Maybe he was drinking alone. That would be great. They could mourn their upcoming firings. She could report to him about Dorrie. She grinned in relief. Christ, she could hardly stand up.

Gloria pushed open the door. "Yoo-hooo," she called. "Got a drink for an old friend?" There was no answer. She went in, looked around. The light, she saw, came from the neon fixtures that were always on—the Olympia waterfall light over the bar and the big neon-tubed clock on the wall. The radio, a portable one near the cash register, was tuned to KISS, the Top-40 station. It sounded very small and tinny. She called. No answer.

Why was the door open? It was locked with a key from the outside and Sully always had that key and always used it. But now she saw the key ring, Sully's, placed on the cash register in plain view. Whoever had last been in here had left the keys, and that was why the door was open. Had left Sully's keys. She picked them up. There was a piece of paper wired to them. *Thanks for the memories* was written on it in ballpoint pen. Gloria rang open the cash register. The till, which always had twenty or so dollars in it, even on deposit nights, was bare.

She screeched out of the parking lot, heading back toward town with two bottles from the bar. After a few miles she stopped to pee. The night world looked empty of humans, except for a distant farm light. It grew and receded in a pulsing kind of rhythm. She blinked hard and looked at her feet. A cool little breeze had come up. She finished and lay down for a minute near the ditch. But she had the whirlies and had to get upright again or she'd lose it. She staggered back and forth across the road a few times and got back into the car. She wanted people, people she knew. She gunned it. She was crying, but she didn't know why. It felt like nostalgic crying, as if she was missing something. That's how she would feel all the time in Great Falls, if she went. She cried some more. The tears were flowing in sheets down her face.

A point of light became two points and then an oncoming pickup, which honked long and angrily at her when it flew by. In the distance, another set of oncoming lights, pinpricks now but coming her way. When they passed, they almost blinded her. She had to get out of the car. It was urgent. She had to get off this road for a minute, get out of the car, and pee or throw up or just breathe some air and rest for a minute. She couldn't tell which.

The far end of her lights caught a gravel turnoff to the left. She braked quickly, the Pontiac shimmying again, a small screech of the wheels, and made the turn. But she was going too fast, and she was sliding sideways on the gravel. She wrenched the wheel around and stepped on the gas to straighten the car out. And then, straight ahead, sealing off the road, was a big metal fence. She heard herself screaming. She felt her sandal catch under the gas pedal as she tried to pull it away, but it wouldn't pull, and the big mesh fence with its silver poles, all that dazzling metal, came rushing in on Gloria Beauchamp and snared her like a fish.

* * *

At 9:56, the buzzer went off at launch control center Q-0. Something had tripped the motion sensor devices at one of the silos. *Waaahnk. Waaahnk.* The big buzzer blared through the room. First Lieutenant Bill Baumgartner located the site of the infraction—silo Q-11, six miles away—and buzzed the security boys topside. Then, to be on the safe side, he buzzed base security to order an armed helicopter over the site.

Topside, lieutenants Skip Johnson and Murray Podhoritz didn't get too concerned about the order to check out Q-11. This had happened a few times before. Once it had been a gopher. It wasn't like the Reds were coming or anything. More like some kids with BB guns from Madrid.

They loaded themselves and several guns into the pickup. Two more guys would follow in the little camo tank because they needed the practice.

They got the call just before 10 P.M. Twenty minutes later, they were radioing for an ambulance. Then the heli showed up and landed with its windy roar. And everyone stood around, guns ready, looking at a very long, sea-green car tipped up on its front end like a crashed rocket.

Podhoritz reached through the shattered window to try for a pulse from the woman inside. He got nothing. She was finished. Her body was kind of tucked into a curl, hanging upside down on the steering wheel, and her hair had fanned out so it covered her face. No one moved it.

Podhoritz unlocked the gate and went inside the site. He picked up part of a taillight from the concrete slab that covered the missile. Everything else seemed in order inside the twenty-foot enclosure.

He locked the gate, struggling for a while with it,

because he was running on very little sleep and the entire scene and that woman shook him up. When he looked up, lights were coming down the gravel turnoff to Q-11. The first, red light whirling, was the ambulance from town. The second was the camouflaged mini-tank.

# Chapter 24

It was a hot day, but you could feel autumn coming, a cold, dry breath on the edges, a thinning out, a burnishing. The big, slow-moving flies of September drifted lazily among the little group of mourners at the grave.

They gathered in one corner of the small cemetery, just outside Heart Butte, on the reservation, up near the shadows of the big mountains. The casket was a charcoal color, covered by a church cloth of some sort, and on top of that some chamois skin that Gloria's grandmother, Rosie Two Guns, had beaded in the pattern of a large star.

The Heart Butte priest, Father Downey, stood at the head of the open grave in a black cassock that was too short for him. He was well over six feet tall and slope-shouldered, with a young, unlined face and white hair. His shoes were badly run over at the heels.

He held a missal in one hand and the silver holy-water shaker in the other, and as he recited the service he shook water crisply over the coffin at intervals, like punctuation.

"May the angels lead you into paradise; may the martyrs welcome you on your arrival and bring you into the holy city of Jerusalem. . . .

"Receive, O Lord, the body of our sister, Gloria, your loyal and faithful servant. We commit her body to the ground; earth to earth, ashes to ashes, dust to dust. . . ."

Sam stood quietly beside Dorrie, holding her hand, staring at the priest. He had taken his first steps at Mrs. Berridge's the day Dorrie shot the horse. Old Rosie stood nearest the grave, her mouth a tight line in her leathery old face. Her daughters Leona and Earlene, and her son Darrel, were there. And Steve McClintock. And Ace Booker. And another airman from Malmstrom who had been sent in some official capacity, because the accident had happened at a missile site. His Air Force uniform looked two sizes too big for him.

Two high school friends of Gloria's were there, Sherry Newell and Mary Patan.

And Candy Kampen was there, tiny little Candy, who stared at the casket and wept with quiet, shuddering sobs. Candy had fixed Gloria's hair at the funeral home. At the Rosary, when everyone filed past the open casket, she had reached in and adjusted a spit curl.

"Let us pray," Father Downey said, and the mourners bent their heads and urged whatever might remain of Gloria toward happiness. Sam began to wriggle, and Dorrie picked him up. She hugged him hard and kissed his downy little head, and he gave a loud happy chirp. Candy buried her face in her hands.

Father Downey used all the old church language, although he substituted English for Latin here and there. A teenage boy stood next to him with a guitar, which he now started to strum. His reedy voice floated over the group. "How many roads must a man walk down, before you call him a man?" he began. And when he got to the chorus, he sang it louder than the rest. "The answer, my friend, is blowin' in the wind; the answer is blowin' in the wind."

Most people kept their heads bent, but Rosie's popped up, and she stared at the guitar player with those icy wolf eyes as if he were out of his mind.

As he began the third verse, a pink car, rusty and low-slung, turned into the cemetery and bobbed slowly down the rutted little road toward the grave. All the heads went up. The car stopped about ten yards from everyone, and Bernice Beauchamp got out of the passenger side, heaving the balky old door open with an angry push.

She had always been a large, powerful-looking woman, and she was even larger now. Her hair had turned a wild steely gray and flared up from her head. Her large breasts strained against a white sleeveless blouse, which was tucked into a tight wool skirt. The skirt looked as if she had pulled it out of a box she had packed away years before. Her face was large and full-lipped and furious. A deep furrow ran vertically between her small, smudgy eyes.

The driver followed her. He was a fat man with oiled pewter-colored hair. He had on a big, flapping shirt and baggy slacks that were cinched down near the tops of his legs beneath his ponderous belly. He wore sunglasses.

The two of them walked over to the grave. Bernice stared at the casket. Everyone else stared at Bernice, except the man in the sunglasses, who stood behind her and looked around at the countryside.

The boy stopped playing his guitar, and everyone was absolutely silent, even Candy.

"Let us pray," Father Downey began again. All the heads went down, including Bernice's, though her eyes stayed open. And it seemed that everyone stayed that way for quite a while, even when the priest was finished talking.

As the mourners drifted away from the grave toward the cars at the edge of the cemetery, Steve came up to Dorrie and put his arm around her. She looked up at him, purely surprised. They hadn't spoken since the day she shot the horse. He wasn't quite looking at her—he seemed to be looking just past her face—but the muscle in his jaw twitched and he kept his arm around her shoulders for a few more seconds as they walked silently. She put her arm quickly around his waist, but couldn't look at him because she would cry. He left her at her car.

The pink car passed her. Three people now sat in the front seat: Bernice, and Bernice's big oily partner, and between them, very tiny and black, Bernice's mother who had given up on her. Old Rosie.

They would be going back to a house, Dorrie supposed, Rosie's house, where everyone could mill around and yell at kids and seek out all those small antidotes to the grave—black coffee and whiskey, hot dishes from the neighbors, comments on the hot dishes, the clink of knives and forks, cigarettes, solemn murmurs, the guilty relief of laughing for a moment or two.

And then, as the day wore on, people leaving, and the others bending their heads together over dirty dishes or cups of coffee, and somebody crying again, and maybe another drink.

But maybe not. Because there really weren't very many people at Gloria's funeral, after all. And as for Bernice and Rosie, what could they say to each other after all these years? Bernice had showed up to bury her second child. What on earth would there be to say?

Buddy was buried in that corner of the cemetery too. His burial was in November, and the wind blew so hard his classmates could scarcely stand. The priest murmured Latin only, and flung holy water that blew away from the casket into the children's faces. He turned the pages of his black book, and the men lowered Buddy into a cave in the hard ground.

And now Gloria was there. The baroque, masked, physical part of her was. Ticker. The Swamp Kitten.

She had bashed, drunk, into a fence around a rocket, setting off buzzers and lights, summoning war vehicles and men with machine guns.

They rushed toward her as her body went quiet forever. And she floated west, beyond the tabletop of the high prairie, away from the buried rockets, to the shouldering foothill country. Where her old grandmother put leather with brilliant beads over her corpse, and her wayward mother drove up in an old pink car to say goodbye, and the hills folded her in.

# Chapter 25

The weeping birch was thirteen years old now, and as tall as two men. Dorrie and Earl had planted it on the patch of grass between the sidewalk and the street, and somehow it had survived. It was the only tree of any size for a couple of blocks in either direction, because the houses on Skyline Boulevard got smacked so hard by the wind that the water in the toilets rocked mysteriously and most new trees just lay down and died.

Dorrie sat on the front step in her big winter coat, drinking coffee. She could see the pale prairie through the gaps in the houses across the street. It would be a brilliant, hard October day. The blue and golden time, though the gold was almost gone. Thick frost lay in all the shadows. The sky was a blank, new violet. She watched her breath, and the steam from the coffee, and the flickering leaves on the white-barked birch. And as she did that, she began to think about Gloria.

For almost a month, since it had happened, Gloria's death had felt, to Dorrie, like a wavering, emerging absence she couldn't look at. A growing hole at her feet, with terrible contents. You know it's there but can't look down, because whenever your eyes even begin to drift downward, they straighten, shocked. This morning, though, she stared through the steam of her coffee and her breath, and let her eyes fall, as slowly as night. And when the first jolt came—*you could have done something, could have been a friend, could have made her going from this earth less unhappy*—she closed her eyes and answered herself. *Yes.*

Regret could become a giant. She could let it pump up, expand before her eyes until she could never see around it to anything else. It was a grinning rubber clown, with her own face, its fat white finger pointing. She bowed her head and said it again, *Yes, I didn't,* and the clown collapsed with a slow sigh at her feet, and she let the warm tears flow out the corners of her eyes.

The sun raised itself a degree, and now the entire birch tree was trembling brass medallions. She thought of Gloria, what most people saw when they saw Gloria's brittle surface, and a small gust of wind stirred through the tree, stirred it like a gentle spoon, and hundreds of gold leaves swirled upward, then floated, rocking, to the ground.

She watched them all the way down. Another stronger blast of moving air, then, and the long tassels lifted and flicked their ends, the way Gloria had waved her favorite customers out the door. Then they dropped and swayed. And the tree stood almost bare, its white arms raised.

Rosemary drank her coffee at the table in the pink and green kitchen. Her upper face peered over the top of the china, the tufted eyebrows like new, unlicked fur or feathers—no longer the lovely wings of the first Rosemary or the amazed pencil lines of the second.

She had waited for them, in her red coat, in the reception room that smelled of Lysol. She had smiled calmly at them and let them hug her. Her body was heavy and spongy. She had touched Sam's chubby little arm and said hello in a voice that sounded soft and creaky.

Where was the person who had lit candles at dinner so that the light fluttered across her bare shoulders; who had run laughing along a pair of metal tracks, the pitch of her laugh rising as they caught her like an animal and wrapped her in a tobacco-colored blanket; who had twice made it to the dismissal office of that huge gray institution, then done something, anything, to force them to make her stay? Where was *she?*

What had gone on during this short year, this nine months, of her time and Dorrie's? What had made her know it was time to go home? A drug? A decision?

Where did she think she had been?

The first note said, *Dear Margaret, I am sorry. I didn't know he was your horse.* She scratched out *he* and substituted *it.*

The second note said, *Dear Margaret, Your father just told me the horse I shot was yours. I have had some troubles, and I am not well. . . .*

The one she gave to the nurse to mail said, *Dear Margaret, Please forgive me. Your friend, Dorrie.*

She heard nothing, for a week, two weeks. Then a rumpled-looking envelope arrived, addressed in penciled block letters. The letter said, *I have tried to forgive you, but I can't. I will keep trying. Sincerely, Margaret Greenfield.*

She took Sam to Roy Greenfield to have him

checked, and Greenfield discovered an ear infection. "Has he been crying a lot? Really crying?" Greenfield asked.

"Yes."

"How long has he been doing that?"

"Well, there was his digestion. When we started the new formula?"

"No, no," he said impatiently. "That was something else. An ear infection is really painful. You know something is wrong. Makes 'em crazy."

She thought of those few days before the shooting—the way Sam had cried as if he would never stop. He had been hurting, on and off, for a month now. It was too sad. She had to lie.

"This is recent."

"I see," he said gently. He had seemed to be examining her—her look, her eyes, her responses—since she came in the door. And he was so calm and courtly about it that she wanted to explain herself to him in detail, the way she had been that day. How depleted she had been. How everything had accumulated.

They had discussed it briefly, matter-of-factly, her second day in the hospital. She would reimburse the Greenfields in some way when she was able. He had understood she was under strain; a situation had gotten badly out of hand. There was no point in hashing it over all at once, he said. There was time. He had drawn some blood in the hospital and told her she was anemic. She was taking iron.

And he had kept quiet. Miraculously, word of the shooting did not get around town. Gloria had died before she said anything, if she was going to at all. Rosemary didn't know; they had kept it from her. That left Earl, Steve, probably Ace, Roy Greenfield, and Margaret. And Greenfield's wife, MaryEllen.

You knew when people were talking about you in

Madrid—they looked at you too attentively; they were a shade too nice. There may have been some vague talk, a hospital nurse's straying speculation. But if there had, it had evaporated. And no one else said anything. It was a shared secret.

She saw Margaret once at the drugstore, by herself, staring through the glass top of a display case full of wristwatches. She looked awful. Her knee socks had slipped down around her ankles. Her fringed jacket was buttoned wrong. She held her slipping glasses with a finger on the nose bridge while she bent her head over the glass. She was even thinner than usual, and too pale. She seemed mesmerized by the watches, oblivious to anyone around her. Dorrie moved away, behind a shelf of bath products, out of Margaret's sight.

Dorrie, Rosemary, and Sam walked out into the late afternoon, past the bare birch tree, past the Presbyterian church, where a very tall person with a young boy's face swept the steps. "There's Jay-Jay Tweet," Rosemary murmured.

The casual, proprietary comment startled Dorrie. She gave her mother a sharp glance. Rosemary returned a mild smile. "He grew too fast," she said.

At the Inland Market, though, Rosemary kept her head down. She looked remote and docile. She did not look Dorrie or anyone else in the eye. She kept a hand on the handle of Sam's stroller.

It was late afternoon, a Saturday, and the store was very quiet. Steve McClintock stood at the far end of one aisle, reading the labels on motor oil. He had on his Air Force uniform, including an overcoat, and looked formal and out of place. At that moment, Marie Cotten came around the corner of the long row of shelves, wheeling a loaded cart. Steve looked up. She smiled at him and touched his arm.

Rita Kay and two other girls trailed behind Marie. They all wore white lipstick and huddled together while Marie greeted Dorrie and Rosemary very elaborately and sweetly. She put a freckled, ringed hand on Rosemary's arm, as if she were a child, and told her how glad she was to see her again. She wore a puffy, pink little jacket over jeans, a teenager's jacket, and her eyeliner curved up at the corners.

Rosemary bent over Sam, pretending to adjust his little hat, and he sneezed loudly and wetly in her face. She jumped but stayed bent over him, and Rita Kay and her friends clamped their hands over their mouths and snorted at her. Marie gave them an indulgent, disapproving look and pushed off to the butcher counter, where Ray Rondini scowled and slapped hamburger angrily onto a large piece of white paper.

Steve's heels rapped loudly on the wooden floor. Rosemary looked up as he approached, her fingers brushing the stroller handle in a steady, delicate, whisking motion.

"My mother," Dorrie said, touching her shoulder. She felt, sometimes, this surge of protectiveness, the way she had felt toward the twirling Margaret at the Trail's End street dance.

Dorrie and Steve shook hands gravely.

"How are you?" he asked. He'd lost his summer tan and looked a little gray-faced. He had a new, very short haircut.

"Fine," she said. Sam reached out a chubby hand and touched Steve's pant leg, then looked up to Dorrie for some kind of confirmation. She smiled at him, and he touched the pant leg again.

"I just got some news today," Steve said. "I'm

being transferred in a couple of weeks. Grand Forks. I'll be doing the same thing. Launch control center. Just be sitting under North Dakota dirt instead of Montana dirt." He shrugged complacently.

Sam touched Steve's pant leg again and squealed happily.

"Well," Steve said.

"Well."

"Good luck," he said, extending his hand again.

"Maybe I should say that," she said.

"Well, say it, then."

"Good luck." And she knew as they shook hands like lodge brothers that she would forget the way Steve McClintock leaned against the bar at the Bull's Eye, and she would forget his stifling trailer parked out in the middle of nowhere, and she would even forget their three nights in the same bed. What she would remember would be his finger in a paper lei and the petals, pink and white petals, drifting to the sidewalk in the dark. And she would remember him stretched across the backs of her knees, gasping, while Gloria's small shrieks floated to them from far, far away. That's what she would remember.

Grease crackled in the kitchen. The television chattered from the next room. Earl stood in front of the stove, wielding a spatula, a dish towel tucked into his belt. He was whistling.

Earl should have been worried and tight-lipped. He had lost $10,000 in the Bull's Eye, maybe more. A week earlier, he and the other partners had watched a burly crew move the building to town. The crew had dismantled it and lifted the pieces straight up off their foundation onto three long-beds, which took them into Madrid to become the new Moose Hall.

They had left the sign, though, because there

wasn't much to do with it. You can see it to this day—a big arrow sunk in the middle of a black-and-white target—sitting on the ground next to a square of cement out on the empty prairie. The arrow, of course, doesn't light up anymore. The cement surface where the building once sat looks very much like a missile site without a fence around it. Same slab of concrete, ordinary as a service station floor.

Earl should have been strained and worried. The Bull's Eye had been a fiasco. His daughter and her fatherless baby had moved into his quiet house full of his magazines, his stacked papers and diagrams. His wife slumped quietly in a chair and watched him cook, her face a plump white oval, her fingertips moving slowly around the tabletop like a groggy old war veteran mapping dense, imaginary battles.

But Earl seemed invigorated by it all. He had real, tangible, noisy problems all around him, and he liked it. It was some sort of quietness that had been terrifying him, Dorrie thought. Now he was like a man who has removed his earplugs. And it seemed to affect, this new hearing, the way his eyes looked. He was awake. He was here.

Things were happening. She could imagine Skeet Englestad's booming voice as the Hi-Line Investors discussed the disposal of the Bull's Eye building. Then the Bull's Eye being wrenched from its foundation with a groan, and the sound of hammers cracking through the quiet prairie air.

Inside the house, horses clattered, guns went off, deep-voiced announcers urged everyone to think young. The hatless, grinning president toured the country and the crowds roared. The hash browns in the frying pan spitted and hissed. Sam cried. A TV camera zoomed in on the House of Parliament. A gavel came down, and rows of jowly, suited, steely men were toppled by a tiny prostitute.

Rosemary did the dishes for the first time since she got home. Earl and Dorrie gave each other hopeful looks. A plastic box on the windowsill above the sink had Rosemary's pills in it. She studied them a moment or two, as if trying to figure out the right combination for an evening, an imaginative combination, then took the two she was supposed to take. Sam smiled a wide little baby smile at her, and she smiled back.

The phone rang. Dorrie said hello and listened. There was no sound. Her face flushed. He hadn't stopped. He was still out there.

"Hello?" It was Margaret.

"Margaret." She tried to sound encouraging but not overwhelming.

"Well, we're selling this certain salve, and the school gets a movie projector if we sell enough." Her words came all in a rush. "And we're supposed to get pledges." She drew a deep breath. "And some movies, too. Some movies to go with the projector. Nature movies. Nature and space. Space shots, I think." The phone made a huge racket. There was a pause and some rustling. "I dropped the phone on the table. That was the sound you just heard."

"What kind of salve?"

"All-purpose," came the prompt reply. "It's called Robinson Brand All-Purpose Salve. It's for all purposes." Paper crackled. "Colds, burns, chafing," she read in a monotone. "Insect bites." The paper crackled. "Minor irritation?"

"How much?"

"Two dollars and forty-nine cents a can. For each can, you get one credit for the projector, and then they send it to you if you—if everybody—gets two hundred and fifty credits, I think it is. Not each person, but, like, a group. If you get two-fifty, you get to put your name in for a chance for a projector." She paused. "I understand it, but I can't explain it."

"Well, I could pledge to buy five cans."

"You could? Good." She sniffed deeply. "I have a bad cold. It started with this *horrible* headache, the kind you can get with spinal meningitis." She tossed the term off casually. "But it didn't turn out to be that."

"Good."

"Um-hum."

"When do you deliver this salve?"

"It's supposed to come in . . ."—the paper crackled—"ten days to two weeks."

"Do you bring it by?"

"Yes, we do."

Dorrie was reluctant to end the conversation. "Is it okay for babies?" she said. "Sam's the one with the minor irritations."

"Maybe," Margaret said. "It smells kind of sweet. Like a Big Hunk plus a kind of plastic smell, like if you sniff the inside of one of those little cases for pocket combs?" She let the image register. "Sam likes Big Hunks. They remind him of what he gets to have when he's older and has more teeth."

# Chapter 26

She arranged her legs on the wide seat, curving them sideways beneath her, the way Dorrie did when she sat on the floor to play with Sam. It was a very graceful look. It was the way Rima sat on the jungle floor among the dangling vines, her head cocked for messages from her animal friends, messages that sounded like nothing more than shrieks or thumping if you didn't know the jungle code. She wished more people would walk down the aisle, past her, so they could glance over and notice how absolutely at ease she was.

Rita Kay and her new friends never sat so poised. They sat tailor style, which was knotted and boylike. If Rita Kay were here, she would be squirming around, pointing out the window, talking too loudly. She would go up to absolute strangers and tell them she had just spent the night in a motel in Williston, North Dakota, on a bed that hummed and shook when you put a quarter in it. She would tell everyone she'd eaten a steak in a huge dining room that had velvet wallpaper and a white life-sized statue of a naked goddess, and that dessert was cherry pancakes that were set on fire at the table. She'd run right up to anyone on the train who would listen, blab out every detail she could remember, and everyone would know she was just a dopey girl who'd never been anywhere. It would show through.

The two women in the forward seat were laughing again. They laughed a lot. They were iron-haired older women, buxom, in tweedy suits with circle pins at the necks of their blouses. They didn't laugh loudly, but once they started, they laughed steadily—throaty, automatic laughs like quiet burp guns. One would murmur something, and they would both laugh—*heh-heh-heh-heh-heh*—and then the other would murmur something, and they would do it again.

Across the aisle and two seats forward, a teenage girl with dead-looking yellow hair, a blotched face, and a high, hard little voice told lies to a man who leaned against the window. "I've taken this train fifty times," she said. "I have a very wealthy aunt in Seattle who begs me to visit her. She cries on the phone if I don't come."

"I've been seeing her every other week for, what, two months now," Roy had said to MaryEllen. "Checking her blood count, checking the baby. Talking with her. She's fine. She is, MaryEllen."

MaryEllen was silent. Margaret crouched down to the grate to hear better.

"I think we should let Margaret go with her," he said. "We're talking about one day. One day on the road, a night in a motel. Then Dorrie goes on to Chicago, and Margaret comes home on the train."

"We're not talking about the most stable person in the world," MaryEllen said.

I'm stable, Margaret thought, surprised. She listened. The grate was in the corner of her bedroom, over a corner of the kitchen, and she could smell the leftovers of fried chicken. As she bent over it, her gum dropped out of her mouth, straight through the grate. She heard it tick lightly on the floor below, but her parents didn't seem to notice.

"How do we know she's not going to turn out just like her mother?" MaryEllen added. And in that little flash of a moment before she knew they were talking about Dorrie, not her, she answered the question. I'm not. I'm not going to turn out like my mother. She mouthed the words as if repeating information from someone else, knowing it to be true, feeling the loneliness of it.

"She was anemic," Roy said patiently, as if he'd said it quite a few times. "Exhausted as hell. I'm surprised she could get out of bed in the morning."

"Anemia makes someone pick up a gun and start shooting?" MaryEllen's voice had a shrill edge.

"Things had caught up with her," he said. "She's had a lot to deal with in the last year. Her mother, of course. And then the baby's father took a powder, it seems. He was apparently some kind of nightclub performer."

Margaret jumped a little. Nightclub performer! What would *that* involve? She saw the pale and handsome Fitzgerald on a small stage, telling jokes, juggling knives, swooping a pigeon from a dark hat, smiling his dazzling Bobby Kennedy smile, his Woody Blankenship smile, at Dorrie and the rest of the audience. She saw him running offstage in mock horror, leaving a faint trail of baby powder. It was hard to think of him that way, to make the switch in her mind from a perfect husband to a performer.

"Margaret should go because it's safe for her to go. And because she wants to go," Roy said. "She seems able to put the business with Señor Roja behind her—so we should too."

MaryEllen said nothing.

"I think we should give Dorrie the benefit of the doubt," Roy said. "I think she needs to know that she's trusted. Especially since she's going to give Chicago another try."

"It's so frightening when people just lash out like that," MaryEllen said in a quiet voice. "When they just feel free to do something cruel, something . . ."—she searched for the words—"something so out of character."

There was a quietness between them. It sounded as if MaryEllen was accusing Roy of something, but Margaret couldn't think of what it might be.

"Sometimes our imaginations just run away with us," Roy said. Margaret put her face right down to the grate to see him walk over to MaryEllen. MaryEllen shook her head. Then she raised her palms to the skies, giving up, and let Roy hug her.

Margaret dug around in her duffel bag for the Nancy Drews she was rereading and discovered, with a small shock, the bumpy drawstring sack with the toys she had meant to give Sam. Now he would forget her. When Dorrie went off to her college classes and her part-time job, Sam would have a new babysitter named Helen. A divorcée babysitter. Helen would be around all the time, because she was going to be Dorrie's roommate. So how would Sam ever remember Margaret? He would need something to remind him, and it wouldn't be there.

She couldn't believe she had forgotten to give him

the toys, and took them out, one by one, to appreciate fully her mistake. There was a big plastic rattle shaped like a diamond engagement ring; a small stuffed bear that she had snagged with a toothy little crane at the county fair; some pop beads, which were a bad idea because he'd think they were candy; a plastic rocket with doors, one of them broken off so you could see the praying Virgin Mary inside; a Chinese puzzle box, which was also dumb because Sam wouldn't be able to learn the moves; an empty Intimate cologne bottle that she had filled with bubble bath so he could shake it and watch it foam.

A man with smooth black hair sat across the aisle, almost at the front of the car. She couldn't see much of him at all, except that he wore a big overcoat, like a detective's overcoat, and the collar went halfway up the side of his face. He looked very mysterious. Occasionally, he dangled one arm off the side of the seat, let it swing, sometimes with a cigarette held limply between the fingers. There was a gold ring on the pinkie finger, the kind rich Englishmen wore in movies. It was the most sophisticated, world-weary man's arm she had ever seen. She stared at it, watched it rock with the movement of the train, listened to the wheels frantically tock-tocking their way through empty farmland and range, and the wild wail in the distance that said, Here they come! I'm bringing them through!

She pulled the shade on her window so she could think about being on a train that rushed through groves of pretty trees in Europe, past parapeted cities and peasants on bicycles. A train with compartments, where all the women sat like she did, and smoked, and leafed through magazines, and all the men had arms and hands like the one up ahead.

The girl with the pimply face ambled to the front

of the car and got a drink of water in a tiny white paper cup. On her way back to her seat, she spotted Margaret and sat down right next to her in the empty seat. Margaret made a very small smile.

"Where did you get on?" the girl demanded. She smelled like Noxzema.

"Williston," Margaret said. She paused. "I was there with my sister Dorrie, who is moving to a penthouse in Chicago. I've been helping them move. Dorrie and her son. We had a night on the town. We had dinner at the Mediterranean Garden in Williston." She raised the shade and looked out the window, smiling to show that she savored the memory.

"I've been on this train more times than I can count," the girl said. "My aunt in Seattle lives in a mansion. She begs me to come and stay with her."

"My sister had a nervous breakdown," Margaret offered. She turned to the girl. "Did you ever see the movie *Cat People?*"

"Sure."

Margaret let the lie go. "A lady in *Cat People* had a breakdown something like my sister's," she said. "Her name was Irena. She was from a foreign country, and she moved to this country to be a fashion designer. But a curse followed her. She had a panther inside her that sprang out if she got jealous of her husband or fell in love with him too much. At night, she had to stay in her own bedroom and lock the door. Because of the problem with the panther."

"A dog bit me once on my face," the girl said. "I could have lost my eyesight."

"She couldn't help it," Margaret said. "It was a strong curse. When her husband started to like a lady at his ship-designing office, the panther jumped out of Irena and ripped the other lady's bathrobe to shreds while she was in a swimming pool."

The train rocked gently, and they were quiet for a few moments.

"I had rheumatic fever, the worst case they ever saw." The lying teenager's metal voice drifted over everyone's heads. "They didn't think my heart would ever be the same. I'm lucky to be here now. Luckier than I'll ever know."

At the beginning of the trip, when Dorrie pulled up in the heavy blue car, her face had been damp-looking. But she had smiled at Margaret and even hummed a little as she stowed Margaret's red duffel bag in the trunk. The car was plush and warm inside, and jammed with suitcases and boxes. Some of the boxes in the back seat jingled and clinked whenever the car stopped or turned a corner.

Dorrie speeded up at the city limits, where Main Street became Highway 2, and Sam tried to stand up and look out the window. Margaret pulled him into her lap and found a baby book on the floor to read to him. The car had a deep, whining sound, like an old man humming.

A skiff of snow smoked across the highway as they drove toward the lifting sun. It was early November, cold, mostly dry. Dorrie sniffed daintily from time to time, blew her nose, drove intently. But her face looked peaceful. Margaret concentrated on reading to Sam. One duck, she crooned. Two penguins. Three ponies.

At Wolf Point, they had stopped at a place that said LOUNGE, LANES, MOCCASINS to eat a hamburger at a counter next to the bowling lanes. The woman who served them had turquoise and silver rings on every finger except her thumbs. She moved with a quick, distant efficiency, smoking the stub of a cigarette as if it were fuel. There was a blurry color photo on the wall of a snarling coyote. The camera had been held above its face, so you could look down on the bared fangs and the tangle of metal trap.

"My son trapped it," the woman with the rings said curtly. "He took the picture right before he shot it. Stood on the hood of his pickup and took that picture." Her voice was brusque with pride. "It don't look too happy, I'd say."

Sam sat on Dorrie's lap, and chirped, and threw saltines on the floor. Margaret thought about the coyote, about that last moment when its eyes were alive in its head. And when she did, grieving anger returned to her in a flood. She thought that feeling had gone away. She *felt* it had gone away. But here it was, back again, and she was helpless before it. She felt embarrassed, trapped. Like she did when she knew she might throw up in front of other people. You go to school not even suspecting you're sick, and then there you are, about to throw up. It was a horrible feeling.

She thought it had gone away because she had been able, one day, to call up Dorrie and just talk about the Robinson Brand All-Purpose Salve as if nothing in the world was wrong. What a relief that had been!

She had been able to call Dorrie on the phone because of empathy. Her father had told her about Dorrie's anemia, and she had thought about it. And then she had suddenly known exactly what it must feel like, which is what empathy was. It felt, anemia did, like your blood was blindfolded and staggering around, not knowing how to act, not knowing where to go. It doesn't have enough oxygen so it's gasping and desperate, and it makes the person on the outside of the blood feel so panicky she just blows up without even wanting to.

Margaret had always had empathy with Sam. She always knew what he was thinking. But it wasn't until she thought a long time about Dorrie's blood that she found she also could have empathy for an adult. For Dorrie. She had felt poised between Sam and Dorrie, able to beam her mind either way. And that's when she had said yes about this trip. The horrible feelings had faded, dropped into the background where she didn't have to look at them, and she could beam her mind into Dorrie's, and understand the feeling of having desperate blood cells, and say yes.

But now the quivering fury was back. She tried to push it away, but it stayed. The sun dropped behind them and gave the car a shadow. Margaret could see her head in the window of the car shadow, and she raised her hand and saw the shadow hand too. She waved at it bleakly, trying to distract herself.

The road was absolutely straight and almost empty. A mile or so passed between every car. The prairie was snowless, except for patches in the low spots. The barbed-wire fence lines, the telephone lines, were thin silver ropes. She stared at them, trying to keep her eyes open wide so the tears wouldn't squeeze out and show. She thought of driving across the grass to Señor Roja. *Never would she see him again, never, never.* She felt her face burn, like it did just before she threw up, and she knew there was nothing she could do about what she was going to say. Her empathy wasn't working anymore. It had fled.

"You shot my horse," Margaret said in a choking voice. She turned to face Dorrie and said it again. "You just *shot* him."

Dorrie slowly pulled the car to the side of the road

and stopped. Sam, curled like a shrimp on the seat, stirred, sighed deeply, slept.

"And I don't happen to *care* about your red blood cells!" Margaret cried. She jumped out of the car and stood on the shoulder of the road, eyes clenched shut. She heard the distant drone of an oncoming car.

"Blood cells?" Dorrie's voice sounded faint, confused.

Margaret screwed her eyes closed. She felt the tears streaming down her face, dropping off the end of her chin and jawbone. She felt Dorrie's eyes on her, and the sharp chill of the day, seeping through her sweater.

Then there were arms around her. She realized that she was quite a lot taller than she was when she met Dorrie. Her head rested against Dorrie's shoulder. She just stood there, arms at her sides, and cried for a while. Dorrie didn't say anything.

Then she said, "You helped me when it counted, Margaret. I know that seems like I'm changing the subject. But you did."

Margaret didn't answer.

A battered pickup came to a halt on the other side of the road, and a florid old man in coveralls leaned out the window. A speckled dog with a black ring around one eye put its paw on the edge of the pickup bed and barked.

"Any trouble here?" the man shouted in a creaky voice.

Dorrie shook her head.

He struggled out of the driver's seat and walked, stiff legs bowed, across the narrow highway to them. "You got some trouble here?" he asked, peering at the tires.

"Please forgive me," Dorrie said to Margaret in a rush. "If you can, just keep going with us to Williston. Try to forgive me. If you can." The farmer glanced sharply from Dorrie's face to Margaret's. He waited. They all waited. The dog with the pirate eye patch barked twice, sharply.

The farmer looked hard at Dorrie and Margaret and their strained young faces. He wheezed a little as he breathed. Then he turned to Margaret. "Go on to Williston," he advised. He waited for her nod, then made his slow, rocking way back to the pickup. He gave the dog a pat, heaved himself into the driver's seat, and roared off. When it was quiet again, a dark arrow of Canadian geese flew high over their heads, calling faintly, hurrying south.

To calm down, Margaret had pretended she was driving. She had studied the road intently, as she did when she really drove, and pressed her gas foot harder to the floor. They gathered speed. Forty, forty-five, fifty-five, sixty. She blew her nose, keeping her eyes on the road. A car appeared like a bug in the distance and took a long, long time coming to them. When it passed, the driver signaled hi with a friendly wave of his index finger. Margaret returned the index-finger wave. They speeded up a little.

Dorrie turned on the radio. A man was talking. "Noooo," he said. "He *doesn't* want that kind of attitude. But the thing is, it's out of your hands. Let me give you an example. Let's say you commit just three sins a day. That's not very many. Things done, things left undone, the whole ball of wax. Well, that's twenty-one sins a week. That's eighty-four a month. That's one thousand and eight sins a year." He let the numbers sink in. "In a normal lifetime, that's in excess of *seventy thousand* sins. There's no way, just no way, that you're going to clean those off on your own."

Sam's sleeping breath whistled a little. Margaret felt her own eyelids begin to fall. The radio sound fuzzed out, and Dorrie reached over to turn it off. She put her hand gently on Margaret's leg. Margaret's eyelids dropped again. She thought about the way a car shadow can get so long at the end of a day: the way it skims across the grass, glides through telephone poles, wavers, pulls in, stretches again; stretches so far it seems to grab the skyline.

One of the big women with the circle pins rustled deep in a carry-on bag and brought out something that sounded like crackling paper and sent the smell of ham and mayonnaise back to Margaret. She had already eaten in the dining car. They had seated the pimply girl, the one who told the lies, at her table. The girl had ordered a BLT and told Margaret that B, L, and T were the initials of her boyfriend, who was in the service and looked like Bobby Darin.

Margaret mentioned that when she'd eaten dinner the night before at the Mediterranean Garden, she'd had some wine, and everyone at the table had toasted her. The inch of wine in her glass had tasted so strange and European that she smiled, remembering it. She and Dorrie had clinked their glasses three times. She could still hear the sound, like a miniature bell. She could hear Sam's delighted squeal.

The pimply-faced girl said she had drunk a Coke bottle full of Old Grandad on her birthday.

The day darkened. When the train ran close to the highway, car lights came at it like tiny animal eyes. Here and there, out in the flat dimness, a pale yard light came on. She was sleepy. But she worried that, if she slept, she would miss Madrid. She reviewed the whole meal at the Mediterranean Garden so she could tell her parents. She dug around in her duffel bag and found the napkin she'd saved. It had some ancient ruins drawn on it—some crumbling columns—and a bunch of grapes coming out of a basket. Below the grapes, it said *In Vino Veritas* and under that it said *In Wine There Is Very Much Happiness.* Which was probably true.

She opened her Chinese puzzle box. The note from Dorrie, asking for forgiveness, was still there. She read it and folded it up until it was very small and put it on the very edge of her seat. Then she looked out the window, and when she looked back it had dropped to the floor, where she left it.

She walked to the front of the car to get a drink of water in one of the tiny paper cups. On the way back to her seat, she arranged her face and looked directly at the man in the trench coat. He was slumped sideways, the coat over most of his head, his arms hidden.

She practiced her posture. She walked slowly. When she got back to her seat, she tucked her legs under her and cleaned her glasses. The women laughed their low laughs. *Heh-heh-heh.*

She went up into the empty dome car, where it was dark. The sky was turning inky blue, and two stars had appeared. Three more. Far out across the grass and the fields, solitary lights sparkled at wide distances from each other like mirrors of the sky stars or pinpricks in the earth.

And then Madrid appeared, a short string of solid rhinestones scattered along the horizon. It was beautiful. It brought a lump to her throat. She ran back down to her regular seat and got her coat and her duffel bag together. She sat with her face close to the window and practiced her new personality, silently, to herself.

Her new personality was, like Dorrie's, perfect for a city. It was calm and brave and adventurous. It looked around, and took in the world, but didn't panic at anything. Or if it did, it recovered quickly. It was ready for anything. It didn't fit someplace like Madrid, but it didn't mind being there for a while.

She cleaned her glasses again, put them back on, and tipped her head up a little.

The train slowed. Its harmonic shriek wedged into the darkness. The lights grew. Some were bluish now. Some were warm.

*Shrieek. Tock TOCK, tock TOCK. Shrieeeeeeeek.* The train crawled out onto the trestle and then came to a dead stop. It waited. It didn't move.

Margaret looked around nervously. Why weren't they moving? What were they waiting for? No one else seemed nervous, though a few people peered curiously out the window. The train inched forward, then stopped again with a screech. Maybe there was a disaster ahead. Maybe the trestle was about to break in two. Maybe they would have to be extricated—slide on endless ropes down to the river below. The bragging girl would burst into tears. Margaret would tell her to clap her trap. The man in the trench coat would stride to the engine to see what the trouble was, and when he came back he would thank Margaret for keeping everyone calm.

The train lurched ahead, lurched again, and smoothed out. The two women began to laugh. Margaret was standing now, so she could see their faces over the top of the seat. Their necks wobbled when they laughed. She thought about kuru. Kuru was a disease in which you laughed to death. The article in *Time* said it had been discovered among some tribespeople of New Guinea, as many as a hundred of them. They started laughing, and then if they were "authentic victims"—that's how *Time* put it—they laughed themselves right to their deaths. Maybe these women were authentic victims but didn't have a clue. Maybe they had picked up kuru someplace but didn't know they had it and were going to get off in

Madrid and give it to the whole town. They thought they were laughing, but they were really dying.

One of the women got up and walked back toward the tiny bathroom, still smiling. The other woman sneezed loudly, then was silent. Margaret saw Roy and MaryEllen standing at the station door, small clouds coming out of their mouths. MaryEllen was huddled in the doorway and had a big scarf over her head. A newspaper flew past her legs.

The train passed them. It passed the Madrid station sign. But it was going very slowly. And when it finally stopped, Margaret was already at the door.